# RISING

Death is just the beginning...

a novel by

## T.C. Zmak

ISBN: 0692672257
ISBN-13: 978-0692672259
Library of Congress Control Number: 2016904908
Zmak Creative, Marina, CA

For information: www.tczmak.com

CreateSpace, Charleston SC
Printed in the United States of America

First paperback edition, September 2016

*For ocean lovers everywhere—human and otherwise*

# RISING

# Prologue

The surfer faded in and out of consciousness. He felt himself being carried through the ocean. Cool salt water rushed beneath him. He struggled to lift his eyelids but didn't have the strength. He felt a sharp, stabbing pain in his heart. *Leilani*, he thought as he drifted into blackness again.

When he awoke that evening, he was startled to find a blue-eyed man in a white lab coat staring at him. He tried to escape the man's glare but couldn't move. He felt drugged. He attempted to lift himself, but something hard and cold pinned his ankles and wrists to the bed.

The doctor leaned down and placed his lips next to the surfer's ear. "I know what you are," he hissed. "I know what you do. And you will never leave here alive."

# 1 – Fresh Catch

Thirty-five miles to the east, a great white shark patrolled the waters off the Orange County, California coast. Seeing a lone diver near the ocean's surface, the shark rocketed toward the long limbs dangling above her. As she opened her jaws and prepared to clamp down upon her prey, he disappeared. The shark lunged into the air and saw the diver being hoisted out of the water on a small crane attached to a boat. She snapped her jaws closed, missing his feet by only an inch or two.

"Higher, dammit, higher!" the diver, Matt, yelled. "C'mon, Jules! Drop the net!"

"Got it!" The blond woman raised the black lever on the research vessel's control panel to lift Matt out of the hungry shark's reach. With her other hand, she smacked the red button, dropping a large net into the ocean. She watched the shark splash down on top of the net. "And, Matt, unless you want to be chum, stop calling me Jules! You know I hate that. It's 'J'—short and sweet like me."

"Okay, J," Matt snickered.

Feeling the mesh beneath her, the shark quickly reversed course. She zoomed upward, hoping to leap out of the water and over the edge of the net rapidly encircling her.

"Get her, J! She's getting away!" Matt shouted.

"I know!" J hit the red button again to retract the net.

The net closed just as the shark reached the surface. She burst through the water but immediately crashed down, completely ensnared. She thrashed wildly but couldn't escape. She morphed from her shark body into her human body, thinking she could use her hands to open the top of the net.

J lifted a red lever and raised the net out of the ocean. She guided the lever to the right to move the net over the deck of the boat. "Hey! Graysuit!" she taunted. "Or should I call you Lily?"

"Let me go *now* or I'll kill you," Lily, the brunette in the net, threatened.

"I can't do that, Lily." J pointed at the diver hanging from the crane. "You were gonna kill my buddy, Matt, here. I'm sure he's not the first either."

"No. He's not," Lily glowered, her fangs reflecting the soft glow of the peach-colored sunset.

"Nice fangs," J jeered, "but where we're going, you won't be needing those anymore." She pulled down the red lever to lower the net into a secure holding tank below deck.

As Lily disappeared into the tank, she struggled to shred the net.

"You're wasting your time," J laughed. "That's no ordinary net. It's made of a special alloy that can't be torn apart, even by vampire sharks." She gazed down at the captive woman, slammed the steel cover closed, and locked it from the outside.

J grinned at Matt, who was still suspended above the water. "What are you doing just hanging around? We have work to do."

"Funny," he said. "Forget marine biology. You should be a comedian."

"No way! You're the funny one. Let's get you down so we can take our catch back to the lab."

"Sounds good," Matt said. "By the way, J, that was close. Too close. I almost lost my toes to that one."

"You were totally safe the whole time."

"Uh huh," he smirked, "right."

J maneuvered the arm of the crane toward the boat and released Matt. He landed on the deck with a thud. "With Lily and the male vampire shark who was brought in this morning, it looks like you and Finn will be busy in the lab," he said.

"Yep, looks that way," she said. "Why don't you radio in and tell Dr. Finnegan we're on our way?"

# 2 – Reflecting

A few hours later and several miles down the coast, Leilani Waters and Jake Ryder boarded the red-eye flight from San Diego to Honolulu.

After the plane reached a safe cruising altitude, Leilani turned on her laptop. She completed her paperwork to request a 30-day leave of absence and emailed it to the special agent in charge of the FBI's San Diego Division. She claimed the reason for the leave was that she was brutally attacked by two vicious, possibly rabid, dogs. She couldn't state the real reason—that she'd been brutally attacked by two vicious, definitely psychotic, vampires.

Leilani glanced at her watch. *1:15 a.m., Saturday. Was it really only 30 hours ago,* she wondered, *that Dean and Logan tried to kill me? And that Tristan asked me to marry him and then died alone in the ocean?* She shuddered, feeling nauseated by the memory of Dean and Logan puncturing her skin with their fangs and sucking her blood. She self-consciously tugged at her long cotton sleeves and kicked her feet beneath her ankle-length skirt to make sure no one could see the wounds, even though they were already hidden beneath bandages under her clothing. She sighed heavily. *Three days ago, I didn't believe vampires existed. And vampires who can turn into great white sharks in the ocean? Whoever heard of such a thing?*

As Leilani considered how she and Jake would track Dean once they landed in Waikiki, her mind drifted. Feeling sleepy from the pain medication she took, she reclined her seat and closed her eyes. Sixty seconds later, she was out.

# 3 – Returning the Favor

Seeing Leilani's head loll to the side, Jake gently propped a pillow under her ear and covered her with the thin airline blanket. He tilted his seat back and rubbed his eyes. It had been a long day. Twenty-four hours ago, he had searched for Tristan in the ocean, but he never showed. Jake knew the only thing that would keep Tristan away was if he didn't survive.

*Is Tristan really dead? It doesn't seem possible. He always seemed so powerful—so in control of everything.* Jake glanced at Leilani. *What about her? She was supposed to marry Tristan.*

Jake remembered how he felt when his best friend, Cody, was killed. How fresh and raw and all-encompassing the hurt and grief and pain were. How different his life became afterward. He was grateful to Leilani for being there for him during that difficult time. *Now it's time for me to return the favor.*

Leilani whimpered in her sleep and scratched at one of the many bites on her arms.

"It's okay. You're safe," Jake whispered. He wrapped his arm around her and settled her head on his shoulder. *Tristan asked me to take care of you if he didn't make it back, so that's what I'm gonna do. And my first order of business is to find Dean and make him pay for what he did.*

# 4 – Putting the Past in the Past

While Jake and Leilani slumbered on the flight to Honolulu, Skylar and Dean swam along the Waikiki coast under a starlit sky.

Skylar's mind wandered to Tristan. *Does he know I'm gone? Does he even care?*

Skylar painfully recalled how, a couple of nights earlier, Dean told her that Tristan proposed to Leilani. She felt a fresh wave of hurt wash over her. *No! I can't think of Tristan anymore. He said he didn't love me and that he never would. I have to put him where he belongs—in the past.*

Dean swam up to Skylar. "Everything okay?" he asked.

"Yeah. Why wouldn't it be?" She smiled, but a melancholy look in her eyes betrayed her emotions.

"I know it was hard for you to leave Tristan, but it was the right thing to do. You know he was never going to be with you. That wasn't what he wanted," he said.

Skylar nodded. She knew it was true, but that didn't make it hurt any less.

"But that's not me," Dean said. "I know exactly what I want. I want you. And I can give you everything you want. We're having fun so far, right? We had a great meal yesterday. We're swimming under the stars in a tropical paradise. I promise this is going to be great. *We* are going to be great."

"Sorry," Skylar said. "It's not that I don't want to be here with you because I do. I just can't help feeling that I should call Tristan to tell him I've left and I'm not coming back."

Dean shook his head, tired of having the same conversation over and over with Skylar.

"Then I should at least call Torrey and Cruz, or Logan," she insisted. "It feels wrong to disappear on them. I don't want them to worry about me. Even if Tristan wasn't the guy I thought he was, they were my friends."

Dean clenched his jaw and forced the corners of his mouth up into a smile. He knew he had to keep his cool so Skylar wouldn't get suspicious and start asking questions. He knew she'd never approve of him killing her friends, no matter how good his reasons were. She still had no idea that he had sent Logan to infiltrate Tristan's crew, the Nomads, to find out who murdered his fiancée, Andi. She also had no clue that he'd plotted to kill Tristan, that he personally killed Cruz, or that he'd instructed Logan to kill Torrey and Leilani. As far as she knew, everyone was alive and well.

"I understand how you feel," he said, "but you can't contact them. Ever. They'll tell Tristan, and you'll never be free. You need a clean break. Trust me. It's for the best. I've known Tristan longer than anyone. This is the only way."

Skylar sighed, still feeling uneasy about breaking off communication with her closest friends.

Dean cradled her face in his hands and stared into her eyes. "Promise me you won't contact them. I couldn't live with myself if anything bad ever happened to you."

"Okay, I promise," she said reluctantly.

"Good, then it's settled. And I promise I'm going to make you so happy that you'll forget all about Tristan. He had 10 years with you, and what did he bring you? Nothing but heartache. Just give me a little time," Dean said.

"I will, but you need to give me a little time to get used to this. They were all a part of my life for so long, and now they're not," Skylar said.

"Okay," Dean agreed. "But you're happy now? With me?"

Skylar wasn't sure if she actually felt that way but promised herself she'd try.

# 5 — Shiver

Leilani opened her eyes. She felt Jake's arm around her. Seeing him sleeping, she gingerly lifted his arm over her head and placed it on the armrest between them. She had the feeling she'd been having nightmares but, thankfully, couldn't remember them. Her real life over the last two days had been horrific enough. She didn't need to relive it in her dreams.

She gazed out the airplane window into the night sky. *Tristan.* She stared at the engagement ring he gave her as he lay dying from the stake wound near his heart. The midnight blue round cut sapphire shimmered under the overhead light, as did the small white diamonds surrounding the stone and the band. *Torrey and Jake tried to save him, but it was too late. The wound was too deep. I can't believe I'll never see him again.* Leilani tried to stop thinking about Tristan. She didn't want to cry. Not here on a plane full of strangers. Not here next to Jake, who saved her life and tried his best to save Tristan's.

Her thoughts turned to Dean. *We have to find him before he kills again.* Thinking of him made her shiver. She pulled the blanket up to her chin, shut her eyes, and tried to push the bloody memories of Dean from her mind.

# 6 – Missing in Action

When Dean and Skylar returned to their hotel room, Skylar stripped off her bikini and sauntered to the bathroom. She turned on the bathtub faucet and closed the door.

Dean quietly stepped outside onto the balcony. He dialed Logan's number. "Logan, it's Dean. Again. Dude, where the hell are you? I need to know you finished things with Torrey and Leilani. Call me as soon as you get this."

Dean paced between the balcony and the bed. *Why isn't Logan calling me back? Is he blowing me off because he's on a plane to Australia or he's already there surfing? He knows he's not working for me anymore, so he doesn't have to check in like before. He's got $100,000 in his bank account, from me, for his time with Tristan's crew. I know Cruz is dead because I staked him myself. But what about Torrey and Leilani? I left Logan to kill them, and he's M.I.A.*

*And what about Lance? He's been missing since I left him and the other graysuits to kill Tristan. There's no way Tristan could've survived an attack like that. Nine against one? No way. But I should've heard from Lance by now. Unless …*

"Dean!" Skylar called from the bathroom. "The bath is ready. Are you coming?"

"Be right there!" He buried his phone in his luggage and dropped his boardshorts to the floor. *No. There's no way Tristan can be alive,* he reassured himself.

# 7 – Checking In

Jake and Leilani landed in Honolulu before dawn on Saturday morning. They rented a car using the fake California driver licenses Jake had obtained from a friend of Tristan's in San Diego. They headed to the beach where two surfers were killed the previous morning and scouted hotels in the area. They parked on a side street and called each hotel, asking to speak with a guest by the name of Dean Delsur or Skylar Sirena but came up empty.

"Do you think they're using other names like we are?" Jake asked.

"Maybe. Let's check into the hotel closest to where the attack happened. We'll get two rooms with ocean views so we can keep an eye on the beach in case they return. Then we can plan our next move," Leilani said.

"Sounds good. It's almost sunrise, which means they're probably not going back out anytime soon. And I should get inside."

"Oh yeah. I forgot about that. So, now that you're a graysuit, does that mean no sun at all?" Leilani asked.

"For a while. I need to build up a tolerance. Sunscreen will help a little with indirect light, but I should definitely avoid direct sun. Extra crispy is not a good look for me," Jake said.

"Let's get you inside then." Leilani still wondered about Jake's decision to have Tristan turn him into a vampire shark. *Jake said that it was because he discovered it's who he really is—that he's meant to be more a part of the ocean. I just hope he didn't become a graysuit for revenge so he could gain an edge in tracking Dean.*

Jake started the car and drove to the hotel. They carried their bags to the front desk.

"Aloha!" exclaimed the desk clerk who, in Leilani's opinion, seemed way too chipper for the early hour. "How may I help you this beautiful Hawaiian morning?"

"Hi. Do you have any rooms available with an ocean view?" Leilani tried her best to sound like a happy tourist on vacation, but her wounds throbbed beneath her bandages.

"Let's see. We have a convention here so we're completely sold out, but maybe something's become available." The clerk tapped away at his keyboard. "You're in luck! We have exactly one room available, and it's an ocean view."

Leilani glanced at Jake and shrugged. "We'll take it."

"Great! I'll need a credit card and ID, please," the clerk said.

Leilani handed him their new California driver licenses and her credit card. She immediately realized her credit card had her legal name—Lani Marley—on it, unlike her license. "Um, I understand you need the card for incidentals, but we'd prefer to pay cash when we check out," she said.

"That's fine. We just need to have it on file. It's policy." The clerk recorded the credit card number, glanced at their licenses, and returned them to Leilani. He placed two keycards in a paper sleeve and slid it across the granite countertop. "Room 1015. We hope you enjoy your stay, Mr. and Mrs. Pierce."

Leilani fell silent. *Mr. and Mrs. Pierce.*

"Thanks," Jake said. He touched Leilani's arm. "You ready?"

"Yeah. Sorry. Just tired from the flight," she said.

As soon as the elevator doors closed, Jake turned to her. "I'm sorry. That was stupid of me to give us Tristan's last name. I thought it was a tribute to him because he said we were like the only family he had left. I didn't think people would assume we were married."

"It's okay. It just surprised me. I know you meant well. And you were right when you said Tristan would've wanted it this way. You were like a brother to him, and I ..." Leilani stopped.

She knew if she said anything else, she'd break down. The pain of losing Tristan was still too fresh, and she felt too exhausted to hide her emotions.

The elevator doors opened. "It's been a long night," Jake said. "Let's get some rest, okay?"

They headed down the hall and opened the door to their room. "Wheeeeew!" Jake whistled. "Fancy digs."

They walked inside and stopped. There was only one bed.

"You take it. I can sleep over there," Jake said, pointing to an armchair in the corner of the room.

"No," Leilani said. "We're both exhausted. We need to get some rest if we're going to find Dean and Skylar. You won't get any sleep in a chair. It's a king-size bed. There's plenty of room."

Jake hesitated.

"It's fine. Really." Leilani rummaged through her carry-on bag. "I'm going to wash up and change my bandages."

"Okay, but only if you're sure. Do you need any help with your bandages?" he asked.

"No, I've got it. Thanks though." Leilani headed to the bathroom and shut the door.

Jake set his bags in the corner. He closed the curtains, stripped down to his underwear, and climbed into bed. He pulled the sheet up to his waist and scooted as close to the edge as he could.

Fifteen minutes later, Leilani emerged from the bathroom wearing a pale pink tank top and matching boxer shorts. Fresh white bandages covered her arms and legs. She climbed into the cool cotton sheets and stared at the ceiling, hoping sleep would come quickly. "Good night, Jake."

"G'night. Or maybe that should be 'good morning' since the sun's already up," he said.

After a minute, Leilani rolled onto her side. "Jake? I'm glad you're here."

"Where else would I be? Try to get some sleep, okay?"

# 8 – Awakening

While Jake and Leilani sat at the airport in San Diego waiting to board their flight to Honolulu, Tristan awoke again. He tried to open his eyes but couldn't.

*"I know what you are. I know what you do. And you will never leave here alive."* Tristan had a hazy memory of a man telling him that, threatening him. He struggled to clear the fog that clouded his brain. With great effort, he managed to raise his eyelids a fraction of an inch. He glimpsed a door to a small bathroom on his left. He glanced down his body and saw he wore a thin cloth gown. Metal cuffs bound his wrists and ankles to the bed. An IV pumped clear liquid into his inner arm, and an electrocardiograph recorded his slow heartbeat.

*A hospital?! I can't be in a hospital! I'll be a lab rat for the rest of my life once they realize I'm not human.*

The smell of salt water punctured Tristan's panicked thoughts. He looked to the right and saw a large circular pool. *A saltwater pool? This isn't a hospital. But if it's not a hospital, then what is this place?*

Before Tristan could formulate a theory, he succumbed to the powerful sedative the IV pumped into his body. His eyes closed, and he slipped into blackness again.

Dr. Luke Finnegan entered Tristan's room. Nicknamed "Finn" by his friends, he had very short brown hair, fair skin, a prominent forehead, a flat nose, and blue eyes.

Finn stood next to the bed and examined the devices monitoring Tristan's condition. He noted the day and time—Friday, 9 p.m.—and recorded Tristan's vital signs on the chart attached to his clipboard.

Finn spoke softly so he didn't wake Tristan. "It was touch-and-go for a while, but I think you're going to make it—for now. When you're well enough to wake up, I'm hoping you'll help me. I need to know who created you and how many of you guys are left in the world so I know what I'm up against. You vampire sharks are a pretty violent species, and it's time that comes to an end. So, I'm going to have to keep you here until you tell me what I want to know. I realize great white sharks don't do well in captivity, and that means you'll probably die here. Cody says you're a nice guy, so sorry about that. But if you help me, maybe I can help you. I'll be back to check on you tomorrow. Sleep tight."

# 9 – Visitor

Finn left lab #1. The door automatically locked behind him. He turned down the hallway and stumbled into Cody Hansen. "Cody! I didn't see you. What are you doing down here so late?"

"Sorry, Finn," Cody replied. "I didn't mean to run you down. I was looking for you though. I want to see how Tristan's doing."

"His condition is still very serious," Finn said.

"Can I see him?"

"Not yet. I'll let you know as soon as he improves enough to have visitors. I'm in a hurry. Can we talk later?"

"Yeah." Cody started to leave but turned back toward Finn. "Thanks for what you're doing. I know I shouldn't have brought him here, but he's a good guy."

"So you say," Finn replied, failing to keep the sarcasm out of his voice. "I've gotta go. I'm late for dinner, and J hates it when I'm late. We'll talk tomorrow."

"Yeah. Later, man." Cody watched Finn rush down the hall and through the door to the stairwell. Cody turned the doorknob to Tristan's room, but it was locked. He looked at the digital keypad next to the door. He had no idea what Finn's entry code might be.

Cody pressed the intercom button next to the door. "Hey, Tristan, it's Cody," he said quietly. "Sorry I can't get in to see you, but you're gonna be okay. I'll visit as soon as Finn lets me. Take care, man."

As Cody climbed the stairs to his apartment on the top floor of the compound, he recalled the first time he saw Tristan. It was the same day Cody was killed—or at least his human body was.

# 10 – Cody's (Re)Birth

Cody had spent that entire afternoon surfing with his best friend, Jake. After the sun set, he wanted to stay out a little longer, so he sent Jake ahead to the shore. That seemingly inconsequential decision ended up costing Cody his life.

A newly created vampire shark named Rick mistook Cody for the head of a territorial surf gang and attacked him. Tristan tried to stop Rick but was too late. By the time he arrived, Cody's body had been bitten so badly there was no saving him.

As Cody lay dying underwater, he watched Tristan argue with Rick on the ocean's surface. At that moment, a dolphin approached from below. The dolphin inspected Cody's wounds and shook his head from side to side. *I'm not gonna make it*, Cody thought. His memory flooded with experiences from his life. Through it all, there was one constant—Jake.

Cody felt himself swaying in the current. He saw a body. Bright red blood dissipated in the water around it. It took him a moment to realize he was staring at his own dead body.

Cody, who was now a free, formless soul in the water, gazed at the dolphin. The dolphin spoke through whistle-like sounds. Without the restrictions of a human brain and human senses, Cody understood him perfectly.

"Hi, I'm Luke Finnegan. You can call me Finn. I'm sorry about what happened to you, but it's lucky I found you when I did. Most humans don't realize this, but right here, right now, you can make a choice. If you want, you can stay here on this planet, in this dimension. I can transport your soul to a new body like mine. Or you can move on to whatever the next step is on your soul's path. The choice is yours, but you have to make it now. You have only a couple of minutes before your soul connects with its new path and moves on."

Cody instantly thought of Jake surfing these waters. He didn't want his friend to die in the brutal, painful, terrifying way he did. "I want to stay," he decided. "But how?"

"I know you have a lot of questions, but we don't have much time. Are you sure you want to stay?" Finn asked.

"Yeah."

"Then hang on," Finn said. "It's going to be tight quarters until I can get you to a new body."

Finn closed his eyes and concentrated. Cody felt a swirling sensation as his soul began to move toward Finn. Within seconds, he felt himself inside the dolphin's body.

"There. It's done. My soul is now in the left side of my brain, and your soul is in the right side of my brain. Let's get out of here before the vampire sharks notice us. Some of them find dolphins even more tempting than humans." Finn turned and began swimming northwest.

Cody marveled at the velvety feel of the cool water on the dolphin's skin as they glided through the ocean. It felt invigorating and soothing at the same time. "So, I'm inside your brain?" he asked.

"Yes, for now. Sorry. You may feel a little cramped until I can get you your own dolphin body," Finn said.

"How is this even possible?" Cody asked.

"Dolphins are different from other mammals like humans. One big difference is in the way our brains work. Unlike humans, we dolphins sleep with only one hemisphere of our brain."

"Yeah, I think I heard that somewhere before," Cody said.

"Well, that serves a few purposes," Finn explained. "At a basic physical level, because we sleep with only one brain hemisphere—instead of our entire brain like humans do—we can watch out for predators because half of our brain is wide awake. We can literally sleep with one eye open. At an intellectual level, it means that our consciousness and our thoughts are not limited by the need for sleep the same way a human's are. We can engage in lucid thought 24/7. It's more powerful, of course, when we're using both hemispheres simultaneously. But we can function really well using one hemisphere or the other, which means that a dolphin's brain is not only more flexible but more powerful than a human's."

"Hold up, dude. I'm still getting used to the fact that you're a dolphin and I'm inside your head. Could you maybe take it a little slower? Pretend I don't know anything about dolphins … which I pretty much don't," Cody admitted.

"Sorry. Okay, Cody, you as a human have two brain hemispheres—a left brain and a right brain. These hemispheres are connected. Some people might use one hemisphere a little more than the other. But they typically use both brain hemispheres when they're awake, and they also sleep with both hemispheres. Dolphins have two brain hemispheres too, but the difference is that we can consciously operate each hemisphere independently of the other. That means my soul can use one hemisphere of my brain, and I can temporarily place your soul in the other hemisphere of my brain. I can have two souls in one body, and we can coexist for as long as needed. Of course, my goal is to get you your own dolphin body as soon as I can. It's exhausting having two souls in one body. I'm sure you're a great guy, but I don't want to live with you inside my head day and night."

"So, my soul is inside your head. And you're a dolphin. That's such a trip," Cody said. "Do humans ever do that—two souls in one body?"

"Sometimes, but I wouldn't recommend it. You've heard of possession, right?" Finn asked.

"You mean like demonic possession? Like in horror movies?" Cody asked.

"That's one form of possession, but not every soul that hijacks a human brain is evil," Finn explained. "Sometimes it happens by mistake—a soul loses its connection to its path, accidentally enters a person, and gets trapped. Other times, a soul purposely ignores its connection because it doesn't want to leave. Since it can't go back to its old body because it's dead, it finds a vulnerable person nearby and invades his or her brain. Most instances of schizophrenia and dissociative identity disorder are mental illness, but every once in a while, it's a case of a soul living in a body it's not supposed to."

"No way."

"Yeah, and the person is miserable because there are two souls trying to occupy the same brain. The human brain isn't designed for that. It can't handle it. Anything beyond one soul in there wreaks havoc with the person's mind and body," Finn said.

"Whoa. So, what are you?" Cody asked. "Some kind of super-dolphin?"

"You humans still have no idea how smart dolphins really are, do you? That's a shame. Dolphins could help you with so much. But you never think to ask."

# 11 – Compound

Finn and Cody swam to Finn's home, a three-story compound on the coast of Catalina, a small island in the Pacific Ocean off the Southern California coast. Situated northwest of Avalon, on the outskirts of the island's most populous city, the nondescript sand-colored building blended in with the landscape, so it was nearly invisible from the air and the sea.

The first floor of the building was below ground. It housed a research facility that had been abandoned decades earlier by the U.S. military. It was secretly built during World War II when Catalina Island was closed to tourists and used for military training. This subterranean level had only two access points: a hidden entry in the sea and a locked interior door. The door opened to a stairwell, which climbed to an interior door on the ground level of the building.

When Finn's mentor, Terrell Lincoln, purchased the compound from the U.S. government, he modernized it. The subterranean level now boasted six state-of-the-art labs, each equipped with an array of medical equipment and tools, computers, video and audio surveillance, and saltwater pools. During World War II, the Navy used the labs to study marine mammals to determine if they could be trained for military uses. Unbeknownst to Cody, Finn used the labs to imprison and study vampire sharks.

The ground level of the compound was outfitted with 12 offices, a conference room, a gym, a multimedia room, and a mess hall—all of which surrounded a large courtyard. A small tile fountain adorned the center of the square. The fountain was encircled by herb and vegetable gardens, fruit trees, flowering plants, and succulents. Four long wooden benches lined the perimeter of the courtyard.

Terrell added the top level of the building shortly after he bought it. He built six apartments above the ground floor, each with a balcony overlooking the open courtyard. Terrell's former apartment, which featured an ocean view, now belonged to Finn and his girlfriend, J.

All the apartments were designated for dolphins with human souls—or "finners" as they called themselves—who preferred to spend most of their time in their human body rather than their dolphin body. Not all dolphins had the ability to shapeshift into a human form. Only those dolphins whose souls had been human could do it—if their human body died in the ocean and their soul was rescued by a finner. Once the human soul had its own dolphin body, it could teach itself to shapeshift back into the body it had when it was human—right before it was injured or attacked and died.

If a finner wanted to work in the compound but didn't want to live there, he or she could choose to live in Avalon, where most humans reside on Catalina Island, or Two Harbors, a rustic seaside village located at the isthmus of Catalina. Or they could choose to go anywhere in the world—as long as they didn't return to their former lives and loved ones since everyone thought they were dead.

To reach the compound's subterranean level, Finn and Cody swam into a secluded cove and entered an underwater tunnel. A few twists and turns led to a sea cave. On the far wall of the cave, next to a rocky ledge, Finn entered a code on an underwater keypad. To the left of the keypad, a round panel slid open beneath the ocean's surface. Finn and Cody passed through the opening, and the panel closed behind them. They continued swimming and emerged in a saltwater pool inside one of the research labs.

Cody surveyed his surroundings. "Where are we?"

"This is one of our labs," Finn replied.

"This is where you work?" Cody asked.

"And live. When you get your new dolphin body and learn how to change back into your human form, I'll show you around our offices and the apartments upstairs. We have a few vacancies if you're interested," Finn said.

"Uh, I think an apartment here might be out of my price range, especially since I don't have a job or any money now."

"Don't worry about that," Finn said. "You can live here for free while you get used to your new life and figure out what you want to do next."

"For free? Thanks, man. That's really generous," Cody said. "So, when can I move out of your head and into a dolphin body of my own?"

"Soon. We'll see what becomes available. If a baby dolphin is born with no soul, you can take that body. Or if an older dolphin decides its soul has spent enough time in this world and is ready to move on, you can take that body when his or her soul moves out. Any preference?"

"Nope. I guess I'll take the first available," Cody said. "It's kind of crowded in here."

"Tell me about it," Finn chuckled. "You know I can see your thoughts, right? Part of dolphin communication consists of sending and receiving sound pictures. But when you're here in my head, I can see everything you're thinking. You think about sex a lot, don't you?"

"Yeah, dude. I'm a guy," Cody replied. "Don't you?"

"Yeah, but it's tapered off since I became a dolphin and realized how many more things there are to think about. Just try to keep it in check until you're out of my head, okay?"

"I'll try, but I can make no guarantees."

# 12 – Moving In

Fortunately for both Finn and Cody, early the next morning a dolphin named Cristobal decided to vacate his body and offered it to Cody. Cristobal, a dolphin who had never been human, had grown tired of life in the oceans of planet Earth and was ready to move on to something different. Cody moved in before Cristobal moved out so he could explain a few things.

"I like fish but squid is my favorite, so it'll probably be the same for you in this body," Cristobal began. "You know that dolphins breathe through their blowholes, right? Try to avoid polluted waters because this blowhole is kind of sensitive. If you see a cruise ship, swim away as fast as you can. They dump their waste, and it makes it really hard to breathe. I nearly died from that once. Humans can be pretty disgusting. But you probably know that already since you were one of them, right?"

Cody bristled inside Cristobal's head.

"Too soon? Sorry." Cristobal thought for a moment. "What else? Oh. I have excellent hearing. You should know that all dolphins are fast healers, but I'm really fast—except for the blowhole, as I mentioned. I think that's it. All in all, it's a really good body. It's about five years old now, so it's still pretty young. Good luck with it."

"Thanks, man. I really appreciate this," Cody said.

A moment later, Cristobal vacated the left side of the dolphin's brain, and Cody moved into both brain hemispheres. He felt at home right away.

# 13 – Finners

Finn let Cody settle into his new body for a few hours and then went to meet with him to explain the rules of being a finner.

"Here's the deal, Cody. Many humans believe in reincarnation, but it's mostly based on faith. We can't be the ones to prove to them that transmigration—the movement of a soul into another body after death—is real or even possible. That's not our job. And it would have devastating consequences for dolphins around the world. Humans would enslave them and force their souls into dolphin bodies that already have souls. It would be disastrous for everyone. Do you understand? You can't tell anyone about being a finner," Finn said firmly.

"I guess that makes sense," Cody said. "There are already too many people around the world who hurt dolphins. I don't want to be the one to make it worse."

"Good. Part of that means you can't go back to your old life. You have to let your loved ones grieve and move on."

Cody swallowed hard. "Yeah. I kind of figured it had to be that way. I'm sure my friend Jake saw my body wash up. There's no way I could explain to him how I'm alive after being attacked and killed like that."

"Right. I'm glad you get all this, Cody. It's really important. Do you have any questions for me?" Finn asked.

"Yeah. Since a dolphin can carry a human soul to a new dolphin body, does that mean we can live forever—jumping from dolphin to dolphin?"

"No. Several have tried, but it doesn't work. I don't know why, but it only works once. Maybe it's like a fail-safe in the universe. For whatever reason, we're not meant to be immortal."

"So, my lifespan is now limited to whatever this dolphin's lifespan is?" Cody asked.

"Yep."

"I guess I can't complain. Every minute I'm alive is a minute longer than I should've had, right?"

Finn smiled. "That's a good way to look at it. We've all been given a second chance at life here. We're very lucky."

Cody nodded in agreement. "How long do dolphins live?"

"Bottlenose dolphins like us can live up to 40 or 50 years. Like humans, females generally outlive males by a few years."

"Huh. I'm not surprised," Cody chuckled. "You know, I always thought it was so stupid that some guys talk about women as the weaker sex. First off, women live longer than men. That right there proves they're one up on us, right?"

Finn smiled. "I bet you were really popular with women in your old life."

"I did alright," Cody shrugged.

"I'm sure you did."

"Yeah, but I wasn't a dick about it. I was raised by a single mom," Cody explained. "She died a few years ago. But while she was alive, she was one tough lady. I know how hard she worked to try to make a good life for me. So, I appreciate women—and they appreciate me appreciating them."

"I bet they do. What else do you want to know?" Finn asked.

"Why are we called finners? Are we named after you?"

"No, but you're not the first to ask that. Terrell Lincoln, the very first finner, came up with the term. The word 'finner' comes from the 'phin' in 'dolphin.' But using an 'f' seemed simpler than a 'ph,' so that's why it's 'finner' and not 'phinner.' Terrell already had the name before he even met me. I took this place over from him after he died," Finn said.

"How did he die?" Cody asked.

"How do you think?"

"Uh … men in gray suits?" Cody guessed. "That's surfer slang for sharks in case you didn't know."

"Yeah, Cody, I know. And yes, it was a vicious, senseless attack by a vampire shark—a graysuit," Finn said bitterly.

"You saw it?"

"I was there. It still haunts me to this day." Finn paused to purge the memory of Terrell's violent death from his thoughts. "Cody, I know you think Tristan is your friend and that you can trust him, but it's like a human trusting a grizzly bear or a lion—or a shark. They're wild animals. Even when you think you understand them, they can turn on you in an instant. Remember that documentary about the guy who lived with the grizzlies? Or that performer in Las Vegas who was bitten on stage by his tiger? You can't trust apex predators. Ever."

"I know, but Tristan's not a straight-up shark," Cody said. "He was human once too."

"Yes, but a shark is still a shark. Any other questions?"

"How do I shift back into my human body? I'd like to be able to walk around and talk like normal instead of doing these whistles and pictures and stuff."

"You'll get used to that. Some finners find they actually prefer being in their dolphin bodies. But to morph, you have to concentrate and picture yourself transforming into your human body. It's more than just visualizing it though. You have to feel it with each and every one of your cells. You've heard of muscle memory, right?" Finn asked.

Cody nodded.

"This is like cellular memory," Finn said. "The first time is the hardest. After that it gets easier. I'll leave you alone so you can give it a try. If it works, you can find some men's clothes in the cabinet over there by the door. If you don't get it right away, don't worry. It'll happen. But you should also take time to get used to your dolphin body. That can be an adjustment. You've got no arms or legs or opposable thumbs. It's important you learn how to survive in that body too."

# 14 – Bodysurfing

When Finn saw Cody later that afternoon, he was amazed at how quickly Cody had adapted and that he had already mastered changing from his dolphin body to his human body.

"You're doing great, Cody. I've never seen anyone take to being a finner so fast," Finn said.

"Maybe it's because I spent almost all my free time in the ocean when I was human," Cody grinned.

A bright look crossed Finn's face. "Do you like to surf?"

"No, dude. I *love* to surf."

"You want to have some fun?" Finn asked.

"Always," Cody answered.

"I want you to meet someone. She's an awesome bodysurfer." Finn led Cody from lab #3 to lab #5. He entered his code into a digital keypad outside the door and let Cody inside.

A blond woman strode across the lab to greet them. Cody guessed she was in her early to mid 20s. She had a pretty face with delicate features, straight blond hair, and a petite but athletic frame. *She's hot*, Cody thought. *I'd like to …*

"Hey, after spending time in your head, I know what you're thinking and knock it off," Finn warned with a smile. "Cody, this is Julianna. Julianna, meet Cody. He's the soul I saved in the most recent attack."

Julianna extended her hand. "Hi, Cody. You can call me J. Everyone else here does except Matt. He calls me Jules, but that's just to annoy me because he knows I hate it."

Cody grasped her hand. *She's just my type*, he thought, *but then again, they're almost all my type.* "Nice to meet you, J."

Finn nudged Julianna. "Cody wants to have some fun."

Julianna flashed a conspiratorial smile at Cody. "Some fun, huh? Are you sure you're ready for this?"

"Uh huh," Cody said, wondering exactly what she meant by 'fun.'

Julianna began unbuttoning her blouse. "Okay. Let's do it."

"Wait." Finn placed his hand over Julianna's hand. "Cody, until you get used to this, turn around. I'd prefer to have you not staring at the love of my life as she takes off her clothes."

"What?" Cody said uneasily. "Why is she taking off her ..."

"Turn around," Finn said as he dropped his pants to the floor.

Cody turned away from them. Finn and Julianna finished removing their clothes and left them next to the saltwater pool. They jumped into the pool and transformed into dolphins.

"Oh! I get it. If you transform while you're dressed, your clothes get torn apart," Cody said. "Be right there!" He peeled off his clothes, climbed into the pool, and morphed.

"Let's surf," Finn whistled.

Finn entered his code into a keypad above the gate that separated the pool from the ocean tunnel. The gate slid open, and they swam through it. When they approached a round panel at the end of the tunnel, Finn entered his code again. The panel opened, and they swam into a dark sea cave. From there, Finn led them through another underwater tunnel to a cove and then to the open ocean.

When they found a nice surf break, Cody watched Finn and Julianna bodysurf. The mechanics were different for a dolphin than for a human with gangly arms and legs. Cody realized that because his dolphin body was tapered at both ends, he could now swim much faster. He swished his tail fin, which he learned was called a fluke, to propel himself toward a growing wave. He used his pectoral fins, together with his entire tail section, to direct his body. Suddenly, he was in the wave. The surfing felt incredible—a thousand times better than it did when he was human. *It doesn't feel like I'm riding the surf,* Cody marveled. *It feels like ... I am the surf.*

When Cody finished the ride, he dove underwater and swam out to catch another wave and another and another. *This is better than sex,* he thought. He glanced over at Julianna. *Almost.*

After an hour, Julianna took a break. Seeing her treading water as a human, Cody morphed too.

"What's up?" Cody asked.

"Nothing. Sometimes I like to feel the ocean on my human skin," she said. "It's so different than being a dolphin, you know?"

"I do now, thanks to you guys," he said. "I really appreciate what you and Finn are doing for me—helping me adjust and stuff."

"It's no problem. Hey, Cody," Julianna broached, "do you mind if I ask you a personal question?"

Cody instantly became aware of Julianna's naked body in close proximity to his own naked body in the ocean. *Dude, she's Finn's girlfriend. Don't even think about it,* he reminded himself. *Just pretend she's wearing a bathing suit—one of those really big, ugly ones from 100 years ago.*

"No, I don't mind," he replied. "Ask away."

"I just want to see if you're doing okay. You lost your life—I mean, your old life—only yesterday. You've been through a lot. Did you have family? Or a girlfriend?"

"No. My mom died a while back. My best friend, Jake, is—I mean, was—my only family. He was with me when it happened—not when I was bitten but right before that. We were surfing. He went ahead to shore, and I got attacked. But if my body washed up on the beach after it happened, he's probably the one who found it. I really hope he didn't have to see me all shredded like that."

"I know what you mean," Julianna said. "When I was attacked, I was alone. My husband was on the beach, so he didn't see it happen. But he probably found my body afterward.

That must've been really hard for him to see me like that."

"Yeah," Cody said quietly.

"It's not easy—wondering what life is like for them when you know they're missing you and there's nothing you can do to ease their grief. It's hard enough to deal with the trauma of the attack and losing your own life. But to know the people you care about are in pain? That's even harder. It just sucks," she said.

Cody nodded. He quickly dipped his head in the salt water to hide the tears forming at the corners of his eyes.

"If you ever need to talk, I'm here. I've been where you are, and I can help you get through this. For now, what do you say we get back to bodysurfing? I surfed nonstop when I first became a finner. I found that if I exhausted myself, I didn't have the energy to lie awake in bed, worrying about everyone I left behind. It helped me get through the hard times," she said.

"Surfing's never failed me before, so that sounds like a hell of an idea to me. Thanks, J," Cody said.

Finn swam up and joined them. "Everything okay?"

"Yep. Just taking a break. You guys ready to hit the waves again?" Julianna asked.

"Yeah. Cody, how about you?" Finn asked.

"More waves? Yeah, man." He smiled at Julianna. "It's just what the doctor ordered."

# 15 – Worrying

After bodysurfing for hours, Cody, Finn, and Julianna swam back to the compound. Exhausted, Cody declined their dinner invitation, so they showed him to his new apartment and left.

Cody collapsed on the bed. His thoughts turned to Jake. He felt bad that Jake was probably grieving for him. *If I left Jake out there and he got attacked by a shark and I saw his dead body wash up, I don't know what I'd do. I do know I'd feel like complete shit.*

Cody began to worry. *Jake could be pretty sensitive about stuff, so he's probably taking this really hard.* He smiled when he thought of how he used to tease Jake by telling him he should have women crawling all over him because he was already so in touch with his feminine side. Jake would then punch him in the arm. Cody would punch him back. It would continue until their arms went numb or they gave up because they were laughing uncontrollably. *But Jake is all alone now. What if he can't handle this by himself?*

The next morning Cody warily approached Finn. He didn't want to lie to him, but he knew he needed to check on Jake. He told Finn he felt ready to explore the ocean in his new body. Finn warned him about the many dangers lurking in the vast Pacific Ocean, but Cody didn't back down.

"I need to do this. I'm feeling smarter already from being part dolphin, and I feel like I'm languishing here. See? I just said 'languishing.' I've never used that word before. I know I haven't been here long. But I need to get out and get some mental stimulation, or I'm gonna go crazy," Cody said.

"Really? I don't remember Cristobal feeling so claustrophobic here," Finn countered.

"I'm not Cristobal."

"No, but you're not the old Cody anymore either. You cannot, under any circumstances, go back to where you came from. If humans know dolphins can transport souls, they'll enslave us—even more than they already do for their stupid amusement parks, tourist attractions, military operations, and who-knows-what-else. No one can know you're alive."

"No one will know," Cody promised.

"Okay. I'm trusting you. When do you want to leave?"

"I'm ready now."

"Leave through lab #5. I'll open the gates," Finn said.

Cody left the compound and swam at a leisurely pace toward the North County San Diego coastline. He didn't know that his dolphin body had been microchipped while Cristobal had it or that Finn and Julianna could trace his journey.

Later that evening, Julianna entered Finn's office. "Ready for dinner?" she asked.

"Almost," Finn said.

She noticed him staring intently at his computer screen. "What'cha doin'?"

"Watching Cody do exactly what he said he wasn't going to do."

She looked over his shoulder at the GPS signal on his screen. "He's swimming home?"

"That's what it looks like."

"We've experienced this before. Usually they just want to make sure their loved ones are okay—from a distance and in their dolphin bodies. I don't think Cody will do anything stupid like change into his human body and talk to people. He probably wants to check on his friend Jake. Then he'll come right back," Julianna said.

Finn sighed. "I hope you're right."

# 16 – Paddle Out

The next day, Cody swam up and down the coast from Del Mar to Encinitas, hoping to spot Jake out surfing. Near sunset, he stopped in at Seaside Reef, the beach where he surfed his last wave with Jake. From underwater, he saw what looked like hundreds of legs dangling from surfboards. *No way. This can't be for me, can it?*

Cody had attended a few paddle outs before—for older surfers who died—but he'd never seen one this large. To get a closer look, he swam to the middle of the circle of surfers. He lifted his dolphin head out of the water. He found himself surrounded by flowers and in the midst of at least 100 surfers who splashed water toward the sky, chanting "Cody! Cody!"

*Wow! I can't believe this is really all for me.* Cody glanced around the circle. As soon as he spotted Jake, he heard someone in the group yell, "Hey, Cody's here!" Cody ducked underwater. *Oh my god! Finn's gonna kill me. But wait ... How could they know it's me? I'm a dolphin.* Then he heard laughter echoing above. *Oh, it was a joke. Ha ha. Good one! I guess since I'm here and no one actually knows it's me, I might as well go out with a splash.*

Cody swam upward as fast as he could and leapt out of the water, arcing his body. As he sailed through the air, he looked toward Jake again. He saw him sitting next to their friend Carlos. *That's good. Since Carlos is a minister, he's probably helped lots of people through this before. He'll know what to say to make Jake feel better.*

Cody splashed down into the water and swished his fluke to say goodbye to everyone. He heard the circle burst into applause as he swam away, back toward Catalina Island.

# 17 – Chipped

Cody entered the sea cave and saw Finn waiting for him at the gate. He didn't like the expression on Finn's face but followed him into the compound. They entered the saltwater pool in lab #5, then exited the pool and pulled on their clothes.

"You have something you want to tell me?" Finn asked.

"Not really," Cody replied.

"You went home, didn't you?"

"Yeah," Cody confessed. "I just wanted to make sure Jake was okay."

"You can't do that, Cody," Finn said.

"I didn't think there'd be any harm. I was a dolphin. Nobody knew it was me."

"It doesn't matter. You have to let him go."

"I know. You're right," Cody said. "So, how did you know I went home?"

"We're all microchipped. That way we know where everyone is in case there's a graysuit attack. When we're dolphins, we can just send each other a picture. It's easy. But as humans, we're more limited in our communication. We have to rely on technology," Finn explained.

"So, you knew where I was the whole time?" Cody asked.

"Yep," Finn said. "When you took over Cristobal's dolphin body, you took over his chip. When you morph into your human body, that chip morphs with you like any other body part."

"I'm really sorry, Finn. I was just worried about Jake. He's probably taking this really hard."

"I get that, but we need to be careful. No one can know about us or about what we are. You get that, don't you?"

"Yeah," Cody said. "And I swear I'd never do anything to put us at risk."

"I promise it'll get better in time. Julianna and I are here if you want to talk about it. She's helped a lot of finners get through this transition period. She can help you if you want," Finn said. "Listen, I have to get back to the lab."

"Okay. What exactly do you do here anyway?" Cody asked.

"Research."

"That's kind of obvious," Cody grinned. "What kind of research?"

"We're conducting research on vampire sharks. Our mission is to save lives and prevent the killing of humans like you."

Finn explained a few details about vampire sharks and their physiology. "We'll fill you in on the rest after you've had more time to adjust to life here. If you want to stick around, you can help. For now, just focus on working through whatever you need to work through. We're here if you need us."

# 18 – Vampire Shark Adrift

For the next couple of weeks, Cody bodysurfed every day as hard as he could and as long as he could. *Julianna's right*, he thought. *The best medicine for grief is sheer exhaustion.*

When he wasn't surfing or sleeping though, he still worried about Jake. So, once a week, he'd swim from Catalina to the North County shoreline and spend a day or two looking for him up and down the coast. He kept moving so Finn wouldn't see him lingering in any one place and get mad at him. Cody didn't know what he'd do if he actually found Jake since finners weren't allowed to reveal their human forms to anyone from their past. But that didn't stop him from looking.

It was on his third trip, late one night, that he found Tristan alone, clinging to a surfboard. Cody saw he had been staked in the chest. Since Tristan was still alive, Cody deduced that the stake must have narrowly missed his heart—otherwise, he would've died and turned to ash. But the gash was so deep, Cody thought he'd probably bleed to death before his body could heal. Seeing Tristan in excruciating pain, Cody had a déjà vu to his own experience three weeks earlier when he was attacked by a vampire shark. That was the first time he saw Tristan. He remembered Tristan arguing with the blond man who attacked him. *It looked like Tristan swam out there to try to stop that guy and save me. Maybe I should try to help him.*

Cody watched as Tristan attempted to morph into a shark. But due to the severity of his injury, Tristan couldn't muster enough energy to hold his shark form. He tried again. He flickered back and forth between forms—human, shark, human.

As Tristan gazed into the dolphin's eyes, a spark of recognition flickered across his face. "Is that really you?" Tristan asked.

*No way. How could he possibly know it's me?* Cody wondered. *Sense of smell, maybe?* He bobbed his bottlenose up and down.

As Tristan shifted from human to shark again, he felt the dolphin's movement with his lateral line. The nerve impulses traveled to his brain, helping him hold his shark form.

Cody wriggled his body and swam closer. Tristan felt a tingling sensation across his head as his vast network of electroreceptors detected Cody's electrical field. Tristan focused all his energy to hold his shark form. But after a few seconds, he felt himself fade back into his human body. He looked at the dolphin and tried to morph again but couldn't.

"Thanks for trying, Cody. I guess it wasn't meant to be." Tristan placed his hands back on his surfboard and rested his head on his hands.

Cody changed into his human form. He knew it was a violation of Finn's rules, but he thought an exception could be made in a life-or-death situation—and with someone who wasn't entirely human either. He draped his arms across the surfboard, opposite Tristan.

"Jake really misses you," Tristan whispered.

"You know Jake?! How is he?" Cody asked.

"Okay."

"I've tried to find him—in my dolphin body, I mean. I can't let him see me like this. He thinks I'm dead. I'm pretty sure he saw my body wash up on the beach after I got attacked."

"Yeah," Tristan said. "It messed him up pretty bad."

Cody nodded. He felt terrible his best friend had to see him like that. He wondered again how he would've dealt with it if the situation were reversed—if it was Jake's bloody, mangled body that washed up on shore. And again, he shuddered at the thought.

Glancing across the board, Tristan saw Cody shiver and

steered the conversation away from Jake. "I've heard rumors of this dolphin/human reincarnation thing but didn't know if it was true. I've never met one before. I thought it was a myth," Tristan smiled weakly, "like vampires."

"Nope. It's true," Cody said. "This dolphin came along when I died. He offered to carry my soul. He let me live in his brain until I could get a dolphin body of my own. Good thing it didn't take very long. Man, it was crowded in there. What happened to you? It looks like you got staked."

"Yeah. By my best friend." Tristan glanced down at his wound. Blood seeped through his torn stitches and into the ocean. "Make that former best friend. He had a bunch of graysuits attack me. Then he went after my fiancée. Jake's the one who saved us."

"He did? Whoa! Jake's a hero. I always knew he had it in him, even if he'd never believe it about himself."

"Yeah. Jake's a good guy." Tristan lifted his eyes and looked at Cody. *He's so young. He must've been 22 or 23 when Rick killed him—or at least his human body.* "I'm really sorry about what happened to you. I tried to stop Rick, the vampire shark who attacked you, but I was too late."

Cody swallowed hard. The searing pain from the bites still felt fresh and raw in his memory. "I saw you there. I heard you guys arguing. That's how I know your name. And his."

Tristan's face twisted in pain. Cody couldn't tell if it was from the stake wound or from guilt.

"Hey man, it's not your fault," Cody said softly. "I saw you grab him. I know you tried. But the damage was already done."

"I know. I'm so sorry," Tristan whispered.

"Dude, you weren't the one who killed me."

"No, but …" Tristan sharply sucked in his breath. His face contorted in agony. "I don't think I'm gonna make it, Cody. I think this is it."

"What can I do? Tell me what to do."

Tristan was too weak to answer. He couldn't hold his eyes open.

"I'll stay with you," Cody promised. He swam to Tristan's side of the board and put his arm around Tristan's shoulders. The water lapped against them as they clutched the surfboard.

Cody racked his brain, but he had no idea how to help Tristan, who was very close to death. He felt Tristan's hands slip off the surfboard and saw his face drop into the water. He lifted Tristan's head. "Tristan?"

*What do I do?* Cody looked around frantically. *Finn! He knows all about vampire sharks. He'll know what to do.*

Cody removed the leash from the surfboard. Gripping the leash in one hand, he pulled Tristan's arms over his shoulders so Tristan rested against his back. He wrapped the leash around Tristan's wrists to bind them together in front of his neck. "Hold on," he said, though he didn't know if Tristan could hear him. He shifted into his dolphin body and raced to Finn's compound, carrying Tristan on his back.

Tristan, barely conscious, felt his arms locked around Cody's neck as cool salt water rushed beneath him. *Leilani*, he thought, before blacking out again.

# 19 – Stitches

When Cody reached the sea cave, he wriggled backward and slipped out of Tristan's arms. He gently rolled Tristan up onto the rocky ledge. Cody pressed a button on the underwater keypad and whistled for someone to open the gate. He raced toward lab #5.

Once inside the lab's saltwater pool, he changed back into his human body and climbed out of the water. He pulled on his shorts, then darted out the open door and down the hallway. "Where's Finn?!" he demanded of the first person he saw.

"In his apartment. Why?" Lucia asked.

"No time!" Cody sprinted upstairs and banged on the door to Finn's apartment.

Finn flung open the door. "Cody? Do you know what time it is? The sun isn't even up."

"I need you. Hurry!" Cody pleaded.

Julianna appeared in the bedroom doorway. "Finn, what's going on?"

"I don't know yet. Go back to bed. I'll take care of it." After she stepped inside the bedroom, he turned to Cody. "What?"

"Come with me!" Cody grabbed Finn's arm and started running. "He's dying! He needs your help!"

Cody guided Finn to Tristan, who was still lying on the ledge. As Finn approached, he wrinkled his nose in disgust. "A graysuit?! What the hell is he doing here in our cave?"

"You've gotta save him," Cody said.

"You brought me a vampire shark? To save? Are you out of your freakin' mind?" Finn turned toward the tunnel.

"No!" Cody gripped Finn's shoulder and refused to let go. "He tried to save me when I was attacked. He knows Jake. We have to try to save him!"

"No. No way I'm saving one of those things! Do you know how many people they've killed?"

"He's not like that," Cody argued. "The day I died and you rescued me, he was there. He tried to stop the graysuit who killed me."

"Cody, you have no idea what you're asking me to do."

"I'm asking you to save a life," Cody said. "That's your mission, right? Saving lives?"

The hardness in Finn's face softened ever so slightly.

"Please!" Cody begged.

Seeing Cody's concern, Finn relented. "Help me get him to the lab. But if this goes wrong, it's your head."

"Yeah, whatever," Cody said. "Just help him!"

Cody pulled Tristan onto his back again and shifted into his dolphin body. Finn opened the entry tunnel to the compound, and they swam to lab #1. When they were inside the saltwater pool, they morphed. Cody released Tristan and removed the leash from his hands. He grasped Tristan's upper body while Finn gripped his feet. They lifted him out of the water and onto a gurney. They rolled the gurney across the room and hoisted him onto a hospital bed.

"Restrain his arms and legs," Finn said.

While Finn washed his hands, Cody pinned down Tristan's wrists and ankles, using the metal restraints on the bed.

Finn placed electrodes on Tristan's chest to monitor his heart rate. It was incredibly slow, which was normal for a vampire, but faint. *Too faint*, Finn thought. He inserted an IV in Tristan's arm and administered a strong anesthetic.

Finn appraised the stake wound. "This is huge. I can't believe he's survived this long." He opened up what was left of Tristan's stitches and peered inside. "Whoever stitched him up saved his life. You can see where they tried to repair the damage, and it helped. But it's still a mess in here. Cody, this is going to take some time. Go home. I'll call you when I'm done."

"No, I want to stay." Seeing the hard look on Finn's face, Cody added, "If that's okay."

"Fine, but it's going to be bloody." Finn glanced down at the gash. "Well, more bloody. If you're at all squeamish, you should leave now for your own good."

"I'm staying." Cody sat in a chair on the other side of the bed, looking at everything in the room except Tristan's bloody chest.

Finn set to work repairing the damage. Hours later, he placed the final stitch.

"Are you done? Is he gonna be okay?" Cody asked.

"I don't know. I've done everything I can," Finn said.

"Now what do we do?"

"Now we wait," Finn answered. "And Cody? Never do this again."

# 20 – Lockdown

Finn trudged home. He washed up and climbed into bed.

Julianna opened her arms and wrapped them around him. "I must've fallen asleep waiting for you. What was up with Cody?"

"You're never going to believe what he brought me to save," Finn said.

She cocked her head to one side. "What?"

"A vampire shark."

Julianna's eyes widened. "To save? Why in the world would he do that?"

"He thinks this guy tried to save him from being attacked. He says this is one of the good ones—as if such a thing even exists," Finn said.

"Where is he now?" Julianna asked.

"The graysuit? Restrained in lab #1."

"Can I see him? I'd like to see if he's the one who killed me when I was human."

"He's not," Finn said. "He looks nothing like the one you showed me. But he's still a vampire shark, which means he's dangerous. While he's here, that lab is on lockdown. I don't care if Cody knows him. There are no exceptions to the lockdown policy."

"I'd still like to see him," Julianna said. "I'm curious."

"I know, but I'm exhausted. Can we talk about this later?"

"Sure." Julianna kissed Finn's cheek and nestled against his shoulder. She glanced up at his tired face. "I love you."

"I love you too."

# 21 – Ripple

Finn listened to Julianna's restful breathing, wishing he could fall asleep.

*A graysuit!* Finn thought to himself. *Cody brought me a graysuit to save. Not to study. Not to kill. But to save. What the hell was he thinking? And what was I thinking doing it?*

To Finn, it felt like yesterday … the day that Terrell, his mentor—his carrier—was killed by a vampire shark. *Terrell saved my life, but I couldn't save his.*

Finn remembered the day Terrell rescued him. Finn had been out surfing. A particularly vicious wave threw him headfirst into a large craggy rock on the ocean floor. The blow, which took a huge chunk out of his forehead, killed him instantly. Terrell was there.

"Hi. I'm Terrell. I saw what happened."

"What?" Finn asked, disoriented. He felt woozy like he was rippling along with the ocean current. He saw a lifeless body floating near a rock. Blood gushed from the man's head. Finn was shocked when he realized it was his own face he was looking at. He turned to the dolphin and then back to the body. He gulped. "Is that me?"

Terrell nodded yes.

"Am I dreaming?" Finn asked.

"No," Terrell answered.

"Am I dead?"

"Yes," Terrell said. "And you have a choice to make, but you have to do it quickly. Your soul has left its body. If you want to stay here on this planet and in this dimension, you can. I can help you. It's important you understand you can't have your old life back. That's gone. But if you're not yet ready to leave this plane of existence, you can stay. If you don't want to stay, you'll move on to your next destination."

"Where?" Finn asked, still staring at his own body.

"Wherever your soul needs to go to progress on its unique path. I don't know. It's different for everyone," Terrell said.

"I don't understand," Finn said.

"I know and I'm sorry, but you have to decide now. Your soul doesn't have a body. It's not tethered to this dimension anymore, so it's going to move on unless you make a conscious decision to stay. If you stay, you need a body to anchor you here. I can take you to one—a dolphin—but you have to choose now. What's it going to be?" Terrell asked.

Finn looked at his 37-year-old body. *I'm not done here yet,* he thought. *I'm too young to die or move on or whatever.* "I want to stay," he answered.

"Are you sure?" Terrell asked.

"Yes."

"Okay," Terrell said. "Let's go find you an empty dolphin."

# 22 — Guest

Finn finally drifted into a fitful sleep. He dreamed of bodies—bitten, battered, and bloody—floating in the ocean. He jerked awake and followed the smell of coffee to the kitchen, where Julianna was pouring herself a steaming cup.

She looked at the dark circles under his eyes and handed her coffee mug to him. "You need this more than I do. Did you even sleep? You look terrible."

"Good afternoon to you too," Finn said, pretending to be annoyed.

"Sorry. Bad dreams?" Julianna threw her arms around his neck and gave him a kiss.

"Yep."

She pulled her head back and peered into his eyes. "Lemme guess. Vampire sharks?"

"Yep." Finn pulled away and took a sip of coffee.

"Are you going to be able to deal with this? Having one of them here as Cody's, uh, guest?" she asked.

"I don't know. I made the decision last night to save him. Now, in the cold light of day, it seems like a really stupid decision, but I guess I'm stuck with it."

Julianna watched Finn's face slowly brighten. "What?" she asked.

"We have to be careful how we handle this with Cody, but since this graysuit is Cody's friend, maybe we can use that to our advantage," he said. "Maybe this one will actually cooperate and tell us what we want to know. Maybe we can find out who created him, how many of them there are, where they live, where they congregate—that is, if they do congregate. Maybe we can finally get some information that will help us."

"Maybe. But be careful."

"I will." Finn kissed Julianna, set the coffee mug on the counter, and headed for the shower. "I'm going to get ready and then go check on Cody's graysuit friend."

"All right, but call and let me know when you think you'll be home. With that thing in there, if you're late and you don't call, I'll worry. Then I'll have to round up a posse, break into the lab …"

"I'll call," he smiled. "Don't worry. Have a good day."

"You too. Or at least an uneventful one."

# 23 – Captivity

Since Tristan was the only graysuit in captivity at the moment, Finn stopped by his office first to catch up on paperwork. Shortly after he arrived, Julianna's voice called out over the intercom.

"Finn? We have a vampire shark sighting. Jamal sent a sound picture to Matt. It's Lily. Matt and I are going to take the research vessel and play 'dangling diver' with the graysuit. Sunset should be the perfect time to catch her. Are you okay here with Cody's graysuit?" Julianna asked.

"Yes," Finn replied. "You and Matt be careful, okay?"

"You too. Love you."

"Love you more," Finn said.

"Ha ha." Julianna glanced at her watch. "See you in a few hours. Looks like we'll be having a late dinner tonight."

"That's fine. I can finish up here and check on Cody's friend. I'll have dinner ready when you get back."

"Sounds good," she said. "Over and out."

Finn typed away at his computer, documenting the details of Tristan's arrival and surgery. *All right, now it's time to see how the patient is doing.*

Finn strolled to lab #1, entered his code, and walked inside. Tristan lay in bed, unconscious. Finn took his vitals. As he listened to the slow beat of Tristan's vampire heart, he thought about Julianna and grew anxious. He knew Julianna and Matt had successfully captured and brought many graysuits back to the lab. But, before he could stop it, his mind flashed to Julianna and what happened to her when she was still human and savagely killed by a graysuit.

Brimming with years of anger and resentment over what he'd seen graysuits do to humans—and to Julianna and Terrell in particular—Finn leaned over Tristan. He saw Tristan's eyes flutter open as he bent down next to his ear. "I know what you are," Finn hissed. "I know what you do. And you will never leave here alive."

Finn stormed home. He set a pot of water on the stove to boil and opened a beer. He drank it alone as he stared out the window at the darkening ocean, worrying about Julianna. After a few minutes, Matt's voice called out to him on the ham radio. He reported that they had captured Lily, the graysuit, and were on their way back to the compound.

Relieved, Finn turned his attention to dinner. He boiled some pasta and chopped fresh herbs and vegetables from the courtyard garden. He dumped everything into a bowl and tossed it with olive oil and vinegar. As he placed it in the refrigerator, he realized he forgot to record Tristan's vital signs on his chart.

Finn hastily returned to lab #1. He didn't know Tristan had awoken just a few minutes before and was alarmed to find himself in a place that looked like a hospital room but with a saltwater pool inside it. Tristan fell asleep again before Finn entered the lab.

Finn re-examined the various devices monitoring Tristan's condition and noted the results on his chart. Outside the lab, he ran into Cody who asked to see Tristan. Finn said no, but he promised to let Cody know when Tristan would be well enough for visitors. He hurried home.

Finn arrived at the same time as Julianna. "Perfect timing!" He gave her a quick kiss and opened the door to their apartment. "The pasta salad is in the fridge. I'll get some bowls."

"That sounds great. I'm starving," Julianna said.

"Everything go okay with your graysuit?" Finn asked.

"Yep, Lily's on lockdown in lab #4. How's Cody's graysuit?" she asked.

"On lockdown in lab #1. Cody is begging to see him. Maybe tomorrow I'll let him in and see if the graysuit will tell us anything that might help us. So, tell me about your evening."

Julianna recounted how she pulled Matt from the water just as Lily was about to attack. "Matt was all worried about his toes, but I had him the whole time," she laughed. "You should've seen Lily when we trapped her in the net! She's all, like, 'Let me go now or I'll kill you.' It was hilarious. Then she showed us her fangs, like that's supposed to scare us. She's in a net! Then she tried to tear it apart. Classic."

Finn reached across the table and clasped Julianna's hand. "It sounds like we're both going to be busy over the next few days. But for now, I'm glad you're here safe and sound with me."

# 24 – Rest

The next morning, Finn punched his code into the keypad at lab #1. He closed the door behind him and approached the bed. Seeing Tristan awake, he tried his best to sound cheerful and friendly. "Tristan, I see you're awake. That's good!"

"Where am I?" Tristan croaked.

"You're in my lab. I'm Dr. Finnegan. Cody found you and brought you here."

"I need salt water," Tristan said.

"Yeah, I've heard you guys need to submerge yourselves in salt water every three days or you age and die pretty quickly. Is that right?" Finn asked.

Tristan wondered how this doctor knew so much about graysuits. But he also knew he desperately needed to submerge himself in salt water, so he nodded.

"Hang on," Finn smiled. "I'll call Cody, and we can help you to the water." While Finn could've easily helped Tristan to the pool on his own, he knew he'd feel safer having Cody there when he removed Tristan's restraints.

Finn glanced at his watch. "It's only been about 30 hours since you were last in the ocean—when Cody brought you to me. But maybe in your weakened state, you need the salt water sooner?"

Tristan tried to shrug but didn't have the energy to raise his shoulders. He'd never been staked or come that close to death before, so he had no idea.

A minute later, Cody rapped on the door. Finn opened it and Cody entered, breathless.

"That was quick. Did you run here?" Finn asked.

"Yeah. I wanted to see Tristan," Cody replied.

"I need your help walking Tristan to the pool," Finn said.

"Yeah, sure." Cody's face lit up upon seeing Tristan with his eyes open. "Tristan! Hey man, it's good to see you."

Tristan smiled weakly through cracked lips.

Finn unlocked the metal cuffs on Tristan's wrists and ankles, and detached the monitors. Together, he and Cody helped Tristan into the pool. After a few minutes, the redness in Tristan's face began to dissipate. After a few more minutes, he felt well enough to talk. "Cody. Good to see you."

"Are you feeling better?" Cody asked.

"The salt water helps," Tristan said. "Where are we?"

"This is Finn's place. Finn's the one who saved me. And you," Cody said.

Tristan dunked his head underwater and surfaced again. He wiped his fingers across his eyes. "How did I get here?"

"I brought you," Cody said. "You blacked out. I didn't know what to do. I thought Finn could help. He's a doctor and a marine biologist. He knows a lot."

Tristan looked over Cody's shoulder at Finn. "You saved me?"

"Yeah," Finn shrugged, "I stitched you back up. I've had to keep you sedated to prevent you from moving while your body heals."

"Oh." Tristan blinked groggily. "How long have I been here again?"

"A little over a day," Cody answered. "I brought you here early yesterday morning."

"But I'm so dry. It feels like longer." Tristan glanced at the pool around him and then at Finn. "How do you know about what I am? About the salt water?"

"I've been studying vampire sharks for a while now," Finn said.

"You have? Why?" Tristan asked.

"We can talk about that later. You need your rest. Cody and

I are going to leave. We'll come back in a few hours. If you want to get out of the pool before then, press that button." Finn pointed to a large red button on the side of the pool, just above the water's surface. "It'll ring my office and my apartment. Then Cody and I can help you back to bed."

"Okay," Tristan said, "but first I need to call …"

"Later," Finn interrupted. "You need to recuperate from your surgery. No excitement, just rest."

"But …"

"Later," Finn said firmly.

The sedatives in Tristan's body made it difficult to think. He looked at Finn again. There was something about his manner. Tristan couldn't say what, but something was … strange.

"We'll be back soon! Get some rest," Cody called over his shoulder as Finn ushered him from the lab.

# 25 – Venom

While Tristan slept in the salt water, Finn left Cody and strode down the hall to lab #4. He entered as quietly as he could.

Julianna glanced up. "Come on in. I'm just getting to the good stuff." She turned away from Finn and skillfully extracted a fang from the heavily sedated, unconscious graysuit lying on the surgery table. She examined the venom sac inside the bleeding gum, which used to house the fang. She surgically removed the sac, sealed it in a small glass jar, and quickly stitched up the hole in Lily's gum.

"Well?" Finn asked.

"This one seems to be exactly like the others. I'll do the other fang next. Then I'll analyze the blood sample I took earlier and the venom to be sure, but this gal here looks like a regular old vampire shark. She's not the creator."

Finn sighed. "Then we'll just keep trying till we find the creator. When she wakes up, do you think you can get her to talk?"

"I doubt it. We haven't been able to get any of the others to reveal who their creator is," Julianna said glumly.

Finn moved behind her and rubbed her shoulders. "No, we haven't." He placed his lips near her ear. "But you can be very persuasive when you want to be."

Julianna smiled. "That's true. But here in captivity without her venom, Lily's only got a few days to live—a week at most." She turned to face Finn. "You still look really tired. You should go home and take a nap."

"I was actually on my way to do that, but I wanted to stop in and see you."

"I'm glad you did. Do you think you'll be able to get any sleep without the nightmares?" she asked.

"I wish," he said. "I try not to think about it. But as soon as I shut my eyes, I keep seeing Terrell's body or your body or other bodies. I don't know how to stop it. You still have nightmares about your attack, right?"

"Yeah, but they've diminished. At first, I had nightmares all the time. They were so vivid. I'd see myself with my husband at the beach. I'd smell the scrambled eggs he was cooking over the fire. I'd stroll into the ocean to rinse our dishes. Then I'd feel the teeth sinking into my legs and the vampire shark carrying me out to sea. I'd feel gnashing and slicing into the right side of my neck and shoulder—the pain getting sharper and sharper until I blacked out. That's when I met Terrell."

Finn hugged Julianna tightly. "I'm so sorry you had to go through that. We'll find who's responsible—either the one who attacked you or the one who created him."

Julianna nodded. "What's going on with the graysuit in your lab?"

"Nothing. I think Cody wants to be best friends with him, hang out, surf."

"You haven't told Cody what we do with vampire sharks yet?" she asked.

"Not everything. He knows we study them, but he doesn't know they never leave here alive. He's not ready to hear it. He's really attached to this one. You'd think with what he went through when he died that he'd want nothing to do with them. But he keeps saying this vampire shark is a good guy."

"Well, with many things in nature, there's an exception to every rule. We do occasionally see dolphins who are violent and who kill for pleasure. Maybe at the other end of the spectrum there are vampire sharks who are actually nice guys," Julianna said.

"Doubtful."

"So, what's Cody's friend's name?" Julianna asked.

"Tristan," Finn said.

"That's funny. That was my husband's name."

"I know. That's why I didn't bring it up. I'm still kind of jealous of the guy. He got to be married to you," Finn teased.

Julianna groaned. "Not this again."

"I'm only joking. How can I be jealous of someone you were with 40 years ago?"

"I'm not talking about that," she said. "I'm talking about the marriage thing."

"Is it so terrible I'd like to be married to you? We've been together 11 years. I'm pretty confident it's going to work out," he chuckled.

Julianna, however, wasn't amused. "I told you I don't want to get married again. Ever. There's no reason for it. I was married before. I loved him completely. But I always felt like he was holding something back from me, like there was part of his life he was unwilling to share. I thought after we were married he'd feel safe enough to open up to me, but he never did."

"What does that have to do with us?" Finn asked.

"Nothing. All I'm saying is you don't have to be married to fully commit to someone. I love you, and I love how things are. Let's leave it at that."

"Fine. But if you change your mind, you know where to find me," he said.

"At home in bed having nightmares?" she smirked.

"Nice. You're so understanding."

"Sorry. I really do hope you sleep well."

"Me too," he said. "I'll see you tonight."

After Finn closed the door behind him, Julianna settled at her desk. It had been a long time since she'd thought about Tristan. *I really did love him ... and, oh my god, he was so sexy.* She remembered Tristan's hypnotic dark brown eyes, smooth dark brown hair, and perfectly toned body. *I wonder what happened to him—if he met someone else and married again after I died.*

Julianna felt a tiny flare of jealousy imagining Tristan married to another woman. Once aware of it, she quickly extinguished it. *I do hope he finally found someone he could confide in—someone who could truly share his life. Because that obviously wasn't me.*

# 26 — Late for Dinner

Later that afternoon, Finn and Cody returned to lab #1. They helped a semiconscious Tristan back to his bed. Finn reattached the monitors and clamped on the restraints.

"Do you really have to cuff him down like that?" Cody asked. "I told you, he's a good guy. He tried to save me."

"I'm responsible for a lot of people here. I can't take any chances until I complete my own evaluation," Finn said.

Cody rolled his eyes. "When will he be awake enough for me to talk with him again?"

"It's hard to say. It depends how his recovery goes. For now, the best thing is to keep him sedated. The less he moves, the more his body will heal. The gash in his chest is the worst I've ever seen. He would've died if not for you. We need to give him time. I know it's difficult, but it's what's best for Tristan right now," Finn said.

"Okay," Cody reluctantly agreed.

"I'd like to talk with you more about the work we do. I'm hoping you and Tristan can help us," Finn said.

"Sure, man. Whatever you need."

Finn glanced at his watch. "Damn. I'm going to be late for dinner. She hates it when I'm late."

"Julianna?" Cody asked.

Tristan, still sleeping, jerked against the restraints. Somewhere through a thick gray fog he heard Julianna's name. *Julianna. Julianna's waiting for me, Dean. I can't be late for dinner again,* he said to himself, lost in the ether between memories and dreams.

"Yes, Julianna," Finn replied to Cody. "We'll talk about this later. Let's leave Tristan so he can sleep."

# 27 – Sighting

Across the Pacific Ocean, Jake and Leilani slept through the day. They awoke at dusk. Jake went surfing while Leilani watched from shore.

She saw two people stroll to the water to catch the last glimmers of color before the sky turned dark. Something seemed familiar about them. She walked toward the couple, careful to stay on the dry sand so she didn't get her bandages wet. She turned toward them. "Beautiful sunset tonight."

"Yeah," the man said somberly.

*The witnesses! They're the ones who saw the shark attack.* Leilani recalled their faces from the news interviews on the beach, shortly after the attacks occurred. Since they still looked stricken, she decided not to mention it.

"May I ask you a question? I was supposed to meet some friends here earlier, but my flight was cancelled and then my next flight was delayed. Anyway, I haven't been able to reach them. I was wondering if maybe you've seen them? A man, about 6 feet tall, good-looking, brown hair, light blue eyes. And a woman, 5-foot-6, tan, big brown eyes, wavy brown hair, really pretty. They're both around my age, and they're really good surfers."

The man and woman looked at each other. Their faces brightened a little as they both said, "Yeah."

"You've seen them?" Leilani verified.

"It was before dawn—before those surfers got killed," the man said.

"You saw them though? That's a relief! Did you happen to see if they're staying here at the hotel?" Leilani asked.

"They came from that direction, but I can't say for sure," the woman replied.

"Thank you," Leilani said. "You've been a big help. At least I know I'm in the right place."

Leilani returned to her towel and stretched her legs in front of her. The wounds beneath her bandages ached, but she didn't want to take her painkillers while she was awake. The pills made it difficult to think, and she needed to have her head clear if she was going to find Dean and Skylar.

An hour later, Jake emerged from the ocean with his surfboard. He ran up to Leilani and reached for his towel, careful to keep his distance so he didn't drip salt water on her. "They were here," he said. "I talked to a couple of surfers who saw Skylar the morning of the attack. They said she was with a guy but couldn't remember anything about him."

"I talked to two people who said they saw them before the attack. We're in the right place. The question is, are they still here?" Leilani asked. "Jake, how often do vampire sharks feed?"

"If you have a big meal like they did, you can easily go for three days without eating."

"So, if they're going to kill again, we don't have much time to find them. I'm going to question the hotel staff. There may be people on duty now who I haven't talked to yet." Leilani set off toward the hotel.

"Hang on. I'll go with you," Jake said.

"It'll be better if I talk to them alone. They might be willing to share more if there's only one of us asking questions," she explained.

"Is there anything I can do to help?" he asked.

"Nope, I've got this."

Jake watched her march toward the hotel. *I guess that's that. If Tristan were here, he'd know what to do. He'd know how to find them. But I'm not Tristan.*

# 28 – Home Again

An hour later, Leilani returned to their hotel room. She explained to Jake that a bellhop remembered seeing Dean and Skylar leave with their bags around the time she and Jake checked in.

"So, we just missed them?" Jake hung his head. "I'm sorry. I wish I was better at this. I thought I'd be able to sense where they are, but I'm not helping at all."

"You helped tonight when you told me those surfers remembered seeing Skylar. And you're helping just by being here. My state of mind is … not what it should be. I know I haven't fully processed what Dean and Logan did to me, or losing Tristan, but I can't deal with that now or I'll break down. We don't have that kind of time. We need to find Dean and Skylar before they kill again. I need you here, Jake."

He gave her a feeble smile. "Okay. I'm here for whatever you need. And you don't have to keep all that stuff bottled up inside. You can break down if you need to. I know you're strong, but you're still human—unlike some of us."

"Thanks, but it's better for me right now if I don't," she said. "The bellhop told me he thought Dean and Skylar were headed for the North Shore. He overheard them talking about Sunset and Pipeline. Let's head over now while it's dark. Maybe we'll get lucky."

Jake and Leilani checked out of the hotel and headed up the highway. He glanced at her as she dozed in the passenger seat. *She really is beautiful.*

Leilani awoke and caught Jake staring at her. "What? Am I drooling?" She quickly wiped her mouth.

"No. I was just … Hey, didn't you used to live in Oahu?"

"Yeah, when I was a teenager," she said.

"Are your parents still here?" he asked.

"I don't know. I haven't spoken with them since I left for college."

"Really? Why?"

"It's a long story," she said.

"Sorry. If you don't want to talk about it …"

"No, it's just that I don't think they ever liked having me around. When they had me, they thought they'd get this little version of themselves. But I was pretty much their polar opposite. I always felt like I was in the way—like I was keeping them from the life they really wanted. When I left, I felt like I was doing them a favor," Leilani explained.

"That must've been tough growing up like that," Jake said.

"Most of the time I felt like I was the parent and they were the kids. It really wasn't much of a childhood. Whatever. It was a long time ago."

Jake knew he should take that as his cue to stop asking questions, but he had one more. Having lost his parents, he had a hard time hearing that hers were still alive but that she didn't want to see them. "Do you think you'll ever see them again? Maybe they've changed."

"I don't know. Can we drop it for now?"

They drove in silence. Leilani stared out the passenger window. *See my parents? That's not a good idea, is it?*

Jake and Leilani arrived at Pipeline. They wandered around but didn't see anyone. At Sunset, Jake thought he caught a whiff of Skylar's scent—the ocean mixed with tropical fruit—but it quickly disappeared. They scoured the local hotels and several other beaches but found no trace of Skylar or Dean.

*There are so many awesome surf breaks here. I don't know if we'll ever find them,* Leilani worried. She did a quick search online to see if they were missing anything. On a whim, she typed in her parents' names, Jeff and Linda Waters. One listing popped up. Leilani gasped. *It's nearby.*

"Did you find something?" Jake asked.

"My parents."

Fifteen minutes later, they parked across the street from a tiny, ramshackle cottage. They could see the silver light of the television flickering through the front window.

"We're here. What do you wanna do?" Jake asked.

"Good question," Leilani said.

They saw the front door open. A tan, weathered-looking woman with bleached blond hair stood in the doorway as a freckled, red-headed woman stepped outside with a brown paper bag in her hand.

"Some things never change," Leilani said ruefully.

"What?" Jake asked.

"The blond in the doorway—that's my mom. The woman leaving just bought pot from her. That's what's in the bag." She watched her mom go back inside the house. The woman with the bag walked to her car and drove away. Leilani reached for the car door handle. "I'm going in."

Halfway to the front door, Leilani turned around and walked back to the car. She opened the car door. "Will you come with me? I know it sounds stupid, but I'd rather not go by myself."

"Whatever you want," Jake said.

As he climbed from the car, Leilani extended her hand to him. "For moral support?"

Jake clasped her hand and walked her to the front door. Leilani raised her other hand in front of the doorbell but couldn't bring herself to ring it.

"You can do this," Jake whispered.

She pressed the button and waited, but no one appeared. "It probably doesn't work." She knocked. She heard a ruckus inside. It sounded like someone hastily putting things away.

Jake grinned sheepishly at Leilani. "You knock like a cop."

She grimaced. "Oh yeah. Force of habit."

Finally, the door opened a crack. "What do you want?"

Leilani stepped forward, under the soft glow of the porch light. "Mom? It's me. Leilani."

Linda Waters reared back her head. "Leilani?" She opened the door wider and appraised the petite but fully-grown blond woman standing in front of her. "Leilani! But I haven't seen you since you left for that *college*."

Leilani detected disdain in the word "college." *Yep, I'm home.*

# 29 – Drive, She Said

"Well, come in, I guess." Linda stepped aside to let them enter. "It's such a surprise to see you here. And who's this?"

"My friend Jake. Jake, this is my mom, Linda."

Linda spied the engagement ring on Leilani's finger. "Friend, huh?" She guided them to the family room and waved her arm in front of a couch with faded blue and yellow plaid upholstery. "Don't just stand there. Sit."

Linda sat in a wicker chair across from the couch and glared at Leilani as she and Jake settled on the lumpy cushions. She saw Jake caress Leilani's hand. "I can't believe you're here, Lolo. We thought you'd written us off."

"That's funny. I thought you'd written me off. When I was in school, I called and left messages. When you didn't respond, I wrote a few times, but you never wrote back," Leilani said.

"You didn't really want us to though, right?" Linda countered.

Leilani tried her best to ignore the nastiness in her mother's tone. "If I didn't want to hear from you, I wouldn't have tried to contact you."

"C'mon, Lolo. When you graduated from high school, you couldn't get out the door fast enough. And all that talk of being a cop or whatever? You know we sell weed. We didn't want you coming back and shutting us down. This is how we make our living."

Leilani released Jake's hand and clenched her fists in her lap. "Do you really think I'd do that?"

Linda searched Leilani's face. "I dunno. You were always such a stubborn girl and so self-righteous. It just seemed like you were done with us so …"

Leilani shook her head and tried to quell her rapidly growing agitation. "Where's Dad?"

A curious look darted through Linda's eyes. Jake couldn't identify what it was. He glanced at Leilani but thought she must've missed it. He noticed Leilani's knuckles were turning white. He softly touched her wrist and smiled when her eyes met his. When she unclenched her fists, he clasped her hand in his.

Linda glowered at Leilani. "Your dad? Do you really want to know?"

"Yeah," Leilani said. "I mean, I'm here, aren't I?"

"Your dad," Linda sniffed and wiped her eyes, "isn't here anymore."

"What do you mean?" Leilani asked. "He left?"

"No, Lolo. He died," Linda said.

"He died?!" Leilani choked back a sob. "How? How long ago?"

"A few years now," Linda replied.

"Why didn't you tell me?" Tears began to well in Leilani's eyes.

Jake wrapped his arm around her. *No. This is too much*, he worried. *All the death she's experienced—Tristan, Torrey, Cruz. And now her dad?*

Linda buried her head in her hands. Her shoulders shook.

"Linda, are you okay?" Jake asked.

"Hahahahaha!"

Jake and Leilani gaped at each other, startled by Linda's behavior.

Across the family room, the bedroom door burst open. A man with craggy, sunburned skin and long, straggly gray hair jumped into the room. "Aargh!"

Leilani and Jake jumped. Leilani instinctively reached for her gun but realized she wasn't carrying one. She eyed the disheveled-looking man in the tie-dyed shirt and rumpled shorts.

"Lolo! It's me!" the man said.

"What?!" Leilani cried.

Confused, Jake turned to Leilani. She looked pale.

Linda gasped for air, struggling to speak through her laughter. "When you knocked … hahahaha … I saw you through the window … hahaha … when your dad was putting away the weed. We thought … hahahaha … it would be funny to …"

"This was a joke?" Leilani asked. "Telling me my father is dead?"

"Yeah," Linda said, "and a good one. You should've seen your face!"

"C'mon, Lolo. It was funny," Jeff said.

"No," Leilani seethed, "it wasn't."

Flabbergasted, Jake didn't know what to say to Leilani—or to Jeff and Linda.

"You're always so serious, Lolo. Lighten up," Linda scolded.

Leilani glared at Linda. "That's the thing. Your jokes and his jokes were always at my expense. You guys always thought they were hilarious, but they weren't to me."

"Ugh! You're such a little stick in the mud," Linda said. "Some things never change."

"You're right." Leilani jumped to her feet. "Jake, we're leaving."

"Lolo, don't be such a spoilsport," Jeff teased. "We were only kidding."

Leilani took a pen from her purse, scribbled her cell number on a piece of paper, and thrust it at Linda. "This is my number. If you ever want to have an adult relationship, call me. But I'm not a child, and I won't be the butt of your jokes anymore. I'm done."

"Look at you, Miss Fancy Pants Cop, all grown up," Linda said. "Too good for us now? Can't take a simple joke? This is who we are, Leilani, and we're not gonna change for you or anyone. You call us when you can accept that."

"Don't hold your breath," Leilani muttered, grabbing Jake's hand and rushing past them out the front door. She climbed into the car and slammed the door shut.

Jake turned the ignition. "Where to?"

"Just drive," she said. "I don't want to talk. Just get me out of here."

After a few minutes, Jake heard Leilani's breathing calm. "Are you okay?" he asked.

"I should've never gone there. I thought I left all that behind. Then I'm in their house for two minutes and I'm a kid again, feeling alone and ridiculous. Nothing's changed. I'm sorry. I shouldn't have dragged you there. 'Jake, meet my parents. Oh, by the way, they're totally immature and kinda psycho.'"

"Don't apologize. I still can't believe those are your parents. They're so uh … uh …"

"At least now I don't have to feel guilty about not talking to them for so long. They haven't changed, and they probably never will."

"Are you all right? That was pretty rough," Jake said. "And after everything else that's happened …"

"I'm fine. Forget about it." Leilani crossed her arms, winced, and uncrossed them.

"What do you say we call it a night?" Jake suggested. "We can find someplace to sleep, and you can take a painkiller."

Leilani groaned. "Tonight, I don't think there's one strong enough."

# 30 – Reconsidering

At Velzyland, a spot on the North Shore known for its rippable waves and heavy localism, Dean decided to test Skylar. "I'm working up an appetite out here. You hungry?" he asked.

"I could eat," Skylar said. "What do you have in mind?"

Dean nodded toward a lone surfer. "The V-Land special."

"That guy? Why?"

"What do you mean, 'why?'" Dean asked.

"Why him? What'd he do?"

"C'mon, Sky. You don't really follow the Rules every single time, do you?"

"Yeah, actually I do," she said. "I've never killed anyone who didn't deserve it. And I've certainly never killed a child."

"But don't you sometimes wanna break free? I mean, we're vampires. We're sharks. It's only natural we'd want to feed on humans. It's in our nature—times two. It's a food chain thing, and we're at the very top." He gave Skylar his most charming devil-may-care grin.

"Yes, but we were human once too," Skylar said. "Isn't that why Tristan made the Rules? To protect innocent people?"

"Tristan made the Rules out of grief for his dead *wife*," Dean said, knowing the word "wife" would slice through Skylar's heart. "He doesn't care about humans, and he doesn't care about our needs. He created the Rules out of selfishness. Every single thing he does is to serve himself. He couldn't care less about anyone else. You of all people should know that by now."

"Why are you saying this?"

*Pull back. You have to ease her into this*, Dean reminded himself. "I've just been thinking about how we've all been blindly following Tristan all these years. But why? Yeah, he created us. But beyond that, is he smarter than us? Or better than us? He's not a god. He's just a guy. I think we've given him too much power and control over our lives. It's not right."

"So, you wanna dump the Rules?" Skylar asked, shocked.

"I don't know. Regular vampires don't have these 'Rules,' and they seem to get by fine. Humans disappear all the time, and they don't suspect why. We could easily do the same thing in the ocean."

"It feels weird," she said. "I was a human not that long ago." Dean smirked.

"Okay, maybe 10 years is a long time ago," she admitted. "But if it was me, I wouldn't want someone killing me for my blood—on the land or in the ocean."

"But you can't think like a human anymore because you're not. You're better than a human. And most humans eat meat—cows, chickens, pigs, fish, lambs, rabbits, frogs, squirrels, horses, dogs, cats, snails—literally whatever they can get their hands on. They don't care about any of those creatures or if they have families or souls or anything. So, why should we?"

Skylar paused. "I don't know. It just seems wrong."

"I don't think it is anymore," Dean said. "You've got to get Tristan out of your head. He can't control the way you think or act anymore. You should be free to make your own decisions."

*Is it really just because of Tristan that I feed only on so-called 'righteous kills'? Or is it because I remember too well what it's like to be human so I can't think of killing someone who doesn't deserve it? Well, except maybe Leilani,* Skylar joked to herself.

Dean watched Skylar argue with herself in her head. He decided to let the issue rest. "Forget it. We can talk about it another time. How about a big, bloody prime rib? My treat."

"That sounds good," Skylar replied. *I can't believe I don't even know how I feel about this. Can I kill a human who hasn't done anything to deserve it? All I can hear is Tristan's voice in my head. When will I finally be over him?*

# 31 – Kai

Jake and Leilani awoke early the next morning to a police officer rapping on the car windshield. Startled, Leilani quickly assessed his appearance to determine if he was a threat or not. He looked to be about 25 years old. He stood at 5'8", about an inch taller than Jake. He had tan skin and closely cropped black hair. His body was toned but not overly muscular.

Officer Kai Kamaka knocked on the windshield again and pointed to the No Parking sign. "You can't park here overnight. It's illegal."

Jake rolled down the window and placed his hands on the steering wheel to make them clearly visible to the officer. "We're sorry. We were too tired to drive and didn't have a place to stay, so we thought it was safer to pull over. We didn't see the sign."

As soon as Jake started talking, Officer Kamaka jumped back from the car.

"What's wrong?" Jake asked.

Leilani saw the officer's hand move toward his gun. "Officer? What is it?"

"You," he glared at Jake. "I know what you are. Did you kill those two surfers in Waikiki—the ones on the news?"

Jake looked questioningly at Leilani.

Officer Kamaka removed his gun from his holster and pointed it at Jake. "Step out of the car, and put your hands behind your head."

Seeing the gun aimed squarely at his head, Jake did as he was told.

Officer Kamaka read Jake his rights and cuffed him. He looked inside the driver's side window at Leilani. "You're not safe, ma'am. This man is not what he seems."

"What do you mean?" Leilani asked. *Does he know Jake is a graysuit? How?*

"He's not human."

*Alrighty then, I guess he does know.* "Officer, I'm an FBI agent. I can assure you this man had nothing to do with the killings. I can show you my badge. May I get it from my purse?"

"Slowly." Officer Kamaka kept his gun pointed at Jake's head and watched Leilani reach into her purse and produce her badge.

"My name is Leilani. This man here is my friend, Jake. So, you know about graysuits?"

"Yes. What do you know about them?" he asked.

Leilani raised the sleeves on her left arm and peeled back one of her bandages. "Enough."

Officer Kamaka gasped. "Did he do that to you?!" He moved the gun closer to Jake's head.

"No," Leilani said as evenly as she could to try to calm him. "Jake saved me from the men who did this to me. I would've died if not for him. Please, will you uncuff him? You have the wrong man."

"How do you know? It was graysuits who killed those people in Waikiki."

"I know because Jake was with me in San Diego when they were killed. We saw what happened on the news, and we think we know who did it. I think one of them is the same guy who did this to me. He also killed our friends. That's why we're here. We're looking for him."

Officer Kamaka stepped back. "Are you sure this isn't the one who killed them?"

"Yes, I'm sure," Leilani said.

He holstered his gun and uncuffed Jake.

Jake glanced at the brightening sky. Pink clouds illuminated soft pink ripples in the ocean. "Can we finish our conversation inside? I shouldn't be out when the sun comes up."

"Is there somewhere we can go and talk?" Leilani asked.

"Follow me. But if this graysuit pulls anything or tries to get away, I have no problem throwing his ass out in the sun and leaving him there to die. Understand?"

Jake and Leilani nodded.

# 32 – Legends

They followed the police cruiser to a small apartment a few miles down the road. Knowing the sun was about to break through at any moment, Officer Kamaka quickly led them inside.

"Thanks, man. That was close," Jake said.

"Yes, thank you, Officer Kamaka," Leilani said.

"Call me Kai." He closed the curtains and pointed to the couch. "Sit. Tell me about the graysuit—the one you think killed the surfers here."

Leilani and Jake told him about Dean and how he betrayed Tristan and the Nomads.

"What about you, graysuit? You ever kill anyone?" Kai asked.

Jake glanced at Leilani. She nodded at him.

"Only Logan. He was a graysuit and a killer like Dean. He and Dean are the ones who did this to her." Jake pointed his thumb at Leilani, who unconsciously tugged at one of her bandages. "When I saw Logan, I didn't think about it. It was like instinct took over, and I staked him."

"You've never killed any humans?" Kai asked.

"No," Jake replied.

"Would you?"

"No, man. I'm not a monster," Jake said. "I lost my best friend to a graysuit. That's how I got mixed up in all this. Leilani too. We're trying to find Dean so we can stop him from killing anyone else."

Kai looked from Jake to Leilani and back again. "I think we can help each other."

Kai retrieved an ancient book from the shelf above his desk and turned to a dog-eared page in the middle. "There are legends of shark-men here in the Hawaiian Islands. They've been around for generations—stories of men and women who could change between human and shark form. Except here in these stories, they're reincarnations of people who died. Family members would see them in the ocean and immediately recognize them. These shark-people would help their families fish and protect them from danger, like riptides or ocean predators. But some went further. They would target enemies of their families. They'd tear apart their fishing nets or sometimes even kill. According to these legends, two of the strongest shark-men, the brown shark and the blue shark, went to war. The brown shark banned the eating of humans after losing a loved one to an evil shark-man. The blue shark rebelled and sought out lost souls to convert to his cause. He killed and ate those who refused to follow him."

"What happened then?" Leilani asked, thinking of the parallels to Tristan and Dean.

"The blue shark won. That's why people are still attacked by sharks today. It's not the shark that kills humans; it's the lost soul inside the shark," Kai explained.

"So, are graysuits like the modern-day version of these shark-people?" Leilani asked.

"No," Kai said. "The shark-men and shark-women in the legends were reincarnations of people who died. Vampire sharks are something different. They're humans who were turned into vampires who somehow developed the ability to shapeshift into great white sharks in the ocean. They began arriving in the Hawaiian Islands in the late 1970s. Most of them came from California. But we don't know how they were created or how they got the ability to turn into sharks."

"But how do you even know about them?" Leilani asked.

"Same as you. A family member lost someone she loved to a graysuit," Kai said. "We first learned about the existence of vampires here on the Islands toward the end of the 18th century, after the first European invaders arrived. Not all of these, uh, 'settlers' were human. To survive, my ancestors learned to identify vampires by their smell; they smell metallic like blood. Then when the graysuits began arriving 40 years ago, it was the same. We learned to identify them by their smell. They smell salty like the sea. My great aunt's boyfriend was the first Hawaiian to be killed by a graysuit. She saw him get attacked by a shark in the ocean. Then she saw the shark turn into a man and wipe the blood from his mouth. The man spotted her, chased her, grabbed her by the neck, and pulled her to him. That's how she learned what they smell like. Then some locals arrived. When they saw this haole gripping her by the throat, they jumped him. He ran to the ocean and escaped by turning back into a shark and swimming away." Kai looked at Jake. "So, that's how I knew what you were when you rolled down your car window. You smell salty."

"He does?" Leilani sniffed. "He doesn't smell salty to me—at least no more than someone who spends a lot of time in the ocean."

"Once you know what graysuits smell like, it's easy to pick them out—especially if your survival depends on it," Kai explained.

"Do all Hawaiians know about graysuits?" Leilani asked. "I lived here when I was a teenager, and I never heard of them until just a few days ago."

"No. Only those of us whose families go back generations here. With those first Europeans, we learned to be wary of visitors—and especially the ones with fangs," Kai said. "So, do you have any photos of Dean or Skylar?"

Leilani thought of Tristan's photo album, the one Jake gave her when she was in the hospital. "Maybe. There might be some back home. I left so quickly I forgot to see if Tristan had any photos of them."

"Could you describe them to a sketch artist?" Kai asked.

"I can describe Dean, and Jake can do Skylar," Leilani said.

"Good. I'll call one over," Kai said. "I have family members here and on the neighboring islands. I can't circulate the sketches to law enforcement because they think those surfers were killed by sharks. But I can send them to my relatives and some family friends, and have them keep an eye out for these two. If they're still in the Islands, we'll find them."

# 33 – Sympathy

After having breakfast with Julianna, Finn called Cody. "How would you like to learn more about what we do here?"

"Sure. You think I might get in to see Tristan again today?" Cody asked.

"I'll let you know after I check on him. Come down to lab #4. I'd like to show you something. It might help you understand why we need to be cautious around vampire sharks, even those that seem nice," Finn said.

A few minutes later, Cody pressed the buzzer outside lab #4. Finn let him in. Cody saw a woman restrained on a hospital bed.

"Cody, this is Lily. Lily is a vampire shark," Finn explained.

Cody walked closer to the bed and peered at Lily. She didn't look like a killer. She looked like a librarian or a teacher. She had soft brown eyes and long brown hair that tapered below her chin to frame her heart-shaped face.

Seeing concern in Cody's blue eyes, Lily decided to play the sympathy card. "Please," she whispered, "you have to help me. I haven't done anything. They're hurting me—conducting experiments, torturing me." Tears dropped from the corners of her eyes and streamed past her temples into her hair.

Cody glanced at Finn and turned back to Lily.

"Pleeeeease," Lily whimpered. "I don't want to be hurt anymore."

Cody stared into her eyes. "Finn, I don't think …"

"She's pretty convincing, isn't she?" Finn interrupted. "You know what she did before we brought her here? She killed a couple on their honeymoon. They were kayaking. She rammed the kayak, sending them both into the ocean. Then she ripped the bride and groom to pieces, and she ate those pieces for dinner."

Lily shook her head. "He's crazy. You have to help me."

"Give it up, Lily," Finn said. "No one here believes your lies."

"How do you know it was her?" Cody asked.

"He doesn't. He's evil. We have to escape before he does this to you. Please," Lily begged.

"C'mon, Cody. Who are you going to believe?" Finn asked. "Me, the person who saved you? Or a vicious graysuit? A graysuit exactly like the one who attacked you."

"I believe you, Finn," Cody answered, though he still felt terribly uncomfortable seeing the woman restrained and whimpering.

"Good, Cody, good. Let me show you what Lily did. Then you can see for yourself what graysuits are like when they think no one is watching—and what convincing liars they are, like Lily here."

Finn strode to his computer and pressed "play." A video began. Cody recognized Julianna's voice as she narrated.

# 34 – Video

"We're searching for a vampire shark named Lily," Julianna said as she pointed the video camera at the ocean. "She's a night school teacher. There've been a few disappearances at the beach near her school, which is what brought her to our attention. Jamal's been conducting surveillance, posing as a student. He followed Lily to the beach and then contacted Matt and me … There! I think that's her." She turned the camera to a shark breaching the water's surface. In the distance, a yellow kayak appeared.

"Kayakers!" Julianna panned the camera across the water. "I've lost sight of Lily." She turned the camera back to the kayak. As it came into view, something struck the kayak from below, throwing the man and woman into the ocean.

"Matt, it's Lily. Get us to the kayak! Hurry!" Julianna lifted the camera onto a tripod secured to the front of the boat. She grabbed a tranquilizer gun from the gun rack aboard the vessel. She aimed at the kayak but didn't see Lily. "Dammit! I don't know if I can get a clean shot from this far away. The amount of tranquilizer in each dart is calibrated for a full-grown great white shark. I don't want to miss and accidentally shoot the people. It'll kill them."

While Matt raced the boat toward the empty yellow kayak, the camera rolled. The shark surfaced, snatched the stranded man, and crushed him between her jaws. Julianna fired two darts at the shark but missed. The woman in the water screamed. The shark turned, crunched down upon the woman's head and shoulders, and dove underwater.

"Follow her!" Julianna commanded.

The video abruptly cut to a shot of Julianna's face. "We lost Lily," she reported. "There are no survivors."

# 35 – Caught

Finn stopped the video and clicked on a different one. "Now let me show you this."

The video began with Matt dressed as a diver, sitting in a harness, dangling over the ocean. Once again, Julianna narrated. "We think we've located Lily again. We're going to use Matt here as chum. Wave to the camera, Matt."

Matt smiled and waved. "Just make sure you pull me up, J. I'd like to keep my appendages from the waist down. I've grown quite fond of them over the years."

"Sure thing, Matt."

The video showed Matt being lowered into the ocean and then jerked out of the water, up into the air. The great white shark followed, nearly biting Matt's toes. Julianna dropped the net and ensnared the shark. Finn forwarded the video to show Cody where Lily morphed into her human body inside the net and bared her fangs.

"Let me go *now* or I'll kill you," Lily threatened on camera.

"I can't do that, Lily," Julianna replied off camera. "You were gonna kill my buddy, Matt, here. I'm sure he's not the first either."

"No. He's not," Lily glowered.

Finn stopped the video. "Cody, meet Lily. Lily is a cold-blooded killer—like they all are."

Ashen, Cody turned to Finn. "That video's pretty gnarly. Sorry I doubted you, man."

"That first video, where Lily killed those kayakers, was shot early last week," Finn explained. "The second video, where Julianna and Matt captured her, was shot at sunset about 12 hours after you showed up here with Tristan. So, maybe now you can understand my reluctance to save a graysuit."

Lily gasped in surprise. "Tristan's here?"

"You know Tristan?" Finn asked.

She quickly turned away and stared at the ceiling.

"Lily, I asked you a question," Finn said. "Do you know Tristan? Six feet tall, brown hair, brown eyes, good-looking guy?"

Lily stared straight ahead, refusing to acknowledge Finn.

"Cody, I need you to leave now," Finn said.

"But if she knows Tristan, I ..."

"Cody, you are here at my invitation," Finn said, clenching his jaw. "Now I'm asking you to leave. I'll call you when I'm done, and we can continue. I think you can help me save more people from being hurt and killed the way those kayakers were. Right now, I need to talk to Lily alone."

Cody exited the lab. He stole one last look at Lily before the door closed. *How could I have believed her—that she's a victim when really she's a killer? I'm not that gullible, am I? Is Tristan like her? He can't be. He tried to save me. But ... he's still one of them.*

When the door closed, Finn approached the bed. "Lily, we can do this the easy way or the hard way. How long has it been since you were in salt water? We're closing in on 40 hours, right?"

Lily blinked rapidly but refused to make eye contact with Finn.

"You can drop the tough act. You've been defanged, and your venom pouches have been removed. And I know what happens to you guys after 72 hours without salt water. You dry out. Have you ever seen it? It's pretty nasty." Finn leaned closer to Lily and lowered his voice. "Your skin will turn pink, then red, and then purple. It will blister, crack, and break open. Your lips and eyelids will tear and bleed as the skin sizzles away. You'll feel like you're being microwaved as your organs cook from the inside out. It'll grow more and more intense with each passing hour. This is your body aging. It's about five years for every hour you go without salt water after three days, right? Within a week you'll be dead—a worthless pile of ash. But before you turn to ash, the searing will be so excruciating, so unbearable that you will beg me—beg me!—to kill you. But I won't. I'll let you burn and waste away to nothing. You can avoid all that if you tell me what I want to know. Tell me about Tristan. What do you know about him?"

Lily continued to stare at the ceiling. "What do you want to know?"

# 36 – Epicenter

Down the hall in lab #1, Tristan stirred. He opened his eyes and tried to sit up but couldn't. *I'm still restrained,* he thought. *What am I doing here? What does this guy want? Leilani. I have to get to Leilani. Did she survive after Dean and Logan attacked her? Dean! What if she did and Dean's still out there? I have to get out of here. I need Cody to help me ...* Tristan lost consciousness again.

Outside, Cody paced up and down the hallway. After half an hour, he saw Finn exit lab #4. "Finn, can we talk?"

"Not now. I have to find Julianna." Finn removed his two-way radio from his pocket. "J, where are you? We need to talk. ... No, now. ... I'll tell you when I see you. Meet me at home."

Julianna arrived home shortly after Finn. "What's going on?"

"I can't be sure," Finn said, "but we may have found the creator, or at least we're getting closer."

"What?!"

"Lily, the vampire shark you brought in Friday night—she knows Tristan, Cody's friend. When I was explaining to Cody that Lily was captured about 12 hours after he showed up with Tristan, she seemed really surprised and said, 'Tristan's here?'—like it would be really shocking for him to be captured. What could be more shocking than if your creator was captured, right? I was able to get Lily to admit she was turned into a vampire shark in 1974 in San Francisco, but then she clammed up and wouldn't say anything more."

"San Francisco," Julianna repeated.

"Yeah, everything points to San Francisco." Finn walked to his computer and clicked open a map. He pointed at the gray dots on the screen. "As you know, each of these gray dots represents a graysuit and where they said they came from."

"And the red dots are the attacks by graysuits," Julianna said.

"Right. Now when we join the gray dots together, the lines form a small semicircle. And what's in the middle?" he asked.

"San Francisco."

"Yeah. And when we join the red dots together, we get a much larger circle. Again, San Francisco is in the middle. You were attacked just north of there. You're one of these red dots. The creator must've lived in San Francisco and done most of the creating there. Then as graysuits moved away, the attacks began to fan out to broader and broader areas."

"San Francisco," Julianna said. "Where I lived. At this exact time. While all this was going on."

"Yeah."

"So, do you really think the guy we have is the creator? Cody seems to think he's incapable of hurting anyone."

"I don't know. I couldn't get Lily to say anything more about Tristan or who created her, but I'll keep trying," Finn replied. "Hey, J, don't mention any of this to Cody. I want to see if he can help me get to the bottom of this with Tristan, and it's better if he doesn't know his friend might be a mass murderer. I'm going to talk to Cody now."

"Okay." Julianna stared at the gray and red circles on the computer screen. "San Francisco. Shit."

# 37 — A Request

Cody opened his apartment door. He was surprised to see Finn standing outside. "Hey, dude. What's up?"

"I'm sorry about before. Do you want to get some lunch and talk?" Finn asked.

"Yeah, I could eat."

They walked downstairs to the mess hall on the ground level. After they sat down with their meals, Cody asked, "What happened with Lily? Does she know Tristan?"

"I don't know," Finn said. "But she's a pretty convincing liar. You saw her—the way she pretended to be the victim in all this?"

"Yeah. And that video was brutal. That couple she killed was on their honeymoon?" Cody asked.

Finn nodded. "We didn't know it at the time. Later we saw a news report that a honeymooning couple rented a kayak in Dana Point, but they never returned to shore. We put two and two together and …"

"And Lily. Are they really all like that?"

"Cody, I'm sorry to tell you this because I know Tristan is your friend, but I've never met one that's not a ruthless killer," Finn said.

The roast beef sandwich Cody chewed suddenly tasted terrible. He forced the lump of cold meat down his throat and set his sandwich on his plate.

"But maybe you're right. Maybe Tristan is different," Finn said, trying to butter up Cody to make him more receptive to his forthcoming request. "You brought him here to us, so I'd like to think so. And the good news is there's a way Tristan can prove it to us. Do you think you can get him to help us? It could save a lot of lives."

"Yeah, I'm sure he'd help us. What do you need?" Cody asked.

"I need you to find out if he lived in San Francisco in the early 1970s," Finn said.

"Why don't you just ask him?"

"Because vampire sharks are a very secretive species, and Tristan doesn't know me. But he knows you and trusts you, so that means he's more likely to open up to you."

"Why do you want to know where he lived?" Cody asked.

"He may know someone we need to find. This person lived in San Francisco in the '70s, and it's really important we find him or her," Finn explained.

"Is that all you need?"

"For now," Finn said.

"Okay. When do you want me to talk to him?"

"No time like the present." Finn glanced at Cody's half-eaten sandwich. "But finish your lunch first."

"No thanks." Cody pushed his plate aside. "I kinda lost my appetite thinking about Lily and those people she killed."

"I know what you mean."

# 38 – Friend or Foe

Outside the door to lab #1, Finn held a covered bowl of soup in one hand and began entering his passcode with the other. Cody tried to look over his shoulder to see the code but caught only the first number, 5.

Finn turned back to Cody. "Don't push him. Just ask him questions casually, like a friend who wants to learn more."

Finn hit the final number, 3. He led Cody into the lab and smiled brightly. "Hi, Tristan. We brought you some soup. Do you mind if I examine your wound first?"

Tristan shook his head.

Finn set the soup bowl on a cart near the bed and peered at Tristan's chest. "This is healing up nicely. I think we'll be able to reduce the sedatives."

"Please. I don't like feeling like this," Tristan mumbled. "I can't think."

"I know, but it's the only way to keep you quiet so your chest heals. But like I said, we should be able to reduce your meds. I'm going to remove the restraints and leave you guys alone to catch up. Cody, after Tristan eats, do you think you can help him into the saltwater pool on your own?"

"Uh huh," Cody replied.

"When you're done, press the red button. I'll come open the door for you. I'll see you later."

Outside, when Finn heard the lock secure, he leaned against the door. "Finally," he breathed. "Terrell, wherever you are, if you can hear me, we may have finally caught him."

Finn climbed the stairs to his office and turned on the wall of video screens. Each screen showed a lab. He watched Cody and Tristan.

# 39 – Favor

Cody pushed the cart against the bed and swiveled the tray in front of Tristan. Tristan shakily scooped some soup into the spoon. He tried to lift it to his lips, but it spilled on his hospital gown.

"Here, let me." Cody took the spoon from Tristan's hand, dipped it into the bowl, and lifted it to Tristan's mouth.

Tristan swallowed. "Sorry. The drugs … It's too much."

"Maybe you'll feel better after you eat," Cody said.

When the bowl was half empty, Tristan raised his hand. "No more."

"You need to eat. It'll help you gain your strength back."

Tristan felt his head begin to clear a little. "Maybe later." He leaned against his pillow. "Cody, what am I doing here?"

"You're recovering. Remember? Finn stitched you up. He saved your life."

Tristan peered into Cody's eyes. "*You* saved my life. Now I need your help again. I have to call Leilani, my fiancée. She's human. She was attacked the same night I was. I need to see if she's okay, if she's still … alive. If she is, she's in danger. Dean, the guy who tried to kill me, tried to kill her too. He'll come after her again if he knows she survived."

"I'll see what I can do. But I'm supposed to be dead. I'm not allowed to communicate with anyone back home," Cody explained. "None of us are. That's why we don't have any phones in here. There's no need for them."

"Then get me a cell phone," Tristan said.

"They don't work down here in the lab," Cody explained. "We're underground in a totally secure facility. And I can't get you out because Finn keeps the labs locked. I don't know the codes."

"Cody, I have to get out of here. If Leilani is with Jake, Dean will go after him too. They're in danger," Tristan said.

The color drained from Cody's face upon hearing Jake's name. "Let me see what I can do. How about if I help you to the pool, and I'll talk to Finn?"

Tristan nodded. After Cody set him in the saltwater pool, he pressed the red button to signal Finn.

"Dammit, Cody. You didn't even try," Finn muttered to himself in his office. He walked downstairs and opened the lab door.

Cody rushed to him and told him what Tristan said about Dean.

"Let's talk outside," Finn said. "Tristan, we'll be right back."

They stepped into the hall, and Cody repeated what Tristan said about Jake and Leilani being in danger.

"Cody, don't you see? He's using Jake to manipulate you," Finn whispered. "You're smarter than that. Don't let him."

"But what if Jake is in trouble?" Cody asked.

"He's not. But how about this? Give me Jake's full name, address, and phone number, and get me whatever information you can for Leilani and Dean. I have a friend who's a cop here in Avalon. I'll see what I can find out while you work on Tristan. I need to know if he was in San Francisco in the early '70s and what he was doing there."

Finn let Cody back into the lab. Cody gathered the info for Leilani and Dean from Tristan, and then gave Jake's info to Finn too.

"Tristan said to tell you he really needs to call Leilani and Jake. It's a matter of life and death," Cody said.

"No. The work we do here is secret. We can't have people communicating with the outside world. Any security breach would be disastrous for all finners, including you. I will personally go to the police station and talk to my friend. I know I can trust him to be discreet. I'll be back as soon as I have any information." Finn gripped Cody's shoulder. "I'm counting on you."

Finn ushered Cody into the lab again and returned to his office. He called Julianna. "I need to visit Jim at the police station."

"Why? Anything wrong?" Julianna asked.

"No, everything's fine. I'm doing a favor for Cody. He's in there talking to Tristan now," Finn explained.

"Is Cody safe in there by himself?" Julianna asked.

"Yeah. Tristan is too weak to do anything with all the drugs in his system," Finn said.

"Should I come down to your office and monitor them just in case?" she asked.

"No, that's okay. I won't be gone long. I'll call you when I get back."

# 40 – Prisoner

In the lab, Cody sat on the edge of the pool and told Tristan that Finn left to see what he could find out about Leilani, Jake, and Dean.

Tristan shook his head. "It's not enough. I need to get to Leilani. She's not safe."

Tristan closed his eyes. His thoughts felt heavy and clouded. He motioned for Cody to come closer to him. He raised his lips to Cody's ear and whispered, "I don't trust Finn."

Cody's eyes widened. "Why?"

"I don't know. Just a feeling. Is there a way I can slip out of here without him knowing?" Tristan asked.

Cody shook his head. He wondered if the sedatives were making Tristan paranoid. Cody always liked to see the best in people, so he couldn't fathom why Tristan wouldn't trust Finn, who worked so hard to save his life. "Dude, it's literally a fortress here. It used to be a military facility. You need a code to get in or out."

"And you don't have a code?"

"No."

"Then who does?" Tristan asked.

"Finn. And probably Julianna," Cody whispered.

"Julianna?"

"Yeah, Finn's girlfriend or wife or whatever," Cody said. "Have you met her? She's really cool."

"No. I've only seen Finn in here. I was married to a Julianna once, a long time ago." Tristan's eyes darkened. "She was killed."

"I'm sorry." Remembering Finn was counting on him, Cody asked, "Where did she die?"

"Stinson Beach. North of San Francisco."

"Oh. Did you live in San Francisco?" Cody asked as casually as he could.

"Years ago." Tristan rubbed his eyes. "This is wrong. I can't clear my head. Everything's all jumbled. I need to get out of here."

"I'm sure you can leave as soon as you're well enough. We're not prisoners," Cody assured him.

"Oh yeah? Then why do I feel like one?"

# 41 — Alive

Thinking about Cody alone with Tristan, the vampire shark, Julianna grew worried. She walked to Finn's office and checked the monitor for lab #1. She saw Cody talking to a man in the pool. From the angle of the camera, she could only see the back of his head. He had dark brown hair. *Huh, that's funny. This Tristan kind of looks like my Tristan.*

She watched Cody chat with him. Cody seemed to be safe. She turned up the volume but still couldn't hear what they said. She then saw Cody step into the pool to help him walk back to bed. Tristan's head hung low and his shoulders were hunched, his body supported by Cody. As Tristan walked by the camera on the way back to bed, he raised his head.

Julianna's mouth fell open. "Oh. My. God."

At that moment, the buzzer from the lab sounded, making her jump. "Finn? I'm ready to come out," Cody said over the intercom. "Tristan's gonna take a nap."

Julianna stared at the man climbing into the hospital bed. "It can't be." Her mind raced as she marched to the lab. She entered her code and opened the door.

Cody exited past her. "Hey, J. What's up?"

"Huh?" She blinked. "Nothing. Are you all done in here?"

"Yeah, he's pretty tired. He's sleeping again." Cody noticed Julianna's turquoise blue tank top accentuated the color of her eyes. "That color looks great on you, by the way. It really goes well with your …"

"Yeah, okay." Distracted by thoughts of Tristan, Julianna closed the door in Cody's face.

"… eyes." Cody stared at the door. *I must be losing my touch. Maybe I need to get out of here too.*

Inside the lab, Julianna approached the bed. *What if it's him?*

*What if he's alive? What if he's … a graysuit?* She felt sick at the thought. She stood at the foot of the bed and looked at the man's face. "Tristan?"

Tristan stirred at the sound of his name. He saw a petite woman standing near his feet. She had straight blond hair. He strained his eyes. "Leilani?"

"Tristan?"

Tristan stared, expecting to see Leilani's face. But it wasn't her. It was … Julianna. Tristan closed his eyes and opened them again. *I must be hallucinating.*

Julianna watched Tristan open and close his eyes. "Tristan?"

"Julianna?" Tristan struggled to make sense of what he was seeing.

"It's you," she gasped.

"Julianna? Is that really you? You look exactly the same." Tristan struggled with the image of the blond woman standing in front of him, speaking to him. "How are you alive? I carried you to shore, but you were already gone. I grieved for so long. I thought I lost you."

Julianna stepped closer and reached for Tristan's face. As she extended her fingers to touch his cheek, she smelled a familiar smell—the salty scent of a vampire shark. She snapped her hand back.

"What's wrong?" Tristan asked.

She shook her head. "You're one of them."

"What?"

"How long, Tristan?" Julianna asked quietly. "How long have you been a graysuit?"

Through the drug-induced fog in his brain, Tristan again strived to make sense of what he was seeing and hearing. *Julianna's here, alive. She knows my secret—the secret I kept from her our entire relationship.*

"It doesn't matter," he answered. "You're alive! How? Where

have you been all this time? I missed you so much."

Julianna clenched her teeth. "It. Matters. To me. How long have you been a graysuit?"

Tristan could feel Julianna's anger swelling and filling the space between them. He struggled to piece together his thoughts. "Julianna, let me explain …"

"I don't want to hear your explanation. I want to hear your answer. How long?" she demanded. "While we were together? Before? After I died?"

"Before," Tristan confessed. "Ever since I met you."

Julianna recoiled in horror. "It was all a lie? Our entire relationship? Our marriage?!" She abruptly turned and stomped toward the door.

"No! Wait! Please!" Tristan shouted after her.

The lab door slammed. He leaned back against the bed. "Julianna's alive. She's mad as hell, but somehow she's alive."

# 42 – Buzz

Jake hung up his cell phone and turned to Leilani and Kai. "That's weird. The Avalon police department just called and asked if I wanted to submit a bid to design a new website for them. I wonder how they got my number."

"Maybe they Googled web designers and found you?" Leilani suggested.

"Maybe. But I haven't done any work for city governments or police departments before. Why would they call me?" Jake wondered aloud.

Leilani shrugged and smiled. "Maybe you're that good. You've got buzz. What did you tell them?"

"I told them to call my 'associate.' He's actually a friend who's been handling my work since Cody died. I know he appreciates the extra income, and I don't exactly have time to sit at a computer and work while Dean's out there killing people," Jake said.

Kai picked up his buzzing phone and saw a text. "The sketch artist is on his way."

# 43 — Oblivious

Finn returned from the police station, strolled to Cody's apartment, and reported his findings about Jake, Leilani, and Dean. "So, when you see Tristan later, you can tell him not to worry. Jake and Leilani are fine."

"Thanks," Cody replied. "When will Tristan be well enough to leave?"

"It's hard to say. Were you able to find out if he lived in San Francisco?" Finn asked.

"Yeah, he did." Remembering what Tristan revealed, Cody turned somber. "He said his wife was killed at Stinson Beach, north of San Francisco."

Finn's blood turned cold. "What was his wife's name?"

"Julianna."

"I have to go." Finn raced downstairs to Julianna's office, but she wasn't there. He ran back upstairs to their apartment. He glanced inside their bedroom and saw her lying face down on the bed. "Julianna? What's wrong?"

She rolled over. She had a dazed look on her face. "It's him."

"Who?" Finn asked, knowing—and dreading—the answer.

"The vampire shark in lab #1. Tristan. He was my husband. And he was a graysuit the whole time. He was a monster, and I never knew. I never even suspected. How could I not know?" She reached for Finn and wrapped her arms around him.

While Finn held Julianna, his thoughts turned to Tristan. *Tristan was in San Francisco in the early 1970s. He was there in the center of it all. Is he the one we've been searching for all this time? Is he the creator? If not, he must know who is. I mean, it's one thing for Julianna to be married to a graysuit and not know it. But the creator? She'd have to know that. How could you hide such a thing?*

Finn pressed his lips to Julianna's cheek. "Are you okay?"

She nodded. "It's such a shock. Seeing him here. Finding out he's a graysuit. How could I not have known?"

"Because that was before anyone even knew vampire sharks existed. Not even Terrell knew what they were back then," Finn said.

"But people were dying! I remember seeing reports of shark attacks on the news. It seemed like there were more and more all the time. What if I could've done something to help those people?"

"Julianna, stop. It's not your fault."

"But I …"

"No. Listen to me," Finn said firmly. "I know this has been a terrible shock. But if we can gain Tristan's trust, we can get him to tell us who created him. We know he was in San Francisco in the early '70s. He was there in the middle of it, at the beginning. If we can find the creator and capture him or her or them, we can stop the killing."

Julianna sighed. "You're right. Maybe he can help us."

"But if you don't want to talk to him, I can," Finn offered.

"No. I think he'll be more willing to talk to me. I just need some time to gather my thoughts. We'll have to dial down the sedatives some more. I need his head to be clear. I need him to think back and remember everything he can about when we were …"

"When you were married," Finn grimaced.

Julianna nodded. "I'm sorry. I'm sure this isn't easy for you either."

"I'm fine. But the sooner we find out what he knows, the better for both of us."

# 44 – Bristling

A loud rapping at the front door jarred Cody from his nap. He opened the door and saw Finn looking uneasy.

"I'm heading to the lab. You want to come?" Finn asked. "We can tell Tristan what I learned from my friend in the police department."

Cody followed Finn to lab #1. He looked over Finn's shoulder as he punched in his code: 5, 2.

Finn turned around. "Can you step back? You're a little close."

"Sorry. I know Tristan's really anxious to hear about Leilani," Cody said.

*5, 2, and the last digit is 3,* Cody thought. *What are the two numbers in the middle?*

When Tristan heard the door open, he looked up expectantly. He'd been thinking about Julianna and all the years he'd lost with her, believing she was dead. He desperately wanted to see her again to make sure she was real.

Finn and Cody strolled to Tristan's bedside.

"Good news, Tristan," Finn began. "You're healing nicely, so we're going to bring down the sedatives some more. But let me know if anything changes, like if you feel pain or notice any tearing or bleeding, okay?"

"Yeah," Tristan said. "How's Julianna?"

Finn bristled at hearing Tristan say her name.

Instantly, Tristan remembered Cody saying that Julianna was Finn's girlfriend … or wife.

Finn forced a tight smile. "She's fine. She, uh, told me about you. I'm sure it was a shock for you both."

"Yeah. I still can't believe she's alive. So, you and she are married?" Tristan asked.

Finn bristled again and tried to maintain his composure. "No. But we've been together more than 10 years. She's my … everything."

Tristan nodded.

"Hey, what am I missing here?" Cody asked.

Tristan and Finn exchanged a glance.

"Here's the deal, Cody," Finn said. "It turns out Tristan and Julianna knew each other when Julianna was human. They were married."

Tristan noticed the strain in Finn's voice when he uttered the word "married."

"No way!" Cody exclaimed.

"Yeah, until she was killed by a graysuit and brought here." Finn adjusted Tristan's IV drip. "Tristan, your head should start to feel more clear as the day goes on. Julianna will be back here in a little while."

Finn noticed Tristan's eyes brighten. "But before she comes back, I want to give you an update. I had a friend of mine in the police department look into your friends. Jake is fine. He's safe at home designing websites. My friend personally spoke with him on the phone. Leilani's fine too."

Tristan exhaled a sigh of relief.

"She's your fiancée, right?" Finn added sharply.

Tristan nodded. *Leilani is alive. Julianna is alive.*

"Apparently she was attacked by 'rabid dogs' and released from the hospital. She's taking a 30-day leave of absence so she can recover, but she's going to be okay," Finn explained.

"How do you know? Did you talk to her?" Tristan asked.

"My friend spoke with her boss, who spoke with Leilani when she requested the time off," Finn said.

"But what about Dean?" Tristan pressed.

"My friend located the biotech company that hired Dean as a marketing consultant. They said Dean completed his contract and is on vacation in Hawaii. So, you don't have to worry. He's 2,500 miles away from Leilani and Jake," Finn said.

"It doesn't matter where Dean is. If he's alive, then they're not safe," Tristan argued.

"Calm down," Finn warned. "You need to stay still, or you're going to open up your stitches. If that happens, we'll have to sedate you and restrain you again. I know you don't want that, so I need you to remain calm."

"I understand," Tristan replied with all the calmness he could muster, "but Dean will kill her if he knows she survived. He already tried to kill her once—the same night he tried to kill me."

"Listen, if he doesn't know she's alive, he won't be coming back for her, right? Stop worrying. You're going to make yourself sicker," Finn said.

"But …"

"Tristan, I've got this," Finn snapped. "I've been protecting people from your kind for years. You focus on your recovery. Let me worry about the rest."

"You don't know Dean. It's not enough," Tristan said. "When can I get out of here?"

Finn glanced at his chart, pretending to check something. "I'll let you know the moment you're well enough to leave."

The lab door opened and Julianna entered. She directed a quick nod at Finn.

"Cody, what do you say we leave them alone to talk?" Finn took Cody's arm and led him out of the lab.

"Later, Tristan!" Cody called over his shoulder.

# 45 – Reunited

Julianna approached Tristan and took a deep breath, ignoring the salty graysuit scent. She sat beside him on the bed. "I'm sorry. I shouldn't have left like that," she said.

"No, I'm the one who should apologize," Tristan said. "I don't even know where to start. I still can't believe you're alive. I've missed you so much, Jules."

Julianna winced. The entire time she was human, Tristan was the only one who called her "Jules"—usually when they were alone and being intimate. It was why she now insisted everyone call her "Julianna" or "J" for short. Hearing "Jules" was a painful reminder of the life she had—and lost—so long ago.

"Don't call me Jules," she said. "Jules was young and naïve, and believed her husband would never lie to her. That's not who I am anymore."

Tristan cringed, regretting causing her so much pain. "I'm so, so sorry, Julianna. You have every right to be angry with me. I lied to you for our entire relationship. I didn't mean to. But I was afraid you'd leave if I told you what I was, and I couldn't bear the thought of that," he explained. "I should've told you though. I should've told you before I proposed. I just loved you so much. I was afraid of losing you. But I did lose you. By not telling you about me or about graysuits, I put your life in danger. If I would've told you, you would've had a choice. You could've chosen to live a normal life. You wouldn't have had to suffer and die so violently."

Julianna sat motionless, stunned by his apology. Part of her hated Tristan for not telling her, for keeping a secret that big from her—a secret that ended up destroying her human life. But she also knew if he had told her, she wouldn't have believed him. If she did believe him, would she still have married him?

She didn't know. She did love him—but as a human.

"I don't know what to say, Tristan. I always felt like you were keeping something from me. I thought maybe after we were married, you'd trust me enough to open up. It was hard. Sometimes …" she stopped herself.

"What?"

"Sometimes I felt like you were closer with Dean than you were with me," she said.

Tristan flinched upon hearing Dean's name.

Julianna's face dropped. "No. Don't tell me. Dean was a graysuit too, wasn't he? That's why you two were always together and why you'd go surfing by yourselves all the time?"

Tristan nodded. "I'm sorry I didn't tell you, Jules—I mean, Julianna. It was selfish and wrong, and it cost you your life. For that, I will never forgive myself."

"I was surrounded by graysuits, and I never knew it. Were there others in our circle of friends?" she asked.

"Usually when we'd surf with other people, there'd be some around. But mostly they were just acquaintances."

Julianna shook her head. "I can't believe I had no idea."

"So, you're with Finn now?" Tristan asked.

"Yeah. He's a good man. He's saved a lot of people from vampire sharks, and he's given a lot people a second shot at life, like Cody."

"Are you happy with Finn?"

"Yeah, I am," she replied.

"That's all I ever wanted for you," Tristan said. "I'm sorry I wasn't the one to bring you the happiness you deserved."

"You did, Tristan. I felt like I was the one who couldn't make you happy and that's why you felt like you couldn't confide in me."

"That wasn't it at all. I was trying to protect you. But mostly I was trying to protect myself because I didn't want you to leave," he admitted. "When you were killed, it broke me. Something inside me died that day. When I realized you were gone, I hunted the graysuit who killed you, and I killed him."

"He's dead?!"

"Yeah. I killed him right after I found your body. Ever since you died, I've been traveling the world to take out vampire sharks who kill innocent people. I thought it would help ease my grief. But the truth is, it didn't. Nothing did. I missed you so much. I still can't believe you're alive."

"You've been killing graysuits?" Julianna asked, surprised by Tristan's confession. "But you're a graysuit. Why would you do that?"

"Yes, but I don't kill innocent people," Tristan said. "When I lost you, I regained my humanity. I knew what it was like to lose someone who I loved more than anything in the world. I didn't want that to happen to anyone else. So, if a graysuit kills an innocent human, he or she forfeits the right to live. If they take an innocent life, they pay for it with their own."

"I've never heard a graysuit say that before."

"There are others of us, many others, who feel the same way I do. There are some bad seeds, but you have that in every species—humans, even dolphins," he said.

Julianna shook her head in disbelief. In all her years of research, she had never heard a graysuit talk about protecting human life. She peered into Tristan's eyes, trying to figure out what made him different from every other vampire shark she encountered. After a moment, she lost herself. *He has such beautiful eyes. Mesmerizing.* Dazed, she said the first thing that popped into her head. "What about you? Did you ever remarry?"

"No. When I lost you, I didn't think I'd ever be able to get close to anyone again," Tristan said. "I was surrounded by people, but I always felt alone. I always felt … empty. There was a space I couldn't fill—a space that belonged to you. It's still there. When you died, you took a part of me with you. But then a few weeks ago, something happened. I actually met someone who made me think I didn't have to be alone anymore. I don't know how or why, but I fell in love for the first time since I was with you. It came as a huge surprise after being on my own for so long. I even proposed to her. The night I was nearly killed, she said yes."

"What happened?" Julianna gingerly placed her hand on Tristan's chest next to his stitches. "Who did this to you?"

"Dean."

"What?! Dean staked you? Why?"

Tristan relayed the story of the killing of Andi and Andy, as well as what happened at Dean's fake wedding and afterward with Leilani, Torrey, and Cruz.

"I can't believe Dean would turn on you like that! You two were so close. You were like brothers," Julianna said.

"I couldn't believe it either, but he did. And he's still out there. If he finds out Leilani survived, he'll kill her. If she's with Jake, he'll kill him too. That's why I can't be here. I have to stop that from happening," Tristan said.

"But you're not strong enough to go anywhere yet."

Tristan grasped Julianna's hand, which rested on his chest. "Don't you see, Julianna? I have to. For 40 years, I've lived every moment of my life with the excruciating pain of knowing you died because of me. Even now, knowing you survived as a finner doesn't stop me from feeling guilty about what happened to you. I don't think I can live with myself if something bad happens to anyone else I care about. Torrey and Cruz are dead. If Dean gets to Leilani or Jake before I do … You have to get me out of here. I can't stay here while Dean's out there."

"I hear you, Tristan. I do. But you can't leave here yet, or you'll die. You're not ready."

"I'll die if one more person I care about is killed because of me. I would give my life to save Leilani or Jake or anyone else from being killed by a graysuit. If I could've given my life to save you, I would've done it a thousand times over. Please, Julianna."

Julianna rose from the bed. "Give me a minute. I need to think." As she paced, her thoughts turned to Finn. "Tristan, who turned you and Dean into vampire sharks? Who created you?"

"What? Why does that matter now?" Tristan asked.

"Finn and I have been trying to identify the origin of the vampire shark. We think the first graysuit began creating others around 1973 in San Francisco. Since that's exactly where we were, I thought you might be able to help us."

Tristan sighed heavily. "It was a long time ago, Julianna."

"It was." She sat beside Tristan again. She lowered her head and raised her eyes to meet his. "But in some ways it feels like yesterday, you know?"

Tristan clasped her hand. "Yeah, I know."

# 46 – Broken

"No, no, no!" Finn hurled his coffee mug at the video monitor for lab #1. Coffee and ceramic shards splattered across the room. The monitor cracked and went black.

*You had your chance, graysuit. She married you, and what did you do? You got her killed. There's no way in hell I'll let you put her life at risk again*, Finn thought.

He disconnected the broken monitor, placed it in the corner of the room, and set about rerouting the video feed to a new monitor.

# 47 – Moving On

Julianna removed her hand from Tristan's. "I'm sorry. I can't. I loved you. There's a part of me that probably still loves you, but I'm with Finn now. I love him. He treats me like I'm the most important person in his life because I am. We have no secrets from each other. That's the kind of relationship I've always wanted and needed."

"Yeah," Tristan said. "It's just seeing you here …"

"I know. And I know we can't completely erase those feelings, but our time together has passed."

"You're right," he said.

"Did you tell Leilani what you are?" Julianna asked.

"Yes. I did it because of you. I didn't want to keep that secret, knowing what could happen as a result."

"Then you should be with her," she said. "You loved her enough to tell her what you couldn't tell me. If she makes you happy, you should be with her."

Tristan nodded and gazed into Julianna's eyes. "I'm so happy you're alive. You mean so much to me, and you always will." He reached for her hand again. "So, will you help me get out? I can't sit here in bed while Dean's out there. He's nothing like the man you remember."

"You need to recover first. The stronger you are, the better prepared you'll be when you do find Dean," she said.

Tristan decided not to push. He remembered Julianna hated being told what to do, so he decided to give her a little time. "One more thing, Julianna. I'm really glad you're happy. You deserve only the best. I'm sorry I couldn't give that to you."

Julianna smiled. "I'll be back soon. Get some rest."

# 48 – Tired of Waiting for You

By the time Finn reconnected the video feed from Tristan's room to a new monitor, Julianna was gone. Feeling irritable and wanting to take his anger out on someone, he settled upon the perfect victim. *Maybe Lily's ready to talk.* He burst into lab #4. "You have 24 hours before you start deteriorating, so let's get to the point. Who created you?"

Lily refused to acknowledge him.

"We know it was Tristan," Finn lied, "so do yourself a favor and admit it."

She ignored him.

"All right, have it your way. If you want to chop a few centuries off your life, that's fine by me. Personally, I don't care if you live or die. But tomorrow night when you hit the 72-hour mark and desperately need salt water, you'll tell me everything I want to know. Good night, Lily."

Julianna ran into Finn as he exited lab #4. "How's it going with Lily?" she asked.

"Not well," Finn replied, "but I think she'll crack in a day or two—right about the time her skin starts splitting open."

They walked upstairs to his office and shut the door. "How did things go with your husband?" Finn asked.

"Don't say that! He's not my husband anymore," she said.

"But he was. You were *married* to a graysuit, and you won't marry me. How do you think that makes me feel?"

"I didn't know he was a graysuit when I married him!"

"Would it have made a difference? You two seemed pretty chummy in the lab," he said.

"You were watching us?!"

Finn cast his eyes to the floor to avoid her searing gaze. "I was worried! You were alone in a locked room with a killer."

"He's not like that," Julianna said.

"Oh, great. So, now you're like Cody. How does Tristan do that? How does he get you all to completely abandon your common sense? He's a *graysuit,* which means he's a *killer.*"

"You don't know what you're talking about. He's *not* a killer," Julianna argued. "Do you know he actually kills graysuits who murder innocent humans? And that while you have him locked here in the lab, a graysuit is out there killing people? The same one who tried to kill him and his fiancée?"

"While *I* have him in the lab? Like *you* have nothing to do with it! What does this mean? Are you going to abandon me and our work now that you have your husband back?" Finn asked.

"No! And he's not my husband anymore. Why are you being like this?"

"Because I'm tired, Julianna. I'm tired of seeing mangled and dead bodies when I sleep. I'm tired of seeing Terrell being shredded in front of my eyes. I'm tired of thinking about the graysuit who killed you. But mostly I'm tired of waiting for you to love me as much as I love you. Or as much as you loved your husband—who is now here, holding your hand, professing his undying love for you."

"That's not what happened!"

"I saw it!" Finn yelled.

"If that's true, then you would've also seen me tell him that I love you. Did you see that?" Julianna glanced at the broken monitor in the corner of the room. "No, I guess not. I'm going to stay in the vacant apartment next to Cody's. Come see me when you're ready to apologize."

"Apologize? For what? For loving you so much that I want to marry you?"

"No. I want you to apologize for being an ass." Julianna stormed out of the office and slammed the door.

# 49 – Terrell

Later that night, Finn lay awake alone in bed. *How can she be mad at me? She's the one who was married to a vampire shark. Married!* He thought of his mentor, Terrell. *What would Terrell do if he were here?*

From the day Terrell saved Finn and carried his soul to a new dolphin body, Finn looked up to him. Terrell always seemed to have the right answer for everything.

Terrell was a marine biologist who studied cetaceans. He stood as tall as Finn, and had dark brown skin and curly black hair. But he usually shaved his head, which accentuated his square jaw, wise smile, and vibrant brown eyes. Inside and outside the lab, his female friends and acquaintances often held intense debates about what was sexiest about him—his face, his body, or his brain. Terrell, however, was oblivious to their longing gazes since his attention was usually focused on his work.

Terrell bought the research facility in Catalina after the military ceased its operations there. He studied dolphins for years. He believed dolphins to be intelligent, sentient beings, capable of much more than humans gave them credit for.

Finn smiled when he thought of Terrell's favorite rant. "You've got all these people searching for intelligent life in outer space, and it's right here in the oceans of planet Earth! How about we try communicating with an intelligent species right here in our own backyard?" Terrell would ask. "We share a great deal more in common with dolphins than we probably ever could with some beings on some other planet. And I'm sure dolphins could teach us a thing or two. I know it! But instead we put them in amusement parks and make them do silly tricks for fish. We force them into the military and give them dangerous jobs, such as locating underwater mines. They're way ahead of us in the communication game. Did you know they can transmit sound pictures to each other? They know exactly what we want from them, and sometimes they play along. But what do they want from us? What can they give us? We have absolutely no idea!"

Long before Terrell met Finn—on the day Terrell's human body died—he was working in his lab with a dolphin in a saltwater pool. He was attempting to capture the dolphin's sound pictures using a scientific instrument that makes sound visible. Terrell felt he was on the precipice of a breakthrough when a blood vessel burst in his brain, killing him instantly.

"Finally! Hello, Terrell. Do you know how frustrating it is to hear and understand everything you say, and to have you not be able to understand me at all?"

Terrell glanced around underwater, trying to figure out who was talking to him.

"Terrell, there's no one else in the pool. It's me, Kingston, the dolphin. Kingston's not my real name. But it's the name you gave me, so let's go with that for now."

"Have I gone mad?" Terrell asked.

"No. You're just no longer restricted by a human brain," Kingston said. "It's amazing you humans have accomplished as much as you have with such a small organ."

Terrell looked up at his body floating face down on the pool's surface. "Is that me? Am I dead?"

"Your body is. I think it was an aneurysm. I heard a pop, so it must've ruptured," Kingston explained. "Listen, Terrell, I know you've been trying to communicate with me for years. I know you're a kind, compassionate person. You've never hurt a dolphin in your research, and you saved a great many of us when you took over this facility from the military. Unlike those fools, you didn't imprison us or send us off on ridiculously dangerous missions. You gave us free access to the open ocean, which is why we were willing to stick around and help you in your research. Now I'd like to do something else for you. If you want, I can give you a first-hand view into what it's like to be a dolphin. But you have to promise me one thing: that you won't share any of what you learn with humans. We're more advanced than humans, and they're not ready for what we know. We can't alter the course of their existence. They're on their path—self-destructive as it is—and we're on ours. Do you understand?"

"I think so," Terrell said.

"Good. So, would you like to learn what it's really like to be a dolphin?" Kingston asked.

"Are you kidding? I've wanted that my whole life!" Terrell exclaimed.

From Kingston, Terrell learned it was possible to carry a human soul in a dolphin's brain and transport it to another dolphin's body. He learned that not every dolphin is born into this world with a soul. At the last minute, some dolphin souls decide Earth is too primitive and bail, leaving behind an empty vessel.

Terrell's soul moved into one of these empty vessels. As a carrier—a dolphin who can carry a human soul to another dolphin body—Terrell rescued humans who were killed, by accident or by predators like vampire sharks, but who wanted to stick around on Earth. He surprised the dolphins when he taught himself to shapeshift back into his human form. Terrell explained that it was simply a matter of visualization— arranging the cells in his body to assume their previous form. The dolphins were impressed nonetheless.

The day Terrell was killed was devastating for all his friends, dolphins and finners alike.

He and Finn were patrolling the Malibu coastline. Really,

they were bodysurfing, but they always kept an eye out for a human in need. Terrell saw the vampire shark first. She was about to attack a man as his legs dangled from his surfboard in the ocean. Terrell swam as fast as he could, intending to whip the shark in the eyes with his fluke. He transmitted a picture, instructing Finn to stab her when she took off after him.

Finn picked up a razor-edged rock from the ocean floor and raced toward them. But right before Terrell struck, the shark pivoted and unexpectedly chomped down on Terrell's fluke. She pulled him deeper and deeper into her jaws. Unknowingly, Terrell transmitted sound pictures to Finn, who felt every tooth and every tear as the shark lacerated more and more of Terrell's flesh. When the shark clamped down upon Terrell's head, the pictures stopped.

Finn froze, horrified by what he'd seen. Despite the nearness of the shark, he waited for Terrell's soul to escape his body. After a few seconds, he saw Terrell's soul shimmering in the water.

"Come with me," Finn pleaded. "I'll take you to a new body."

"No, Finn. I've already had one lifetime more than I thought I'd get on this planet, and what a life it's been. I'm ready to move on and see what's next," Terrell said.

"Please let me carry you," Finn begged, "like you did for me."

"No. It's time for me to go," Terrell said. "My will is in a blue envelope in the top drawer of my desk. I've left everything to you and Julianna. Please carry on our work. But, Finn, don't let this experience harden you. The graysuits are here for a reason, just like us. We don't know what that reason is, so it's not up to us to extinguish their species. Oh! There's my path. It's beckoning to me. It's ... beautiful. Goodbye, Finn. I hope we meet again."

Finn watched Terrell disappear. He felt dreadfully alone.

Finn's intense loneliness abruptly turned to rage. *The graysuits don't deserve our kindness. They never did. Terrell might have studied and released them, but that's not me. Look what Terrell's kindness got him. It got him killed! The only way to protect ourselves is to bring an end to vampire sharks once and for all.*

It was then that Finn noticed the vampire shark was nearly finished eating Terrell's body. He transmitted pictures recounting Terrell's violent end, hoping other dolphins were nearby. Within minutes, a superpod of 1,000 dolphins appeared. They were shocked and saddened by the news of Terrell's death.

Finn pointed to the vampire shark who killed Terrell. One by one, the dolphins charged her.

The vampire shark, attacked from all sides, felt the force of each hit deep inside her flesh. She tried to lash out and bite the dolphins, but there were too many. The dolphins rammed and pummeled the shark. They whipped their flukes across her eyes, blinding her. They stabbed her with shards of coral and rocks. They battered her until her gills split open, her fins tore from her body, and her organs began to fail. Soon her heart stopped.

When it was over, Finn thanked each member of the pod and swam back to the compound alone.

# 50 – No Way

In the years Finn worked under Terrell, learning from one of the world's greatest scientists, the only time they argued was about graysuits.

Terrell's policy at the lab was "catch, study, and release." He knew that great white sharks quickly deteriorate and die in captivity. He had no desire to cause another species pain or drive it to extinction. His goal was to study vampire sharks to research and document their physiology, and identify their origin. He wanted to know if vampire sharks evolved naturally, like vampires, or if something human-made caused a mutation that resulted in the species.

Terrell examined the graysuits' fangs and studied their venom, which was housed in a small sac buried in the gum tissue beneath each fang. He determined that vampire sharks could create regular vampires by biting the neck of a human and releasing their venom into the human's carotid artery. But he had yet to find a vampire shark who could create another vampire shark. He theorized there must be one vampire shark whose venom was unique. Despite intense questioning, none of the graysuits ever told Terrell, Finn, or Julianna who created them or how.

When Terrell finished his study, he'd tranquilize the graysuit and drive to the middle of the Pacific Ocean. He'd then place him or her in a biodegradable life raft, set the raft adrift, and speed away. A few hours later, the graysuit would awaken and swim home, with no idea of where he or she had been.

With each release, however, Finn grew more and more frustrated. When he'd complain about their failure to identify the creator, Terrell would try to calm him by explaining that graysuits, like great white sharks, are a very secretive species.

"Revealing how they came to be is unimaginable to them. It's against their nature," Terrell would say. "Think about it. Even with all the research humans have accumulated over decades, they still don't know how great white sharks mate. Neither do we. No human or dolphin in the world has ever witnessed that, so we can't be surprised that a creature that's part shark wouldn't want to share the intimate details of its creation."

"But that doesn't mean we stop digging," Finn would argue. "If we can find out who's creating them and how, we can stop new ones from being created and prevent more senseless murders."

Terrell would then counter with a gentler point of view. "True, but we can also be more understanding of their natural tendency to want to keep to themselves. Sharks are not pack animals. They enjoy their solitude and space. When you confine them, you kill them. That's not what we do. It's not who we are. It doesn't mean we stop studying or questioning. The more we can learn about them, the more we can learn about how to deal with them to protect ourselves and humans. But we don't question or study to the point of torture. Even if we know a graysuit has killed a human—which it seems most, if not all, of them have—*we* do not kill."

Finn would then nod but silently and vehemently disagree. He respected Terrell but often thought he was too soft for his own good.

When Finn met Julianna, when he began working for Terrell at his Catalina compound, he became even more convinced he was right and Terrell was wrong. Finn knew Julianna had been murdered by a graysuit, but he didn't know how barbaric and senseless the killing was until he saw it for himself.

After he and Julianna had been together a few months, they knew it was serious for both of them, and they became exclusive. In a moment of intimacy, at Finn's urging, Julianna agreed to transmit pictures of her attack to him. As he saw her memories of the attack, he felt her pain and terror as the shark bit into her. When the images stopped, he felt his heart constrict. Finn and Julianna held each other wordlessly for several hours afterward. Finn became more determined than ever to find the graysuit creator and put a stop to the killing. *There's no way I'll let a graysuit do that to another person if I can help it. No way in hell.*

# 51 — Confidant

Early Monday morning, Julianna paced inside the empty apartment next to Cody's. Her mind raced. *Tristan said he kills graysuits who kill humans. He said there are lots of graysuits who don't kill innocent people. Does that mean we've been wrong about them all these years and that not all of them are murderers? Have we inadvertently killed innocent creatures under the guise of research?*

Still angry from her argument with Finn, Julianna stormed into lab #1. "I need to talk to you, Tristan, and I need you to tell me the truth—no lies, no holding back."

Tristan knew that tone of voice. *Whoa, Finn must've done something to really piss her off. Or maybe she's still mad about me lying to her when we were together.*

"I'll tell you anything you want to know," he said calmly. "First tell me why you're so upset. Is it because of me?"

"No. It's just … Hang on." Julianna entered a code in a wall panel to turn off the video and audio surveillance.

"What did you just do?" Tristan asked.

"Nothing," she said curtly.

He decided not to press her. "Are you okay?"

"Yeah. Finn just makes me so angry sometimes," she said.

"Why? What'd he do?"

"Sometimes he has a narrow point of view. Things are very black and white with him." Julianna debated the merit of airing her grievances about Finn to her former husband, but she realized she actually liked—and missed—talking with Tristan. "Finn is mad at me because I won't marry him."

"Why don't you want to marry him?" Tristan asked.

Julianna shrugged.

"Do you love him?" he asked.

"Yes, of course, I love him. But I don't think you need to marry someone to show how much you love him. The relationship Finn and I have is the relationship we have, and a stupid marriage license won't change that," she said.

"It's me, isn't it? I'm the one who ruined marriage for you," Tristan said. "You thought if we got married, I'd change and open up to you. But I didn't. I held back. So, now you think, 'What's the point?'"

Julianna met Tristan's gaze and quickly looked away. "I just don't think marriage changes the relationship you already have. Marriage didn't make you and me any closer. We loved each other, but it wasn't enough."

"Don't let your relationship with me cloud your relationship with someone else," he said. "Do you think Finn is keeping something from you?"

"No," she replied. "And I know he loves me."

Tristan sighed heavily. *I can't say I like the idea of Julianna marrying Finn, but she's already been with him for years. I don't want what happened with me to keep her from finding happiness with someone else—even if that person is Finn.* "Well, if you love him and trust him and marriage is that important to him, maybe you should consider it. If you truly love the relationship you have—and as you said, a marriage license won't change that—then why not do it?"

Across the room, a red light flashed and an alarm blared.

"What's that?" Tristan asked.

"Red siren," Julianna said. "I have to go."

"Go where?"

Julianna strode to the door. "A yellow siren means there's been a killing, but we don't know where the graysuit is. A red siren means there's been a killing, and one of us is tracking the graysuit. We're going to try to capture it."

"Wait! Maybe I can help," Tristan said. "What if it's Dean?"

"No," she said. "Not in your condition."

As Julianna exited the lab, she smacked into Cody in the hallway.

"Red siren. Can I go this time?" Cody asked.

"You're not ready. You haven't even started your training." Julianna held the door open to lab #1. "Here, keep Tristan company."

# 52 – Risks

Julianna met Finn, Matt, and two other finners, Jamal and Lucia, at the cove.

"Everybody ready? We have to move if we're going to catch this one," Finn said breathlessly. "Emma is tracking the graysuit. It's the one who killed those two surfers in San Clemente. He hasn't noticed her yet. Let's hope he doesn't. Matt, when we reach him, you get his attention."

"Why am I always the chum?" Matt joked.

Finn ignored Matt's attempt to lighten the mood. "The rest of us will run the standard figure-eight formation. I'll deliver the first blow. Julianna will stick him with the sedative. We'll have about a minute before it takes effect. So, we'll need to keep ramming him so he can't get his bearings and attack. Okay?"

All four finners nodded and boarded the boat. Julianna grabbed a large elastic band, which held six syringes of a powerful sedative, and slipped it around her waist.

Finn reached for Julianna. "I'm sorry about last night. I overreacted," he said. "I love you. You know that, right?"

"Yes. I love you too," she said.

Finn started the boat and sped toward Emma's GPS signal from her microchip. When they reached her location, they drove past it a bit. Lucia dropped anchor. They all jumped into the ocean and transformed into dolphins.

"They should be here any minute," Finn whistled. "Everyone see the picture Emma's sending us?"

They could sense the graysuit approaching and moved in that direction. Finn's clicks increased as they got closer. He whistled, and the pod dispersed.

Matt swam head-on toward the vampire shark who passed right over him. Matt turned around at the same instant the shark did. He lunged for Matt's face. Matt turned, but the shark still managed to sink his teeth into Matt's side.

Half a second too late, the rest of the pod appeared. Finn delivered the first blow, disorienting the graysuit. Julianna shifted into her human body and reached for the band around her waist. She grabbed a syringe and jabbed it into the shark's side.

Emma, who had been trailing the graysuit for miles, climbed aboard the boat and prepared the net.

While Finn, Lucia, and Jamal battered the vampire shark, Julianna swam over to help Matt. He had a large gash in his side, one of his pectoral fins was torn, and his breathing was halting and shallow. She helped him to the surface while the other three finners waged battle below, slamming repeatedly into the shark until the sedative knocked him out.

Emma dropped the net. The dolphins shoved the vampire shark into the net, and she reeled it in.

Finn approached Julianna, and they changed back into their human bodies.

Julianna placed her hand on Matt's head, above his bottlenose. "He can't morph. His injuries are too severe. But as a dolphin, I'm pretty sure he can recover. A human would never have survived this."

"We'll drop a harness for him. You help him into it, and we'll lift him into the saltwater tank. Would you like to stay with him on the ride home?" Finn asked.

"Yeah," Julianna said.

"Don't worry. He'll be okay. You did great today. I'm the one who screwed up. I was a half-second too late," Finn said.

"It's not your fault. We all did the best we could. We know the risks every time we do this," Julianna said.

Finn groaned. "I'll lower the harness."

# 53 — Warmth

Emma drove the boat back toward Catalina Island and docked in the cove outside the compound. Jamal and Lucia helped get Matt from the boat into the ocean while Julianna raced ahead to get lab #2 ready for him. Julianna unlocked the lab door and turned up the heater in the saltwater pool to ensure it would be comfortable for Matt, a native Hawaiian who preferred warmer temperatures. She was ready for them by the time they reached the underwater gate to the lab's pool.

Jamal and Lucia guided Matt to the smooth ledge at the far end of the pool. Then the two dolphins morphed and climbed out of the water.

"What do you need, J?" Jamal asked.

"Yeah, how can we help?" Lucia added.

"I'm going to clean up Matt's wounds and stitch him up. He'll have to stay here a few days. If you could visit and keep him company, I'm sure he'd appreciate it."

Matt gave a weak whistle of acknowledgment.

Julianna stroked Matt's head. "Quiet. You're going to be fine. Just rest, okay?"

Jamal and Lucia said their goodbyes and promised to visit. Julianna treated Matt's injuries and stayed with him through the rest of the day and night.

# 54 — Frying

While Julianna tended to Matt, Finn and Emma lowered the unconscious vampire shark, still trapped inside the net, into the ocean. They pulled the net through the rocky tunnel into the sea cave and then into the tunnel leading to the labs. Finn opened the gate to lab #6 and pushed the net into the saltwater pool. He closed the gate behind them.

"Thanks, Emma. I can take it from here," he said.

"Are you sure?" she asked. "This one's pretty nasty. He ripped those two surfers apart. There was so much blood. By the time I got there, their souls had already moved on. I'm sorry I couldn't save them."

"Don't apologize. It's because of you we captured him. Get some rest. We can debrief later," Finn said.

After Emma left, Finn stood above the pool and gazed at the vampire shark sleeping inside the net. "I'll be back soon. For your sake, let's hope I'm in a better mood than I am now."

Finn thought about checking on Matt but felt too upset. He stomped to lab #4. "Lily, how are we doing tonight?"

Lily, still shackled to the hospital bed, panted. Her skin glowed deep pink, bordering on fuchsia. It peeled and flaked.

"Is it hot in here?" Finn fanned himself and laughed cruelly. "Nope, it's just you." He hovered over Lily and whispered in her ear. "I hear it feels like you're frying on a skillet. Is that right? Or is it more like being microwaved and cooking from the inside out? I bet you could use a cool, refreshing saltwater bath about now."

"Yes," Lily breathed.

"First tell me what I want to know. Who created you?"

She closed her eyes.

"Lily, I don't know why you're protecting the graysuit who

created you. I want to help you, but I need you to help me. Tell me who created you, or I'm going to leave you here until you're nothing but ash. It's going to take a few days for that to happen. If you think you're miserable now, just wait until tomorrow."

"Fuck you, Finn," Lily rasped. "I don't have to tell you shit."

"You're right. You don't. See you tomorrow."

Finn left Lily and walked down the hall to lab #2. He saw Julianna sitting next to Matt in the pool, caressing the top of his head to soothe him. Not wanting to disturb them, he headed to lab #1. Finn didn't know that Cody had spent the day with Tristan or that they were plotting his escape.

# 55 – Trapped

When Julianna let Cody into Tristan's room, the lab door locked, trapping Cody inside until Finn or Julianna returned—which was exactly what Tristan wanted.

"Did they all leave?" Tristan asked.

"Most of 'em. Graysuit siren," Cody explained.

"That's what Julianna said. You didn't go?"

"No. I'm stuck here," Cody said.

"That sucks, but I could use the company. It's so boring in here by myself."

Cody glanced around. "Yeah, I bet."

"Could you come a little closer? My voice is kind of hoarse," Tristan said.

Cody leaned over Tristan.

"Closer," Tristan rasped.

Cody put his ear above Tristan's mouth.

"My voice is fine," Tristan whispered, "but don't move, and keep your expression casual. We're under surveillance—video and audio, I think. There's a panel in the corner of the room, but you need a security code to disable it. Julianna turned it off, but it might've re-engaged when she left. I need you to help me walk over there. I'm too weak to stand on my own. Believe me, I've tried. Pretend you're helping me, like physical therapy or something. I'll make it look like I'm tired and lean against the wall so I can check the panel. I've had security systems in some of the places I've lived, so I can probably tell if it's on or not. Now lean back and say, 'Yeah, I'll help you walk around.'"

Cody raised his head. "Sure, I'll help you walk around."

He helped Tristan stand and supported him as they walked toward the wall and strolled the perimeter of the room. When they reached the corner, Tristan leaned against the wall.

"Give … me … a minute," Tristan panted. He glanced at the panel and saw the surveillance was on. He tried entering Julianna's birthday. When they lived together, she used her birthday as the combination to the safe where she kept her grandmother's jewelry. The digital display showed an error message. He figured he had two more tries before he set off the alarm. On a whim, Tristan entered his and Julianna's wedding anniversary. The surveillance system turned off.

"It's off," Tristan said. "Help me back to bed. Then get a glass of water from the pool, knock the splashguard off the panel, and dump the water on it. I'll tell Finn I felt dizzy, fell into the panel, and threw up. He'll think it shorted out. Then we need to talk."

Cody did as he was told. He pulled a chair next to Tristan's bed and sat down.

"Something's wrong, Cody," Tristan explained. "I don't know how much you know about graysuits, but both vampires and sharks have accelerated healing—like dolphins do. I should be perfectly healthy by now. I think the sedatives are messing with my natural healing processes, and that's why I'm so weak and still partially have a hole in my chest."

"You think Finn is doing this on purpose?" Cody asked.

"I don't know. Do you know anything about the research they do here?" Tristan asked.

"Not much. I know they study graysuits, but that's about it," Cody said.

"I knew a graysuit once who told me she was captured and taken to some kind of research center. She thought it was a military facility. She told me the researcher took a sample of her venom from beneath her fangs. She was sedated but remembered hearing the guy say, 'This one's like the others. Let's sew her up and set her free.' She woke up on a raft in the middle of the ocean but had no idea where she'd been. I didn't think twice about it at the time. I thought she made the whole thing up—she was kind of dramatic—but now I'm not so sure. Have they told you anything about what they might be looking for or why they're keeping me here?" Tristan asked.

Cody hesitated.

"Please, Cody. You can trust me. I hope you know that."

"I do. But they're finners like I am now … and you're a graysuit," Cody said.

"And you think all graysuits are bad?" Tristan asked.

"No. I just …"

Tristan could see Cody struggling. "I need to leave. It's not just for me. I have to get to Leilani and Jake. They're in trouble," Tristan said.

"Finn says they're safe."

"Finn doesn't know Dean," Tristan said. "I do. Leilani and Jake are all alone. They think I'm dead, and they don't know how to go up against a killer like Dean on their own. Plus, I can feel myself deteriorating every minute I'm trapped here. Great white sharks aren't meant to live in captivity. If they keep me here, I'll get weaker and weaker until I die."

Cody sighed heavily. "I want to help you, but I don't even know the code to the door. I only know a couple of Finn's numbers. I can't get you out of here."

"Can you at least tell me why Finn is keeping me here? It's not for my recovery. I know that now. What does he want from me?" Tristan asked.

"Before you and Julianna saw each other, he wanted me to ask if you lived in San Francisco in the early 1970s," Cody said.

"But he knows I lived there because I was with Julianna then. Why would he care where I lived?" Tristan asked.

"I don't know. He said you might know someone he needs to find, and it's really important."

"What else?"

"Dude, that's everything. I'm new. They don't tell me much," Cody said.

"What about you? Why are you still here?" Tristan asked.

"I dunno. Because I'm still getting used to this, and I'm not sure where to go. I can't go back to my old life. We're not allowed to see people we knew before. I was thinking of staying and seeing if maybe I could help Julianna with her work or something. She's been really cool to me since I've been here—helping me adjust and stuff," Cody said.

"Yeah, Julianna is a really good person. But she doesn't realize they're killing me by keeping me here. When they get back, can you ask her to come here? Tell her it's urgent."

"I'll try, but they're usually pretty busy when they bring in a new graysuit. I heard Matt say this one killed some surfers," Cody said.

"What happens when they bring in a new vampire shark?" Tristan asked.

"They bring him to a lab and do some kind of research."

"Here's the thing that worries me, Cody. You've seen graysuits come in, but have you ever seen any leave?"

"Uh, no," Cody replied. "But I haven't been here long."

Tristan sighed. "I'm going to trust you with a secret. This secret could kill me or any graysuit, so I'm pretty much trusting you with my life here. But you already saved my life once, so I know I can rely on you."

Cody nodded.

"When a vampire's venom sacs are removed, it's like removing their life source. Since a graysuit is part vampire, without this venom we die within days. It's like when we can't get to salt water. If my friend, the dramatic one, was right, that's what they're doing to graysuits in the lab. I think that several years ago they used to study the venom and release the graysuit unharmed. But they don't do that anymore. I think graysuits are dying here. My guess is that Finn is trying to find out how vampire sharks are created and is willing to sacrifice lives for it," Tristan said.

"But if the graysuits they bring in are killers, isn't that okay? You told me you take out killers, like when you killed Rick after he attacked me," Cody said.

"Yes, but I don't kill innocent graysuits—and I'm dying here. If they take my venom, I'll be dead within a week. They might not mean for it to happen, but it will."

"They wouldn't do that," Cody said.

"Are you sure? Because right now I'm not willing to bet my life on it," Tristan said.

"I would," Cody assured him. "Finn saved you. Why would he do that if he was just going to let you die?"

Tristan didn't want to play the "Jake" card but knew he had no other option. "Would you be willing to bet Jake's life on it?"

"I already told you that Finn said Jake is fine," Cody said.

"That's not what I mean," Tristan said.

"What then?"

"Jake should really be the one to tell you this, but I will because it could save his life someday. Jake is now a graysuit like me," Tristan revealed.

Cody jumped up from his chair. "No. No way, dude. Now I know you're messing with me. I can't help you."

"I'm not messing with you. It's true."

"No! Jake's no graysuit. If he was, I'd know," Cody said.

"No, you wouldn't. It happened, or at least it started, the day you died," Tristan said.

Cody looked at Tristan with a heartbreaking mix of doubt, confusion, and anguish on his face.

Tristan explained how he accidentally nicked Jake's toe as he swam by racing to get to Cody before Rick killed him. While the tiny amount of venom wasn't enough to completely turn Jake, it was enough to begin the transformation. Tristan told Cody about how on the night of Dean's attack, as they floated in the ocean, Jake asked him to finish the job and turn him completely.

"Why?! Why would he do that?" Cody demanded.

"Because he said it's who he is," Tristan said.

"Jake's not a killer!"

"You're right. Jake's not. Not every graysuit kills innocent people. That's where Finn has it wrong," Tristan said.

"You're lying," Cody said.

"I'm not. Jake is a graysuit. I know Jake would never kill a human. But if he gets captured and brought here, he'll die here—like I am."

Cody paced around the room. "How do I know you're not lying to me?"

"Because I've never lied to you," Tristan said.

Cody gazed at the stitched-up hole in Tristan's chest. It did look terrible. He also noticed Tristan's skin was ashen and his eyes were dull. "Swear to me, Tristan. Swear on Leilani's life that you're telling me the truth about Jake."

"I swear."

Cody heaved a sigh. He knew he had no choice. He couldn't risk Jake being brought in if what Tristan said was true about graysuits never leaving the lab alive. "So, how do we get you out of here?"

"Thank you, Cody. You won't regret this. Help me to the pool. I want to see if the code I used to disable the surveillance works on the gates."

Tristan entered his and Julianna's wedding anniversary, but an error message flashed. With Cody's help, he hobbled back to bed.

"There are two codes then—one for the surveillance and one for the exits. Earlier you said you knew part of Finn's code? Which code?" Tristan asked.

"The door. It's 5, 2, something, something, 3," Cody said.

"That's good! Do you think you can get the other two numbers?" Tristan asked.

"Maybe. But Finn doesn't like me standing over his shoulder," Cody said.

"See what you can do."

# 56 – Motives

Finn entered lab #1 to check Tristan's vital signs. He nearly dropped his clipboard when he saw Cody sitting next to the bed. "How'd you get in here?"

"Julianna let me in before you guys left. Did you catch the graysuit?" Cody asked.

"Not before he attacked Matt," Finn said.

Tristan frowned. "Is Matt okay?"

"Is he okay?! He was attacked head-on by a vampire shark!" Finn said.

"C'mon, Finn," Cody said gently, "he's just asking."

"Matt is critically injured," Finn said. "If he was human, he wouldn't have survived."

"Is Julianna okay?" Tristan asked.

"Yes. She's staying with Matt in the lab tonight," Finn replied.

"So, he'll recover?" Tristan asked.

"Yes," Finn said. "What have you two been doing?"

"Talking. Cody helped me walk around a little, but I felt dizzy and threw up," Tristan said. "Then I had to lie down. That's actually what I wanted to talk to you about. I'm feeling sicker, and it's because …"

"I'll increase the sedatives," Finn interrupted.

"No! They're making things worse. I should be healed, and I'm not. It's because I'm not out in the open ocean. Keeping me here is making me sicker." Tristan quickly glanced at Cody while he waited for Finn's response.

"You think you're feeling worse because you're here? No, you just need to get some more rest," Finn said.

"That's not it," Tristan argued. "If you'd just …"

"Listen, Tristan, it's been a long day," Finn said. "You're

tired. I'm tired. Get some sleep, and we can talk again later. I'm sure you'll feel better tomorrow."

"I won't," Tristan said. "You need to let me go …"

"Enough!" Finn shouted. "I said we'll talk later. Cody, let's go. Tristan's had enough excitement for one day. You can see the toll it's taken on him."

Tristan raised his eyebrows at Cody, imploring him to question Finn's motives. Cody shrugged and followed Finn out the door.

# 57 – Barely Breathing

Outside the lab, Cody decided to press Finn about Tristan's condition. "Hey, Finn?"

"What?!" Finn snapped.

Cody flinched. "Tristan does seem weaker, and he looks terrible—definitely worse than yesterday."

"Tristan is not at the top of my concerns right now. I have Matt recuperating in a lab after almost being torn to pieces. The graysuit who did it is in another lab. Lily is being as stubborn as ever. I'm a little busy," Finn said.

"But if we could just …"

"Not now." Finn marched down the hall to lab #6.

Cody decided to check on Matt and talk to Julianna. Seeing the door open to lab #2, he tiptoed inside in case Matt was sleeping.

A high-pitched shriek erupted from down the hall. Cody peered into the hallway. *Must be coming from lab #6—the new graysuit. Do I even wanna know what Finn's doing to make him scream like that?* He heard another bloodcurdling shriek. *Probably not.*

Cody carefully closed the door to lab #2 and approached the saltwater pool. "How's Matt?"

"He's resting," Julianna replied. "Here, take a look."

Cody glanced at the stitched-up gashes in Matt's body. He shuddered, knowing all too well the excruciating pain of having one's flesh torn open by rows of jagged teeth.

Matt coughed.

"It's okay, Matt. Just rest here on the ledge so you can get the oxygen you need," Julianna murmured. "Cody's here. He came by to see how you're doing."

Matt opened his eyes.

"Hi, Matt. I'm glad you made it home," Cody said softly. "Finn just went in to see the graysuit who did this to you. I would not want to be that guy right now. Anyway, I hope you feel better. Let me know if you need anything, okay?"

Matt blinked in acknowledgment and closed his eyes again. Julianna rested her hand on the top of his head.

"Julianna, can I talk with you for a minute?" Cody asked.

They stepped a few feet away from Matt.

"It's Tristan. He says he's getting worse because he's trapped here," Cody explained.

"He's got a pool full of fresh ocean water in his room. And we're not holding him captive," Julianna said.

"Aren't we though? He wants to leave, but he's locked inside a lab. He's worried about Leilani and Jake. We need to release him," Cody said.

Matt coughed. Julianna saw spots of blood dissipate in the water around him.

"Cody, get Finn now! Matt's bleeding internally. He's barely breathing. We need to operate," Julianna said.

Cody ran to the door. "I can't get out! What's your code?"

Julianna dashed over and punched it in. Cody saw her hit 1-1-5 but couldn't see the last two numbers.

Cody raced to lab #6. He pressed the intercom button outside the door. "Matt's in trouble! Julianna needs you in surgery now!"

Finn dropped the graysuit's venom sac into a small jar, sealed it, and set it inside the lab refrigerator.

"Hurry!" Cody yelled.

Finn ran out of the lab, leaving the graysuit restrained on the table and bleeding from his gums. "Go home, Cody. I'll get you when we're done with Matt. Until then, stay in your apartment."

# 58 – Escape

Cody walked toward the stairwell. His thoughts turned to Tristan. *Tristan tried to save my life when Rick came after me. I brought Tristan here to save him, but now he's getting worse. Finn and Julianna are tied up with Matt. Who knows for how long? I can't let Tristan die here. And what if he's telling the truth about Jake?*

Cody turned around and ran to lab #1. He pressed the intercom button. "Tristan, I have the first three numbers of Julianna's door code: 1-1-5. I don't know the last two. Do those numbers mean anything to you?"

Tristan racked his brain. *1-1-5. 1-15 maybe? Or 11-5? 11-5. No, that'd be too easy.* He pressed the intercom button near his bed. "Try 11-5-72."

Cody entered the numbers. The door buzzed open. "We have to go now. Can you walk?"

Tristan sat up and then fell back, dizzy. Cody removed his IV and tried to stand him up, but Tristan lost his footing and fell to the floor.

"Forget walking. Just drag me to the pool," Tristan said.

Cody gripped Tristan's feet and pulled him across the floor to the pool ledge. Cody quickly removed his clothes and dropped them on the floor. He climbed into the water and pulled Tristan deeper into the pool. He removed Tristan's hospital gown and tossed it outside the pool. Holding Tristan with one arm, he entered Julianna's code on the panel above the gate that separated the pool from the ocean tunnel. The gate slid open.

"Can you morph?" Cody asked.

Tristan tried but didn't have the energy to transform, so Cody pulled Tristan's arms over his shoulders. Tristan laced his fingers together in front of Cody's neck.

"Take a big breath, and hold it," Cody said.

Cody morphed and pulled Tristan through the maze of twists and turns to the next gate. He entered Julianna's code. The gate opened, and they swam into the sea cave. Cody surfaced so Tristan could get some air. Gasping, Tristan filled his lungs. After a minute, he nodded to Cody.

Cody dove underwater again and transported Tristan through the rocky tunnel to the cove and the open ocean. Once there, Cody surfaced, changed back into his human body, and lifted Tristan's hands over his head. He thrust his arm under Tristan's armpit and treaded water behind him. "Are you okay?"

Immediately, Tristan felt a surge of energy from the cool ocean currents rippling around him. He smiled and turned to Cody. "I am now, thanks to you."

After several minutes Tristan felt strong enough to morph. "I have to find Leilani. I'm sorry to leave you like this. Finn's gonna be pissed."

"Do you really think Leilani and Jake are in danger?" Cody asked.

"If Dean's still out there, I know they are," Tristan said.

"Then I'm coming with you."

"How?" Tristan asked. "No one can know you're alive."

"I'll be careful no one sees me. I know I can't risk exposing finners to humans. But if this guy is as dangerous as you say, you're gonna need backup," Cody said.

"No. I won't risk your life."

"You're not," Cody said. "I'm doing this for Jake. Are we going or not?"

Tristan nodded and morphed. He led Cody toward the North County coast of San Diego, gaining more strength with each minute he spent in the ocean. *Leilani.*

# 59 – Pieces

When they finished operating on Matt, Finn left him in Julianna's care. He felt too wired to go home and sleep, so he burst into lab #4. "Hey, Lily. Hot enough for you?"

Lily lay on the table, breathing heavily. Her lips cracked and bled. Across her body, her skin blistered, ruptured, and peeled.

Finn strolled to the saltwater pool. He dipped a glass into the water and brought it to Lily. He waved it in front of her. "Is there anything more refreshing than a cool dip in the ocean?"

He lowered his index finger into the glass and positioned it a few inches above her mouth. A droplet of water clung to his fingertip. Lily tilted her head up but couldn't reach it.

"Lily, I know you're suffering," Finn said. "Believe it or not, I don't like this any more than you do."

Lily glared at him with dry, bloodshot eyes.

"It's true," he said. "I don't want to hurt anyone, and I don't want anyone to get hurt. That's why we do what we do here. You killed people, Lily. You inflicted pain on them. You took their lives. You had no right to do that. Now, as you sit here roasting alive in your own body as it ages, you know what excruciating pain feels like. I don't want you to die, but you have to help me. Can you do that?"

Lily managed a slight nod.

Finn leaned closer. "Was that a 'yes'?"

"Yes," she croaked. "Water."

"I'll give you this glass of salt water if you tell me who created you. If I think you're being truthful, I'll help you into the pool. It'll take some time, but you'll recover. You'll be a lot older, but it's not too late."

Lily's mouth felt too dry to form another word.

"I'm trusting you." He dribbled the salt water over the top

of her head, face, neck, and chest. "Better?"

She grunted.

"Good. Now who created you?" he asked.

Lily remained silent. She nodded toward the glass.

"No," Finn said. "We had an agreement. No more water until you tell me what I want to know. Who created you?"

She raised her head, signaling Finn to come closer. He lowered his head near her face.

Lily opened her mouth and licked her cracked, bloody lips. "Fuck. You. Finn."

Finn grimaced. "That was your last chance, Lily."

She struggled against the restraints. Large pieces of her skin flaked and crumbled onto the bed.

Finn gave her one last hard look. "I'm sorry it had to be this way. Just remember, you chose this. Rest in pieces."

# 60 – Makaio

While Leilani and Jake described Dean and Skylar to the sketch artist, Kai made breakfast. He set a plate of fresh papaya, pineapple, and bananas on the table, next to a bowl of hard-boiled eggs. He looked at the sketches. "Pretty," he said, appraising the pencil drawing of Skylar.

"Yeah, and the worst girlfriend ever," Jake said.

Leilani nodded in agreement.

"I'll keep that in mind." Kai scanned and emailed the sketches to his family while Jake and Leilani ate.

"Thank you for breakfast, Kai. This is great," Leilani said.

"Yeah, awesome, man," Jake mumbled with a mouthful of fruit.

Leilani yawned, which made Jake yawn.

"You guys get any sleep last night?" Kai asked.

"Maybe an hour or two before you woke us," Leilani said.

"It's a good thing I did though," Kai said. "Right, graysuit?"

"Right. Call me Jake."

"Why don't you guys crash here?" Kai suggested. "I have to get back to work. I can meet you here after sundown."

"Are you sure it's no trouble?" Leilani asked.

"I'm sure. There are clean towels in the cupboard outside the bathroom. See you later," Kai said.

Leilani stretched out on a lounge chair on Kai's balcony while Jake napped on the couch inside, safe from the sun. She awoke first, then showered and dressed. Jake followed. He opened the door to let the steam out and toweled off his hair.

Kai burst through the front door. "My cousin saw Dean and Skylar last night at Maui Brewing Company. That means they're probably staying in the Ka'anapali area of Maui. There are lots of resorts there. Let's go!"

A short while later, Kai, Leilani, and Jake arrived at the airport in Kahului, Maui. A handsome man with brown skin, long black hair, and a broad smile greeted them.

Kai shook his hand and threw his arm around the man's shoulders. "Leilani, Jake, this is my cousin, Makaio. Makaio, this is the woman and graysuit I told you about."

At 23, Makaio was three years younger than his cousin. He towered six inches above Kai and had a more muscular physique, which he liked to show off as often as he could.

Cautiously, Makaio shook Jake's hand. He turned to Leilani. "You're as beautiful as your name. Did you know Leilani means 'heavenly flower'?" Makaio leaned in close to her and whispered, "Kai didn't tell me I'd be meeting someone like you here today. For a cop, he's not very observant, is he?"

"I, uh, thanks," Leilani sputtered.

"Ignore him, Leilani," Kai said with a grin. "Makaio's name means 'gift of god.' When it comes to women, he likes to think he's god's gift. But really he's more like a white elephant—the gift nobody wants that you can never seem to get rid of."

"Brah, you're just jealous my side of the family got the good looks," Makaio teased.

"Good thing because you definitely got skipped in the brains department," Kai said.

They climbed into Makaio's car and drove away from the airport. Once they hit the coast, they skimmed along the edge of the island on Route 30, heading north. Leilani gazed out the window, spotting arid hills and bare trees on the right. She saw the midnight blue Pacific Ocean on the left. She opened her window and breathed in the warm night air.

They drove past Lahaina and into Ka'anapali. Makaio pulled off the Honoapi'ilani Highway and onto Lower Honoapi'ilani Road. They continued past hotels and condos, and turned into a modest apartment complex situated behind an oceanfront resort.

They exited the car, and Jake took a deep breath of salty ocean air. "This is great! You live so close to the beach."

"It figures the graysuit would love it," Makaio snickered.

"The name's Jake, not graysuit," Jake said.

"You naming your pets now, Kai?" Makaio laughed.

"Hey, Makaio, Jake saved my life. Give it a rest, okay?" Leilani flashed a friendly but firm warning smile.

"For you, Heavenly Flower, anything. My apologies, gray— uh, Jake," Makaio said. "Welcome to my humble abode."

They settled into Makaio's studio apartment. He opened the windows so they could get some fresh air and listen to the wind rustle through the palm trees.

"How far are we from the brewpub where Dean and Skylar were spotted?" Leilani asked.

"Maui Brewing is just under two miles away—about five minutes by car," Kai said. "You want to start there?"

"That sounds good. How late are they open?" she asked.

"Midnight," Kai and Makaio answered simultaneously.

Jake shifted in his seat. He didn't like the way the two cousins were gawking at Leilani—like lovestruck teenagers. He decided to break the spell. "Well, what are we waiting for? Let's go!"

Jake stood and offered his hand to help Leilani to her feet. Since their arrival in Hawaii, he noticed that her arms and legs stiffened up at night from all the puncture wounds. He continued to hold her hand as they strode toward the door. Out of the corner of his eye, he saw Makaio shoot a questioning glance at Kai, who shrugged his shoulders. *Yeah, she's with me, God's Gift or whatever your name is. So, keep your eyes and hands to yourself,* Jake thought.

At the brewpub, Kai ordered a round of Coconut Porters.

"None for me, thanks," Leilani said.

"What? You don't like beer? It's got toasted coconut in it," Makaio said in a singsong voice to make it sound more enticing.

"I like beer fine. I'm taking medicine I can't mix with alcohol," Leilani explained.

"Yeah, don't pressure the lady," Kai said.

"My apologies, Heavenly Flower." Makaio's eyes danced as he gazed into Leilani's blue eyes.

"Does that really work for you?" Kai teased. "Forget the Coconut Porter. How about some pineapple wine to go with that cheese, brah?"

Watching Kai and Makaio good-naturedly rib each other, Leilani thought Kai seemed a lot younger and far less threatening than he did when he rapped on their windshield and pointed his gun at Jake's head earlier that morning.

"Leilani, do you want to talk to the staff?" Kai asked. "We can ask about Dean and Skylar, and see if anyone knows where they're staying."

As Leilani rose from her chair, Jake stood to accompany her.

"Jake, it'll be better if you wait here," Kai said.

"It's fine. I'll be back soon," Leilani said to Jake. She headed to the kitchen with Kai.

"Looks like we're out in the cold," Makaio said. He raised his glass to Jake. "Cheers, brah."

Jake noticed Makaio smirk before taking a drink. "What's so funny?"

"Nothing," Makaio said. "It's just the first time I've ever toasted a graysuit. It feels pretty weird."

Jake lifted his glass. "Right back at 'cha, dude."

# 61 – Impression

Ten minutes later, Kai and Leilani returned to their seats. "Apparently Skylar made an impression," Kai laughed.

Leilani threw a worried glance at Jake. He shrugged.

"What? Was she your girlfriend, graysuit?" Makaio asked.

"Dude, it's Jake, not graysuit! And I'd rather not talk about it," Jake said.

Makaio nudged Leilani. "Does he still love her?"

"Definitely not," Leilani said.

"Rawr! Cat fight," Makaio joked. "Heavenly Flower, I've seen her, and she's got nothing on you."

"You got that right," Jake mumbled. *Damn! Did I say that out loud?* He gave Leilani a bashful smile. "Well, it's true."

A woman sauntered up to the table. "Hi, Kai. I hear you're looking for a couple that was in here last night."

"Hi, Alana." Kai held up the sketches. "You talk to them?"

"Yep," Alana replied. "The guy was pretty cute, and the girl was pretty … demanding."

Leilani snorted, trying to suppress a laugh.

"Do you know where they're staying?" Kai asked.

"No. But the guy was talking about martinis, and the girl was talking about Tiffany's. Maybe Wailea?" Alana guessed.

"Thanks, Alana," Kai said. "You've been a big help."

"Good. Then maybe you can take the help to dinner sometime and show your appreciation," Alana suggested.

"Yeah, sure." Kai turned to the others. "Let's go."

"But I'm not done with my beer," Makaio said.

Kai rolled his eyes. "You wanna drink beer or catch graysuits?"

Makaio slammed the rest of his porter and grinned. "Why not both?"

# 62 – Martinis

Dean and Skylar relaxed at a table in the open-air beachside restaurant at the Four Seasons Resort in Wailea. They sipped their ice-cold martinis under a canopy of stars.

Skylar plucked the skewer of three olives from her drink, wrapped her lips around the first olive, and slowly pulled it into her mouth.

Dean smiled appreciatively. "God, you're sexy."

Skylar beamed. "Thanks for bringing me here. It's beautiful."

Dean raised his glass to her. "No, you're beautiful."

"Stop," she giggled and took a sip of her drink, breathing in the cool juniper scent of the gin.

"Isn't this the best martini you've ever had? You wanna know their secret?" Dean asked.

"What?"

"C'mere," Dean whispered.

Skylar moved toward him.

"Closer," he breathed.

Skylar leaned in so their lips almost touched.

"The secret is these martinis are stirred, not shaken," Dean divulged.

"I see. And how does one stir a martini?" Skylar leisurely pulled another olive from the skewer into her mouth.

"I was just about to get to that. You see, the bartender takes the gin and gently drizzles it over ice into a beautiful crystal cylinder," Dean murmured. "Then the bartender takes a long—very sizable, actually—crystal stirrer and eases it into the cylinder. He swirls it around and around very softly, very slowly. He repeats this—removing the stirrer, adding more gin, gliding the stirrer into the cylinder—again and again and again. Then at just the right moment, he plunges the stirrer into the cylinder, swirling deeper, harder, and faster this time, until everything melts together into bliss."

Skylar grazed her lips across Dean's cheek and raised them to his ear. "It sounds like the bartender knows what he's doing."

"Oh, he's very, very good," Dean said.

"Maybe you'd like to mix me a martini? How about in the ocean?" Skylar suggested.

"I think that can be arranged."

# 63 – Closer

Makaio, Kai, Leilani, and Jake climbed into Makaio's car and headed south. Makaio turned off Highway 31 and drove toward the Four Seasons, nestled among palm trees and tropical gardens on the sandy crescent of Maui's southwest coast.

Makaio pulled into the self-parking garage. They strolled down the sidewalk to the hotel and looked around inside.

"This, Heavenly Flower, is how the other half lives. You can't do this on a cop's salary like Kai's," Makaio joked.

"Or a flunkee's like Makaio's," Kai retorted.

"Or an FBI agent's," Leilani mumbled.

Kai and Leilani showed the sketches of Dean and Skylar to every hotel staff member they could find, but no one recalled seeing them.

"Kai, your friend said something about martinis. Let's see if any place is still serving drinks," Leilani suggested.

They walked through the Lobby Lounge and restaurants, but they were closed. "Maybe tomorrow we can talk to more staff. There aren't many on duty this late," Leilani said. "Let's split into pairs so we can cover more ground. We'll meet back in the lobby in 20 minutes."

Kai and Makaio left to search the pools while Jake and Leilani walked toward the open-air restaurant by the ocean.

# 64 – Swirling

From the warm Pacific Ocean, Skylar stared up at the hotel. Her arms and legs were still wrapped around Dean, who breathed a contented sigh. She saw a silhouette of a man standing in the restaurant where they'd been earlier. The way he stood reminded her of Jake.

She released Dean and dunked herself underwater to drown the thoughts of the past now swirling around in her head.

# 65 – The Other Half

Standing next to Leilani, Jake felt distracted. He noticed the sweet smell of her skin and the scent of her hair blowing softly in the wind. He wanted to reach up and tuck a loose strand behind her ear. He heard her strong, steady heartbeat and …

"You see anything or smell anything?" Leilani asked.

"Huh?"

"Skylar and Dean? Anything?" she asked.

Jake lifted his nose into the breeze and scanned the ocean. "No, nothing." He watched Leilani reach into her purse and toss a painkiller into her mouth. "Are you all right?"

She gulped down the pill. "Uh huh."

"C'mon, I know you're tough, but it's okay to say you're ready to call it a night. I mean, you were just in the hospital a few days ago," he said.

"Yeah. Half of my body is throbbing. I should probably get some rest," she said.

"Why don't we get you a room here? I can explore, maybe go for a swim. I'll let you know if I find anything."

"I don't want you going by yourself. There are two of them and only one of you. Take Kai and Makaio with you," Leilani said.

"I'll be fine. I don't want to leave you alone with those guys though. I think they like you," Jake teased.

"Shut up." Leilani playfully pushed Jake but winced as she extended her arm.

"Let's get you inside," he said.

They walked past the fountain pool and cabanas, then back up the steps to the hotel lobby. They got a room and waited for Kai and Makaio.

"We're staying here for the night," Jake said.

Kai and Makaio eyed each other nervously.

"Uh, like I said before, I'm not exactly making Four Seasons money. Neither is God's Gift here," Kai said. "How about if we head back to his place, and we can meet you down here first thing in the morning?"

"You guys don't have to drive all the way home. Leilani and I can get you a room," Jake said.

Kai shook his head. "We couldn't."

"Do you have anywhere you have to be tomorrow? Work or anything?" Leilani asked.

"No," Kai answered.

"Then stay," Leilani said. "You'd be doing us a huge favor by helping us look for Dean and Skylar."

Makaio nudged his cousin. "Kai, a beautiful woman asks you to stay with her in a swanky hotel, you say yes! Leilani, we'd love to stay with you."

"You're not staying *with* her. I'll get you guys your own room," Jake said. "Then you can see how the other half sleeps."

# 66 – Reminder

By the time Dean and Skylar emerged from the ocean, Dean noticed her mood had changed.

"You okay?" he asked.

"Yeah." Skylar smiled and added a lilt to her voice to mask her gloomy mood. "Why wouldn't I be?"

Dean gave her his best "c'mon, you can tell me" look.

Skylar rolled her eyes. "It's nothing. I just saw someone who reminded me of my last boyfriend. It made me sad."

"Why?"

"Because I hurt him, and I never got to apologize," she said.

"You don't still have feelings for him, do you?" he asked.

"No, of course not. But I feel bad. I didn't treat him well, and he didn't deserve it. He was actually a nice guy."

"I'm sure he's fine. That's all in the past anyway, so let it go. How about we head back to our room?" Dean placed his hands on Skylar's hips and pulled her close. "I'll mix you another martini, just the way you like."

# 67 – Falling

While Leilani got ready for bed, Jake jogged back down the path to the beach. Seeing it deserted, he dropped his trunks on the golden sand and strode into the warm water. He turned into a shark and swam as fast as he could.

He felt unsettled. He was annoyed with Kai and Makaio and their snide graysuit comments. He was disturbed by the way Makaio, God's Gift, openly fawned over Leilani despite the engagement ring on her finger. He was angry that chasing Skylar and Dean made him think of Skylar and the way she blatantly lied to him about her relationship with Rick and how Rick killed Cody. He was frustrated that they always seemed to be a step behind Skylar and Dean, and that his heightened graysuit senses did nothing to get them any closer to catching them. But mostly he was upset with himself … because he knew he was falling for Leilani.

After several hours of swimming out his frustration and aggravation, Jake returned to shore. He pulled on his trunks, climbed the steps to the resort, and shuffled back to the room he shared with Leilani. He entered as silently as he could, but he heard Leilani stir. "Sorry. I was trying to be quiet. I told you I should've gotten my own room."

"Why pay for two rooms when you're going to be out most of the night? How was your swim? Find anything?" she asked.

"Swim was good. But no, I didn't find anything." Jake quickly changed out of his trunks in the bathroom and pulled on a pair of boxers. He walked past Leilani's bed to the other queen-size bed and climbed in. He stretched out and stared at the ceiling. "I'm sorry, Leilani. I thought I'd be better at this."

Leilani turned on her side to face Jake's bed. "I know we talked about this already … but did you have Tristan turn you because you thought it would help us catch Dean and Skylar?"

"No. I already told you that. That's not why I did it at all. But if I'm being totally honest, I did think it would help," he said.

"Don't beat yourself up. What about me? I work for the Federal Bureau of *Investigation*. I do this for a living, and I'm not exactly finding them either."

"Well, that's true," Jake chuckled in the dark. "Good night, Special Agent Waters."

Leilani grinned. "G'night, graysuit."

# 68 – Shift Change

Leilani awoke before dawn to a ringing phone. She clumsily reached for it. "Yeah?"

"Shift change in 20 minutes," Kai said. "Let's canvas again and see if anyone's seen the graysuits."

"I'll come by your room in 15 minutes." She hung up and swung her feet over the side of the bed.

"Who was that?" Jake mumbled.

"Kai. There's a shift change in a few minutes. We're going to see if any of them have seen 'the graysuits,'" Leilani mimicked.

"Nice," Jake smirked. "Can I help?"

"No. Get some rest. The sun's coming up soon."

Jake groaned. "Man, that's one thing I miss—being able to go out in the daylight like a normal human."

"But you can build up a tolerance, right? Tristan used to walk me to my car sometimes in the daylight."

"Eventually. I just need to gradually expose my skin to the sun—first from the light of the moon and then up to a point where I can go out sometimes like Tristan and Skylar did," Jake explained.

Leilani studied Jake's face. She thought he seemed a little down. "Are you going to be okay here by yourself?"

"Yes. Go."

"Call my cell if you need me. I'll call you if we find anything," she promised.

# 69 — Bad Boys

Leilani and Kai scoured every inch of the hotel, asking every staff member they could find if they'd seen Dean or Skylar. They struck out until they got to the beachside restaurant and approached a beautiful but tired-looking bartender.

"Yeah, they were here last night till closing. I remember this guy," she said, pointing at the sketch of Dean. "Tsssss! He was hot. He wanted to know how we make our martinis here. I told him that the secret is in the stirring. I even offered to give him a private demonstration after closing, but he turned me down. You believe that?" The bartender shook her long black hair and smiled at Kai.

"No," Kai smiled back.

"Then he went back to her," she said, pointing to Skylar's sketch. "They were a little too cute, you know? Whispering in each other's ears, holding hands, kissing. They couldn't keep their hands off each other."

"Did they charge their food or drinks to their room?" Leilani asked.

"I can't tell you that," she said.

Leilani flashed her badge. She knew she shouldn't since she was on medical leave—not officially investigating a case and not even using her current legal name—but she thought it might help. "Please, it's really important we find them."

"Why?" the bartender asked.

"Sorry, classified," Leilani replied. "So, did they charge their items to their room?"

The bartender eyed Leilani and Kai, and relented. "No. They got four martinis and paid cash. The gorgeous guy is also a generous tipper."

"Are they staying here at the hotel?" Kai asked.

"I don't know. When I asked for his name for our guestbook, he laughed and said he could tell me, but then he'd have to kill me. The way he stared into my eyes? Ooh, you can just tell he's a bad boy," the bartender said longingly.

"Why is that?" Kai asked, annoyed. "Why do beautiful women always go for the bad boy type?"

"Because they're so …" The bartender struggled to find the right word.

"Lemme guess," Kai offered. "Hot?"

"Tsssss," the bartender replied.

# 70 – Alarm

Leilani and Kai picked up Makaio. They went back to her room so they could tell Jake about Dean and Skylar.

"They were here last night?! Ugh! I couldn't sense them at all," Jake lamented. "Do you think they're still here?"

"I don't know," Leilani said. "We only found one person who remembered serving them drinks last night, but she didn't know if they're staying here. We gave the front desk their names but no luck. If they're here, they're not using their real names."

"What do we do now?" Jake asked.

"Pool party!" Makaio exclaimed. "Have you seen the adults-only pool? It's got a swim-up bar!"

"Sorry about my cousin, Leilani," Kai said. "He's all beauty. No brains."

"Dean and Skylar won't be outside during the day, right? So, are they sleeping here in the hotel, or did they leave last night?" Leilani asked.

"The bartender said they each had two martinis. Those are pretty strong. They wouldn't drive after that, would they?" Kai asked.

"They're killers, dude. I don't think they care about drinking and driving," Makaio said.

"No. Skylar would care," Jake said. "Her parents were killed by a drunk driver. I went swimming last night, and there was no sign of them. It's a big ocean, but they'd probably stick around if they're having a good time. Now it's daylight. If they're here, they're inside the hotel."

"Then there's only one way to flush them out. Fire alarm!" Makaio nodded at Kai. "Who's got the brains now, brah?"

Kai sighed. "I hate to say it, and I don't want to create a panic or misuse public resources like that, but it's not the worst idea

I've ever heard."

Makaio grinned at Leilani.

"Jake, if it was broad daylight, would they respond to a fire alarm and evacuate the building?" Leilani asked.

"I don't know. It's not like they're new to the vampire thing. If they cover up with clothes, hats, and sunglasses, they'd be fine for a little while at least," Jake said.

Leilani nodded. "Then let's go. Jake, you stay here. No reason for you to expose yourself to the sun. We'll call you or send Makaio if something happens."

"But ..."

"Please, Jake," she interrupted. "I don't want you risking your life. I couldn't stand to lose another person I care about. How about if you take this side of the building and watch from the window?"

Jake gave her a disappointed nod.

"Can I pull the alarm?" Makaio asked.

"No!" Kai and Leilani answered together.

# 71 – Pursuit

"Let's each take a different area adjacent to the hotel rooms," Kai instructed. "Makaio, you head that way and call me if you spot them. Leilani, you take that side. I'll pull the alarm and take this area in the middle."

Leilani and Makaio walked in opposite directions. Kai slipped on his sunglasses and flipped his hood up over his head. He covered his hand with his sleeve and activated the fire alarm.

Immediately, the alarm blared. People flung open their doors and looked around. Seeing no imminent danger, they calmly evacuated the hotel and assembled outside in their pajamas and robes, murmuring to each other about possible causes for the alarm.

Leilani, Kai, and Makaio milled through the crowd. Jake watched from his room. He scanned the throngs of people below. Something caught his attention—a large, floppy hat. It looked like the same hat Skylar wore the morning they visited Tristan's house—the morning Tristan invited him surfing and then later told him the truth about Cody, Rick, and his own transformation. Jake noticed the woman in the hat was holding hands with a man wearing a San Francisco Giants cap. The man quickly led her away from the building.

Jake dialed Leilani. "I think I see them. Wait! They disappeared. They're headed for the lobby. She's in a big, floppy hat. He's in a San Francisco Giants baseball cap."

"Got it," Leilani said. "Meet us at the entrance. We'll try to keep you out of the sun."

"Be right there."

Leilani called Kai, who then called Makaio. She showed the sketches to the front desk and then to each of the valets. Makaio ran up the hill to retrieve his car from self-parking while Kai monitored the exit. Makaio drove up to Kai, who shook his head. Kai climbed into the passenger seat, and they zoomed to the lobby entrance. Jake, dressed in a cap, long sleeve shirt, long pants, and running shoes, dove into the back seat. Leilani climbed in next to him.

"Go! They're in a silver BMW!" she said. "It must be Dean's favorite car. He was driving one the night I first met him, when Tristan and I had dinner with him."

At the intersection, Kai told Makaio to head north. "They're probably on their way to the airport."

Jake fidgeted in the back seat. He was sweltering wearing all that clothing and a cap, but that wasn't what made him uncomfortable. Something gnawed at him, but he didn't know what.

As they raced up Highway 31 toward Kihei, Jake bolted upright. "That's it!"

Leilani jumped. "What?!"

"That's what's been bugging me! The silver BMW! That night I went to find Tristan at the cove—the night Dean tried to kill everyone ... When I got there, a silver BMW pulled out. I snaked the parking spot from another car and pulled in. It had to be Dean. He must've been leaving just as I got there. Dammit! If I had known it was him, I could've stopped him. Then he wouldn't have been able to hurt you, Leilani."

"Jake, it's not your fault. Plus, I'm the one who let Logan into Tristan's house, not you," Leilani said. "Kai, can you call all the rental car companies and ask about silver BMW rentals? I'm on medical leave, so I shouldn't be waving my badge around here."

"I'm on it." Kai began dialing.

# 72 – Soaring

"Why are we leaving?" Skylar pouted. "It's just a fire alarm."

"There was no fire. Are you sure you haven't tried to reach Tristan?" Dean demanded.

"Tristan? No. Why? You think this is Tristan?" she asked.

"I don't know. I told you if you contacted him, he'd come after us. If that's true, we're not safe."

"I didn't call him or anyone else for that matter!" Skylar insisted. "What's your problem?"

"Sorry. It's a work thing. It's got me stressed," he said. "Lance was supposed to report back to me on something important, and he hasn't."

"Then call him!"

"Wow, what a great idea, Skylar," Dean said sarcastically. "You don't think I've been calling him? He's not picking up!"

"So, fire his ass and get a new assistant. What's the big deal?" she asked.

"It's complicated. Can we not talk about this right now?"

"You're the one who brought it up." Skylar stared out the window. "Where are we going anyway?"

"Makena. It's just south of here," he said.

They drove in silence until Dean finally caved. "I'm sorry. Okay? But I've survived this long by trusting my instincts. Something wasn't right back there. If I have to choose between leaving and making you mad at me, or staying and something bad happening to you, I'll choose your wrath any day of the week."

Skylar didn't acknowledge his apology.

"So, how long do you think this wrath might last?" Dean asked.

"Hard to say," she said.

"Give me a ballpark. Days? Months? Decades?"

"Depends," Skylar said nonchalantly.

"On what?" he asked.

"On how you plan to make it up to me," she said.

Dean flashed a megawatt smile at her. "Well then, wanna go for a ride?"

An hour later, Dean and Skylar climbed aboard a helicopter. They soared above the Pacific and arrived at Honolulu International Airport. They stared at the departure board.

"Still mad?" Dean asked.

"Maybe."

"Well, what destination might lighten your mood?" he asked.

Skylar scanned the digital displays listing all the departing flights. She saw a flight to San Diego and thought of Jake. *I really did treat him badly by lying to him about Rick. I should call him and apologize.*

"Well?" Dean asked. "What's your pleasure, Sky?"

# 73 — Abandoned

Kai hung up his phone. "The Kahului Airport is where they rented the car. It's due back in two days. If we stake out the rental car return, we may be able to find them."

"What names are they using?" Leilani asked.

"Dean Tiburon. Skylar wasn't listed on the vehicle."

"You're kidding," Jake said. "His last name is 'shark' in Spanish?"

As they approached Kahului, Kai's phone rang. "This is Kai. … I see. So, we don't know where they're headed then? … What about the address on file?" Kai retrieved a pen and small notebook from his pocket. "Got it. Thanks."

"What?" Leilani asked.

"The car was found abandoned in Makena. There was no sign of Dean or Skylar." Kai passed his notebook to Leilani and Jake. "Does this address mean anything to you?"

"That was Skylar's address," Jake said. "She doesn't live there anymore though."

Kai took his notebook back. "Then I guess we've hit a dead end."

"Why?" Jake asked.

"They can charter a helicopter in Makena and fly to any of the other islands. From there, they can take a plane anywhere," Kai explained. "Do you have any idea where they'd go?"

"Jake, did Skylar ever mention anyplace she wanted to go?" Leilani asked.

"No," he said.

"Let's go back to the hotel and get our things," Leilani said. "Then I guess we'll drive to Makaio's place."

# 74 – Relax

When they arrived at Makaio's apartment, Jake asked Leilani, "What now?"

"I don't know. Makaio, is it okay if we hang here while we figure out our next move?" Leilani asked.

"For you, Heavenly Flower, anything," he answered.

Jake rolled his eyes.

"Jake, since it's daylight, why don't you crash for a while?" Leilani suggested.

"What are you gonna do?" Jake asked.

"Go for a walk on the beach." Seeing a bright smile appear on Makaio's face, Leilani added loudly, "By myself. I need to clear my head."

Leilani left the apartment. The palm trees lazily swayed in the breeze, beckoning her to the ocean. As she strolled, she thought of Tristan and how he was truly able to live in the moment. *Unlike myself—always thinking about what's up ahead or around the next corner.* She took a deep, cleansing breath. *Maybe I'm trying too hard. Maybe I should let go and see what happens. Dean and Skylar are bound to turn up. Dean's reckless and Skylar's, well, Skylar.*

As she walked through the resort near Makaio's apartment, she noticed the sun reflecting off the palm fronds created a dazzling light show in the morning breeze. She stopped and closed her eyes. The wind whipping through the palm trees sounded like white noise on a television with the volume being turned up and down at unevenly spaced intervals. She opened her eyes and began walking again.

*This is good. Tristan was right. I do live too much in my head. I need to appreciate my senses and spend more time living in the moment. Who knows? Maybe that'll help us find Skylar and Dean. Maybe I just need to relax, free my mind, and open myself up to what's around me. What was it Tristan told me? "All you need to do is be. Just be."*

Leilani arrived at the ocean and marveled at the brilliant cobalt blue water. She turned left and walked along the shoreline. She stared at the water, trying to empty her head of Tristan, Jake, Kai, Makaio, Dean, Skylar, her parents—everyone.

# 75 – Break

When Tristan and Cody were several miles away from Catalina Island, Tristan slowed to rest. He and Cody changed into their human bodies so they could talk.

"Sorry. I need a break." Tristan flipped over on his back and floated under the darkening sky.

"No problem," Cody said as he drifted next to Tristan. "Do you think Finn will come after us?"

"Maybe. But they've got their hands full right now. I think if I could explain to Julianna, she'd understand why I had to go. I hate to leave her without telling her why. I found her after all these years, and now I've abandoned her," Tristan said.

"She'll understand," Cody assured him.

"Maybe." Tristan morphed back into a shark and circled underwater. The salt water around him felt so good he couldn't tell where his body ended and the ocean began. He sighed with gratitude at the vastness of the Pacific Ocean as cool, healing currents of energy washed over him.

# 76 – Call

Leilani and Jake took Makaio up on his offer to stay the night. Leilani slept on the couch while Jake went surfing.

The waves weren't very powerful, so the rides were brief. *Short and powerless—just like me,* Jake lamented. *I can't believe we were so close to Skylar and Dean, and I couldn't find them.*

A half hour before dawn, he headed back to Makaio's apartment. As he made his way through the thick morning air, he felt billions of microscopic water droplets explode on his skin. He bumped into Leilani as he neared the apartment, and his mood immediately lightened. Before he could stop himself, his face broke into a huge smile. "You're up early! How'd you sleep?"

"Good. I thought I'd get out for a sunrise walk, and then maybe we can talk about what to do from here," she said.

"Okay. I'll make us breakfast," Jake offered.

"That sounds great. I'll see you soon."

On the beach, Leilani gazed at the brightening pre-dawn sky. The clouds cast pink and yellow swaths across the calm, glassy water as if part of a rainbow had been overlaid on transparent film and stretched across the ocean's surface.

Walking up the beach, she felt the sand squish beneath her bare feet. It seemed softer than she remembered it—softer than her favorite worn t-shirt or the jersey cotton sheets she liked to sleep in during the winter. As she skimmed the water's edge, letting the waves rush in and out over her bare feet, she glanced at the neighboring islands of Lanai and Molokai. Clouds clung to the island mountains, afraid to move for fear of dissipating into nothingness.

She thought of Jake. *He dropped everything to come here to find Dean and Skylar. I can't believe Skylar was so terrible to him. He's such a great guy.*

Leilani felt the soft pelt of raindrops on her skin. She turned back toward Makaio's apartment, noticing the islands again. She spotted long sheaths of moisture with diagonal rainbows, purple to red and red to purple.

Her thoughts turned to Tristan. *Thank you, Tristan, for helping me take the time to notice the world around me. You changed my life in so many ways, and for that I will always be grateful.* Salty tears trickled from her eyes and rolled down her cheeks, mixing in with the cool raindrops. She huddled under a tree and cried, releasing days of grief and frustration.

When she arrived back at the apartment, Jake had breakfast waiting for her. Makaio had left for work, and Kai had returned to Oahu so he could be home in time for his next shift.

"Looks like you got caught in the storm." Jake went to the hall cupboard to get a towel and handed it to her. He noticed her eyes were red. "Have you been crying?"

"Yeah, but I feel better now." She peeled the soggy bandages from her arms and legs, and threw them in the trash.

Jake glanced at the fang marks. "Are those feeling any better? They're starting to look better."

"Yeah. They should be gone soon, except for the scars."

Jake felt a ball of anger spin in his stomach as he remembered what Dean and Logan did to her. The ringing of his cell phone interrupted his dark thoughts.

"Do you mind if I take this?" he asked Leilani, who sat down to eat. She shook her head and lifted a forkful of fruit to her mouth.

Jake fished his phone from his pocket and stepped toward the bedroom. "Yeah, this is Jake."

"Jake, it's good to hear your voice. It's Skylar."

"Skylar?"

Leilani dropped her fork. She turned slack-jawed to Jake.

*Oh my god. It worked*, she thought. *I relaxed and let go, and now Skylar's calling!*

"Yeah. How are you?" Skylar asked.

"I'm okay," Jake said. "How are you?"

"Good. Listen, the reason I'm calling is I want to apologize for what happened between us," Skylar said. "I'm sorry I lied to you. I should've told you about Rick and Cody. But I thought you'd be really upset and wouldn't want anything to do with me if you knew I was with Rick when he ... when he did what he did to Cody. But by not telling you, I hurt you even more. You didn't deserve to be treated like that. I was only thinking of myself, not you."

Jake stared at Leilani, dumbfounded. He raised and dropped his shoulders to signal that he had no idea why Skylar got the sudden urge to call.

Skylar continued her apology. "I know you're probably mad, and you have every right to be. If you don't want to talk to me, I'll leave you alone and won't bother you again."

"No, I want to talk to you." Jake saw a frown form on Leilani's face. He grimaced and pointed to the phone to show that he didn't really want to talk to Skylar but wanted to find out where she was. "So, where are you?"

"The Monterey Bay," she replied.

"What are you doing in the Monterey Bay? Did you drive from San Diego?" he asked.

"No. I actually just got back to California. I went to Hawaii with an old friend. He's out right now. I wanted to call you earlier but thought I should wait a few days. You were pretty mad at me before, and I know I deserved it."

"I'm glad you called," Jake said. "I went by your place to talk to you, but the landlady said you moved."

"You did?" Skylar smiled.

"Yeah. I wanted to see if you were okay," Jake said.

"Why?" Skylar asked. "I was the one who hurt you."

Leilani saw a puzzled expression form on Jake's face.

"I went there because I was worried about you—you know, after what happened to Leilani and Tristan, and Torrey and Cruz," Jake explained.

"What happened to them?" Skylar asked.

Jake's eyes widened. He covered his cell phone and whispered to Leilani, "She doesn't know."

Leilani shook her head. She had a hard time believing Skylar didn't know anything about her supposed best friends, especially since she'd spent the last few days with their killer, Dean.

"Jake, what happened to them?" Skylar asked again.

"I don't know how to tell you this but … Torrey and Cruz are dead. And Tristan is …"

Leilani snatched the phone from Jake's hand. "Don't tell her Tristan's dead," she whispered in his ear. "Remember? We don't want Dean to know." She handed the phone back to him.

"What?! What are you talking about?" Skylar demanded. "What do you mean, 'Torrey and Cruz are dead'? And what were you saying about Tristan?"

"Sky, who are you with? Is it Dean?" Jake asked.

"Yeah. How did you know? Wait, tell me about Tristan, Torrey, and Cruz," Skylar said.

"She's with him," Jake whispered to Leilani.

"Let me talk to her." Leilani put the phone to her ear. "Skylar, it's Leilani." She swore she could hear Skylar scowl into the phone.

"Leilani? What are you doing with Jake?" Skylar asked. "Shouldn't you be with your *fiancé*?"

Leilani sighed. "I need you to listen to me. Is Dean with you right now?"

"No. How do you guys know I'm with Dean?" Skylar asked.

Leilani ignored her question. "Jake and I have to tell you something. It's going to be a shock, so you should probably sit down."

"Really?" Skylar sneered. "Because I don't think anything could be more shocking than me hearing that you and Tristan are engaged."

"Would you just shut up for a minute?" Leilani blurted out. "This is important. If you're with Dean, you're not safe."

Skylar rolled her eyes and wondered for the thousandth time, *What is with this woman? What can Tristan possibly see in her?* "Why would you say that? You don't even know Dean."

"Because Dean and Logan murdered Torrey and Cruz," Leilani continued.

"What?! Put Jake back on the phone," Skylar said.

Leilani clenched her jaw. "I'm trying to help you."

"I don't know what you're trying to do, but one thing I do know is that you're insane. Put Jake on the phone!" Skylar demanded. "Now!"

Fuming, Leilani thrust the phone at Jake.

"Sky, she's telling the truth. The night after we had that fight, some serious shit went down. Dean's whole wedding was staged. It was just some elaborate ploy to separate Tristan from everyone so he could kill him and then go after Leilani, Torrey, and Cruz. Logan was in on it with him."

"That's impossible. Dean and Tristan have been friends forever. Dean would never do that. And Logan? He's the sweetest guy." Though as Skylar spoke, alarm bells began clanging, faintly at first but then louder and louder. *Is that why Dean insisted I cut off contact with everyone?*

"Sky, why would I lie to you about this? What possible motive could I have?" Jake asked.

"I don't know, but there must be some mistake," Skylar said. "I know Dean. And Logan."

Jake told Skylar about Andi and Andy, and why Dean and Logan set out to kill Torrey, Cruz, and Leilani while Tristan was at Dean's fake wedding.

"What about Tristan? Is he okay?" Skylar asked.

"Dean's friend staked him," Jake said.

Skylar gasped. "Tristan got staked? Is he alive?"

Jake evaded the question. "The stake missed his heart. Skylar, are you getting this? Dean and Logan murdered Torrey and Cruz. You're not safe with him. Tell me exactly where you are so I can come get you."

Leilani nodded approvingly and handed Jake a pen and pad of paper from her purse. She watched as Jake scribbled the name and location of the hotel.

"Dean should be back any minute now. I still can't believe what you're saying is true. But if any part of it is, he won't get away with it. I'll kill him myself," Skylar vowed.

"No!" He turned to Leilani and shook his head. "She wants to kill him."

Leilani motioned for the phone and put it on speaker. "Don't do anything until we get there," she said.

"But if he did those things ... If he killed my friends ... If he hurt Tristan ..." Skylar stammered.

"If Dean suspects you know anything, he'll kill you. He's a psychopath. Just keep him there until we can get to you. We'll get the first flight we can to Monterey," Leilani said.

"Listen, I'm not some pathetic human who cowers from guys like Dean. If he did the things you said he did, he's the one who should be afraid. Not me," Skylar seethed.

Leilani gritted her teeth. "Yeah, I know you could easily take Dean out if you wanted to. But I'm asking you—no, I'm begging you—not to. Wait till Jake and I get there. We'll make a plan together."

"What about Tristan?" Skylar asked.

"Tristan will be with us," Jake lied. "Sky, please wait for me. You owe me. Do this for me."

Skylar sighed. "All right, I'll wait. But if Dean turns on me, all bets are off."

"We'll text you when we arrive. Then we can meet and hatch a plan, okay?" Jake said.

"Okay," Skylar agreed. "But I'm only doing this for you, Jake."

"Take care of yourself. We'll see you soon," he said.

Leilani and Jake packed their bags. They called Kai and Makaio to update them and thank them for their help. Then they headed to the airport.

# 77 – Jet Lag

Jake and Leilani caught a late morning flight to San Francisco. That evening, they boarded a commuter flight to Monterey. They rented a car and drove northwest to the beach resort Skylar suggested.

The resort was situated on the sand dunes above the ocean in Marina, a 20-minute drive from Carmel where Skylar and Dean were staying. They didn't want to risk Dean seeing Leilani before they were ready to confront him so thought it would be safer to stay a few cities away from him.

After Jake and Leilani checked in, he texted their room number to Skylar.

Down the coast, Skylar and Dean returned to their hotel room after a midnight surf session at Carmel Beach. While Dean showered, Skylar read the text from Jake and deleted it. She still couldn't bring herself to believe what Jake and Leilani told her about Dean and Logan. While she didn't trust Leilani, she couldn't fathom why Jake would lie to her, so she agreed to meet them to try to get to the bottom of it. And she really looked forward to seeing Tristan again.

Dean emerged from the bathroom. "I'm so tired," he yawned. "Maybe it's jet lag. How about you?"

"I'm kind of wired. Maybe it was the waves. I'm going to take a drive, check out the beaches up the coast, and then do some shopping when the stores open. I only packed for Hawaii, and I could use some warmer clothes. It looks like it's going to be a foggy morning, which is nice, but I'll need something more than a tank top and shorts if I'm going to blend in with the humans here," she said.

Dean pulled Skylar into his arms. "Why don't we sleep away the day and go shopping tonight? Anywhere you want."

Skylar sighed. "I could use some alone time."

"You're not getting tired of me already, are you?" Dean joked.

"No. I just want to shop and not feel rushed. I do like to shop more than you. Remember Wailea? I could've shopped there for days," she said.

"How could I forget? You made some sales people really happy."

"Well, now I'd like to spread some joy around the Monterey Peninsula. You get some sleep. I'll be back before you wake up," Skylar said.

"Okay." Dean collapsed on the bed and passed out.

# 78 – Tension

Twenty minutes later, Skylar entered Jake's hotel room. She spotted his open bag on one bed and Leilani's on another.

"You guys aren't sharing a room, are you?" she asked. "Where's Tristan?"

Jake reddened—not because anything was going on but because he had developed feelings for Leilani, so he wished something was going on. "Tristan isn't here yet. Leilani's just keeping her stuff here until he arrives," he lied.

Leilani motioned to a chair at the table in the corner of the room. "Have a seat."

Skylar noticed Leilani's engagement ring as she waved her hand over the chair. A sudden spike of rage tore through Skylar's body. It settled in the pit of her stomach, making her feel like she might vomit.

"Are you okay, Skylar?" Jake asked. "You look a little green."

Skylar glanced at Leilani's engagement ring again. Each time Leilani's hand moved, colorful prisms danced across the diamonds. The glittering stones taunted Skylar, reminding her of Tristan's love for Leilani—and his lack of love for her, even after years by his side. She tore her eyes away from Leilani's ring. "Just feeling a little queasy for some reason," she said. "Now tell me again why you think Dean and Logan killed Torrey and Cruz, and why Dean tried to have Tristan killed. I still can't believe it. I spent an entire afternoon with Dean and Tristan a week ago. It was just like old times. They were best buds. There was no sign of anything weird. I would've noticed."

"We know because we saw it." Jake recounted everything he could about that night, and Leilani quickly filled in what happened with Dean and Logan before Jake and Tristan arrived.

They purposely avoided talking about the severity of Tristan's stake wound or the fact that he never made it out of the ocean.

Skylar shook her head. "Jake, I know you have no reason to lie to me, but I just can't believe this."

"All right. Then maybe you'll believe this. Leilani? Show her," Jake said.

Leilani lifted her sleeves to show Skylar the bite marks from Dean and Logan.

"She has bites like this all over her arms and legs," Jake said.

Skylar recoiled at the thought of Dean's mouth on Leilani's body. "Oh my god. I think I'm gonna be sick."

Leilani shrugged at Jake, baffled by why Skylar would care so much about her injuries.

"Where's Tristan?" Skylar demanded. "I need to talk with him. I've tried calling his cell, but he's not answering. It says his mailbox is full."

"Tristan is lying low," Leilani said. She and Jake had come up with a cover story on the plane, which they now relayed to Skylar. "He doesn't want Dean to know he's alive. He's concerned if he's here with you that Dean might be able to smell him on you or something."

"But Tristan and I need to work together to come up with a plan for how to deal with Dean," Skylar insisted.

Leilani pasted a smile on her face. "I'm sure Tristan would love to meet with you, but this is the way he wants to do it. His mind is made up." She glanced down at her engagement ring and back up at Skylar. "I'm sure you know that once he commits to something, it's impossible to change his mind."

"Listen," Skylar snapped, "I know Tristan better than you ever will, so don't try to tell me *anything* about him."

"Hey, we're all on the same team here," Jake said. "Even Leilani and I can't reach Tristan. He thought we'd all be safer that way."

"*You* don't know where he is?" Skylar asked.

Leilani unconsciously twisted her engagement ring around her finger. "No."

Skylar saw Leilani was genuinely distraught. She smiled to herself. "But Tristan will be there when we confront Dean?"

"Yes," Jake lied.

"I don't like it, but I guess I have no choice," Skylar said. "What's the plan?"

Leilani revealed to Skylar that she was an FBI agent, so her plan was to capture and arrest Dean. She intended to turn him in to the authorities for the murder of Cruz, which she personally witnessed. "I know he'll die in jail pretty quickly since he won't be able to immerse himself in salt water, but I can't think of any other way to keep him from killing again."

"That's probably the worst plan I've ever heard. You really do this for a living?" Skylar scoffed.

Leilani curled her hands into fists. Her fingernails dug into her palms. *Don't let her get to you,* she reminded herself. "Yes, Skylar, I really do this for a living. And because I work in law enforcement, I can't be a party to a murder, even if it's Dean. Why? Do you have a better idea?"

"Anything's gotta be better than your plan." Skylar turned to Jake. "If Dean broke the Rules, he has to pay. And if everything you're telling me is true, I'll kill him myself. But if we're going to deal with him, we need to do it in the ocean. We can dispose of him there—and not involve the authorities. Leilani, we *never* bring human authorities into graysuit matters. I know Tristan would never sign off on such a plan. But Dean is strong. I could probably take him out by myself, but it would be good to have another graysuit as a backup. I'll need Tristan with me." Skylar gave Leilani a wry smile. "Tristan and I have been doing this for years. We're best when we're together."

Jake didn't catch Skylar's smirk. He was too busy noticing

Leilani clench her jaw every time Skylar said Tristan's name. He couldn't tell if she was going to explode in anger or tears. Either way, he knew he needed to diffuse the situation. Skylar and Leilani had to work together if everyone was going to survive.

"I can go with you, Skylar," Jake offered. "That night everything went down with Dean and Logan, Tristan turned me. I'm a graysuit now, so I can help you."

Surprised she hadn't noticed, Skylar inhaled deeply. "He turned you? But why? We broke up."

Jake shook his head and sighed. "Not everything is about you, Skylar."

Skylar sat back, stung by his words. "I didn't say it was. But I don't understand. I didn't choose this life. Why would you if we weren't going to be together?"

"It's a long story. Basically it's because it's who I am. It has nothing to do with you and me," Jake said. "Let's just do this and get Dean."

"Okay, but only if Tristan is there." Skylar wanted to get Tristan alone to talk with him—and talk him out of his engagement to Leilani. "I'm not doing this without him."

"Fine," Leilani relented. She didn't want to keep lying to Skylar but couldn't see any alternative. "Let's figure out a plan. Then when Tristan calls me, I'll bring him up to speed. We can have him stay out of sight until we need him so we don't tip off Dean."

"All right. But if I can't plan this with Tristan, we need to do things *my* way. Other than Tristan, I've got the most experience killing Rogues." Skylar smiled sweetly at Jake. "I've already caused you enough trouble in your life. We need to do this my way, Jake, so I can make sure you make it out of there alive. If you got hurt, I could never forgive myself."

"What's your plan?" Leilani asked.

"Like I said, we need to do this in the ocean. The thing with

Dean is, he's a guy. He likes to think he's in charge even when he's not. So, the only way to get him in the ocean when and where we want is to give him a good reason. Leilani, that's where you come in," Skylar smiled.

Jake glanced nervously at Leilani.

"You'll be our bait," Skylar continued. "I'll tell Dean I saw you at the beach here. We won't be able to keep him away."

"No! We're not using Leilani as bait for that psycho," Jake argued. "He almost killed her the last time. I'm not going to give him another chance."

"But Jake ..." Skylar sputtered.

"No!" he interrupted. "I'm not risking Leilani's life to get Dean. We'll find another way."

Leilani, too, was surprised at Jake's outburst—and delighted at how it visibly upset Skylar. She placed her hand on Jake's. "I'll be fine," she soothed. "As much as I don't want to go near Dean ever again, I think Skylar's right. He'll totally lose it if he sees me alive. That'll throw him off his game and make him easier to capture."

Leilani turned to Skylar. "We're going to capture him, not kill him. That's the only way I'll agree to your plan. I'm not going to be part of a murder. I'll turn him in to the authorities myself. You don't have to be involved with that part. I'll keep you all out of it."

Skylar again eyed the engagement ring on Leilani's hand, which still grasped Jake's hand. *There's no way Tristan will ever agree to her plan to turn Dean in to the police,* she thought. *But maybe I should let her tell Tristan what she wants to do. Then he can see how stupid she really is—and how she's nowhere near ready to be a part of our lives.*

Skylar swallowed hard, trying to squelch the bitterness that threatened to seep into her voice. "We'll do it your way. But if things get ugly, I'm taking Dean out. I'm not risking my life or Jake's."

"Or Leilani's," Jake added.

"Of course," Skylar smiled. "Jake, I know you're worried, but it's the only way. I don't want Leilani to be part of this any more than you do. Believe me. But I know Dean. It'll make him crazy if he hears Leilani is alive. That'll give us the edge we need to ki... I mean, capture him."

Jake turned to Leilani. "I don't like it. I think we should find another way. But, Leilani, it's your call."

Leilani felt a little weird about the fact that it was Skylar who came up with the plan to use her as bait, but she had to admit it was as good of a plan as any. *What better way to lure Dean out than to tell him I'm alive? Skylar wouldn't try anything with me if Jake is there or if she thinks Tristan is watching nearby. Would she?*

Leilani shoved aside her doubts and squeezed Jake's hand. "Let's do it tonight. The sooner we catch Dean, the better."

While Jake and Leilani huddled to hash out the details of their plan, Skylar spied their cell phones on the nightstand between the two beds. She rose from the table. "Leilani, do you mind if I borrow your phone? I want to check the surf report for tonight."

"Go ahead," Leilani said. She turned back to Jake to resume their discussion.

After Skylar looked up the report, she turned off Leilani's phone and discreetly dropped it into her purse. *If you won't let me talk to Tristan, I'll make sure I'm the one he gets when he calls you.*

She quietly turned off Jake's phone and shoved it under a pillow. She joined them at the table, and they settled on their course of action.

"We're all set." Skylar headed toward the door. "I'll see you later tonight."

# 79 – Plastic

After swimming all night and into the morning, Tristan and Cody finally made it to the Encinitas shoreline in northern San Diego County. As they climbed out of the ocean, they realized that they had forgotten to bring along clothing for when they changed back into their human bodies.

"Don't worry. I used to keep some shorts hidden here for times like this. Well, not like *this*," Tristan said. "I've never had to escape from a mad scientist's lab before, but you know what I mean."

In the morning fog, they scurried across the beach to a path carved into the bluff. Tristan dug around in some shrubs and pulled out two pairs of old swim trunks. He tossed one to Cody. After they dressed, he led Cody up the path to the house he'd rented on the bluffs above the beach.

After making sure no one was inside, Tristan reached through a broken pane of glass on the back door and unlocked it. "Wait here in the kitchen, Cody."

Tristan walked into the family room. Pools and splatters of dried blood stained the floor, furniture, and walls. "Oh god. Cody, you do *not* want to come in here."

He returned to the kitchen and sat next to Cody at the table.

"It's bad?" Cody asked.

"Yeah," Tristan said. "There's blood everywhere. I'm definitely gonna lose my deposit on this one."

Tristan searched the house for his cell phone, but it wasn't there. "The sheriff must've taken it. I need another phone. Let's go to 7/11 so I can get a burner."

"Uh, dude, I used to live near here. I'm supposed to be dead. I can't really be going out to convenience stores where I might run into someone," Cody reminded him.

"Right. You hang here, out of sight. I'm gonna get dressed and head down to the store. Feel free to borrow some clothes or anything else you need while I'm gone. When I get back, we can call Leilani and Jake."

Tristan ran upstairs, put on some clothes, and pulled a spare car key from his dresser drawer. He climbed into his black hybrid SUV and raced to the store and back.

He sat at the kitchen table with Cody and wrestled with the disposable phone's hard plastic packaging, which was nearly impossible to open—even for a vampire shark. As he tore open the package and reached inside to remove the cell phone, a ragged piece of plastic sliced open his hand.

Cody watched Tristan's blood spill onto the table. "Now your kitchen matches the family room," he snickered. Seeing Tristan was not amused, he quickly apologized. "Sorry, dude, just trying to lighten the mood."

"It's not you," Tristan said. "I just hate this plastic crap. It litters the ocean and kills sea life. And I swear, every year they make these packages harder to open. Whatever. I'll heal."

He quickly set up the phone and dialed Leilani's cell. It went straight to voicemail. "Leilani! It's Tristan. I'm alive. I was held captive, but I'm back. Long story. Where are you? Jake said you were in the hospital. Call me at this number as soon as you get this, and let me know you're okay. I love you."

He then tried Jake's number. There was no answer, so he hung up. He called the local hospitals, but none had a patient by the name of Leilani Waters or Lani Marley.

"I can't reach them. That's not good," Tristan said grimly. "Let's go to their houses."

Cody followed Tristan to his car. He slunk down in the passenger seat, worried about being seen by someone he knew. Finn's words rattled in his head. *You can't go back to your old life.*

"Hey, Tristan, Jake doesn't know I'm alive," Cody said.

"Oh yeah. I forgot. What do you want to do?" Tristan asked.

"I dunno. If he was human, I wouldn't be allowed to tell him. But I don't know if the rules apply if he's no longer human, you know?"

"Whatever you wanna do, man," Tristan said distractedly as he sped to Leilani's.

Neither Leilani nor Jake were home, and it looked like they hadn't been home in days. Sitting in his car parked outside Jake's place, Tristan turned to Cody. "This isn't good."

# 80 – The Promise

"How did he get out?!" Finn demanded, standing next to Tristan's empty bed.

"I don't know. Maybe in all the commotion with the attack on Matt and the new graysuit here, Tristan and Cody were able to escape?" Julianna said.

"The lab was locked. Cody didn't have the code to the door, and he wouldn't instigate something like this," Finn said. "J, did you let Tristan go?"

"No! How could you even ask that?"

"I'm sorry. I just don't see how they could leave a locked lab when you and I are the only ones with codes to open the door and the gates," Finn said.

Julianna's eyes widened. *My code. It's the date Tristan and I met, 11-5-72. Tristan must've figured it out. Ugh. If I tell Finn, he'll freak. He's already threatened by my past with Tristan. This will definitely send him over the edge.*

"Did you think of something?" Finn asked.

"What? No," she replied. "Wait! Cody's microchip!"

"Yes!" Finn sprinted to his computer. "Checking the GPS … hang on … there! Solana Beach. That's where he's from, right? He knows he shouldn't go home, so what's he doing there?"

"He's probably looking for his friend. He and Tristan were really worried about Jake and Leilani," Julianna explained.

"We have to go find them," Finn said.

"Now? What about Matt? And Lily? And the new graysuit?"

"Dammit! Why is everything happening at once? But we have to find them. We can't let Tristan warn other vampire sharks about our work here. We won't be safe," Finn said.

"He wouldn't do that. I told you, he hunts killers like we do," Julianna assured him.

"So he says."

"How about this? I'll get Tristan and Cody. You finish your work with Lily and the new graysuit, and make sure Matt gets the care he needs," Julianna said.

"No. No way I'm letting you go alone."

"Finn, you're not 'letting' me do anything. I'm going. Plus, I have a much better chance of bringing them back here—willingly—than you do. You know it's true. You said yourself I can be very persuasive when I want to be," she said.

Finn knew she was right, but he felt like he was coming apart inside at the thought of letting her go in search of Tristan alone.

Julianna placed her hand on her hip and glared at him. Her face slipped into a tired expression that warned him not to bother arguing with her. "Finn, it's the only way."

He took Julianna's hand from her hip and grasped it tightly. "It might be the only way, but that doesn't make it any easier for me. I don't like this. At all."

"Why?" she asked.

"Because you could be hurt. Or killed! Tristan might not hurt you, but we don't know anything about the company he keeps," Finn said.

"I'll be fine. I can handle myself with graysuits. And Tristan wouldn't let anything happen to me."

"Just like the last time, right?" Finn snapped, his voice raw with emotion as he once again relived the memory of how Julianna was attacked and killed when she and Tristan were newly married.

"That's not fair," Julianna argued.

"Maybe not. But can't you see how this is killing me inside to let you go?"

"I'm sorry, but I'm going," Julianna said. "Finn, don't you see that what you're doing here to try to protect me is exactly what Tristan and Cody are doing to protect the people they love? They couldn't stay here knowing there's a killer out there. Isn't that why we do the work we do—to protect people from being killed by vampire sharks? For someone so brilliant, you can be so stupid sometimes." Exasperated, she turned toward the door, but Finn refused to release her hand.

"Wait! I'm sorry, okay? I'm *sorry*. But … that's not the only reason I don't want you to go," he said.

Julianna frowned, waiting for him to finish. "What then?"

Finn tightened his grip on her hand. "I'm afraid that if you go after Tristan … that you might choose him and not me."

"What?! Don't be ridiculous."

"Then marry me, Julianna."

"Not this again." Unexpectedly, Julianna's earlier conversation with Tristan popped into her head. *Tristan said if I love Finn and if marriage is so important to him, maybe I should consider it. That if I love our relationship—and as I've said, a stupid license won't change that—then why not do it?*

She gazed at Finn, seeing love and fear whirling together in his pained blue eyes. "Finn, I've told you a million times I don't need a piece of paper to show you that I love you. But if it's that important to you, okay. When I get back, we'll get married."

"Really?" Finn asked, taken aback by her reply. In all the years he'd known Julianna, she'd never seriously considered marrying him. "Do you really mean that?"

"Yes. I love you," she said. "You know that."

Finn's face broke into a huge grin. "Okay, then promise me you'll come back to me as fast as you can. Promise me, J."

"I promise," she said.

Five minutes later, Julianna climbed aboard a speedboat and headed toward Cody's signal.

# 81 – Out of Control

Skylar climbed into her rental car and set out to find some coffee and a bite to eat before returning to Dean. She headed down the road and looped around a small lake. She ignored the fast food restaurants and kept driving until she spotted something appealing. *Coffee Mia Brew Bar & Café. That sounds local and coffee's in the name. That'll work.*

She walked inside, ordered a cappuccino and a warm slice of veggie quiche, and sat down at a table. She tried calling Tristan's cell but still couldn't leave a message since his mailbox was full. She turned on Leilani's phone and scrolled through the missed calls. She saw a call from an unknown number and played the message. She instantly recognized Tristan's voice. "Leilani! It's Tristan. I'm alive. I was held captive, but I'm back. Long story. Where are you? Jake said you were in the hospital. Call me at this number as soon as you get this, and let me know you're okay. I love you."

Skylar hated hearing Tristan profess his love for Leilani. She listened to the message again but stopped it after the word "okay" so she wouldn't have to hear the last sentence again. She deleted the message.

*Why would Tristan tell Leilani he's alive if he's working with them to find Dean? And who would hold him captive? Did the police lock him up again? It doesn't make any sense. Unless they aren't in contact with him,* Skylar speculated. *Maybe Leilani and Jake have no idea where Tristan is. Maybe they lost track of him the night of Dean's wedding. Maybe Tristan regretted asking Leilani to marry him and took off—like he always does when things start to get serious. But if that's true, then why would he call and tell her he loves her?*

She finished her meal and headed toward Highway 1. She

drove south, lost in thought, oblivious to the beauty of the windblown dunes and sweeping vistas of the Monterey Bay.

*Are Jake and Leilani doing this all on their own to capture Dean? Otherwise, why would Tristan have to tell them he's alive and that he was held captive—whatever that means? If that's the case, maybe I can use this to my advantage. I can get rid of Dean, and then Tristan will never even know I was with him. I'll say goodbye to Leilani and Jake. Then I'll call Tristan and have him all to myself. I'll be the understanding friend. I'll tell him all the reasons it would never work to marry a human, let alone one in the FBI. I know I can convince him he made a huge mistake with Leilani. We can hang out, get close again, and it'll be just like before. After Tristan hears I killed Dean for hurting him and for what he did to Torrey and Cruz, maybe he'll finally realize we belong together.*

Back at the hotel, Skylar tucked Leilani's cell phone inside the spare tire compartment in the trunk of the rental car. She hurried to her room, trying her best to look surprised and annoyed. She shook Dean awake. "You'll never guess who I saw when I was getting coffee this morning!"

"Who?" he asked, his eyes still half-closed.

"Leilani. Tristan's ..." Skylar couldn't bring herself to say the word "fiancée." "Tristan's human," she said.

Dean's eyes flew open. Skylar pretended not to notice.

"You saw Leilani? Here?!" Dean's mind raced. Instantly, he thought of all the unreturned phone calls to Logan and Lance. "Are you sure it was her?"

"Yeah. Just the sight of her makes me want to hurl. She is, without a doubt, the most annoying human I've ever met."

Dean clenched his jaw and did his best to even out his voice despite the rage boiling up from deep inside him. "Was Tristan with her?"

The tension in Dean's voice and the burning intensity in his aqua blue eyes told Skylar everything she needed to know. She finally believed everything Jake and Leilani said.

"Was Tristan with Leilani?" Dean asked again.

"No."

Dean's eyes darkened to a dull blue-gray color. "Did you talk to her?"

"Yeah."

"What did she say?" Dean pressed.

Skylar replied with a story she concocted on the drive home after seeing Jake and Leilani. "Well, she seemed surprised to see me. Then—get this—she hugged me and said, 'I'm so glad you're alive.' Can you believe that? And here's the best part—Tristan dumped her. She said he went to your wedding and never came home. Then I said, 'I tried to warn you. That's what he does. As soon as you fall for him, he leaves.'"

"Really? She said Tristan never came home? Didn't even call?" Dean asked.

"Nope. Then she started crying, so she ran outside to try to calm herself down ..."

"Did you go after her?" Dean asked.

"No. She's pathetic. It's no surprise Tristan left her. I always knew he would," Skylar said.

"That's it? That's all she said?"

"Yeah. Then I left. Honestly, what did Tristan ever see in her? At least now she's out of our lives for good." Skylar stopped, waiting for Dean's reaction.

Dean clasped his hands together and tapped his thumbs against his chin. "You know, I only talked with Leilani once or twice, but I had no idea she was so unstable. I'm worried because she knows what we are. Tristan told her our secret."

"You're right!" Skylar said, feigning surprise. "She could be dangerous to all of us." *Keep going, Dean. You're on the right track*, she thought.

"That's exactly what I'm worried about. I have an idea. Before you say anything, hear me out," Dean said.

"Okay," Skylar agreed.

"Leilani has been a thorn in your side since you first met her, right?" he asked.

"That's putting it mildly."

"I know you were loyal to Tristan, and I know you've followed the Rules all this time because that's what Tristan drilled into your head. But there are exceptions to every rule, and Leilani should be one of them," Dean said.

"What do you mean?" Skylar asked innocently. *Keep going, Dean, keep going.*

"We should get rid of her. If she talks to Tristan and tells him she saw you, we won't be safe," Dean said. "I told you, he can't be trusted. He's dangerous to us."

Skylar nodded and tried to maintain her composure as she exploded inside. *It's more like the other way around, you asshole! You tried to kill Tristan! Your best friend! And you murdered Torrey and Cruz, who were not only two of my best friends but two of the best people I ever met!*

"I followed Tristan for four decades," Dean continued, "and I'm done. I'm done with him and his Rules. You say you never liked Leilani. Now she's a danger to us. She could expose us—tell our secret to humans. Let's take her out."

Skylar pretended to wrestle with the idea. "Just like that?"

"Yeah. Why not?" he asked.

"Uh, I don't know. How would we do it?" Skylar asked.

"Call Leilani. Tell her you're worried about her," Dean said. "Ask her to meet you at the beach near where you saw her. Invite her surfing. But keep the call brief. Don't let her talk, or she might say no. Tell her to save it for when you see her in person."

As Dean rattled off his plan, Skylar smiled with satisfaction. *You think you're in charge of this? Ha! You're doing exactly*

*what I knew you'd do. Tonight you'll get what's coming to*
*you. Then I'll call Tristan and tell him you're dead. He'll be*
*so happy that he'll forget all about Leilani.*

When Dean finished, he pulled Skylar close to him and planted a kiss on her mouth. He noticed Skylar didn't return his affection as enthusiastically as before. "Anything wrong?"

"No," Skylar said.

"Are you sure?" He flashed his sexiest smile. "How about I mix you a martini? Just the way you like?"

Skylar smiled but panicked inside. She knew there was no way she could be intimate with Dean after hearing what he did to her friends. "As amazing as that sounds, I don't think I can now. All this talk about Leilani has made me feel sick. How about we save it for afterward? I'll feel much more in the mood when I don't have to think about her anymore."

Dean forced an understanding smile. "Sure."

# 82 – Now or Never

After Skylar left, Jake and Leilani decided to rest up for the long night ahead. They awoke at sunset, two hours before Skylar and Dean were supposed to arrive.

"Do you want to go for a walk on the beach?" Jake suggested. "If I sit here, I'm gonna stress myself out about tonight."

"Me too. A walk would be good," Leilani said.

They strolled down a red brick path to the sand dunes and hiked to the water's edge. They walked north, with the churning Pacific Ocean on their left and the rugged sand dunes on their right, until they were the only ones on the beach.

Jake spread a blanket on the soft sand. They sat and watched the waves. He covered himself and Leilani with another blanket to shield her from the cold wind. They gazed at the turquoise blue sky streaked with pink cotton candy clouds. As the sunset colors grew more intense, the pastel hues reflected off the wet sand, which shimmered like the inside of an abalone shell.

To distract herself from thinking about seeing Dean again, Leilani picked up a handful of sand. Together, the grains of sand in her palm were the color of a toasted marshmallow. As she looked closer, she noticed the individual specks were all different colors—goldenrod, pumpkin, beige, olive, gray, white, black, and every shade in between. She parted her fingers and watched the sand fall.

As the blue sky darkened and the clouds turned from bright coral to dusty rose, Jake grew more and more worried about using Leilani as bait. He shuddered at the memory of her drenched in blood after Dean and Logan fed on her.

"Cold?" Leilani asked.

"No. You?" he asked.

"Yeah. It's a lot colder here than San Diego."

"That's for sure." Tentatively, Jake wrapped his arm around Leilani and pulled her close. "Warmer?"

"Yeah. Thanks."

Jake rested his head on hers, feeling the softness of her hair. "I'm worried about tonight. I don't think you should be there. We know Dean's dangerous. Aren't you scared to be anywhere near him again?"

"Yes, but I'll have you and Skylar with me." Leilani hoped she sounded confident. She wanted to put up a brave front for Jake. But inside, her stomach twisted into tangled knots at the thought of facing Dean again—staring into his cruel blue eyes, hearing the harshness in his voice, seeing his fangs and knowing what they felt like on her skin. She leaned into Jake, using his warm embrace to soothe her frayed nerves. "As much as I hate to admit it, Skylar knows what she's doing. We'll just stick with the plan. If anything goes wrong, I'm pretty sure Skylar will kill him. I think she's looking forward to it actually."

"I still don't like it. I wish Tristan was here," Jake said.

Leilani stared at the indigo ocean and sighed. "Me too."

"So much has happened. I know it's not easy losing someone you care about so suddenly."

"Yeah," she said. "It's like Tristan was this shooting star. He came out of nowhere, lit up my life, and disappeared just as quickly as he arrived. And now I'm here, taking a leave of absence from my job hunting so-called 'monsters' to hunt an actual monster."

"And I'm here with you," Jake said.

"I'm really glad about that."

Jake took a deep breath. *It's now or never, dude. A million things could go wrong tonight. You need to do this now.* "Leilani, I don't know what's going to happen tonight, but I want you to know that I will protect you with my life."

"Jake, you don't have to …"

"Just let me say this, okay?" Jake said. "I wish I'd met you earlier—before I met Skylar, before you met Tristan—so we could've had a chance to see … what might have happened. I know you love Tristan, and you just lost him. I don't expect anything from you. But if something happens to me tonight, I need you to know that I love you."

"I love you too. You've been such a good friend …"

"No, Leilani, I mean I *love* you. Not just as a friend."

"Oh." Surprised by Jake's admission, Leilani instantly became hyperaware of his arm around her shoulders.

Feeling Leilani's shoulders tense up, Jake dropped his arm to his side. "It's okay. You don't have to say anything."

"No, I want to," she said. "I think you're great, Jake. If I had met you before Tristan, this could be a very different conversation. Or maybe … in time … it could be different. But now it's too soon. I love Tristan. I know he's gone, but my feelings for him are still as strong as they ever were. I'm sorry. I don't want to hurt you. But you should also know that if I had met you earlier and I was with you, I'd be very lucky. No one could ask for a better guy than you. I'm sorry I can't be more to you than a friend."

"Don't apologize. I know that," he said. "I just wanted you to know how I feel in case something happens. If there's one thing I've realized from all this, it's that life is too short to not tell the people around you how you feel about them. You never know when it could be your last chance. No matter what, I'll always be here for you."

"I'll always be here for you too," she promised.

# 83 – Prove It

As Tristan sat in his black SUV outside Jake's house with Cody, he tried dialing Jake's and Leilani's cell phones again. There was still no answer. In his rearview mirror, he saw a cab approach and stop. A blond woman exited.

Tristan jumped out of his car. "Julianna!"

"You're looking better." Julianna smiled, but Tristan could tell she was angry that he left the compound without saying a word to her. "Where's Cody?" she asked.

Tristan pointed through the driver's side window to the passenger seat. "He knows he's not supposed to be seen by anyone he used to know, so he's hiding."

Julianna leaned inside. "Hi, Cody."

Cody gave her a quick nod. "Hi."

"What are you doing here?" Tristan asked.

"I'm looking for you guys. It's not safe for either of you to be out here." She raised her finger to Tristan's chest. "Especially in your condition."

"I'm fine now that I'm free again. How did you find us?" Tristan asked.

"Cody's body is microchipped. I tracked him here," Julianna explained.

Tristan poked his head inside the car window. "Cody, did you forget to tell me you're chipped?"

Cody slouched down further in his seat. "Oh yeah. Sorry. Guess it's not exactly a clean getaway if they can track you."

"Uh huh. Anything else I should know?" Tristan asked.

"Nope. Not that I can think of," Cody said.

"Have you guys found Jake and Leilani?" Julianna asked.

"No. They're not home, and they're not answering their phones," Tristan said.

"Do you know anyone who can track their cell phone signals?" Julianna asked.

"Yes! Why didn't I think of that?" Tristan reached inside his car for his disposable phone. He made a few calls and quickly found a graysuit who could tap into cellular networks. After a couple of minutes, he hung up. "Both phones were tracked to the Monterey Bay. Leilani's phone is in Carmel, and Jake's is in Marina. It'll take too long to swim or drive there. I'll get us a flight or charter a jet, whichever is quicker." He opened the driver's side door and motioned to Julianna. "You coming?"

Julianna nodded and reached for the door to the back seat.

"No, you drive. I'll arrange our flight," Tristan said.

Julianna climbed in and started the car. "Why does it smell like French fries in here?"

"You're not the first woman to ask that," Tristan chuckled. "My car runs on biofuel."

"Oh. Nice," she said.

"Hey, Julianna, I'm sorry we left so suddenly," Cody said. "We were just worried about Jake and Leilani. How's Matt?"

"Much better," she replied. "Finn's with him."

"Good," Cody smiled.

Tristan smiled too, relieved that Matt was doing better—and that Finn was still back at the compound.

They drove to the McClellan-Palomar Airport and boarded a private jet. Tristan sat beside Julianna. Cody sat behind them.

"So, Julianna, what are you really doing here?" Tristan asked.

"Like I said, I was worried about you," she replied.

"Why? I feel great now that I'm no longer being held prisoner," Tristan said. "Were you ever going to release me?"

Julianna stared straight ahead, unable to meet his gaze.

"I don't get it. What are you guys doing in those labs?" Tristan asked.

"Studying vampire sharks," she said.

"But why?" he pressed.

Julianna knew Tristan wouldn't give up without an answer, so she relented. "Our predecessor, Terrell, started the lab. When he realized it was vampire sharks—and not just regular great white sharks—that were killing humans, he wanted to study them to find out where they came from. He said it was like a whole new species came out of nowhere. He used to capture vampire sharks, study their blood and their venom, and release them. Finn and I took over the lab when Terrell was killed—quite viciously, I might add—by a vampire shark. We go after vampire sharks who kill people, but we do things differently than Terrell. After we study their venom, we don't reattach the venom sacs, which means they die. But we can't give them their venom back and release them into the wild because they'll just kill again. It wouldn't be right."

"But why are you even studying their venom if you already know what they are?" Tristan asked.

"We're trying to find the creator of the species. If we can find him or her, maybe we can prevent new graysuits from being created and prevent more lives from being lost," Julianna said.

Tristan took a deep breath. "And if you find this creator, what will you do? Kill him?"

"We'd study him to see what makes his venom different from the others," she replied. "We'd try to find out how he became the creator and how he creates new vampire sharks."

"And then what? You'd remove his venom sacs and let him die?" Tristan asked.

Julianna looked down at her hands.

"Because what if this vampire shark isn't really creating anymore?" Tristan asked. "What if he learned his lesson in the harshest way possible? What if someone he loved was killed by a vampire shark? What if he did everything he could—lived his entire life—trying to make sure that never happened again?"

Julianna lifted her head. "What are you saying?"

"I'm asking a question. Would you kill him? I know Finn would, but would you?" he asked.

"Don't do that. Don't shut me out again. You held back from me the entire time we were together. Don't do that now," Julianna said.

"Okay. But first I want to know why you wouldn't let me go when you could see I was getting sicker every day. With all the 'research' you do, you have to know that great whites die in captivity," Tristan said.

"Uh, hey guys, can we not do this now?" Cody asked.

Tristan and Julianna turned to the seat behind them. They had forgotten Cody was there.

"Sorry, man, but no. We have to do this now." Tristan tossed a pair of headphones to Cody. "How about if you go to the back of the jet and listen to some music? Loud."

Cody ambled to the other end of the small plane. He put on the headphones and tried to drown out their voices.

"We were trying to find out if you were the creator—like we do with all vampire sharks," Julianna admitted. "I didn't even know it was you at first!"

"But after you did know, why didn't you let me go?" Tristan demanded.

"Because it looks like the genesis of the vampire shark was in San Francisco in the early 1970s. Unbeknownst to me, I was right there in the middle of it. I know you lied to me the entire time we were together. It's time you finally tell me the truth. The *whole* truth," she said.

"You're right. No more secrets." Tristan looked Julianna squarely in the eye. "I'm the one you've been searching for. I'm the creator."

Julianna stared at him in astonishment.

"You should know I'm the only one who can create vampire

sharks. Plain old vampires are another story. But all vampire sharks came from me, from my venom. I created hundreds of vampire sharks from 1973 to 1975. Dean and I thought we were doing people a favor, giving them the ability to surf for centuries and experience the ocean in a way that exceeded their wildest dreams," Tristan explained. "We didn't realize what could happen as a result until you were killed—or at least your human body was."

"Oh my god. You were creating the entire time I was with you? What about all of the reports on the news about shark attacks?"

"It wasn't us," Tristan explained. "I was creating. I wasn't killing, and neither was Dean back then. But I guess others were. After you died, we tried to get a handle on it, but we couldn't control it completely and people died."

Tristan explained the Rules to Julianna and how he and the Nomads go after vampire sharks who indiscriminately kill humans. "If I could go back and undo what I did and never have turned anyone, I would. I told you, I would give my life a thousand times over if I could've saved you."

"Julianna, it's true," Cody said.

Once again, they were so wrapped up in their conversation that they didn't notice him.

"Sorry. I couldn't help overhearing. Tristan tried to help me," Cody continued. "I think he would've sacrificed his life to save mine if he could've. My friend Jake knew Tristan. Jake wouldn't have saved Tristan's life if he was some kind of monster. And he definitely wouldn't have asked Tristan to turn him if he didn't trust that Tristan was an okay dude."

"Wait … Jake is a graysuit?" Julianna asked.

Cody and Tristan nodded.

"Enough. I need to think." She walked to the rear of the plane, then sank into a seat and closed her eyes.

Ten minutes later, she returned to them. "All right, Tristan, I believe you. I believe you didn't know how things would turn out. If you had just talked to me, maybe things would've turned out differently. Maybe I could've talked you out of creating vampire sharks. But what's done is done. We can't change the past, but we can learn from our mistakes. I think you've tried to learn from yours and fix things. Having you out there enforcing your Rules actually helps me and Finn. But I need you to promise me that you will never create another vampire shark ever again."

"Not all vampire sharks are bad. And I rarely create new ones now anyway," Tristan said.

"Promise me," Julianna insisted.

"I don't know if I can do that," Tristan said. "Let's find Leilani and Jake, and then we can talk about this. We need to get to them before Dean does. I will never lie to you again. That means I can't make you a promise if I'm not sure I can keep it," he said.

"Tristan, you said you'd give your life for me. Now's your chance to prove it. I need you to stop creating. I need you to give up that part of your life. Forever," she said.

Tristan carefully considered her words. "Yes, I said I'd give my life for you, and I meant it. So, I guess if that's the only way you can feel safe … if that's what you need … then I'm done. I won't create anymore."

"Swear to me, Tristan. Swear to me, on my life, you will never create another vampire shark again," Julianna said.

"All right. I swear."

# 84 – Unfinished Business

While Dean watched, Skylar pretended to call Leilani to tell her she was worried and to ask her to go surfing so they could talk more. She set down her phone. "We're good."

Dean smiled with satisfaction. "Great. I'll take our stuff to the car. You rest up for tonight."

Dean couldn't say what was wrong, but he knew something was up with Skylar. Thinking about how his previous plans with Lance and Logan didn't turn out as expected, he decided to call for back-up to make sure there were no loose ends this time. He strapped their boards to the roof racks and dialed a few buddies in Santa Cruz who were good friends of Andi, his fiancée, and Andy, her best friend.

"It's Dean. I'm in the area. … Yeah, remember my plan with Tristan and the graysuits who killed Andi and Andy? … Well, it turns out there's some unfinished business—Leilani, Tristan's fiancée. I'm taking care of her tonight. Wanna come along for the fun? … Cool. Here's the plan …"

Later that evening, Skylar and Dean left Carmel and drove to Marina. They pulled off Highway 1 and turned west. They made a quick right and a left into the hotel parking lot. They drove up the hill, and Skylar pointed to the left. "After I get my stuff, park over at the beach. Give me 20 minutes to get Leilani in the water. Then she's all yours."

"Ours," Dean corrected. "What's mine is yours, baby."

Skylar smiled and opened the car door.

"No kiss?" he asked.

Skylar held her breath and kissed Dean, trying to keep her mind focused on calling Tristan when everything was done. "See you in 20. Till then, stay out of sight."

Skylar retrieved her bikini and towel from the trunk and

shoved them in her beach bag. She quietly reached into the spare tire compartment, removed Leilani's cell phone, and buried it inside her bag. She then lifted her surfboard off the roof racks and walked toward Jake's room. She glanced over her shoulder and smiled at Dean.

# 85 – Signal

After they landed at the Monterey Regional Airport, Tristan called his friend again. While Julianna rented a car, Tristan's friend pinpointed the location of Leilani's and Jake's phones.

"Got 'em!" Tristan exclaimed. "They're together—only about 15 minutes from here. Let's go!"

# 86 – Control

Leilani answered the door, dressed in a wetsuit. A holster around her waist held a tranquilizer gun, darts, and waterproof night vision goggles. Jake stood behind her, wearing boardshorts. Even though the Monterey Bay was a chilly 55 degrees, his body's superior thermoregulation made it possible to swim without a wetsuit for as long as he wanted.

Skylar brushed past them. "I just need to slip into my bikini and we can go." She walked to the bathroom, changed, and stuffed her clothes in the bottom of her beach bag. She placed Leilani's cell phone near the top of her bag and folded a flap of her beach towel over it. She motioned toward the front door. "Let's go."

As Jake and Leilani strolled through the door, Skylar quietly dropped Leilani's phone on the bed. She led them down the red brick road to a fenced sandy trail. They descended the dunes and marched to the ocean.

Leilani glanced up and down the beach. To the south were the twinkling gold lights of Monterey and Pacific Grove. To the north was Santa Cruz. "Good," she said. "It's deserted."

"Dean will be here soon. You ready?" Skylar asked.

"Yeah," Jake and Leilani replied.

"Jake, you swim out. Then hang out below our boards. Go now in case Dean gets here early," Skylar instructed.

Jake dropped his trunks in the sand and waded into the ocean. Leilani turned away from Jake's naked body.

Skylar noticed Leilani blushing and smiled to herself. *Maybe it'll be easier to pry Leilani and Tristan apart than I thought.*

"Let's paddle into position," she said to Leilani. "Once Dean's in the ocean, I'll jump in the water and watch from below. Then Jake and I will drive him up to the surface, and you can shoot him with the tranquilizer gun. If anything goes wrong, Jake and I will attack him. So, if you want to do this your way, don't miss. Make sure you get a good look at Jake and me before Dean gets there. We don't want you shooting the wrong shark."

Leilani smirked as she considered shooting Skylar with a tranquilizer dart.

"What's so funny?" Skylar asked.

"Nothing," Leilani replied.

Leilani and Skylar dropped their boards in the ocean and paddled out. After they passed the last line of breaking waves, Leilani put on her night vision goggles. She plunged her head into the water. Jake, in his shark body, made eye contact and gave her a quick nod. Leilani couldn't explain how, but as she peered into the shark's eyes, she knew it was Jake. She felt a warmth and friendliness emanating from him. She took a good look at Jake's shark face and body so she could tell him apart from Dean when he arrived.

Skylar jumped off her board into the ocean. She wiggled out of her bikini and tied it to her leash.

After she morphed, Leilani studied her. Again, staring into the shark's eyes, she knew it was Skylar. She felt the same agitation and awkwardness she always felt around Skylar. She lifted her head out of the water and pulled her goggles down around her neck.

Skylar transformed into her human body and climbed onto her board, naked. "This doesn't bother you, does it? It seems stupid to put on my bikini when it's dark and there's no one else out here."

"It's fine," Leilani said, though it did make her uncomfortable. She tried to avert her eyes from Skylar, but it was easy to see what Tristan and Jake saw in her. *She's perfect. Well, perfect-looking*, she corrected herself. *Her personality is another story.*

While Jake circled below Leilani's feet, his mind again flashed to her tied to the chair, bleeding to death because of Dean and Logan. He knew that as soon as Dean swam into view, it would take all his self-control not to kill him on the spot.

Down the beach, Dean watched two cars pull into the parking lot. Three men and two women piled out and greeted him.

"Thanks for coming, guys," Dean said. "It means a lot. This, tonight, is for Andi and Andy. Tristan took them from us, so we're taking Leilani—and anyone else who gets in our way."

A moment later, the alarm on Dean's watch sounded. He and his five friends strode toward the ocean.

# 87 – Waiting

Leilani floated on her board, facing the dark horizon. An apricot-colored sliver of the waning crescent moon smoldered in the sky above her. Skylar faced Leilani and the beach, keeping an eye out for Dean. An awkward silence stretched between them. Leilani decided to break it.

"Skylar? Thank you for helping us catch Dean. I'm sure it must've been a shock for you to hear what he did. I have to say, you're handling all of this really well. I don't think I could've done nearly as good of a job getting him here without making him suspicious."

"Men are easy," Skylar said. "They like to think they're in control, and that's where they go wrong."

"Yeah," Leilani laughed uneasily. "Listen, I know we haven't always gotten along, but I'd like to start over ... if you want to."

Skylar sniffed the air. "There's Dean," she announced, purposely ignoring the olive branch Leilani extended. She sniffed again. "And he's not alone."

Skylar waved her hand underwater, motioning for Jake to come up.

Jake transformed and poked his head out. "What? He should be here any minute."

"Something's wrong. Dean's got company. I think there are five other graysuits with him."

"Five?!" Leilani hastily pulled on her night vision goggles and removed the tranquilizer gun from her holster.

"What are we gonna do?" Jake demanded.

"Shh! They'll hear us. We can do this. There are two of us, and Leilani's got the tranq gun," Skylar said.

"I knew this was a mistake!" Jake hissed.

"Calm down," Skylar said. "We've got no choice now

anyway. You and I need to get underwater. We'll take them by surprise."

She jumped into the ocean and morphed next to Jake. They swam back and forth beneath Leilani's feet, waiting.

Leilani sat alone on her board. She scanned the beach and the ocean but saw nothing. She gripped the tranquilizer gun, ready to fire at anything that breached the ocean's surface.

# 88 – Lone Surfer

Tristan, Cody, and Julianna arrived at the resort and drove toward the cell phone signals. They followed the brick road up a hill. They drove past a restaurant to a one-story tan and green building on the northern edge of the property, facing the gently sloping sand dunes. As they passed the second door down from the edge of the building, Tristan exclaimed, "This is it!" Julianna stopped the car.

Tristan thanked his friend who had been directing him to the location of Jake's and Leilani's cell phones. "We've got it from here. I owe you big time. Just let me know when I can return the favor."

Tristan leapt out of the car, ran to the room, and banged on the door. "Leilani! Jake!" There was no answer. He walked back to Julianna and Cody, who were now parked in front of the room.

A cab pulled up and screeched to a stop. Finn jumped out.

"Finn!" Julianna cried. "What are you doing here?!"

"I followed your microchip," he replied. "I can't let you do this alone."

"What about the lab?" she asked. "And Matt?"

"He's doing a lot better. Lucia and Jamal are taking care of him," Finn said.

"And Lily?"

"Lily's not cooperating. I don't think she'll survive the night." Finn briefly met Tristan's gaze and looked away. "What's going on here?"

"We tracked Jake's and Leilani's phones here," Julianna explained.

Unlike Julianna, Tristan wasn't happy to see Finn, and he had more than a few things he wanted to say to him, but he didn't want to get distracted from finding Leilani and Jake. "Let's try the beach. Maybe they're there."

They jogged toward the ocean. From the top of the dune, Tristan scanned the water. He spotted a lone surfer and sniffed the air. "It's Leilani!" His face broke into a grin that instantly faded. "But what's she doing out there all alone?"

Tristan saw six fins heading toward her. "Rogues!" He peeled off his clothes as he raced toward the ocean. Julianna and Finn followed. Cody lagged behind them, gathering up Tristan's clothes along the way.

"Wait here!" Tristan yelled over his shoulder as he splashed into the water.

"We're going with you," Julianna insisted.

"No," Tristan said. "I lost you once to a graysuit. I won't lose you again. I'll take care of this. This is what I do."

"And this is what we do." Julianna began undressing. "We're going!"

Finn called behind him to Cody, "You haven't been trained to fight. Wait here!"

"No way!" Cody dropped Tristan's clothes in the sand and removed his own clothing. "I'm going with you. There are too many of them. I can help."

"Then follow our lead, and don't try anything on your own," Finn said. "We don't want you getting killed by a vampire shark. Again."

# 89 – Done

Sitting astride her surfboard, Leilani felt the bite wounds on the left side of her body begin to throb. The pulses of pain grew more intense the closer the sharks got. *The throbbing—it's coming from where Dean bit me. He's here!*

One of the vampire sharks raced ahead and jumped out of the ocean, brimming with excitement about the prospect of a kill. Leilani aimed and fired the gun. The first tranquilizer dart pierced the flesh behind the shark's eye. The second struck his snout. He splashed down, writhing in pain. A few seconds later, he floated on the ocean's surface.

Underwater, Dean glanced up as he swam past his unconscious friend. *I knew something was up! Glad I brought reinforcements,* he thought. *We could've really had something, Sky, but I guess you can never trust a graysuit.*

Dean found Skylar next to a vampire shark he didn't recognize. He shifted into his human body and motioned for his remaining four friends to wait behind him.

Skylar followed Dean's lead and morphed. She signaled to Jake to wait next to her. Then she and Dean surfaced.

"Skylar, what the hell are you doing?" Dean demanded.

"Oh no! Don't turn this on me," Skylar said. "You're a traitor. Everything you told me was a lie. I know you killed Torrey and Cruz! I know what you did to Tristan! That's why you didn't want me to call anyone."

"You don't know anything! Torrey and Cruz murdered Andi," Dean seethed. "She was mine, and they killed her for breaking Tristan's stupid Rules. They got what was coming to them."

Skylar looked away, disgusted.

"C'mon, Sky. Don't ruin what we have for her." Dean

motioned toward Leilani, who pointed the dart gun at his head. "She's nothing but a worthless human."

"You're nothing! You killed my friends, and you lied to me about it this entire time," Skylar said.

"If you'd just let me explain my side of it …"

"No," Skylar said flatly. "We're done."

"That's really the way you want it? After everything we've had together?" Dean asked.

"Yeah," Skylar said. "I can't believe I fell for you and your lies. I knew Tristan would never betray me. I'm done with you—for good. Goodbye, Dean."

"If that's the way you want it," Dean said. "Goodbye, Skylar."

Behind Dean, they heard a commotion. One of the vampire sharks breached the surface and thrashed wildly. Leilani used the distraction to fire a tranquilizer dart at Dean. He snapped his head to the right, and the dart whizzed by his ear. He ducked underwater.

Skylar glared at Leilani. *Pathetic.* She dipped underwater and morphed.

Skylar and Jake followed Dean, who raced to the graysuit in distress. Dean saw his friend being shredded. He looked into the eyes of the brownish-gray shark attacking her and stopped cold. *Tristan.*

Feeling the graysuit go lifeless in his jaws, Tristan released her. He saw another graysuit approach. *Dean.*

Julianna led Finn and Cody to Leilani. They swam in a protective circle beneath her.

Leilani felt the ocean move under her feet. She quickly lifted her legs and tucked them beneath her on her surfboard. Kneeling, she scanned the water, ready to fire if Dean or his friends surfaced again.

# 90 – Distress Call

Tristan and Dean swam toward each other, jaws bared. They wrestled, each trying to bite the other. They gnashed back and forth, but neither was able to make contact. One of Dean's friends slammed into Tristan's left side and sank his teeth into Tristan's pectoral fin.

Skylar darted toward the attacker. She made eye contact with Tristan for one brief euphoric second. Then she rammed the vampire shark that bit Tristan. The graysuit took off. Skylar chased after him.

Jake faced off with another graysuit who approached on Tristan's right as Tristan took another swipe at Dean.

They all failed to notice the third remaining vampire shark break off in search of Leilani. The graysuit spotted the dolphins swimming under the surfboard. He zoomed toward them.

Julianna saw the vampire shark first. As he furiously swam toward Leilani's surfboard, Julianna whipped her body in front of him to prevent him from breaking through their circle. The graysuit rebounded off her body. He quickly regained his bearings, repositioned himself, and hurtled toward them.

Finn and Cody used their bodies to bash the vampire shark from the side, but it wasn't enough to completely derail him. The graysuit's head smashed into the underside of the surfboard, knocking Leilani into the ocean. Still grasping the gun, she kicked toward the surface. Finn whistled to Cody, instructing him to get Leilani out of there.

Leilani surfaced and spun around, searching for her board. She felt something beneath her. She struggled to get away until she heard a series of whistles and clicks. She'd heard stories about dolphins rescuing humans from sharks, but she'd never seen it in person.

Cody positioned himself beneath Leilani so she could climb onto his back. She kept one hand on the tranquilizer gun, wrapped one hand around the dolphin's dorsal fin, and held on tight as the dolphin swam toward the beach.

Finn and Julianna took turns slamming their bodies into the attacking graysuit. They pummeled his eyes, blinding him. They delivered blow after blow to his snout and body. Before long, they heard his heart deliver its last beat.

Out of the inky depths, two more vampire sharks appeared, drawn to the blood in the water. The graysuits weren't friends of Dean. They were just vacationing in the Monterey Bay National Marine Sanctuary. With its giant kelp forests and an undersea canyon deeper than the Grand Canyon, the Monterey Bay is home to hundreds of species of fish and marine mammals as well as surfers, paddleboarders, divers, kayakers, and sailors— making it an appealing destination for hungry vampire sharks.

The two graysuits chased Finn and Julianna, who got separated trying to evade them. Finn swam as fast as he could and disappeared into a dense kelp forest. A moment later, he and Cody gasped in horror as Julianna unwittingly transmitted a sound picture to them. She felt white-hot bursts of pain as serrated teeth punctured her flesh.

As Cody swam with Leilani, he heard something on his left. He saw the graysuit jump out of the water with Julianna in his mouth.

Still wearing her night vision goggles, Leilani turned toward the noise and was surprised to see the shark so close to them. She saw a dolphin trapped between the shark's jaws, struggling to break free. Leilani rested her right wrist on top of her left forearm, which was still wrapped around the dolphin's dorsal fin, to try to steady the gun—at least as much as she could steady it aboard a moving dolphin. She fired a tranquilizer dart. It missed the shark by a few feet. She aimed again and fired two darts in quick succession.

"Yes!" she yelled triumphantly as one of the darts struck the shark's side. Instantly, the shark released the dolphin.

Finn swam toward Julianna, but something hit him from the side. Stunned by the blow, it took him a few seconds to get his bearings—just in time to see a face full of jagged teeth barreling toward him. Finn dove into the kelp forest again, darting in and out of the underwater towers until the shark was no longer behind him. He sent out a distress call to any dolphins close enough to hear him.

Cody received Finn's call. He hoped other dolphins were nearby. He swam toward the shore. Cody deposited Leilani in the shallow water and whistled to tell her to stay there, even though he knew she couldn't understand him. Then he raced back out to find Finn and Julianna.

Cody swam past the unconscious vampire shark with the dart sticking out of his side. He quickly located Finn, who was now with Julianna. Blood streamed from her mid-section. A pod of seven dolphins surrounded them.

"Graysuits! I don't know how many there are," Finn said. "Can you help me get Julianna out of here?"

The pod formed a tight circle around Finn and Julianna, and helped them to shore.

When they were near the beach, Julianna shifted into her human body. "Finn," she said, gasping for breath. She collapsed in the water.

# 91 – Confrontation

Dean and Tristan faced off. With Skylar and Jake in pursuit of Dean's remaining two friends, there was no one else around. Dean morphed, confident Tristan wouldn't take the coward's way out and attack him when he was in his human body. Tristan transformed and followed Dean to the surface. Tristan's arm bled where the vampire shark had sliced into his pectoral fin.

"Where's Leilani?!" Tristan demanded.

Dean acknowledged him with a condescending sneer. "Now you know what it feels like. That burning hatred that's coursing through your veins? That's exactly what I felt when Andi was killed because of you and your stupid Rules."

"Completely different! Andi was a killer!" Tristan argued.

"No! I loved her. That makes it exactly the same!" Dean countered. "You killed Andi for nothing—for feeding on humans. This is what we do! You think because you have some code about who you kill that you're better than me? You're not. We both kill humans. We're predators. Vampire. Shark. What part of that don't you get?"

"What part of the Rules don't you get? We don't kill kids, and we don't kill people who don't deserve to die. Remember Julianna? Didn't you feel bad about what happened to her? We caused that when we turned all those surfers into graysuits," Tristan said.

"Yeah, I felt bad about Julianna. And what did you do when she was killed? You went out and killed the bastard who murdered her. That's exactly what I did when I went after Torrey and Cruz. You and I? We're no different," Dean said.

Tristan shook his head. "I can't let you leave here, Dean. We finish this now."

Worried about going up against Tristan on his own, Dean

knew he had to buy some time. "So, then I guess you don't want to know about Skylar."

Tristan's eyes widened. "What about Skylar?"

"Skylar's with me now. I think she'll tell you she's found our time together to be quite pleasurable."

Tristan clenched his fists underwater. "Where is Skylar now?"

Dean didn't answer. He had no idea where Skylar was. He also knew Skylar wouldn't hesitate to side with Tristan. But he was desperate to stall until his friends could find him so they could all attack Tristan at once. *If they're still alive. If not, I'll take on Tristan by myself but only as a last resort.*

"She's safe as long as I'm alive," Dean lied.

From below, Skylar approached. She saw two naked men treading water. *Dean and Tristan.*

"I'm not screwing around, Dean. Where's Skylar?" Tristan hadn't yet picked up on Skylar's scent since she was underwater and he was above. "What have you done with her?!"

*Tristan really does care about me!* Skylar rejoiced, listening from below.

"If I tell you, you'll just kill me. So, no. I'm going to leave here, and you're going to let me leave," Dean said. "Then my friends will release her."

"I'm not bargaining with you. You leave and you're dead. Tell me where Skylar is," Tristan demanded.

"I'll tell you where she isn't. She isn't with you anymore. She's done with you. You wasted 10 years of her life. You think that's fair? You think that's right? She loved you, and you tossed her aside the minute a new blond showed up. Skylar deserves someone who can give her what you've denied her all these years. You use people, Tristan. We were friends when it was convenient for you. When you left San Francisco after Julianna died, you didn't think twice about me after that, did you? You

RISING     221

left to go on your adventures and sleep your way across the Pacific, and you never thought about me."

Tristan treaded water in silence. He knew Dean wasn't entirely wrong.

"If you happened to be passing through, yeah, you might stop in and say hi for five minutes. But then you were out the door and on to your next conquest. You're a shitty friend, and you always have been," Dean continued. "You don't give a damn about anyone but yourself, and you never have. You created the Rules because you like to kill. You just need to give yourself an excuse—to make you feel like you have some noble cause to fight for, like you're some great avenger. I'm done with your bullshit. Skylar is too. You know the night you went to see her and she sent you away, and I said I'd smooth things over for you? That was our first night together. She couldn't wait to get away from you."

Tristan wondered if Dean was telling the truth or trying to bait him into doing something stupid.

*Shut up, Dean,* Skylar willed from several feet below, *or so help me* ...

"Skylar's been with me ever since. If you kill me, you'll have to kill her because I haven't done anything she hasn't done," Dean said. "How do you think I found Leilani? How do you think I got her out here alone in the ocean? It was Sky…"

With a gasp, Dean disappeared underwater.

Tristan dunked his head and saw a brown 15-foot shark pulling Dean deeper and deeper into her jaws.

Skylar punctured Dean's heart with her jagged teeth and tore into his body until he was nothing but slivers of dead flesh. She morphed, wiped Dean's blood from her mouth, and jumped into Tristan's arms. "I never thought I'd see you again! Dean lied to me. He told me terrible things about you. I didn't know what he did to you or Torrey and Cruz. Jake and I were going to capture him tonight. We didn't think he'd bring friends ..."

"It's okay. He's gone now, thanks to you." Tristan cupped Skylar's face in his hands. "I know you would never betray me. We've been together too long."

Skylar stared into Tristan's warm espresso-brown eyes. She felt her insides melt despite the chilly temperature of the ocean around her. "I love you so much," she whispered.

Tristan pulled Skylar into his arms. "I love you."

A broad smile illuminated her face. *Finally!*

"You're my best friend, and you mean the world to me. But we have to find Leilani." Tristan extricated himself from Skylar's embrace.

Skylar's insides froze. She stared at Tristan, numb. *I'll never be enough. At least not as long as she's around.*

"I haven't seen any of the graysuits Dean brought with him," Tristan said. "Maybe they're all dead, but let's split up and look around. If we don't find her or the graysuits, we'll meet on shore."

# 92 – Rage

Jake continued chasing the graysuit who had approached Tristan when he faced off with Dean. Jake nipped at her tail fin but couldn't quite reach her. Abruptly, the graysuit stopped. Jake's snout slammed into her. The sudden blow blinded him. While he struggled to see past the blackness, the graysuit whipped around and sank her teeth into his snout.

The flash of pain instantly restored Jake's vision. He lashed out, feeling weeks of anger surge through him. He thought of all the carnage he'd witnessed because of vampire sharks. *I'm sick of the killing. I'm sick of seeing Cody's bloody body wash up on shore. I'm sick of seeing Leilani tied to a chair, bleeding to death.* He focused his fury on the graysuit in front of him. As he tore into her flesh, he felt nothing but pure, unadulterated rage. Before he knew it, the graysuit was dead. Just as suddenly as it came, the rage disappeared.

# 93 – Communication

Leilani looked up the beach and spotted two figures in the sand. She warily approached them. She saw a naked man holding an unconscious naked woman. Blood seeped from her abdomen and legs. There was a t-shirt tied around each leg above her wounds and a towel stretched across her stomach and hips, but blood continued to spill from her. Leilani watched the man cradle the woman and cry.

"J, please," he sobbed. "Please, baby. Wake up. I love you. You said you'd marry me. Please come back to me."

Leilani couldn't tell if the man was a graysuit or a human, but there was something about the way he held the woman that made her feel unafraid. "Hello? My name is Leilani Waters. Would you like me to call an ambulance?"

"No. Human doctors can't help," he said.

*Human doctors? I guess they are graysuits*, Leilani thought. "Then what can I do to help you?"

Finn shook his head. "She's dying. There's no way I can save her here."

"What's your name?" Leilani asked softly. Seeing the man covered in the woman's blood, she worried he might go into shock from seeing his loved one hurt so badly.

"Finn. This is Julianna."

"I understand why you don't want a doctor," Leilani said. "Is it because she's a graysuit?"

Finn's expression flashed from grief to anger. "A graysuit is what did this to her!"

Leilani jumped, startled by Finn's outburst.

Seeing Leilani's fear, Finn softened. "I'm sorry. It's just that graysuits …" He looked down at Julianna and then gazed up at Leilani, his eyes wide. "Wait! There is something you can do for me. You said your name was Leilani, right? Leilani Waters? Find Tristan. He's here somewhere. Tell him Julianna's dying." Finn's eyes darkened as he spoke. "Tell him I need him here now!"

"Tristan?" Leilani gasped in surprise. "Tristan Pierce?"

"Yes."

"Tristan's alive?! Where is he?"

"In the ocean. But don't go out too far. There are vampire sharks everywhere. If you can't find Tristan, call out for dolphins. My name is Luke Finnegan. They'll know who I am. Tell them to find a dolphin named Cody and that Cody should find Tristan, tell him Julianna's dying, and I need him here now."

"I don't understand. You want me to call out to dolphins?" Leilani asked.

"You don't need to understand," Finn said. "Just do it! She's dying!"

Leilani ran to the ocean, trying to make sense of Finn's words. She waded in knee-deep and yelled, "Dolphins!" She glanced around nervously. *Am I actually calling for dolphins? Is this really what that guy wanted me to do? I feel so stupid.* Seeing no one around her, she quashed her doubts and embarrassment, and tried again. "Dolphins! Luke Finnegan needs you! Now!"

A dolphin bodysurfed toward her. It raised its head out of the water and nudged her with its bottlenose. Leilani jumped. She couldn't believe it. The dolphin remained there, waiting for her to continue.

Leilani shrugged and spoke to it. "Finn wants you to find a dolphin named Cody. Tell him to tell Tristan that Julianna's dying and that Finn needs him here now on the beach."

The dolphin nodded and disappeared underwater.

Leilani raised her eyebrows. *Did that just happen? Did that dolphin understand what I said? The world is definitely a freakier place since I met Tristan ... and it keeps getting weirder every day.* She scanned the black ocean. *Tristan, where are you? Are you really alive?*

She ran back to Finn. "I found a dolphin and told him." Even as she said the words, she felt silly. But when she saw the relief on Finn's face, she felt like she actually did something useful.

Finn continued his plea in Julianna's ear. "Please, J, please come back to me."

Leilani felt terrible, not knowing how to help him. "Is there anything else I can do?"

Finn looked up at Leilani as tears streamed down his face. "Can you go back to the ocean? We don't have much time. Scream as loud as you can for more dolphins. Tell them to tell Cody to get Tristan here now!"

# 94 — Saved

Leilani ran into the ocean again. She opened her mouth to yell, but a rogue wave knocked her off her feet, and a riptide swept her out to sea. Before she knew it, she was 100 yards from shore. She knew if she swam directly against the current toward the beach that she'd quickly exhaust her energy and drown. So, instead, she swam parallel to the shore. When she finally broke free of the deadly current, she began swimming toward the beach but found it difficult to get very far without fins. "Help!" *Oh, what the hell?* "Dolphins!"

Underwater, Skylar heard a scream. She surfaced. Instantly, she recognized Leilani's voice. Skylar knew she had a choice to make. She could let Leilani drown—if Tristan didn't come to her rescue—and finally get him all to herself. Or she could do what she knew Tristan would want her to do and save Leilani. Skylar sighed and comforted herself with the thought that she was absolutely certain Tristan would tire of Leilani, and sooner rather than later.

She quickly found Leilani. "Quit screaming! Do you want to attract every graysuit in the Monterey Bay? What are you doing out here?"

"A riptide," Leilani panted, "dragged me out."

"Okay. And were you just yelling for dolphins?"

"What? No."

"Right," Skylar said. "Let's get you to shore. I'm gonna morph so we get there quicker. Hang onto my fin."

# 95 – Teamwork

The dolphin relayed Finn's message to Cody, which he then passed along to Tristan. As they headed toward the beach, Cody heard something. It sounded like someone being hurt underwater. Immediately, he thought of Jake. He broke off from Tristan and swam in the direction of the noise. He spotted two graysuits battling. Both were injured and bleeding. *The smaller shark—that's Jake!*

Cody slammed into the larger shark's injured body. The impact was so sudden and fierce, it sent the shark hurtling backward several feet. Expecting to see Skylar or Tristan, Jake turned to see who hit the shark. Instead, he saw a dolphin looking at him expectantly. Jake didn't know why, but when he looked into the dolphin's friendly eyes, he instantly thought of Cody.

The vampire shark, now recovered from Cody's blow, rocketed toward them. Jake bit his snout repeatedly. Cody whipped his fluke at the shark's eyes and pummeled his gills. After several minutes of unrelenting bites and blows, the shark perished. Immediately sensing the shark's death, Cody halted his assault and backed away. It took Jake another minute to notice the shark's heart had stopped beating.

Jake peered into the dolphin's eyes again. *I know it's impossible, but it feels like Cody's here.*

Jake shifted into his human body and surfaced. The dolphin poked its head out of the water. Suddenly, Jake remembered seeing a dolphin at Cody's paddle out. "Cody?" he asked tentatively.

The dolphin opened its mouth like it wanted to say something. Then it abruptly turned and swam away.

# 96 — Need

On the beach, Tristan pulled on his shorts and quickly found Finn and Julianna. They looked bloody and disheveled.

"What happened?" Tristan asked.

"What do you think?!" Finn snapped.

Tristan gingerly peeled the towel and t-shirts away from Julianna's abdomen and legs. The ragged bite marks across her stomach, pelvis, and thighs oozed bright red blood.

"She's been unconscious since we got to shore. She's bleeding to death," Finn said.

"What about you? Are you hurt?" Tristan asked.

"No. This is her blood on me," Finn replied.

Tristan closed his eyes. *I can't go through this again—seeing her die like this because of a graysuit.*

"You need to make this right," Finn said. "Everything points to you. You're the creator, aren't you? You're the one we've been looking for all this time."

Tristan paused, wondering if he should tell Finn the truth.

"I'll take your silence as a yes. We can talk about what that means another time. Right now, I need you to do something for me." Finn peered into Tristan's eyes. "I need you to turn Julianna."

# 97 – Revealed

As they approached the shoreline, Leilani climbed from Skylar's back. Her hand was so numb from the cold water that she didn't feel her engagement ring catch on Skylar's dorsal fin and slide from her finger.

Feeling Leilani drop off her back, Skylar morphed. She glimpsed something sparkly in the water and reached for it. It was hard and round. She held it in front of her eyes. *Leilani's engagement ring.* "Hey! Did you forget something?"

Leilani turned toward her. "What?"

Skylar quickly closed her hand around the ring. "Uh, could you get my towel? My bikini is still strapped to my surfboard. I'm naked. I don't want to be arrested for indecent exposure."

"Be right back." Leilani retrieved a towel for herself, pulled a towel from Skylar's bag, and jogged back to the ocean.

Skylar toweled off and pulled on her clothes. She casually dropped the ring inside her bag and put her wet towel on top of it.

"Come with me." Leilani led Skylar toward Finn and Julianna. "A woman is hurt. The guy, Finn, has been asking for Tristan. Maybe he's there now!"

Skylar frowned. She wanted to delay Tristan's reunion with Leilani as long as she could.

Jake arrived on shore behind Skylar and Leilani. He dropped Leilani's surfboard in the sand, pulled on his boardshorts, and called out to them.

"You're hurt!" Leilani cried, seeing his face and torso covered in blood.

Jake shrugged. "I'll be fine. It looks worse than it is. I have accelerated healing now, remember? I'll be as good as new in no time, right, Skylar?"

"Right," Skylar agreed.

"Where are you guys going?" Jake asked.

"We're looking for Tristan," Leilani replied. "This guy on the beach was asking for him. He says he's here!"

Jake gasped in disbelief. "What?!"

"Yeah!" Leilani led Skylar and Jake back to where she'd left Finn. They saw Tristan leaning over a blond woman.

*Great,* Skylar thought, *another blond.*

They approached quietly, not wanting to startle Finn, who cradled the bleeding blond woman in his arms. They heard Tristan arguing with him.

"I can't do that, Finn," Tristan said quietly but firmly.

"Can't or won't? Because I know you can," Finn hissed.

"I won't. If she asked me to do this and knew what she was getting into, I'd do it, okay? But she made me promise I'd never create another graysuit again. I gave her my word," Tristan said.

"When?" Finn asked. "She didn't know you were the creator."

"Earlier—just before you arrived," Tristan explained.

"It doesn't matter. I'm not going to let her die because of a graysuit. You have to turn her—to save her," Finn said.

"No, I can't break my promise to her," Tristan said.

"Listen! I don't like this any more than you do. But she's going to die. It's the only way to keep her here," Finn said.

"Can't you do your dolphin carrier thing, like you did with Cody when he was attacked?" Tristan asked.

"No. It only works on someone once," Finn said. "You're the only one who can save her now."

Tristan raised his eyes from Finn and saw Leilani, Skylar, and Jake. Overcome with joy, he jumped up, raced to Leilani, and swept her into his arms. "Leilani!"

Leilani threw her arms around him. "You're alive! But how? Where were you?"

"Tristan! This has to happen now!" Finn demanded.

Tristan pulled back from Leilani. "I'm sorry." He quickly squeezed Skylar's hand, patted Jake's shoulder, and ran back to Finn. He gazed helplessly at Julianna's injuries. He knew Finn was right. If he didn't act, she'd die.

"Do you need me to say I'm sorry, Tristan? I'm sorry. About everything, okay? I was wrong. I should've never locked you up. I thought I was doing the right thing. I didn't know you hunted killer vampire sharks like we do. Maybe you're not all bad. Okay? But we're out of options here," Finn said. "Julianna's dying. You know what it's like to lose her. You can't let that happen again. You're the only one who can save her. Please. I'll do whatever you want. Just save her."

*Julianna?* Skylar looked at the woman in Finn's arms. With her straight blond hair and petite frame, she noticed the resemblance to Leilani. *As in Tristan's wife, Julianna? I thought she died.* Skylar shot a quick glance at Leilani to see if she was thinking the same thing.

Leilani's eyes widened. She raised her eyebrows at Skylar. *Julianna?*

Skylar saw a worried expression cloud Leilani's face. *Good,* Skylar thought. *Now you know how I feel every time another blond shows up. Doesn't feel so good, does it? And now I've got two of you to deal with. Awesome.*

"You have to turn her," Finn pleaded. "We're losing time!"

"Finn, I don't want to see her like this any more than you do. It's killing me inside to see her hurt again. But she wouldn't want this," Tristan said.

"You don't know her! I've been with her every day for the last 11 years. I know this is what she'd want," Finn insisted.

Tristan had to admit that he didn't really know what Julianna would want, so he had no choice but to trust Finn. "I'll do it but only if you're 100 percent sure."

"I am. Do it!" Finn said.

Tristan gently pulled Julianna into his arms. He glanced at Leilani. He wished she wasn't here to see this.

Finn looked away as Tristan pressed his mouth to Julianna's neck. Tristan lowered his fangs and pierced her flesh. As he sucked her blood, he released his venom into her bloodstream. After a few minutes, he lifted his head. He quickly wiped his mouth—but not before Leilani saw him with his fangs, teeth, and lips covered in Julianna's blood.

Leilani covered her mouth and ran toward the ocean. Jake sprinted after her.

Tristan tenderly placed Julianna in Finn's arms. "It's done. It's up to her now."

"When will we know if it worked?" Finn asked.

"It's hard to say," Tristan replied. "It's different for everyone. Usually within 24 hours. But that's with a human. I've never done this with … one of you before."

*One of you?* Skylar wondered. *If they're not human and they're not graysuits, then what are they?*

"24 hours?! That's too long," Finn said.

"Finn, I did what you wanted!" Tristan snapped. "Now we'll have to wait and see if it works!"

Tristan immediately regretted his outburst when he saw the pained expression on Finn's face. He knew he probably had that same expression when he held Julianna in his arms when she was killed by a Rogue shortly after they were married. "I'm sorry. I know you want to help her, but I don't know how long it'll take. Maybe it'll go quicker because she's a finner."

Finn nodded.

Tristan placed his hand on Finn's shoulder. "I've done all I can. I have to find Leilani."

"Go," Finn said.

# 98 — Anything, Anything

*Now's my chance*, Skylar thought. She reached out as Tristan strode past her. "Wait! I need to talk to you."

She quickly led him down the beach to give Finn and Julianna some privacy. "Hey, I know what Leilani saw back there was rough," she said. "Give her a minute, okay? This whole vampire thing can be pretty shocking at first. I should know, right?"

Tristan recalled the night he turned Skylar by mistake. He thought she said yes to his offer to turn her into a vampire shark. She thought she was saying yes to a marriage proposal. Even though Skylar seemed to enjoy her life as a graysuit and a Nomad, he had felt guilty about turning her ever since.

"But I feel like I should go to her. She's never really seen the vampire part of me in action before. She's gotta be freaking out, especially after what she went through with Dean and Logan," Tristan worried.

"Yeah, she probably is, but Jake's with her. He can help her understand," Skylar said. "Believe me, the last thing you want to do right now is run after her and scare her away. Let her come to terms with this. Let her come back to you."

"Do you really think so?" Tristan asked.

Skylar nodded.

"I dunno. Maybe you're right," he said.

She gently touched Tristan's arm where he'd been bitten by the vampire shark. "Does it hurt?"

"Yeah, but it's not that deep." He brushed his fingertips along the side of Skylar's face. "Are you okay? Did Dean hurt you?"

"No. Not physically anyway," Skylar said. "He lied to me and told me terrible things about you. He lied to me about everything. If I had any idea what he did to you or Torrey and

Cruz, I would've killed him long before tonight. I hope you know that."

"I do," Tristan said.

"Can we sit and talk for a minute?" Skylar asked. "I promise it'll be quick."

Tristan hesitated. He wanted to find Leilani and reassure her that he was still the same man she fell in love with—even if he wasn't exactly human.

"Please? So much has happened, and we haven't really talked since that night we had that terrible fight," she said.

Tristan sat in the sand. Skylar settled next to him.

"First, I want to apologize," she said. "You were right. I should've told Jake that Rick was my boyfriend and that he killed Cody by mistake. I'm sorry I didn't listen to you and that I caused Jake so much pain."

"Thanks for that, but have you said that to Jake?" Tristan asked.

"Yeah, sort of. There's something else. It's not easy, but as your best friend, I need to say this. Tristan, I know you love Leilani. I do. I just don't want to see you get hurt. Part of loving someone is accepting who they are. If Leilani can't accept you and love you—all of you, including what she saw here tonight—then she isn't the right woman for you."

"Skylar, don't start," Tristan said wearily. "I just got her back."

"I'm not starting anything. I swear. I'm saying this as your oldest and closest friend. I'm only looking out for you," Skylar said.

"I appreciate that, but Leilani can make her own choices. Either she'll want to be with me or … she won't."

Skylar yielded, not wanting to push too hard or too fast. "You're right. Just know I'll always be here for you, no matter what."

"Thanks. That means a lot. I'm glad we're still friends," Tristan said.

"Me too," she smiled.

"So, what happened after you killed Dean? Were there more of his friends out there?" he asked.

"I don't know. Leilani got caught in a riptide, so I had to help her get back to shore. She would've drowned if no one found her."

"You saved her?" Tristan asked.

"Don't act so surprised, dude. You love her, and I'd do anything for you. So, of course, I saved her. But, Tristan, you have to ask yourself, would Leilani do the same? Would she do anything for you? *Anything?* The way she bolted tonight when things got rough? That worries me, and it should worry you. The life we lead isn't easy. Is she really ready to be a part of it?" Skylar asked.

Tristan sat in silence.

"Okay. I've said enough. Just think about," she said. "You deserve someone who loves you, Tristan—all of you."

# 99 — Doubt

Jake found Leilani a quarter-mile down the beach, sitting with her head buried in her hands. "Are you okay?" he asked.

"No. I am most definitely not okay," she replied shakily. "Do you remember that night in your kitchen, right after I found out what Tristan was? The same night you found out how Cody died and that you were part graysuit?"

"Yeah, I remember," Jake said. "That night sucked."

"Yeah, it did, and I feel like I'm right back there again. I don't know what planet I'm on. Everyone here tonight? Everyone around me? They look human, but they're not. Tristan's wife is back from the dead. Nothing makes sense anymore. I feel like I'm this close," she pinched her thumb an eighth of an inch away from her forefinger, "to losing my mind."

Jake draped his arm across Leilani's shoulders. "I know everything seems crazy right now. While I may be one of the people around you who's not entirely human, I still care about you just as much as I did when I was human. Even more actually."

"I'm not talking about you. Even though you're a graysuit, you're still Jake. But Tristan? Seeing him bite her neck like that? His *fangs* covered in blood? I don't think I can ever get used to that," Leilani said.

"I know it looks pretty gross. I think it's just the shock of seeing him do it for the first time, you know? It's like when Tristan took me out surfing and realized I was part graysuit— right before he told me what really happened to Cody. He asked me to picture my feet as a fin. I thought he was crazy, but I did it. Then I looked down at my feet, and they weren't there. Instead, I had a fin. I swear, Leilani, I nearly lost it. I freaked out. And that's nothing like what you saw tonight. I know it probably doesn't make you feel any better, but it didn't look like Tristan wanted to do it. I think he only did it because that guy said it would save her life."

Leilani wiped her nose with her hand and noticed there was nothing on her ring finger. "My engagement ring! It's gone!"

Jake stared at her hand extended in front of him. "Did you wear it tonight when we left for the beach?"

"Yes! I haven't taken it off since Tristan put it on my finger. Even when I was in the hospital, I refused to take it off," she said.

"Do you think it could've fallen off in the ocean?" he asked.

"I don't know. If it did, it's gone forever. What am I going to do?"

"About the ring or Tristan?" he asked.

"Tristan," she said.

"That all depends. Do you still love him?"

# 100 — Changing

Cody swam up to the beach. He poked his head out of the water. He didn't see Jake anywhere, so he shifted into his human body. He retrieved his clothes and set out in search of Finn and Julianna.

He found Finn holding Julianna in his arms. They were both covered in blood.

"Are you hurt?" Cody asked Finn.

"No," Finn said.

"Is Julianna gonna make it?"

"I don't know. The bleeding has stopped, so that's good." Finn swept Julianna's hair aside to reveal two puncture wounds on her neck. "I asked Tristan to turn her."

Cody's jaw dropped. "What?! But you hate graysuits."

"It's the only way to save her," Finn explained. "I know Julianna. Even as a graysuit, she would never be a killer."

# 101 – Shades

Tristan stood behind Jake and Leilani, motionless.

"Now that you understand what he really is," Jake continued, "do you still love him?"

As Tristan watched them, he thought about how different things would be if they had never become involved with him and Skylar. *Their lives would be so much easier. Leilani wouldn't have nearly died. She and Jake would be safe at home, away from all this.*

Tristan stole another glance at Leilani. *Maybe Skylar's right but not for the reasons she thinks. Maybe it's not that Leilani needs to accept me for what I am. Maybe I need to accept her for what she is. She's human. I can't get her mixed up in this any more than she already is. She and Jake should go home, back to their normal lives. Jake may be a graysuit, but he doesn't have to be a Nomad. Torrey and Cruz died because of what I asked them to do. I won't risk Jake's life or Leilani's life again.*

Leilani lifted her head from Jake's shoulder. "Yes. I still love him."

Jake swallowed hard. He wasn't surprised by her answer, but that didn't make it hurt any less. *Suck it up, man. Put your feelings aside, and do the right thing for Leilani.* "Then you should find him and tell him that."

Leilani stood, turned toward the dunes, and found herself face-to-face with Tristan.

"I love you too!" Tristan said. As he lifted Leilani into his arms, Jake quietly walked away.

Seeing Jake leave, Leilani pulled away from Tristan. She ran to Jake and hugged him. "Thank you. For everything."

When Leilani released Jake, Tristan grasped his hand and pulled him into an embrace. "Thank you for keeping her safe.

I knew you would."

"We kept each other safe," Jake said, embarrassed by the attention. "So, what happened to you? I looked everywhere for you that night, but you weren't there."

"Long story." Tristan gazed longingly at Leilani. "Another time?"

"Yeah. I'll leave you guys alone." Jake turned and walked away.

Tristan placed his hands on Leilani's hips and pulled her close to him. "I missed you so much."

Leilani threw her arms over Tristan's shoulders. "Not as much as I missed you."

Tristan pressed his lips to hers. Instantly, he felt the warmth and familiarity of home. Gone were the loneliness and worry he felt during the time he was away. He kissed her softly at first and then more deeply. When his tongue touched hers, he lost himself in her.

Leilani eagerly returned his kisses, feeling so incredibly grateful to have him here, alive. She felt a tingly rush of warmth spread across her body as she pressed against him.

Breathlessly, Tristan whispered, "We should stop now, or in 30 seconds I'm going to peel that wetsuit off you and kiss every inch of your body, right here, right now. I don't care who else is around. You feel so good."

"Yeah," she said, "so do you. But it might get a little awkward with our friends here milling around the beach."

"Yeah, maybe just a little," he grinned.

As they pulled apart, Leilani slid her hands across Tristan's broad shoulders and down his muscular arms. Her fingertips grazed a ragged cut on his arm. "You're hurt."

"It's nothing. I'll be fine." Tristan grasped Leilani's arms and peered into her eyes. "I'm so sorry about what you saw back there with Julianna and Finn. I know it must've been a shock.

But now you know everything. You've seen me as a human, as a shark, and as a vampire—the three shades of Tristan. Can you live with that? Can you accept me for what I am?"

"I love you, Tristan. As crazy and unbelievable as life is with you, it's also more … real. Before I met you, I was going through the motions of life, but I wasn't really *living*. I was only half-awake. I have to admit I'd prefer not to see that whole vampire thing ever again—the blood and fangs and everything is pretty gross, especially for a vegetarian," she smiled. "But you promised me you'd never kill another human. Did you mean that when you said it?"

"I did. Graysuits are another matter as you saw in the ocean tonight. But, no, I haven't killed any humans—even bad ones— since I made that promise to you."

"Good." Leilani paused. She wasn't sure if it was the right time, but she had to know. "There's something else I have to ask you. That woman who you bit or turned or whatever … Is that Julianna, your wife?"

Tristan sighed to himself. *How in the world am I going to explain this?* "Yes."

"I thought she died."

"So did I," he said.

Leilani didn't want to, but she knew she had to say it. "Listen, I know how much you loved her. Now that she's back, if you and she …"

"No," Tristan interrupted. "There's a part of me that will always love her, but I'm not in love with her anymore. Our time together was special, but it's over. She's with Finn. I'm with you."

"But if you want to be with her, I'd understand," Leilani said.

"I don't want to be with anyone but you. I love you. You. Are. The. One." Tristan smiled and reached for Leilani's hand. "Your ring—you stopped wearing it?"

"No! I haven't taken it off since you placed it on my finger the night you were hurt."

"And *you* were hurt," Tristan said glumly.

"Yes, but I'm okay now. Really. I must've lost my ring when I got caught in the riptide," she said.

"The ring doesn't matter. It's you that matters. We can always get another ring ... if you still want to marry me."

"Yes, I want to marry you. How could you think I wouldn't?" Leilani touched Tristan's chest where he was staked. "That night we were attacked, when I was in the hospital and Jake came back without you ... I thought I lost you forever. I know you told Jake to come and make sure I was okay, but I wish you would've let him stay with you."

"No. I made Jake leave me because I needed him to check on you. And everything happens for a reason." Tristan explained what he knew about finners, how he was taken to Finn and Julianna's compound, and why he wasn't able to contact her or leave.

Leilani did her best to accept that yet another wild and crazy story—this time about dolphins—was now a part of the world around her. But she knew it had to be true based on her own experiences with the dolphins she encountered earlier that night.

"There's something else you should know," he said. "The finner who saved me in the ocean that night I got staked is the same one who helped me escape and find you. It's Jake's best friend, Cody."

# 102 – Found

Jake stumbled down the beach, feeling lost and utterly alone. *Every time I feel like I have someone, I get the rug pulled out from under me. I thought it was Cody and me against the world, but he died. I thought I'd found a place with Skylar, but she lied to me. Then I thought I'd found a place with Leilani, but now that Tristan is back, she'll want to be with him, not me.*

As Jake ambled along with his eyes cast down to the sand, he slammed into something. He looked up, dazed, and saw Cody. Jake scrunched his eyes closed and opened them again. Cody was still there. Both of them stood with their mouths agape.

"Finn, it's Jake," Cody whispered out of the side of his mouth. "What do I do?"

"It's too late now to do anything," Finn said. "Say hello to your friend, and let's hope he can keep a secret."

"Cody?" Jake asked, still not believing his eyes.

"Yeah, uh, hi, Jake," Cody said sheepishly.

"Wait a minute," Jake said. "I saw your body wash up. I went to the hospital. I talked to the doctor. He said you were dead."

"Yeah. About that …" Cody led Jake up a path through a notch in the sand dune. They climbed to the top of the dune and sat facing the ocean.

Cody told Jake what happened when Rick attacked him. He revealed how he became a finner and why he couldn't contact anyone from his old life—even his best friend. He then explained how he and Tristan left the compound to find him and Leilani. "Which brings us to tonight," he finished.

"So, you're part dolphin now? That's crazy, man," Jake said. "Hey, that was you at your paddle out, wasn't it? And here tonight when I was fighting that graysuit?"

Cody grinned. "Yeah, but let's not mention to Finn that I was at my own paddle out. Would *not* be good. Trust me."

Jake laughed. "Okay, but that was pretty righteous. Everyone was like, 'Cody's here!' when they saw the dolphin. I remember how much I wanted it to be true. And I guess it was."

"So, I know you're a graysuit," Cody said, "but I still don't get why. Did you get bit or did you, like, choose to be one?"

"A little of both," Jake chuckled. He explained about how Tristan accidentally nicked him when he was racing to save Cody from Rick. He then told Cody about how he asked Tristan to finish the job and turn him completely.

"Aren't graysuits killers?" Cody asked. "I know you, Jake, and you're not a killer."

"No, not all graysuits are killers."

"So, you've never attacked anyone?"

"No," Jake said. "I might be a graysuit, but I'm not a murderer. I've only killed Rogues like the ones you saw tonight—the ones who kill people. I'd never attack a human."

"I know," Cody smiled. "I just wanted to hear you say it."

# 103 – All Apologies

Cody and Jake heard someone cough and gasp below them. They sprinted down the dune to Finn.

Finn noticed Julianna's wounds were slowly but noticeably healing. "Julianna? Baby, are you awake?"

"Water," Julianna rasped.

"You want water?" Finn asked. Seeing Cody approach, he said, "Cody, go find Julianna some water!"

"No," she croaked. "Ocean."

"We need to get her into the ocean!" Jake clarified. "It'll help her heal."

Finn carried Julianna to the sea and waded in waist-high. Cody and Jake followed and watched from the sand. As soon as Julianna was deep enough, she ducked underwater and instantly transformed into a great white shark.

"Whoa! She sure took to that fast!" Jake said. Seeing the hard look on Finn's face, he quickly added, "Sorry," but wasn't sure why he was apologizing.

"Finn, this is a good thing," Cody said. "This is what you wanted."

"This *is* good," Jake said. "She'll heal quicker in her shark body—at least that's what Tristan said when he got hurt."

Jake heard his name being called. He looked down the beach and saw Skylar waving to him.

Cody nudged Jake. "Who's that?"

"My ex. And don't even think about it," Jake warned.

Cody grinned. "Nice, man. I always knew you had it in you. I guess a little shark blood in your veins finally gave you the confidence you needed."

Jake shook his head. He'd tell Cody about Skylar another time. He strode toward Skylar, who gave him a big hug.

"Can we talk?" she asked. "There's something I need to tell you."

They strolled south to a secluded spot away from Cody, Finn, and Julianna, and away from Tristan and Leilani, who were wrapped up in their own conversation at the north end of the beach.

Skylar sat and patted the sand, asking Jake to sit next to her. "I want to apologize again for the way I treated you when we were together," she said. "I was wrong about so many things."

"What's done is done," Jake said. "I've moved on. You've moved on. I don't need your apology."

"Maybe not. But if it's okay, I'd like to do this. I want to let you know that I finally get it. I get why you were so angry with me. At the time, I thought I was doing you a favor by not telling you that Rick killed Cody. I thought it was better to put all that pain you felt when Cody died in the past and move on. I didn't realize that not telling you would hurt you even worse. All this stuff with Dean—all the things he didn't tell me about what he and Logan did—made me realize that a lie of omission is still a lie. I was wrong for not telling you what I knew. Tristan begged me to. I thought he was trying to drive a wedge between us. He hasn't always been totally supportive of my boyfriends. But that's not what he was doing with you. He wanted me to tell you because it was the right thing to do. I'm sorry I lied and caused you so much pain."

Jake had never seen Skylar so humble or distraught. "Uh, thanks. I appreciate that."

"Do you think you can ever forgive me?" she asked.

"Yeah, I can forgive you. As it turns out, things didn't happen the way we thought. You see that guy in the ocean—the blond one? You're never gonna believe it, but that's Cody. By some miracle, he was saved by that other guy, Finn."

"I thought you saw his body wash up," Skylar said.

"I did. But through some kind of weird, secret dolphin reincarnation thing, Finn saved Cody's soul and put him in a dolphin's body."

"What?!"

"I don't fully understand it either, but he's alive," Jake said.

"So, Rick killed him, but he's not actually dead? He's here, and he's part dolphin? Huh. I guess that means we're not the only shapeshifters of the sea," Skylar said.

"Nope," Jake laughed. "I guess we're not that special after all."

Skylar giggled. "I've missed you, Jake. Do you think we can be friends?"

Jake looked around the beach. *Cody's alive. Tristan's alive. Leilani's happy and safe. Maybe I can cut Skylar some slack.* "We can be friends as long as we promise to never lie to each other. Deal?"

Skylar grasped Jake's hand and gave it a firm shake. "Deal! Thanks for being so cool. I'm going to get my board. I left it out there when Dean showed up with his friends."

"You want some company in case there are more graysuits out there?" Jake offered.

"No. I think we got them all. I'll be fine."

# 104 – Spencer

The two graysuits Leilani shot with tranquilizer darts awoke within a few minutes of each other.

The vampire shark who bit Julianna—the one who simply stumbled onto the scene in the middle of the attack by Dean and his friends—found his companion in the kelp forest. They decided the Monterey Bay wasn't as hospitable to graysuits as they'd heard. They bolted north without looking back.

Dean's friend, Spencer Delacourt—the first graysuit Leilani shot—awoke with a vicious headache. He shook the tranquilizer darts loose from his head and set out in search of Dean and his buddies. Instead, all he found were pieces of shark flesh.

From beyond the breaking waves, Spencer watched Skylar swim out to retrieve her board. He sighed to himself. *I knew Dean's plan wouldn't work. You don't go up against your creator unless you've got an army. And you don't go after his ex-girlfriend either. Five or even 10 graysuits aren't enough to battle a warrior like Tristan. If we want to do this and get rid of the Rules once and for all, we need to do it right.*

Spencer ducked underwater and headed west.

# 105 – Span

After Tristan finished telling Leilani about Cody, he asked, "Do you want to meet him?"

"Cody's here?" she asked.

"Maybe. He's been trying to avoid Jake. Finners aren't supposed to reveal to their loved ones that they're still alive. But I think after everything that's happened, an exception can be made. And Jake's not technically human, so it's probably okay," Tristan said.

"So, are finners named after that guy, Finn?" Leilani asked.

"No. It's just a coincidence," Tristan explained. "His name is Luke Finnegan. He goes by Finn for short. It was his and Julianna's mentor, Terrell, who stumbled onto the whole dolphin/human transmigration thing and named them finners. Dolphin-human, phin-man, fin-man, finner. Get it?"

"Kind of," she said. "I still have a lot of questions about how it all works."

"I'm sure you do. Let's go find Cody," Tristan said.

They strolled along the ocean until they spotted Jake and Cody standing together at the water's edge.

Tristan smiled. "I guess you guys have talked." He looked up the beach to where he had left Finn and Julianna, but they were gone. "Where's Julianna?" he asked, fearing the worst.

"She's here," Finn answered, rising from the ocean. He stroked the shark fin protruding from the water.

"Already?! I've never seen it happen so fast," Tristan said.

"Yeah, well, dolphins take to things pretty quickly, so it's no surprise she was able to change into a graysuit so fast," Finn said.

"Is she okay? Can she talk?" Tristan asked.

"Not really," Finn answered. "She's still recovering. That's why we're here in the ocean."

"Good. She'll heal faster here in the salt water," Tristan said. "What can we do to help?"

"Nothing," Finn sighed with relief. "I think we're through the worst of it. Thank you, Tristan, for saving her."

"Jake, would you like to introduce Leilani to your friend?" Tristan asked.

"Leilani, this is Cody. Cody, Leilani," Jake said.

Cody offered his hand to Leilani. "Great to meet you." *She's cute too,* Cody thought. *Damn! Jake's been busy while I've been gone!*

"Wow, I never thought I'd get the chance to introduce you to everyone. It's still hard to believe you're really here," Jake said, grinning at Cody.

"It's funny," Cody said. "I haven't been gone that long, but in that time, it's like you've lived this whole other life. You've got these new friends, and you're a graysuit!"

"Cody, do you mind if I ask you a question?" Leilani asked.

"Not at all. Shoot," Cody said.

"I'm still trying to understand the whole finner thing. If you guys can carry human souls to new dolphin bodies and save people, why couldn't you or Finn do that with Julianna?" she asked.

"Because it only works once. A human soul can only be transferred to a dolphin body one time. That means that the dolphin's lifespan, however long that is, becomes your lifespan. After that, your soul moves on somewhere else," Cody explained.

"Where?" Leilani asked.

"That, Leilani, is one of life's great mysteries," Cody said.

Jake's eyes darkened. "Cody, how old is your dolphin body?"

"About five years old," Cody replied.

"How long do dolphins live?" Jake asked.

"Bottlenose dolphins like me can live 40 or 50 years. Like humans, females live a little longer. They can live up to 50 years. Males about 40 to 45 years. Just another advantage women have over men," Cody said, grinning at Leilani.

Leilani smiled back. "So, that's why Finn couldn't help Julianna. I get it now."

Jake, however, couldn't smile. *In 40 years, I'll lose my best friend again*, he thought. *It's 40 more years than I thought I'd get. But compared to my lifespan of, like, 800 years, it's nothing.*

Cody sensed Jake's worry. "Listen, man, I know it's not graysuit years, but it's a few more decades than I would've had otherwise. Plus, since I was already 22 when I was killed, another 40 years puts me at around 62. That's not too bad for a human."

Skylar removed her bikini from her leash, slipped it on, and caught a wave into shore. She set her board in the sand, dried off, and dressed again. She walked along the beach in search of Dean's bag, which had the rental car key in it. She quickly spotted it, set it next to her own beach bag, and joined the group.

"Now that you're all here, what happened tonight? You guys went after Dean?" Tristan asked.

"Yeah, we thought it would just be him out here. We didn't think he'd bring friends," Skylar said.

"Why was Leilani out there all alone?" Tristan demanded.

Skylar hesitated to answer since it was her idea to use Leilani as bait.

Leilani shot a quick glance at Skylar, recalling how Skylar saved her from the riptide. *Maybe now I can return the favor and save her from having to explain herself to Tristan.*

"It was my idea," Leilani blurted out. "It was the only way to get Dean out here alone—at least we thought he'd be alone."

"What you guys did was incredibly dangerous, but I guess it's done. Dean's dead." Tristan turned to Skylar. "Do you know where Logan is?"

"Uh, yeah, I do," Jake said. "He's in a pile of ash at the bottom of the ocean. That night I went to look for you, I found Logan instead. After seeing what he did to Leilani, I couldn't let him walk away from that. So, I staked him."

"Whoa. Just like that?" Skylar asked, impressed.

Jake nodded.

Tristan sighed. "Normally I'd be pissed about you going after a graysuit all by yourself, but I know why you were in the ocean that night. You were looking for me. So … nice work, man! Your first righteous kill." He shot Jake a conspiratorial grin. "I guess that makes you an official Nomad now."

Jake smiled, proud that Tristan considered him part of his tribe.

Tristan's smile faded as he spoke again. "We know Dean and Logan are gone. But Dean's friends here tonight and the ones at his wedding? He's obviously convinced more than a few graysuits to turn against me, which means they're no longer following the Rules. Skylar, do you know how many were following him?"

"No. He kept all that hidden from me," she said. "I'm sorry."

"You have nothing to apologize for. Dean fooled me too. We'll just have to be vigilant and keep an eye out for trouble. Then I'll take care of it," Tristan said.

"*We'll* take care of it," Skylar said.

"No. I already lost Torrey and Cruz. I'm not going to risk your life," Tristan said. "This is my mess. I'll clean it up."

"Oh god, cut the crap, Tristan. I'm in this as much as you are," Skylar said. "I'm not going to abandon you."

"Me neither," Jake said.

"I want to help too," Cody said.

As the only non-supernatural creature, Leilani felt like the odd person out. "I don't think I'd be much help fighting vampire sharks. Being human, I'd probably be more of a liability than an asset in the ocean. But I can help you track them down."

"You are never a liability," Tristan said, "but I'm glad you'll be staying on dry land."

"Don't sell yourself short, Leilani," Cody said. "You were pretty good out there with a gun. The way you shot that shark that attacked Julianna? That was awesome!"

"That was you who helped me?" Leilani asked.

"Yep," Cody said.

"Oh no." Skylar turned to Jake. "I knew we shouldn't have used tranquilizer darts!"

"What tranquilizers?" Tristan asked.

"The gun Leilani had was a tranquilizer gun," Skylar explained. "That means the graysuits she shot aren't dead."

"How many did you shoot?" Jake asked.

"Two," Leilani said. "I shot one of Dean's friends when they first arrived, and I shot the one who attacked Julianna."

"Let's see if they're still out there. Skylar, Jake, you're with me. Cody, Leilani, we'll be right back." Tristan kissed Leilani, dropped his shorts in the sand, and dove into the ocean. Skylar and Jake followed.

They searched but couldn't find the two graysuits. They morphed into their human bodies so they could talk.

"Why was Leilani using a tranquilizer gun and not a real gun?" Tristan asked.

"We thought it would just be Dean. Leilani wanted to catch him, not kill him," Jake explained.

"Yeah, she didn't want to be a murderer—like us," Skylar said.

"That's not what Leilani said," Jake countered.

"No, but that's what she meant." Skylar glanced at Tristan to remind him of their earlier conversation. "I think there are some things about us she's not ready to accept."

Tristan decided to ignore Skylar and focus on rebuilding his relationship with Leilani—starting now. "It's been a long night. Let's get back to shore," he said.

# 107 – Rooms

Tristan, Skylar, and Jake found Cody and Leilani near where Finn and Julianna floated in the ocean.

"The Rogues are gone," Tristan announced.

"I'm sorry," Leilani said.

"It's not your fault. I'm just glad we're all safe. Everyone, what do you say we call it a night and get some rooms here at the resort? My treat." Tristan reached for his wallet and then remembered he didn't have it with him. "But I have no money or credit cards," he laughed.

"Don't worry. I can take care of it. I got that CD you told me about—the one with your accounts and stuff. Leilani and I have been using your, uh, funds to track Dean. I hope that's okay," Jake said.

"That's what it's there for," Tristan reassured him. "I told you, we're family. Why don't you get rooms for you and Cody, Skylar, me and Leilani, and Finn and Julianna in case they need it?"

"C'mon, Leilani, I'll help you get your things from Jake's room," Skylar offered.

Leilani blushed and shot an embarrassed look at Tristan. "Yeah, Jake and I …"

"No need to explain," Tristan said. "I asked Jake to keep you safe. I trust you and I trust him, so we're good. I want to talk with Finn for a minute. Go get settled. I'll be up soon."

Leilani, Jake, Cody, and Skylar climbed over the dune and walked up the brick path to the resort lobby. Jake arranged for the rooms while Cody chatted with Skylar and Leilani. Jake then handed them their room keys. They declined the golf carts the resort offered, preferring to walk instead.

When Skylar and Leilani left, Jake pulled Cody aside. "I

know you've been cooped up in that compound for a while, but those two are off limits."

"Dude, I know Leilani is with Tristan," Cody said. "But if Skylar's your ex …"

"Nah, man. Trust me. You do *not* want to get mixed up with her. Hot as hell? Yeah. But worst girlfriend ever," Jake said.

"I don't need a girlfriend," Cody grinned. "But a night with her? That could be just what the doctor ordered."

"Forget about it," Jake said. "Seriously. You'll thank me later. Just trust me on this."

# 108 – Here Today, Gone Tomorrow

While Skylar helped Leilani carry her bags to her new room, her thoughts turned to Tristan. *I know he'll tire of Leilani eventually. Even if it takes a while, she's human, which means she won't be around forever. Until she finally does leave, they say you can catch more flies with honey than vinegar, so I wonder if that works with sexy vampire sharks too. I guess there's only one way to find out. It's time for me to become super-sweet.*

Leilani opened the door to her room. She and Skylar set the bags on the floor.

"Leilani, can we talk?" Skylar asked.

"Sure. Let me get out of this wetsuit though. I'm freezing." Leilani pulled a pair of black yoga pants and a seafoam green t-shirt from her bag and went to the bathroom to change. "If you need to borrow anything of mine tonight, feel free," she called out from behind the bathroom door.

Skylar picked through Leilani's clothes, wrinkled her nose in disgust, and closed the bag.

Leilani returned and collapsed on the bed.

Skylar sat next to her. "First, I'd like to apologize. I was really mean to you before, and you didn't deserve it."

Leilani had no idea what to say. An apology from Skylar was the last thing she expected.

"The reason I was such a bitch to you is because I was jealous," Skylar admitted. "I could see Tristan liked you, but I thought you were like all the other women—here today, gone tomorrow. I didn't know Tristan was falling for you and that it was different from all the other times. I'm sorry I treated you so badly. I'd like to start over if you don't already hate me."

"I don't hate you. Yeah, I'd like to start over." While Leilani felt it would be easier to be friends than enemies, she couldn't imagine herself hanging out with Skylar—getting lattes, going out to lunch, surfing. *But*, she told herself, *stranger things have happened, right?*

"Whew! That's a relief." Skylar noticed the scars on Leilani's arms. "I still can't believe Dean and Logan did that to you. I'm sorry you had to go through that. It must've been terrifying."

"Yeah." Leilani had been working so hard to find Dean that she still hadn't processed everything that happened the night Dean and Logan tried to kill her.

"I've only been bitten once—by Tristan when he turned me—and that hurt so bad. I can't imagine what it must've felt like to have two vampires biting you—and more than once."

"As bad as the pain was, it was nothing next to watching them torture Torrey and Cruz. Dean staked Cruz—not through his heart but next to it—right in front of Torrey because Dean wanted her to see him suffer. Logan did the same thing to Torrey while Cruz watched." Leilani shuddered. "Then Dean staked Cruz again. That time he didn't miss. Torrey couldn't do anything but watch Cruz die. I will never get over seeing that—seeing the expression on her face as he turned to ash."

"Oh my god. I knew that what went down that night was brutal and that Torrey and Cruz died because of it, but I had no idea how sick and sadistic Dean and Logan really were. I'm sorry you had to witness that, Leilani. I still can't believe Torrey and Cruz are really gone. I miss them so much. I know you didn't get a chance to know them very well, but they were the perfect couple. If you and Tristan are anything like they were, you're going to be really happy together. Speaking of Tristan, he'll probably be back any minute. I should go. I'm sure you two would like to be alone to … catch up."

"Thank you. I'm glad we talked," Leilani said.

"Me too," Skylar smiled. "Good night."

# 109 – Gratitude

"How's Julianna doing?" Tristan asked.

"Good." Finn's eyes filled with joy. "I can't thank you enough for saving her. I don't know what I would've done if I lost her."

"I'm glad she's gonna be okay. I'm heading up to my room. Do you need anything before I go?" Tristan asked.

"No, we'll be fine. I'll morph so I can get some sleep and keep an eye on Julianna at the same time."

"Oh yeah, dolphins can do that too—sleep with one half of your brain while the other is awake," Tristan said.

"Vampire sharks can do that?" Finn asked.

"Yeah. That's one of the reasons we're such great predators and so rarely prey. If Julianna keeps improving and you want to sleep indoors, we got you a room at the resort."

"Thank you, Tristan, and not just for the room. You were there for us when we needed you—even after the way I treated you in the lab, like you weren't … human. I'm sorry."

"We can talk about it another time, when Julianna's better," Tristan said. "You probably already know this, but in the morning if Julianna wants to shift back into her human body, you'll need to get her inside before dawn."

Finn's eyes widened. "I can't believe I forgot about that! She's part vampire now. Right. Thank you."

"Okay then." Tristan began to walk away but turned back to Finn and smiled. "She really does love you, you know."

Finn gave Tristan a quick smile and morphed. Together, the dolphin and the great white shark drifted in the darkness.

# 110 – Together Again

Tristan opened the door to his room. He found Leilani pacing, waiting for him. He closed the door behind him and smiled. "Alone at last."

"At long last," Leilani grinned. "I still can't believe you're really here. It's like it's too good to be true."

"You're too good to be true." Tristan pulled Leilani into his arms and sighed. "I've been waiting so long to hold you like this again." He bent down and gave her a lusciously soft kiss. "I missed you so much."

"Me too."

"You mean everything to me," Tristan whispered as he gently lowered her onto the bed. "I love you, Leilani. Let me show you how much."

# 111 – Immortal

Skylar dumped Dean's bag in the rental car trunk. She drove over to her room at the resort, growing more and more upset thinking about Tristan and Leilani alone together. She unlocked the door, slammed it behind her, and flung her beach bag against the far wall. Leilani's engagement ring fell out and rolled across the floor.

She picked it up and examined it. *You've always had great taste, Tristan. Except when it comes to blonds.*

She slid the ring onto her finger. *One blond wife. Two blond wives. It doesn't matter. I know you'll find your way back to me. What we have is bigger than a stupid human lifetime. What we have is immortal. We belong together. You just haven't figured it out yet. But you will.*

# 112 – Power

Julianna awoke in the ocean. She swished her fins through the water. In her shark body, she felt stronger than she'd ever felt in her life—as a finner or a human. She quickly became aware of Finn next to her in the water. He was completely asleep—both brain hemispheres. *He must be exhausted*, Julianna thought.

Carefully, she eased away from him. She wanted to try out her new body. She knew what it felt like to swim as a human and a dolphin, but she wondered what it would feel like to be a great white shark. She turned and swam deeper into the Monterey Bay. She noticed that as she moved through the water, other creatures fled in abject terror. Her body felt larger and more cumbersome than a dolphin's but much more powerful. *I feel amazing. So strong. So indestructible.* She detected the heartbeat of a large seal. *So hungry.*

After devouring the seal and a few sand dabs, Julianna felt satisfied. She headed back to Finn. As she approached him, she tried to morph. *It has to be the same for a shark as it is for a dolphin. You think about being human and you are.* Instantly Julianna was human again. She looked down at her naked torso. The shark bites were still there but healing nicely. She touched Finn's cheek, just behind his bottlenose.

Finn opened his eyes and saw Julianna next to him. He wasn't sure if he was awake or dreaming.

"Finn?"

He morphed into his human body. "I must've fallen completely asleep." He looked at her and grinned. "You're almost healed!"

"Almost. And apparently I'm a graysuit," Julianna said.

"Uh, yeah, I can explain," Finn said. "You were dying. It was the only way to save you, so I asked Tristan to turn you."

"Tristan told you he's the creator?" she asked.

"I kind of forced him into it," Finn confessed.

Julianna frowned. "But Tristan promised me he wouldn't create any more graysuits."

"I know. He didn't want to, but I begged him. I didn't know what else to do. I wasn't ready to lose you," he said.

"Finn, no one's ever ready to lose the person they love."

"So, you're not happy?" he asked.

"No, it's not that," she said. "I'm blown away that you would ask to have me turned into a graysuit. If I ever doubted you loved me before—which I didn't, by the way—this would prove beyond a shadow of a doubt that you'd literally do anything for me. But how will you be able to stand being around me? Your nightmares are already bad enough. Now you're going to be around a graysuit 24/7."

"Because I love you," Finn said.

"Even as a graysuit?" Julianna asked.

"Even as a graysuit. Besides, you're still part finner. You'd never hurt anyone because that's not who you are."

Julianna recalled the seal she ate for breakfast. When she was a dolphin or a human and fed on animals like fish, it was just for sustenance. There was nothing more to it. As a vampire shark, when she captured and fed on the seal, it was different. It was ... thrilling. She still had a natural high from it. She quickly pushed the thought from her head.

Finn wrapped his arms around her. Instinctively, his head jerked away from her salty graysuit scent.

"What's wrong?" she asked.

"Nothing. Everything's fine." *This is going to take some getting used to,* he thought. *The scent I've associated for years with terror and death is now Julianna's scent. I wonder if I can get her to start wearing perfume until I can get used to this.*

Julianna nuzzled against Finn's neck. The smell of his

blood—thick, rich, and sweet—permeated her senses. She placed her lips on his neck and began to kiss him softly at first but then more roughly. She felt her fangs descend in her mouth. She ran her tongue over them. They felt smooth and sharp, sensual even.

"You want to do this here in the ocean?" Finn asked as Julianna kissed his neck. "Normally I'd say, what the hell? But it's going to be dawn soon. We need to get you indoors before the sun comes up."

Startled by the thought of the morning sun, Julianna immediately felt her fangs retract. She pulled away from Finn's neck. She felt dazed. *What just happened? His neck smelled so good. Good enough to eat.*

Puzzled by Julianna's expression, Finn asked, "Is something wrong? Is it the 'no sunlight' thing?"

"What? Yeah. Just getting used to all this. Things feel … different," she said.

"Good different or bad different?"

"I don't know yet. Just different," she replied.

"What about you and me?" he asked. "We're still the same, right? You still want to marry me?"

"Yeah."

Finn smiled. "Good. Let's get you inside."

# 113 – Meeting

Later that morning, Skylar woke up to someone knocking at her door. As she opened her eyes, the first thing she saw was Leilani's engagement ring on her finger. She quickly wrapped it in tissue and buried it in her purse. She opened the door.

"Hi. What happened to your face?" Jake pointed to the indentation in Skylar's cheek from where she'd slept on the large center stone of the ring.

Skylar rubbed her cheek. "Nothing. Slept funny. What's up?"

"Tristan wants a meeting with everyone. His room, 10 minutes," Jake said.

Skylar smiled. *Some things never change.* She strolled outside to check the surf. The morning fog felt as thick as gray wool. *No wonder vampire sharks love this area. No sun.*

On the path to Tristan's room, she met up with Jake and Cody. "Hey guys! Did you have fun catching up last night?"

"Yeah. What'd you do?" Jake asked.

"Nothing. Just slept. I have to go to Carmel today and get my stuff from the hotel. Until then, I'm stuck in the same clothes I wore yesterday," she said.

"You look beautiful," Cody said. "But I bet you look good in anything. You could probably wear Jake's sorry outfit here and look absolutely stunning."

Jake smiled and punched Cody's arm. "Don't be a dick this early in the morning. If you wanna talk about sad wardrobes, take a look in the mirror, dude."

"Graysuits," Cody teased. "They're so sensitive."

As they approached the open door to Tristan and Leilani's room, Tristan shouted, "Come on in!" He and Leilani were freshly showered and dressed. They looked happy. Too happy, in Skylar's opinion. And Jake's.

Finn and Julianna arrived a few minutes later. Everyone told Julianna how relieved they were to see her up and looking so well.

When they all settled in, Tristan began. "So, you're probably wondering why I called you all here. I've got an idea." He glanced around the room at all the expectant faces. "I'm sure Finn would be the first person to say we don't exactly see eye to eye on the whole graysuit thing, but I think we actually have the same goal. For years, Finn and Julianna have been working to find graysuits who kill humans. Skylar and I have been doing the same thing. Unfortunately, we've all paid a high price for the work we do. I know Finn and Julianna have lost people close to them. Sky and I recently lost our good friends Torrey and Cruz. And Julianna and Cody *were* killed, but fortunately they got a second chance at life.

"I haven't yet discussed this with any of you individually because I thought it would be better to discuss it together. We've all kept secrets from each other. But if we're going to do this, we need to be completely open from the start. Here's what I propose: I'd like for us all to work together from now on. I know it may sound crazy, but it's not if you think about it."

Tristan saw Finn cross his arms in front of his chest. He ignored it and continued. "Finn, Julianna, and their predecessor, Terrell, have been studying graysuits at a secret compound—a former military facility—on Catalina Island."

Finn shook his head. "Dude, seriously? Why don't you just broadcast our location to every vampire shark in the Pacific Ocean?"

"Finn, I trust everyone here with my life. You can too," Tristan said.

Julianna reached for Finn's hand so he'd uncross his arms and hopefully keep an open mind. She laced her fingers through his. Finn waved his other hand toward Tristan, telling him to continue.

"So, one of their goals was to find the creator of all graysuits, and they did. They found me. As some of you know, I created hundreds of graysuits from 1973 to 1975 when I was hanging out with Dean. That stopped after Julianna was killed," Tristan said. "Now I may turn one or two people a year and only for a good reason. Other than Julianna, Jake's the most recent, and I'm sure we can all agree we're lucky to have him."

Cody slapped Jake on the back. Jake grinned and caught Leilani's eye as she beamed at him.

"What that means is that the vampire shark population is declining and has been for decades," Tristan said, staring directly at Finn. "The sad fact is that we kill more graysuits than I turn in any given year. And that's not counting the graysuits Finn and Julianna have killed."

"How are they killing graysuits?" Skylar asked.

"They monitor shark attacks like we do," Tristan said. "But when they capture graysuits who kill humans, they don't kill them immediately. They study them first. But we all know what happens to great white sharks in captivity. They die."

"How do we know they haven't captured and killed any innocent graysuits? They held you captive, right? What makes you think we'll be safe with them?" Skylar asked.

Finn smirked. "You're worried about *your* safety?"

"Finn, it's a legitimate question. Skylar, the thing is, they didn't capture me. Cody brought me to them to save me. And Finn did save my life. He just wasn't exactly thrilled with the idea of me leaving before they completed their 'research,'" Tristan said, smirking back at Finn.

"Probably all of us here, except Leilani, are familiar with basic vampire shark physiology. We have venom pouches below our vampire fangs," Tristan continued. "This venom is what allows me to create new vampire sharks, and it's what allows any other vampire shark or regular vampire to create a new vampire—by biting a human's neck and releasing the venom into the carotid artery. If these venom pouches are removed, it's like when we can't find salt water. We age and die within a few days, a week at most. This venom is a life source for our vampire half, just like salt water is a life source for our shark half. In their research, Finn and Julianna removed the venom sacs from the graysuits they captured. After they studied the venom, they didn't put the sacs back. Since the graysuits they captured were killers, they didn't want to release them back into the wild, so they let them die."

"Unbelievable," Finn said. "Why don't you just give them the entrance codes to our facility? You're giving them everything else—where we work, what we do …"

"Because they deserve to know," Tristan interrupted. "Now I'm going to give you something, Finn. You obviously know how to kill vampire sharks in the ocean and in your lab. But do you know how to kill them when they're in human or vampire form?"

"A stake through the heart," Finn answered. "Like in the movies."

"That's right," Tristan said. "Wood works best because it muffles sound better than metal. When you stake a vampire, you need to do it before they realize what's happening or you're dead. It's a lot easier to hear human skin rubbing against metal. That's why wood is the better choice."

"Is there a specialty store that sells wooden stakes for killing vampires, or can I just order them online?" Finn asked. "What about discounts for bulk orders? Can I get them in different colors? That could be fun."

Tristan ignored him. "Anyway, what I propose is that we start working together to ensure no more innocent lives are lost—that means humans, finners, and *graysuits*," he said, staring point-blank at Finn. "The work Finn and Julianna have been doing to track graysuits who kill has been a help to us and to humans, and I'd like you guys to continue doing that. Skylar, Jake, and I will do the same, using our own methods. Leilani is an FBI agent, so she can help us as well. But now that you know I'm the creator, there's no reason to study vampire sharks anymore. I say we go after the killers and take them out immediately. They know the Rules, so they know when they kill children or other innocent humans that they forfeit their right to live. That's it. I've done enough talking. What do you all say?" Tristan asked.

Julianna spoke first. "I think what Tristan is proposing is a good idea."

"Of course you do," Finn muttered under his breath.

"Finn, stop. I'm the only one here—and probably on the planet—who has ever been a human, a finner, and now a graysuit. So, I have a unique perspective no one else does. I think if we value life, we value all life—including graysuits. Tristan, Skylar, and Jake have proven to us that not all graysuits are mindless killing machines. Do you have a problem with that, Finn? Before you answer, I suggest that you choose your words carefully since I'm now the species you're talking about catching and killing."

Finn sat for several seconds without saying a word. "No, Julianna, I don't have a problem with that. As much as I hate to say it, I actually agree with Tristan. Now that we know he's the one who created every graysuit in existence and that no one else has that ability, we don't need to continue our research. So, Tristan, why don't you enlighten us and tell us how you came to have this unique power?"

Finn's question took Tristan by surprise. He had never revealed to anyone how he acquired his ability. He worried that other vampires would go to the Farallons and feast on sharks contaminated with atomic waste, and then they would be able to create new vampire sharks. He believed it was too much power to trust to anyone else. *I guess this is one last secret I have to keep*, he thought. *It's too dangerous.*

"I wish I could tell you what makes my venom different, but I can't," Tristan said.

"C'mon, I find it hard to believe you have no idea how you got this power that makes you different from every other vampire on the planet," Finn argued.

"I don't know," Tristan said. "I spent a ton of time in the ocean when I was a human and after I was turned into a vampire. Maybe my vampire body reacted in a strange way to all the salt water. Or maybe there's something weird in my DNA. It doesn't matter. The point is, I'm the only one who can create new vampire sharks, and I'm not doing that anymore. Let's move on."

Finn wasn't sure he believed Tristan but decided to let the matter drop for the time being. "Okay, let's say we devote all our resources to tracking and capturing killer graysuits. I don't understand how we'd work together—our team and your team."

"We can work that out," Tristan said. "I think we just keep doing what we're doing and keep in regular contact. My team can let your team know if we suspect a graysuit has killed an innocent human, and your team can do the same. Whoever first discovers the attack can lead the investigation and coordinate between us."

"I can help with that," Cody offered. "If you want, I can join your team, Tristan. Then I can receive communications directly from Finn and Julianna or any of the other finners without having to rely on human technologies like cell phones or ham radios. We can just send each other pictures when we're in our dolphin bodies. Easy."

"But Cody, you haven't been trained to fight graysuits," Finn said.

"Then train me. I'm ready," Cody said.

"I can vouch for that. Cody helped me kill a graysuit last night," Jake said. "We did it together, before I even knew it was Cody."

"If that's what you want, Cody, we can give you a crash course in offensive—and defensive—maneuvers," Julianna said. "Remember, it's not always about fighting. Sometimes it's about fleeing. Then you can join Tristan's team whenever you want."

Cody grinned at Jake. And Skylar.

"That sounds like a great idea. We'd be lucky to have you, Cody," Tristan said. "So, we're all in agreement? We work together?"

Everyone in the room nodded.

"Leilani, I have a question for you," Skylar said. "With your professional experience I think you'd be a great asset to the Nomads, but does that mean you're going to keep your job and work with us in your spare time? Or would you quit your job, which would mean you'd lose access to all your FBI resources and stuff?"

Skylar masked her joy as she watched Leilani struggle to answer her question. *C'mon, Leilani. What's it gonna be? Nomad or not? I can't see Tristan with someone who has a day job. So, are you going to keep your job and make him break up with you sooner rather than later?*

"Uh, I dunno," Leilani stammered. "I haven't really had a chance to think about it seriously now that Tristan is back. Right now I'm in the middle of a 30-day leave of absence, but I don't know what I'm going to do when it's up. I guess I'll have to get back to you on that."

It felt strange to Leilani to feel so uncertain about her future. Since she was a teenager, she knew she was bound for a career in law enforcement. There was never a question in her mind.

But now she had no idea what her future might look like. She knew she wanted Tristan to be a part of her future, but she didn't yet know how life with him would actually work day-to-day.

Tristan leaned in close to Leilani and murmured, "Whatever you want to do, we'll make it work."

Skylar smiled sweetly. "Whatever you decide, it's really great to have you on our team."

Jake shot Leilani a quizzical look. She answered with a slight shrug and smile that said, *I don't fully understand Skylar's change of heart either, but let's enjoy it while it lasts.*

# 114 — Announcement

Finn whispered to Julianna, "Do you still want to do this?"

"Yeah. Don't you?" Julianna asked.

"J, I've been waiting years for this," he grinned. "You know my answer."

When Skylar and Leilani finished their exchange, Finn and Julianna stood.

"We have something we'd like to share with you all, but I need to say something to Tristan first," Finn said. "Tristan, I know you and I have had our differences, but I want to thank you again for saving Julianna's life last night. For that, I can never repay you."

Tristan shook his head. "No need. I'm just glad you're *both* happy about it."

"We are." Finn nudged Julianna. "Do you want to tell them what else we're happy about?"

"Finn and I are getting married," Julianna announced.

Leilani saw a shadow sweep across Tristan's face a millisecond before he smiled broadly. "Are you okay?" she whispered in his ear.

"Yeah, why wouldn't I be?" Tristan asked.

After all the hugging and handshaking were done, Finn spoke again. "There's something else. After everything we've been through in the past 24 hours, Julianna and I don't want to wait to start this new phase of our lives together. If it were up to me, we'd fly to Las Vegas and get married today. But we want to have our friends there, and I probably shouldn't take Julianna so far from the ocean. So, we'd like to invite you all to Catalina Island this weekend."

"The wedding will be Sunday at the Catalina Country Club—after sunset, of course," Julianna added. "A friend of ours owns a hotel within walking distance of the country club. You can all stay there for free. He said it's his wedding gift to us."

"Do you want to go?" Leilani quietly asked Tristan.

"Of course," he said. "Don't you?"

"I guess so," she replied.

"Let's go outside for a minute," Tristan said.

They slipped out the door and walked toward the sand dunes.

# 115 – Split Second

"Are you sure you're okay with this?" Leilani asked.

"Okay with what?" Tristan asked.

"With Julianna getting married again. You were married to her. It's not like you guys got divorced. She was taken from you. I know how hard that was for you because you told me about it on our first date. It has to be weird to find out she's alive and that she's marrying another man," Leilani said.

"And I'm marrying another woman. You. So, why are you upset?" Tristan asked.

"I saw the look on your face when she said they were getting married. You looked sad for a second," she said.

"You're too perceptive for your own good. I guess that's what I get for falling in love with an FBI agent."

"I'm serious, Tristan."

"I know. You're right. I was sad for a second—a split second. Then I remembered how happy Julianna is with Finn, and I know how happy I am with you. That look didn't mean anything. Julianna is a good person. She was a great wife, and I wasn't a very good husband. That's what that look was. I just want her to be happy and to have a husband who deserves her. Finn might not be my favorite person in the world, but I know he loves Julianna and that he'd do anything for her. And I think I know how to be a better husband now so I can make you happy," Tristan said.

"You do make me happy," Leilani said. "I still can't believe you're back here with me. I love you so much."

"I love you. So, when would you like our wedding bells to chime?" Tristan asked.

"Oh, uh, I don't know. Let's get through this weekend. Then I have to figure out what to do about my job. Maybe we could, um, take our time setting a date? The last four weeks have been crazy. I think I still need time to adjust to all this."

"Take as long as you need but not a minute more. I want to make you my wife as soon as you're ready. We can elope. We can have a big wedding or a small one with family and friends. It makes no difference as long as I end up with you."

"Family … Yeah … That's not something we'll need to worry about," Leilani said.

"What do you mean?" Tristan asked.

"While Jake and I were looking for Dean and Skylar in Oahu, I dropped in on my parents. It didn't go so well."

"Jake met your parents?" Tristan was unable to hide his disappointment that Jake got to do something he should've had the chance to do.

"Yeah, but you didn't miss anything. I swear! It was a disaster. They haven't changed. I ended up storming out and telling them to call me when they're ready for an adult relationship. Like that'll ever happen," Leilani grimaced.

"I'm sorry. I wish I could've met them though—and that I could've been there for you," Tristan said.

"Me too."

Tristan eyed Leilani's ring finger. "So, future wife, we need to do something about your engagement ring."

"You don't have to get me another ring. We're engaged. I don't need a ring to prove it."

"Maybe you don't, but I do," Tristan grinned. "What do you say we go shopping and pick out a new ring today?"

"Okay, but only if we can get one that looks exactly like the one you gave me," Leilani said.

"Then that's exactly what you'll have."

# 116 – Decisions

Tristan and Leilani strolled back inside and offered their congratulations to Finn and Julianna.

"You'll both be at the wedding, won't you?" Julianna asked.

"We wouldn't miss it. We're really happy for you," Tristan said.

"Yeah, well, I took your advice and here we are," Julianna said.

"Advice?" Leilani asked.

"Tristan is the one who convinced me to stop being so stubborn and to go ahead and marry Finn. He was right. It's made Finn so happy. Marriage is really important to Finn, and Tristan helped me realize that should make it important to me too," Julianna said.

"He really does love you, Julianna, completely—and you deserve nothing less," Tristan said. "So, we'll see you Sunday?"

"No, Saturday. We all decided while you and Leilani were outside. We can use the day to show everyone around the compound and figure out how we can work together." Julianna laughed at the surprised look on Tristan's face. "What? You're not the only one who gets to make decisions around here. Anyway, Finn and I will go home today and brief everyone on what's happened. It's going to be a lot for them to absorb—that we'll be working with graysuits and that I'm a graysuit."

"You don't think that'll be a problem, do you? I mean, you're still yourself," Tristan said.

"Yeah, but I don't know how they're going to react. They've only known vampire sharks to be ruthless killers. Now I, a graysuit, will be telling them something different. It'll be hard for them to believe at first. Some might refuse to believe it at all. I guess I'll see who my real friends are," Julianna said.

"Won't it make it worse to invite a bunch of graysuits to visit in two days?" Tristan asked.

"Maybe. But if they can accept me, then they can accept my friends," Julianna said. "Before you guys arrive, I'll train Cody on how to deal with killer vampire sharks. Since he's already been 'in the field,' we'll do a crash course. He should be ready to join you by the time you arrive. While I'm doing that, Finn and his friend at the country club will work on the wedding details. Then, after the ceremony, we'll leave for our honeymoon. Come to think of it, I don't think Finn and I have ever taken a real vacation together, so this will be good for us."

"Sounds like you've got it all figured out. We'll see you Saturday," Tristan said. "Good luck with your friends back at the compound."

Julianna grimaced. "Thanks. I'll need it."

Tristan gave her a wry smile. "Yeah, I know."

# 117 – Break

After Finn and Julianna left to catch a plane back to Southern California, Skylar sauntered up to Tristan and Leilani. "Looks like we're all going to Catalina," she said.

"Looks that way," Leilani said.

"What are you guys doing now? Do you want to go wine tasting? The Chardonnays and Pinot Noirs here are amazing! If we leave right now, we can be in the Santa Lucia Highlands in less than 30 minutes," Skylar said. "Or we can grab a beer at English Ales or The Otter's Den here in Marina …"

"No. We've got an errand to run." Tristan clasped Leilani's hand and rubbed his thumb over her ring finger. "Yesterday was a long day. Why don't you take some time for yourself and relax? We can meet up again in Avalon."

"Sure." Skylar smiled to mask her disappointment that Tristan didn't want to spend time with her after not seeing her for so long.

Jake walked up. "Sorry to interrupt. Leilani, do you mind if I talk to you before you go?"

"No." Leilani kissed Tristan. "I'll be right back, and then we can go shopping." She followed Jake to his room.

After they left, Tristan and Skylar stood in awkward silence. Skylar smiled seductively. "Alone again at last."

Tristan scowled. "Skylar …"

"I'm joking!" she said. "Loosen up. Besides, that Cody is pretty cute."

Tristan rubbed his eyes. "Jake's best friend? Really?"

"Kidding! What'd they do to you in that lab? Remove your sense of humor? Actually, you'll be happy to know I'm taking a break from men for a while," Skylar said. "Other than Jake, I can see now that I haven't been the greatest judge of character.

And I can't ignore the fact that three of the last four guys I dated are dead. That doesn't exactly bode well for the next guy. I need to figure out what I want so I can be ready when the right guy does come along."

"Sky," Tristan said, "that sounds like the best idea you've had in a long time."

# 118 – Being There

"What's up?" Leilani asked as Jake closed the door behind them.

"I wanted to tell you I'm really happy Tristan is back," he said.

Leilani gulped as she recalled their conversation on the beach the night before, when Jake confessed he loved her. "Jake, I …"

"You don't have to say anything. I know you love him, he loves you, and you guys will be getting married soon. I'm good with that." Jake noted the doubtful look on Leilani's face. "I am! I swear. I'm really happy Tristan is alive. And to have Cody back? I feel so lucky right now. I just wanted to see if …"

"What? You know I'd do anything for you," Leilani said.

"Yeah, so, I wanted to see if you could maybe not mention to Tristan what I told you last night? He asked me to take care of you, and what do I do? I tell you I love you. That's not exactly being a great friend," Jake said.

"I'm sure he wouldn't …"

"No, I'm sure he'd be cool about it. He's cool about everything. But it's kind of embarrassing for me. It was hard enough to tell you, and I'm glad I did. But I couldn't stand for anyone else to hear it. I don't want to be some loser who everyone feels sorry for."

"You're not some loser," Leilani said. "You're one of the best guys I've ever known. But if it's what you want, I won't mention it to Tristan."

Jake exhaled, relieved. "Thank you."

"And I have no doubt you'll find some amazing woman who will feel incredibly lucky to be with you, and I'll probably be a little jealous of her."

He smiled. "Jealous, huh?"

"Yep. I'll be the new Skylar," Leilani grinned.

"Speaking of Skylar, what's up with her? She's like a new person," Jake said.

"I know, right? She said she wanted to start over with me. Who knows? Maybe she does. Maybe she's finally over Tristan."

Jake glanced outside and saw Skylar talking with Cody. "Uh-oh. Skylar may have turned over a new leaf, but that doesn't mean I want her hitting on my best friend. Her boyfriends seem to have an unusually high mortality rate. I've gotta go."

"Wait. Before you leave, I want to thank you for being there for me. I don't know what I would've done without you," Leilani said.

"I was just returning the favor. You have Tristan back. I have Cody. All is right with the world." He glanced at Skylar and Cody again. "Almost. See you in Catalina."

# 119 – Unloading

Jake and Cody left Skylar and drove to the airport in Monterey. Jake parked next to the curb outside the doors to the small terminal.

"I'll see you in a couple of days," Cody said. "By then, I'll be some bad-ass graysuit killer. You better watch yourself, dude."

"You watch yourself. I've already taken out three graysuits. A finner would be no problem," Jake teased.

"It's really good to see you, man. I'm sorry I couldn't let you know I was alive until last night—Finn and Julianna's rule," Cody said.

"Yeah, Tristan has his own set of 'Rules.' Whether you're human or supernatural, there's always someone telling you what to do, right?"

"I guess so. But when that someone looks like Julianna, I don't mind a bit," Cody grinned.

"Dude, she's about to be married," Jake reminded Cody.

"Yeah, well, what about Leilani? I see the way you look at her," Cody said.

"What?"

"Don't even try to deny it," Cody said. "You can't hide that shit from me. I know you better than anyone else—probably even better than you know yourself."

An airport security guard tapped on the window with his knuckles. "You can't park here. Loading and unloading of passengers only, so unload your passenger."

Jake and Cody nodded at him.

"Guess that's my cue to leave," Cody said. "Later."

# 120 — Words

Tristan and Leilani headed to a jewelry store in Carmel. The shop, which was owned by a graysuit Tristan knew, was tucked into a flower-adorned courtyard, half a block south of bustling Ocean Avenue.

Tristan drew the ring on a piece of paper and indicated the center stone should be a dark blue sapphire surrounded by diamonds, and the band should be encircled in diamonds as well. "Make sure they're conflict-free diamonds. I'd also like to place a rush on this—whatever it costs to move me to the front of the line, okay? The sooner I get this ring on her finger, the better. I don't want her changing her mind," Tristan joked.

Leilani shook her head and grinned at Tristan and the jeweler. When they finished, they strolled outside into the mist that blanketed the city like a soft gray cashmere sweater.

"What now?" Tristan asked.

"We don't have to be in Catalina for two days. What do you say we find a cute little hotel by the ocean and seal ourselves away from the world? Just you and me."

"I like the way you think, Miss Waters. Or should I say, the future Mrs. Pierce?"

Leilani smiled mischievously and pulled a California driver license from her wallet. "Actually, I'm one step ahead of you." She handed it to Tristan.

He stared at the picture and the name beside it. "How did you …"

"Jake did it. After you … well, when you didn't come back, Jake had these IDs made for us so we could track Dean and Skylar without using our real names. He did this as a tribute to you. He took your name too. He said you were like a brother to him. It says Jake Pierce on his ID."

"Wow. I had no idea." Tristan eyed the license again. "Leilani Pierce. I think those might be the two most beautiful words I've ever heard."

"How about these two?" Leilani asked. "Bed. Now."

"Ooh, those sound pretty good too."

# 121 – Checking Out

Skylar returned to her hotel and gathered up her things. She hastily threw Dean's belongings in his bag. She planned to drop off his stuff at the first charity or thrift shop she could find.

She checked out of the hotel and drove up and down the quaint streets of Carmel-by-the-Sea, pondering how to spend the next two days until she met Tristan in Catalina. As she approached Ocean Avenue, she spotted Tristan and Leilani departing a jewelry store, walking hand in hand and laughing.

*Go ahead, Leilani,* she thought. *Get another engagement ring. Get a wedding ring. It doesn't matter because he'll come back to me eventually. He always does.*

# 122 – Facts

When Julianna and Finn arrived back in Catalina, they decided it would be best if she went straight to their apartment.

Finn stopped by lab #2 to check on Matt, who stepped out of the saltwater pool as he entered. "You're looking well!" Finn said.

"Thanks. I'm feeling much better," Matt said. "Where's J? I'd like to thank her for all she did to nurse me back to health."

"She's home. We've had a rough 24 hours. We want to get everyone together after dinner and talk about it," Finn said.

"I'll be there," Matt said. "I was actually about to head to my apartment. As nice as this lab is, it's not nearly as comfortable as home."

Several hours later, all 12 members of the research team assembled in the compound's conference room. The team included the finners who lived at the facility—Cody, Matt, Lucia, Jamal, and Emma—as well as those who lived off-site in Avalon and Two Harbors.

Cody sat next to Matt near the head of the table. Other than Finn, Julianna was closest to Matt. She worried he'd take the news about her transformation particularly hard. If he did, she wanted Cody nearby to calm him—or chase after him if he bolted.

Finn and Julianna took their places at the head of the table, facing their friends and coworkers. The room immediately quieted down.

"Whew, Julianna, you must've kicked some serious graysuit ass!" Matt exclaimed. "I can smell it all over you."

Finn exchanged a nervous glance with Julianna and dove right in. "We have a lot to cover tonight, so let's get started. The first thing we want to tell you is, in my humble opinion, the best thing and something I've been wanting to say for a very long time. Julianna and I are getting married!"

Their friends burst into applause and shouted congratulatory cheers.

"Since I've already waited so long to marry this woman, we're definitely rushing the engagement—and no, she's not pregnant," Finn joked. "The wedding is this Sunday at 6:30 p.m. at the Catalina Country Club. They had a last-minute cancellation so slipped us in. You're all invited. It'll be informal, so there's no need to RSVP or bring a gift. Just show up."

"Wouldn't miss it for the world!" Matt exclaimed.

"Thanks, guys. It would mean a lot to have you all there," Julianna said. "Now this next bit of news is much more serious and pretty shocking. We have a lot to share, and it's important we get through all of it."

Their friends nodded.

"Yesterday Finn and I reached a major milestone in our research," Julianna said. "We learned who the creator of all graysuits is. We also learned that the vampire shark population has been declining for years."

Cheers erupted from around the table.

"This decline is thanks to the work of *everyone* here. And surprisingly," she added, "it's also thanks to the efforts of this graysuit creator and his friends."

A hush fell over the room.

"I know. Finn and I were as stunned as you are. We learned that this graysuit, the creator of all vampire sharks in existence, lost someone he once loved to a graysuit. Because of that, he established graysuit laws to ensure no one ever had to suffer that fate again. These 'Rules,' as he calls them, forbid vampire sharks from killing innocent humans. When this graysuit and his team suspect a graysuit is killing, they investigate and if they find it's true, they kill the graysuit."

Julianna ignored the whispers around the table and continued. "Between their efforts and our efforts, their numbers are declining. What this means is that one of our hypotheses has been wrong all these years. It turns out that not all graysuits are murderers. Many have never harmed a human." She paused. She knew this would cause a commotion, and it did. She waited a few moments before moving forward.

"What about all the killings?" Jamal asked. "Are we really supposed to believe that only some graysuits are killers when so many people are dying?"

"Yes, some graysuits are murderers. We know that because we've all seen it. But not all of them are. As with humans or dolphins, we can't judge an entire species by the actions of a few." Julianna saw the finners around the table crossing their arms, shaking their heads, and whispering to their friends.

"Hey, everyone, Julianna and I know all of this because we saw it last night with our own eyes. We watched graysuits kill other graysuits to protect a human and to protect us." Finn glanced around the room to make sure he'd recaptured their attention. "You all know from working with us that Julianna and I are the biggest skeptics of all when it comes to vampire sharks. Julianna's human body was killed by a vampire shark! And I was there when Terrell was killed. But what we're telling you is the truth."

"Who's the creator?" Matt asked. "Was he here in one of our labs?"

Finn whispered in Julianna's ear, "It's up to you, baby. Whatever you want to tell them."

"Yes, Matt. Tristan, the graysuit we had in lab #1, is the creator. And here's the trippy part … I actually knew Tristan when I was human. He was my husband."

A collective gasp echoed around the room.

"I didn't know that he was a graysuit or that he was creating graysuits when we were together. We'd been married only a few weeks when I was attacked. As it turns out, it was my death that caused him to realize what he'd done. He thought he was giving surfers the chance to surf for lifetimes and enjoy the ocean in a whole new way. When I was attacked, he was the one who found me. It was the shock of that—of seeing how I'd been bitten and cast aside to die—that led him to create the Rules. He's been patrolling the ocean ever since and killing rogue graysuits who murder people." Julianna tried to make eye contact with every person in the room. "You have to know this was as shocking for me to learn as it is for you. I was in the middle of it all when this started, and I had no idea."

"How could you not know you were married to a graysuit?" Lucia asked.

"Because no one knew anything about graysuits back then," Finn answered. "It wasn't until the late 1970s, years after Julianna was killed and became a finner, that Terrell even discovered the existence of the species. Back then, everyone thought they were random attacks by great white sharks. Now that we know about graysuits and about the creator, this can work to our advantage."

"How?" Matt demanded. "How can we trust them? How can you?"

"Because if we work together—finners and graysuits—we can be even more effective at finding and disposing of the ones who do kill," Finn replied. "Graysuits are apex predators. They're one of the most effective hunters on the planet. Don't you see? We can use graysuits to prey on graysuits who are murderers."

Finn assessed the doubtful expressions around the table. "Is there anyone here who doubts my commitment to our cause? Or Julianna's? You know us. We're not easily swayed. We're scientists. We work on evidence. Not faith. Not trust.

We live by cold, hard facts. What we're telling you is a fact. Despite what we've believed for decades, not every graysuit is a murderer. Some are even putting their own lives at risk to protect humans—people they've never even met. We hope you'll join us and see for yourselves. We've invited Tristan and his colleagues, Skylar and Jake, here this weekend so we can figure out how to work together."

"You invited graysuits here? To our home? None of us will be safe!" Matt argued.

"Matt, it's okay," Julianna said calmly. "Tristan already knows where we are because he was here, remember? Yes, Tristan, Skylar, and Jake are all graysuits, but they work to protect humans like we do. There's something else you should know. Cody has known Jake for years. He's his best friend. Jake became a graysuit after Cody died and became a finner. When Cody was attacked, it was Tristan who tried to stop it, and it was Tristan who killed the graysuit who did it."

"Yeah, but Tristan also created the graysuit who killed Cody and Terrell *and you* and everyone else!" Matt countered.

"Yes, but he had no way of knowing that any of those graysuits would go rogue and kill. Matt, even with dolphins and porpoises, we have rogues who take pleasure in hurting and killing their own kind and other living creatures," Julianna explained. "Don't you see? It doesn't matter what species you are. Dolphin, graysuit, human—in every species, there are good creatures and bad creatures. We can't judge an entire species by the actions of a few."

Finn jumped in. "There will also be a human joining us, Leilani Waters. Leilani is an FBI agent, and she's also Tristan's fiancée. If she, Cody, Julianna, and I can trust Tristan and his friends, we all can."

"What if we don't want to?" Matt asked.

"You don't have to," Finn answered. "We hope you'll stay

with us, but anyone who isn't comfortable with this is free to leave. We know this is a big change, and the truth is, there are going to be more changes. For starters, because of what we've learned, we're discontinuing our research on graysuits. Now that we know who the creator is, we have no need for further study. That means we can now devote all our resources to tracking and killing the graysuits we know are murderers. With Tristan and his team helping us, we might be able to finally stop the killing."

"I'm sorry, Finn, Julianna, but I can't believe any of this," Matt said. "You want us to trust vampire sharks?"

"Do you trust me?" Finn asked.

"Yes, but …"

"And do you trust Julianna?"

Matt sighed. "Yeah, but …"

"Then there's nothing left to talk about," Finn said. "We found the creator, and he's going to help us. He already has."

"We know this is a lot to take in," Julianna added, "but we wouldn't be doing any of this if we didn't think we could save a lot more lives this way."

Finn and Julianna watched their friends shake their heads in disbelief and mutter to each other. He touched her arm and whispered, "Do you still want to do the rest? I'm worried."

"Yeah," she murmured. "I don't want there to be any secrets or doubts later. We need to tell them everything."

Finn nodded and mouthed, "I love you." He then addressed their friends again. "Everyone, can I have your attention for just a few more minutes? Then you can go home and figure out what you want to do. Please."

Finn waited for the room to quiet down. "Last night, while Tristan and his friends were fighting and killing graysuits, Julianna was attacked and critically injured. We got her to the beach but … she was dying … right there … in my arms …" He paused for a moment to quickly wipe the tears from his eyes. "I asked Tristan to save her. The only way to do that was to turn her into a graysuit."

Another gasp rumbled across the room.

"A graysuit?" Matt choked back a cry of despair. "J, no."

"Yes, Matt. It's …"

Matt dashed from the room before Julianna could finish. She nodded to Cody, who chased after him.

"… true," she continued. "I know all of this is a big shock. Everything you've heard tonight is the complete opposite of what we've been saying and doing for years. But when we learn new facts, we adapt. These are the facts. We hope you'll stay and do the important work we're meant to do, but we understand if you prefer to move on."

"Why don't you all take some time, and we can meet here again tomorrow?" Finn offered. "We'll take your questions then."

# 123 – Temptation

Half of the finners left the room, avoiding eye contact with Julianna and Finn. The others, including Jamal and Lucia, approached one by one to congratulate them on their engagement and express how happy they were that Julianna survived. They said they didn't care what happened or how; they were simply glad to see her alive.

However, as each finner embraced Julianna, she began to feel more and more uncomfortable. Each person who wrapped his or her arms around her smelled better than the last. By the final embrace, Julianna felt fiercely hungry and desperately out of control.

"I'm sorry. I have to go," she called to Finn as she fled the room.

Finn apologized to their friends and took off after her. He found her in their apartment, huddled over the kitchen sink. "Why did you rush out?"

Julianna guiltily looked up at him. Blood ringed her mouth.

"Oh my god! Are you hurt?" he asked.

Julianna shook her head.

"Why are you bleeding then?" Finn asked.

She pointed to the empty package in the sink. "It's not my blood."

He pieced together the paper label that had been torn in half when she ripped open the packaging that surrounded the 10-ounce steak. "You ate this raw?"

Julianna nodded. She reached for a hand towel and wiped the blood from her mouth and hands. "All those people coming up to me afterward …"

"I know it was stressful."

"I didn't leave because I was stressed," she said. "I left

because I had to. I could smell their blood. It smelled so … good."

Finn's face twisted in disgust. "What?!"

"I came home because it was getting harder and harder not to satisfy the urge to …"

"No, Julianna. You might be a graysuit, but you're *not* a vampire. You're a finner! Find that part of you."

"I don't know how. And I don't know how Tristan, Skylar, and Jake do it. How do they resist? How does Tristan keep himself from hurting Leilani every time they're together?"

"Do you want to hurt me?" Finn asked, aghast.

"No, Finn. I don't *want* to hurt you, but I don't want to lie to you either," she said. "You smell really good. Now that I'm part vampire, my sense of smell and taste and everything else is off the charts."

"Maybe we should call Tristan," he said.

"No. Tristan was never this way with me," she said. "I never felt scared of him or like he wanted to rip open my throat and drink my blood."

Finn gulped. "Maybe not, but I'm sure he's dealt with this before."

"No. He and Leilani need some time alone. He'll be here in less than two days. We'll ask him then," Julianna said.

"What do we do until then?"

"I'll train Cody like we planned."

"Will he be safe?" Finn asked.

"I think so. I just won't get too close to him. If I don't feel right, I'll come straight home," she promised.

"What about our wedding?"

"What do you mean? You don't want to marry me now?"

"Yes, of course, I still want to marry you," he said. "But I don't want you to spend our entire wedding fighting the urge to bite me and everyone else."

"I won't. I just need to get used to this. And you're right," she said. "I'm sure Tristan can help. Until he gets here, I'll just limit my contact with everyone."

"What about me?" he asked.

"I'm not a monster, Finn. I love you. I think I can keep myself from hurting you."

"You think?"

"I know." Julianna smiled at him. "Well, I'm pretty sure."

"Then I guess we live dangerously until Tristan arrives. But if things start to feel out of control, let me know."

"If worse comes to worst, you can put me on lockdown in one of the labs," she said, only half-joking.

"That's not even remotely funny," he said.

"Maybe not, but it's an option if we need it," she said. "Hey, you know what might help? Cologne. If you put enough on, maybe it'll mask the scent of your blood—which, I must say, is the most delicious thing I've ever smelled."

"Really?"

"Yes. You are more tempting than any dessert has ever been in the history of humankind."

"Alrighty then. Since you find me so appealing, let's play it safe. There will be no more intimate contact until after you talk with Tristan. We'll save it for our wedding night." Finn waved his hand across his groin and his neck, "This and this are off limits until you're my wife—and you know you can control yourself."

Julianna smiled seductively and bit her bottom lip. "Now I'm looking forward to our wedding even more."

"You are so sexy, even as a graysuit," Finn sighed. "I'm going to take a cold shower and douse myself in cologne."

"You want company?" she asked.

"No!"

# 124 – Training

The next day, Cody and Julianna swam to a deserted part of the coast. Surprisingly, Julianna didn't feel drawn to Cody's blood. Relief washed over her. As she wondered what made Cody different, her thoughts quickly turned to Matt. "Cody, before we start your training, I want to ask you how Matt's doing. He was really upset."

"Yeah, but I think he'll come around," Cody said. "He's just worried about you. He thinks you guys have been brainwashed or something. I tried to reassure him. I told him all about me and Jake, and that Jake would never hurt a human or a finner. I told him again how Tristan tried to save me and about what went down in the Monterey Bay. He just needs time for it to sink in."

"Do you think we'll see him tonight?" Julianna asked.

"I don't know. Maybe."

"Do you think he'll come to the wedding?" she asked.

"I'd bet money on it. He cares about you. A lot." Cody eyed Julianna. "Do you mind if I ask you a question?"

"Go ahead."

"Did you and Matt ever hook up?"

"Me and Matt? No," Julianna laughed. "He's just a good friend. Other than Finn, he's probably my best friend."

"Okay," Cody said. "I was just wondering."

"What about you, Cody? Did you have anyone serious in your life before you became a finner?"

"Serious? No."

"Is that by choice? Or is it because you haven't met the right woman yet?" she asked.

"I don't know. A little of both maybe," he grinned.

"I see. Personally, I think you just haven't met the right woman. But when you do, you'll be a goner—head over heels, worship the ground beneath her feet, the sun rises and sets on her, goner."

Cody flashed a playful smile. "Maybe I have met her and she's about to marry someone else."

"Riiiiight," Julianna said, laughing. "Did that really work for you when you were human?"

"It used to," he chuckled. "I must be losing my touch."

"All right. Enough socializing. Let's get to work."

Julianna trained Cody in offensive and defensive maneuvers. They swam drill after drill. By the time they returned to the compound, they were both exhausted.

"You did great, Cody. I think you're ready to join us on the battlefront," she said.

"Really? Thanks! I bet Jake, Skylar, and Tristan can show us some new moves too," Cody said. "Hey, you wanna grab some dinner? I'm starving."

"I would, but Finn's probably worried. Rain check?"

"Sure," he said. "I'll see you later."

Julianna found Finn waiting for her in their apartment. He enveloped her in his arms and pressed his cheek against hers.

"I'm glad you're home," he said. "I was getting worried."

"For me or for Cody?" she asked.

"A little of both," he admitted.

"No need to worry. I wasn't tempted in the least by Cody. I didn't even notice the smell of his blood all day. He did really well, by the way. I think he's ready for prime time."

"Good. Do you think you're ready to face everyone again tonight?" Finn asked.

"Yeah," she replied. "As long as there's no group hug or anything, I think I'll be able to contain myself."

"Okay then. Group hug is off the agenda. I'll fix you something to eat, and then we can head down."

# 125 – Questions

That evening when the finners assembled in the conference room, Finn and Julianna noticed three empty chairs.

"Sorry to be the bearer of bad news but Emma, Zach, and Morgan have decided not to work here anymore," Jamal explained. "They said it's nothing personal. They just don't want to work with graysuits."

"I understand," Julianna said. "Seeing as how they all lost their human lives to vampire sharks, it makes sense they wouldn't want to be around any."

"Thanks, Jamal," Finn said. "I'm glad you all decided to join us here tonight. It means a lot. I'm sure you have questions. Who'd like to start?"

Over the next hour, Finn and Julianna fielded questions about Tristan, graysuits, and how they could be sure they could trust them. Matt quietly entered the room as the questions wound down. Julianna tried to make eye contact, but he avoided her gaze.

"Matt, thanks for coming," Finn said. "We've been taking questions from everyone. Since you haven't had a chance yet, is there anything you'd like to ask?"

Matt glared at Finn and then Julianna. "Yeah, there's one thing I'd like to know."

"What's that?" Julianna asked nervously.

"Do you guys really think you can just come in here and … throw a wedding together in 48 hours?" Matt's face broke into a huge smile. "I mean, people spend months planning these things. What can I do to help?"

Julianna rushed over to Matt and hugged him. The enticing smell of his blood tickled her nostrils. As casually as she could, she pulled away and returned to the head of the table. "Thank you for the offer, but it's going to be really simple. Just show up. That's all we need."

Finn noticed Julianna's smile looked strained, so he decided to end the meeting. "Okay, everybody, let's call it a night. Tristan, Leilani, Jake, and Skylar will be here tomorrow. Please remember they're our guests, so there's no reason to be nervous around them. We're all on the same team now. We'll show them around, and then you can get to know each other at the wedding."

# 126 – Change

Tristan rose from Leilani's embrace. "I need to get in the ocean before we head to the airport."

"Okay," Leilani sighed, "if you really have to."

"Believe me, I'd love to spend another hour in bed with you, but we've been in here two days," Tristan grinned. "If I don't get some salt water on this skin, I'll be nothing but a pile of ash. Then what fun would I be?"

"All right," Leilani said. "Can I ask you something first? It's something I've been curious about, but I haven't had a chance to ask you or Jake about it."

"You can ask me anything. You know that," Tristan said.

"So, what does it feel like when you turn into a shark? Does it hurt?"

"No. The actual transformation doesn't feel like anything. You think of yourself as a shark, and all of a sudden, you are. It's not like in werewolf stories where it's this excruciating physical change. It's instantaneous. One second you feel like a human, and the next second you feel like a shark. There's no in-between," he explained.

"And what does it feel like to be a shark?" she asked.

"Pretty amazing." Tristan's dark brown eyes glowed with excitement. "When I'm in my shark body, I feel incredibly powerful—invincible, really."

"Even more powerful than a vampire?" she asked.

"A lot more powerful. I think part of it is just your sheer physical size. Full-grown sharks are pretty massive, as you've seen. You also have these extra senses like your lateral line. When water moves around your body, the stimulation triggers nerve impulses to your brain. It's this rippling sensation that feels pretty incredible. You also have these pores around your head that give you the ability to detect the electrical fields produced by other animals. These senses make it really easy to find prey."

"Do you have these shark senses when you're in your human body?" Leilani asked.

"Yeah, but they're not nearly as strong as when I'm a shark," Tristan said. "When I'm in my human form, I can feel when someone is near, even if I can't see or hear or smell them. Their electromagnetic field makes my head tingle."

"What does it feel like to swim in a shark's body?"

"It's like surfing but even better," he said. "You know how it is when you catch a wave and pop up—and you just instantly know it's going to be the perfect ride? How you and your board feel like you're connected to the ocean? It's like that but a thousand times stronger. It's like you're moving through the ocean but you're part of the ocean at the same time. Your body glides through the water with this ease and this pleasure you just don't get when you're human. It's like every little water molecule that bounces off your body is caressing you and energizing you at the same time. It's like a drug. You get this rush from the water moving around you."

"That sounds pretty cool," Leilani said. "I wish I could experience that—but without being turned into a vampire shark."

"I wish you could too," Tristan smiled.

"What about your prey drive? Is it stronger when you're a shark than when you're a vampire?" she asked.

"Yeah. Basically it's like your body is designed for two things: to move and to hunt."

"Do you want to hunt humans when you're a shark?"

"No more than any other animal in the ocean. It doesn't matter what the creature is. To a shark, it's just food—like I explained before. But being part vampire, I also have this human-like consciousness that remains with me even when I'm a shark. So, even though I have a shark's instincts, I still have the thoughts of a human—or vampire," he said.

"Well, I've seen you as a shark and a vampire, but I definitely prefer you like this—Tristan Pierce, the man I'm going to marry," Leilani smiled. "All right. Go do your graysuit thing. I'll get ready to go."

Tristan pulled on his boardshorts. He gave Leilani a passionate goodbye kiss. "Kissing you is one of the things I like best about being human. To be continued …"

After Tristan left, Leilani's phone rang.

"Hey, it's Jake. Is this a bad time?"

"Nope. I was just about to shower and get ready to head to the airport," Leilani replied.

"Cool. I'll meet you there then?" he asked.

"Yeah. How have you been? What have you been up to the past two days?"

"Sleeping. What about you?" Jake asked and then immediately regretted it.

Leilani decided it would be better for both of them if she just ignored his question. "Have you heard from Skylar?"

"Yep. She's gonna pick me up."

"So, you guys are friends now?" Leilani asked.

"Yeah. She said she's sorry for everything, and I believe her. That doesn't mean I'd ever get back together with her, but I can be her friend," he said.

"You're a good man, Jake. I'll see you soon."

# 127 – Therapy

Tristan and Leilani met Jake and Skylar at the airport before dawn. They flew from Monterey to LAX and caught a cab to the ferry landing.

"How about if we take the scenic route and swim to Catalina?" Skylar suggested.

"I don't want to leave Leilani," Tristan replied.

"Right! Sorry, Leilani. I forgot," Skylar said.

"Don't worry about it," Leilani said. "I guess as the only human my limitations are kind of an inconvenience."

"You? An inconvenience?" Tristan planted a kiss on Leilani's lips. "Never."

Finn picked them up at the ferry landing in Avalon and transported them to the compound where they joined Julianna and Cody. They toured the ground level and then went downstairs to the labs.

Leilani felt Tristan tense up as soon as he walked inside lab #1. "What is it?" she asked.

"This is where they kept me." Tristan walked over to the bed. He pointed to the IV drip and metal restraints. "This is why I couldn't get to you."

Finn saw Tristan's face harden as he showed Leilani the restraints. He walked over to them. "Tristan, I'd like to apologize again to you and Leilani for keeping you here. I'm sorry I didn't believe you that Leilani and Jake were in danger. And I'm sorry we kept you here against your will. I hope you can forgive me."

"As long as you don't imprison graysuits anymore, we're good," Tristan said, though he still felt claustrophobic in the lab. "We've all done things we wish we could take back. So, who am I to judge you?"

"Leilani, can you forgive me for keeping him here, away from you?" Finn asked.

"If Tristan can, I can," she said.

After the tour of the labs, Julianna showed them the research vessel they used to capture graysuits and bring them back to the compound. Then they all settled in the conference room.

"How did everyone take the news that we'll be working together?" Tristan asked.

"Not too bad," Finn said. "Three people have decided not to work here anymore, but I think everyone else understands we all have the same goal."

"Good. Julianna, how'd they react to you?" Tristan asked.

"One thing that turning into a graysuit does is it lets you see who your real friends are. The ones who've decided to stay seem okay with it—as long as I don't eat anyone," she said.

Tristan caught something in Julianna's tone that worried him. "Can we take a break for a few minutes?" he asked.

"Sure. I'll take you guys to the mess hall," Finn said.

Tristan touched Julianna's arm. "Can we talk?"

"Yeah, actually there's something I've been meaning to ask you," Julianna said.

"Should I head to the mess hall?" Leilani asked.

"I have no secrets from Leilani, so it's your call, Julianna," Tristan said.

"Leilani, you can stay if you want." Julianna motioned to Finn. "I'm going to talk with Tristan. We'll meet you in a little while."

Julianna closed the door and took a seat across from Tristan and Leilani. "Now that I'm a graysuit, my craving for blood is pretty intense," she explained. "I noticed it during my first swim as a shark, and it hasn't subsided. Finners, humans, marine mammals, fish—everyone, everything smells so good. That's why I've got Finn wearing all that cologne. It helps mask the scent of his blood. Is that normal? And what do I do about it? How do I keep myself from hurting the people around me?"

"I, uh, I'm not sure," Tristan stammered, surprised by her questions.

"How did you do it when we were married?" Julianna asked. "And how do you do it with Leilani? You smell really good, by the way."

Leilani's eyes widened in surprise. "Uh, thanks."

"I don't know, Julianna. I became a graysuit right before I met you, and it was never an issue for me," Tristan said. "I mean, I love the taste of blood. Sorry, Leilani, I know that's a gross thing for you to hear. But since I've been a graysuit, the craving hasn't been overpowering. It was more intense when I was just a regular vampire. But I think that's because I didn't care about anyone, so I didn't think twice about taking a human life back then. When I was with you and living—for the most part—a human life, I didn't really think about drinking blood. I ate my meat rare, I fed in the ocean when I was a shark, and that was it. I didn't think about killing anyone until you were killed. You helped me regain my humanity when we were together, and you made me want to protect humanity when you died."

"What does that mean?" Julianna asked nervously. "That I'm some kind of monster?"

"No. It just means your cravings are stronger than mine. It's different for every vampire and every graysuit," Tristan explained.

"What about all the people you've turned? Has it been an issue for anyone else?" Julianna asked.

"I don't know," Tristan admitted. "I turned a lot of people when we were together. I didn't really keep track of them."

"You just turned them into vampire sharks and left them on their own?!" Julianna asked.

"The ones in the early days—yeah," he said.

"Wow, Tristan, it's good to know you took your role as the creator so seriously," Julianna said.

"I told you, I thought I was doing people a favor. I didn't know how things would turn out," Tristan said.

"What about Skylar?" Julianna asked. "How does she handle the cravings?"

"Skylar has never once told me she's been tempted to kill an innocent person for their blood," Tristan said.

Leilani shifted in her seat. *He doesn't know about the two surfers Dean and Skylar killed in Waikiki.*

"Leilani? Is something wrong?" Tristan asked.

"While you were gone, a couple of surfers were killed in Waikiki, but it must've been Dean. I'm sure Skylar never would've gone along with it, right? She said Dean lied to her about a lot of things," Leilani said.

"What about Jake?" Julianna asked. "He doesn't seem to have any trouble being with humans. He's not tempted by you, right, Leilani?"

Leilani's mind flashed back to sharing a bed with Jake in Oahu. She then remembered their conversation on the beach when Jake said he was in love with her. "Jake? No."

Tristan caught Leilani's blush and her quickening heartbeat. "You're sure?" he asked.

"Yes. Jake has never once expressed a desire for my blood or anyone else's. He's … Jake," she said, as if that explained everything.

"Then it's just me," Julianna lamented. "I'm a bloodthirsty beast."

"Don't say that. You probably just have a stronger prey drive or stronger senses or something. Maybe because you're part dolphin, everything's escalated," Tristan theorized.

"What do I do? I'm supposed to marry Finn tomorrow. I don't think either one of us will be able to stand the amount of cologne he's wearing for much longer. I don't want to feel like I'm a danger to him or my friends or anyone else."

"You'll just have to work at it," Tristan said. "Like anything new, being a graysuit requires a period of adjustment. If you have a strong prey drive, then use it in the ocean like a shark would and eat things that sharks eat. There are probably methods you can use to train yourself to stop finding the scent of blood so appealing. Maybe some sort of conditioning, like what people do to break bad habits."

"Do you really think it could help?" Julianna asked.

"I do. You're a good person. You just have to hold on to that humanity," he said.

"Okay. I'll look into the therapy thing," Julianna said.

"I'll ask around too. I'm sure there are vampire therapists who even specialize in this sort of thing," Tristan said.

"Really?!" Leilani said.

"Yeah," he smiled.

"Tristan, after all the grief I gave you about keeping secrets, it's probably not very cool of me to ask this," Julianna said, "but would you and Leilani mind keeping this to yourselves? Finn is the only one who knows about my problem. I'm having a hard enough time around here without everyone thinking I'm a breath away from tearing out their throats and draining their blood."

Leilani inwardly winced at the image but tried to keep her expression impassive.

"Sure. As long as you're sure you can keep it in check and you know you'd never hurt anyone," Tristan said.

"I'm sure," Julianna said firmly—more firmly than she felt. "I can always remove myself from the situation if it gets too intense, like I've done up to this point. Okay then. I guess I have some research to do before the wedding, and let me know if you find any therapists who can help me."

"I will," Tristan said.

Julianna stood. "I'll show you guys to the mess hall."

As soon as they entered the room, Finn rushed to Julianna. "Everything okay?"

"Yeah," she whispered. "I'm going to see if I can find some kind of cognitive behavioral therapy to help me eliminate the, uh, cravings. Tristan's also going to ask around."

"And the wedding?" Finn asked.

"It's still on. You're not getting cold feet, are you?" Julianna asked.

"Never."

# 128 – Tourists

After sunset, Tristan, Leilani, Jake, Skylar, and Cody left the compound. They strolled along the ocean and continued down a palm tree-lined path to the Avalon Casino. They walked around the massive circular structure, which stands as tall as a 12-story building, and admired the elegant design. As the sky darkened, they noticed the grand white building and its red tile roof contrasted brilliantly with the sapphire blue ocean surrounding it on three sides.

They continued walking alongside picturesque Avalon Bay until they reached Avalon Pier. Then they circled back and ambled down the cobblestone streets, peeking inside the windows of cafes, restaurants, gift shops, and boutique hotels.

As they passed the Avalon Casino again, Skylar decided to make her move. "Who's up for some bodysurfing? We can swim around to the backside of the island and catch some waves at Shark Harbor."

Cody's eyes lit up. "I'm in! Shark Harbor is one of the best surf spots on the island. How 'bout it, Jake?"

"Yeah, why not?" Jake said.

"Tristan, how about you?" Skylar asked, knowing he'd have to leave Leilani behind. "With the wedding tomorrow night, you might not have another chance. You don't want too much time to go by because you never know what might happen. Remember when you were trapped at the sheriff's station?"

"All too well," Tristan said. "You guys go. I don't want to leave Leilani."

"No, Tristan, you should go," Leilani said.

"But …"

"No buts. If we're going to be together, this is bound to happen. A lot. Go get some salt water on you. I'll see you when you get back," Leilani said.

"Only if you're sure," Tristan said.

"I'm sure." Out of the corner of her eye, Leilani thought she saw Skylar smirk, but as soon as she looked, it was gone. She kissed Tristan and returned to the hotel alone.

Three hours later, Leilani awoke from a deep sleep. It felt like someone was in the room, watching her. She glanced around, but nothing looked disturbed. She turned over and drifted back to sleep.

After another three hours, Tristan returned to the hotel. He tiptoed across the room, hung his boardshorts in the bathroom, and slipped into bed next to Leilani.

"Are you just getting home?" she mumbled.

"Yeah," he whispered. "I must've lost track of time. Sorry."

"Don't apologize. You need salt water to live. I get that. We're good," she said.

"For you, good isn't nearly good enough," Tristan said, grinning in the darkness. "You need to be ecstatic."

"Ecstatic?"

"Oh yeah, ecstatic."

"I'm afraid I don't know what you mean, Mr. Pierce," she giggled.

He slipped the straps of her nightgown from her shoulders and pressed his lips to hers. "Well then, Ms. Waters, allow me to demonstrate."

# 129 – Scents

The next morning, Finn, half-asleep, turned to embrace Julianna. As soon as he inhaled her salty graysuit scent, he bolted upright in bed. He quickly looked around, expecting to see Lily or Tristan or one of the many graysuits they'd captured over the years. Instead, he saw Julianna staring at him, concerned.

"Nightmares again?" she asked.

"Yeah," Finn lied.

"Do you think now that we've changed our view of graysuits that the bad dreams might finally go away?"

Finn sighed. "I hope so. But now that I'm wide awake, I might as well get up. There are still some things to take care of before tonight."

"Need any help?" Julianna asked.

"Nope." He rose from bed but stopped. He slumped next to her. "I have to tell you something. Remember how you said you were having trouble with the smell of my blood—how it smelled really good so it would help if I wore cologne to mask it?"

"Yeah."

"I might need you to do the same thing with perfume until I can get used to your new scent," he said.

Julianna sniffed her skin. "Is it that strong?"

"It's not that it's strong. It's a scent I've always associated with very bad things. When I woke up next to you this morning, I thought a graysuit was in the room, coming to murder me. It wasn't a nightmare that startled me awake. It was your scent," he explained.

"I'm sorry."

"Don't be," he said. "This is you. I just need some time to associate this scent with the love of my life, rather than death.

I think perfume will help me with the transition."

"Okay. Maybe we can get some kind of quantity discount with all the perfume and cologne we're buying." She smiled but quickly turned serious again. "We're not making a big mistake, are we? Covering our issues with perfume and cologne while we figure out a way to work through them?"

"No. We're not making a mistake. We're in a period of transition, like any soon-to-be newlyweds. We're being practical, finding a way to smooth that transition. I love you enough to work through anything. A couple of weeks from now, we'll probably look back on all this and laugh," he said.

"Do you really think so?" she asked.

"I do."

"Then I guess we're packing cologne and perfume for the honeymoon. We'll be the best smelling newlyweds in Kauai," Julianna smiled.

"Cheers to that. I'll see you tonight at the ceremony." Finn kissed her and rose to his feet. "I love you."

"Love you."

# 130 – New Beginnings

After sunset, several finners, three graysuits, and a human gathered in the Fountain Terrace of Catalina Country Club. Cody served as the finner/graysuit liaison and introduced everyone. After that, however, the finners and graysuits separated, leaning against opposite walls like boys and girls at a middle school dance.

"They still seem kind of nervous around us," Jake whispered to Cody.

"Give it time. You have to understand that every graysuit they've ever met has been a killer. Several lost their human lives the same way I did. Once they get to know you, they'll feel more comfortable," Cody assured him.

Skylar ordered three mojitos and brought two to Leilani and Tristan. "Cheers!"

"Thanks, Sky. I'll get the next round," Tristan said.

"Yeah, uh, thanks," Leilani said, still puzzled by Skylar's abrupt attitude change.

"So, Tristan," Skylar said, "is it strange for you to see Julianna marrying someone else?"

Tristan coughed as he swallowed the first rum-filled sip of his mojito. "Smooooth," he joked as he caught his breath. "No. Why would it be strange?"

"If it was me, I think I'd feel weird watching the man who was once my husband marry someone else," Skylar said.

"It might feel weird if I wasn't with Leilani, but everything works out as it's supposed to. Life is good." Tristan brushed a stray lock of Leilani's hair from her face and gazed into her blue eyes. "Very, very good."

Skylar raised her glass in the air. "Well then, to old friends and new beginnings."

# 131 – Courtyard Wedding

Finn and Julianna entered the courtyard through the cream-colored arched portico. Since they didn't have time to shop for wedding attire, they donned the same outfits they wore to a formal New Year's Eve party the previous year.

Julianna dressed in a silver, strapless, floor-length gown with a sweetheart neckline and gentle gathered ruching on her hip, which accentuated her petite curves. An azure blue crystal pin adorned the center of the ruching. Silver sandals, embellished with azure crystals across the lower strap, peeked from beneath the soft layers of shimmery fabric.

Finn wore dark gray pants paired with a matching two-button jacket, which held an azure handkerchief in the chest pocket. Beneath the jacket, he wore an azure dress shirt.

Walking arm in arm, they glided across the brick flooring and took their place in front of the blue tile fountain, where Jamal waited for them.

"Thank you for coming here today to witness the wedding of our great friends, Finn and Julianna," Jamal began. "Finn's been waiting a long time for this day, so let's not make him wait any longer. Finn, would you like to start?"

"Abso-freakin'-lutely!" Finn grasped Julianna's hands in his and gazed into her sparkling blue eyes. "Julianna, it's no exaggeration to say I fell in love with you the first time I saw you. I tried to play it cool for a couple of months so I didn't scare you off …"

"Smart move," she laughed.

"But I knew then, even if you didn't, that we were meant to be together, and here we are today," Finn said. "Since you accepted my proposal, I've done a lot of reflecting. In my entire life—or two lives actually, but who's counting?—there have been three days where I've considered myself to be the luckiest soul on this planet. In chronological order, the first day was when I met Terrell, when he saved my life."

Finn shook his head and smiled. "No one knows this—not even Julianna—but Terrell and I had a bet about whether or not this day would come. And Terrell bet me his 1967 Mustang convertible it wouldn't."

"He didn't!" Julianna exclaimed. "He loved that car!"

"Yeah. Not only that, but for our friends who aren't familiar with Avalon, there's a 14-year waiting list to own a car here on the island, so that bet was a really big deal. Terrell was the smartest person I've ever met, and he was rarely wrong about anything." Finn gripped Julianna's hand and raised it toward the heavens. "But, Terrell, wherever you are, you were wrong about this, buddy! She said yes!"

The finners laughed along with them.

Lucia turned around to Cody, who sat directly behind her. "Seriously! Terrell was never wrong about anything."

"What happened to the Mustang? I wanna drive it!" Matt shouted from his seat in the front row in front of the bride.

"Sorry, Matt. The Mustang went to one of Terrell's friends after he died, so I can't collect on the bet," Finn said. "But the car doesn't matter. The only thing that matters is the woman standing here in front of me now—which brings me to number two of the three best days of my life. That'd be the day I met Julianna. I took one look into those beautiful blue eyes, and that was it. I was hers from that day forward."

Julianna released one of Finn's hands to brush a tear from her eye.

Finn grasped her hand again. "As you've probably guessed, number three is today because in a few minutes I'll finally be able to call this brilliant, beautiful, loving woman my wife. I love you, Julianna, and I promise to love you every moment of every day for the rest of our lives."

"I love you too. That was amazing! How in the world am I supposed to follow that?" Julianna gulped. Suddenly, the words she'd written and rehearsed disappeared from her brain. Panic-stricken, she glanced at their friends. Her heart beat rapidly. "I don't know why I'm so nervous …" She tried to pull together her scrambled thoughts. "Well, Terrell was kind of right. I didn't think this day would come either—the day Finn would be here wearing a gray suit and marrying a graysuit," she tittered.

No one laughed with her.

Feeling her anxiety, Finn gave her a reassuring smile and gently squeezed her hand.

"Let me try this again." She took a deep breath. Slowly, the words she'd prepared began to trickle back into her brain. "So, life has many twists and turns as all of us here are very aware. Through them, this man—this gorgeous, smart, and sexy man—has been by my side. The entire time I've known him, he's never faltered, never wavered in his feelings for me. Now that we've finally made it to the altar, I can't believe I made him wait so long. This is exactly what I want.

"Finn, you are everything I ever wanted, everything I ever needed—even when I didn't know what that was. I'm grateful you were smart enough to figure that out for the both of us—and that you gave me 11 years to catch up and reach the same conclusion you reached on day one. I love you with all my heart. I'm so happy that, when Jamal does his magic here, I will finally get to call you my husband. Do your thing, Jamal! I've already made him wait long enough."

"Finn, do you take Julianna to be your wife?" Jamal asked. "To love, honor, and cherish her, to keep her in sickness and in health, for as long as you both shall live?"

"I do!"

"Julianna, do you take Finn to be your husband? To love,

honor, and cherish him, to keep him in sickness and in health, for as long as you both shall live?"

"I do."

"Can we have the rings, please?" Jamal asked.

Matt jumped up, pulled the rings from his pocket, and handed them to Jamal.

"Finn, please place this ring on Julianna's hand," Jamal said.

Finn's hands shook as he slid the simple silver band on her finger.

Jamal smiled. "Now you, Julianna."

As Julianna placed the silver band on Finn's finger, it stuck on his knuckle. She twisted it and forced it down to the base of his finger.

"Repeat after me," Jamal said. "I give you this ring as an eternal symbol of my love and commitment to you."

Finn and Julianna gazed into each other's eyes and repeated Jamal's words.

"By the power vested in me by the state of California," Jamal said, "I now pronounce you husband and wife!"

Finn wrapped his arms around Julianna and dipped her backward. When they pressed their lips together, they forgot about all their friends watching them and enjoyed the intense pleasure of their very first kiss as husband and wife.

# 132 – Timing

Tristan clutched Leilani's hand throughout the ceremony. She thought he seemed genuinely happy for Julianna, which was a relief.

When the bride and groom kissed, Tristan pressed his mouth to Leilani's ear. "I can't wait for that to be us."

Leilani smiled. She knew she wanted to marry Tristan, but she also wanted them to take their time adjusting to life together. Leilani's life was pretty traditional, and Tristan's life was anything but. She knew it would take time to find something in the middle that felt right for both of them. But if they couldn't make it work, she didn't want them to be too far down a road they weren't ready to travel.

"Let's take our time enjoying being engaged ... and ecstatic," Leilani whispered back. "Right now I'm having fun with the fiancée thing."

"If you like that, you'll like the wife thing even more. I promise," Tristan said.

Leilani sighed to herself. *I guess the first compromise we'll have to make is on the wedding date.*

Skylar, who sat behind Leilani, heard their entire exchange. She couldn't understand Leilani's hesitation to walk down the aisle with Tristan. *When a man like Tristan proposes, you don't crawl; you run to the altar as fast as you can! What's her problem?*

Jake also overheard the conversation and wondered about Leilani. He thought now that she had Tristan back, they'd get married right away. But she didn't appear to be in a hurry.

Cody nudged Jake. "What's up?"

"Nothing," Jake said.

Cody sighed. "Uh huh, right."

# 133 — Species Relations

Tristan ordered another round of mojitos at the bar. Matt stepped beside him and ordered a Corona with lime.

"Matt, good to see you," Tristan said. "Nice wedding. More traditional than I would've thought considering how few humans are here."

"I know, right?" Matt squeezed the lime wedge into his beer. "Now it's time for the time-honored tradition of drinking heavily and embarrassing ourselves with our friends, who will tease us mercilessly about our drunken escapades for years to come."

"Finners do that at weddings too? Awesome! I thought it was just humans and graysuits," Tristan laughed.

"Nah. I think every species does it. Speaking of species, now that you graysuits know where we live, you're not going to massacre us in our sleep, are you?" Matt teased.

Tristan gave him a sardonic smile. "In your *sleep*? No. It's much more fun when you're awake."

"A graysuit with a sense of humor—nice!" Matt clinked his beer bottle against Tristan's glass. "Cheers, Killer."

"Dude, I'm the creator. That's *Mr.* Killer to you," Tristan grinned. "And you finners aren't trying to get us drunk so you can take us back to the lab and dig out our fangs, right?"

"No way," Matt assured him. "We don't care about your fangs. It's the venom sacs, man. That's where the action is."

Tristan slapped his palm against his forehead. "Riiiiight." He held his glass out to Matt. "I'm glad we'll be working together."

Matt tapped his bottle against Tristan's glass again. "Me too, Killer. Cheers, man."

# 134 – Lucky

Jake got in line behind Lucia at the bar. Lucia had long blackish-brown hair, sparkly dark brown eyes, naturally full lips, and a curvy build. She was the same height as Jake but her three-inch heels made her tower over him.

Smelling a vampire shark, Lucia turned to see who was behind her. "Hi, Cody's graysuit friend. What's your name again?"

"Jake. You're Lucia, right?"

"That's me." She stepped aside to let Jake approach the bar. "What's your poison, Jake?"

"Bloody Mary."

"Nice graysuit drink," she mocked. "You like that with O positive or O negative blood?"

"I dunno," he said with devilish grin. "What are you?"

Lucia wrinkled her nose in disgust. "Dude, that's creepy."

"You're the one who started it," Jake said. "I just ordered a tomato-based adult beverage, and you start throwing around these negative stereotypes. What are you drinking?"

"Club soda with lime. Unlike you, I actually like having all my brain cells," Lucia said. "It's a dolphin thing."

"I see," Jake said. "And are all finners as friendly and nonjudgmental as you? Or did I just get lucky?"

Lucia quickly appraised Jake's appearance. *He's nowhere near as gorgeous as Tristan, but he is pretty cute.* She studied his greenish-brown eyes. *And he seems friendly enough.* "I don't know, Jake. I usually go for women. But play your cards right, and yeah, you just might get lucky."

# 135 – Bad

After Finn and Julianna left for their honeymoon, the finners took off to a local dive bar. Tristan, Leilani, Skylar, Jake, and Cody lingered in the country club's courtyard, enjoying the warm evening as they finished their drinks.

"What's next, Tristan?" Skylar asked. "Where to?"

"I don't know. Things seem to be quiet on the graysuit front," he said.

"I should probably get home and check on a few things at work," Leilani replied.

"Me too," Jake added. "I don't want my clients getting too comfortable with my friend who's been helping me out while I've been gone, or I won't have any clients left. No clients—no money. No money—no home, no food, no beer."

"You don't have to worry about that, Jake. If you really do want to be a Nomad, I'm happy to provide like I did for Torrey and Cruz ... and Logan, unfortunately. The same goes for you, Leilani. You don't have to go back to work," Tristan said.

Leilani thought she detected wistfulness in Tristan's voice. But she didn't feel ready to give up her career to be a Nomad until she fully understood what that meant and how her life and Tristan's life would mesh together. "I should go back. So much has changed in the world—or at least what I know of the world—that it'll be good to do something 'normal.'"

"Why be normal when you can be paranormal?" Tristan grinned.

"Damn straight!" Skylar fist-bumped Tristan, and then Jake and Cody.

Leilani frowned, feeling awkward again as the lone human. Tristan settled into a wrought iron chair and pulled her onto his lap. "You might be human, Leilani, but you are so much more than 'normal.'"

"Yeah, Heavenly Flower," Jake joked.

"Heavenly Flower?" Tristan asked.

Leilani shook her head and laughed. "When Jake and I were in Hawaii, we met a couple of locals. One of them said my name meant 'Heavenly Flower,' so he kept calling me that."

"And flirting with you nonstop," Jake teased.

"That had nothing to do with me," Leilani insisted. "I'm sure he flirts with every woman he meets."

"Whatever you say, Heavenly Flower," Jake chuckled.

Leilani punched Jake's arm. "Quiet, graysuit."

"Dude, for the last time! The name's Jake!" he laughed.

"So, I take it you two had fun?" Tristan asked.

"I wouldn't call it fun. We were just trying to make the best of a bad situation," Leilani explained.

"All right then, Heavenly Flower, what do you say we call it a night? Guys, let's meet up for brunch tomorrow and figure out what's next," Tristan said.

After Tristan and Leilani left, and Skylar headed to her room, Cody and Jake piled into a golf cart and drove down to the ocean.

"You've got it bad, dude," Cody said.

"What?" Jake asked.

"Leilani, that's what. You can lie to them. You can even lie to yourself. But you can't lie to me," Cody said.

"Then I plead the Fifth. It doesn't matter anyway. She's engaged, and Tristan's my friend."

"Maybe," Cody said. "But engaged isn't married. That's all I'm saying."

# 136 – Brunch

The next morning over brunch, they discussed their plans.

"Leilani and I are heading back," Tristan said. "We're going to live at her place so she can go back to work."

"But what if there's an attack?" Skylar asked.

"Then we'll do what we always do. We'll go find out what happened and do what needs to be done," Tristan said.

Skylar smiled to herself. *Good. He said 'we.'*

"Jake, do you want to head back with us?" Tristan asked.

"Okay. I can pack up my stuff," he replied.

"Pack? Where are you going?" Leilani asked.

"Cody and I talked last night. He can't go back home. Everyone thinks he's dead. So, I'm going to move here until we figure out where we want to be," Jake said.

"You're leaving?" Leilani asked.

"Yeah. But when Tristan needs us, Cody and I will go meet you guys wherever," Jake explained.

Skylar couldn't pinpoint exactly what was going on, but she sensed a weird dynamic between Leilani and Jake. She decided to push it.

"I have an idea. What if we all stay here for a while?" Skylar suggested. "I gave up my place in Encinitas, so I have no place to be. And, Tristan, I didn't want to say anything, but do you really think it's a good idea to go back after what happened in your house? I mean, it must be a bloody mess. You know we never stay in a city after something like that goes down. What if you get called in again by the sheriff? You could die there. We can't put you in danger like that." She pointed her gaze at Leilani. "Leilani just got you back. I'm sure the last thing she wants is to put your life at risk."

"I'll be fine," Tristan said. "They think dogs attacked Leilani, not vampires. Plus, I'm not even going back to my house. I'll keep a low profile."

"Tristan, you can do a lot of things, but keeping a low profile isn't one of them. Wherever we go, you know graysuits, vampires, and surfers. And even if Leilani said that dogs attacked her, if the sheriff hears you're back in town, they're going to want to question you because it happened at your house," Skylar said.

"She's right," Leilani said. "I could probably convince Garrison to drop it, but he still might want to talk to you. And after what happened the last time, I can't trust he won't be violent or lock you up for no reason. It was stupid of me to think we could go back like nothing happened."

"But if that's where you want to be, we'll make it work," Tristan insisted.

"No. Maybe we can go back after things settle down. For now, I can try to get a transfer to another office on the coast or extend my leave of absence," Leilani said.

"But you love your work," Tristan countered.

"Yeah, and I love you. I won't risk your life with someone like Garrison. We'll figure something out," Leilani said.

"Are you sure?" Tristan asked.

"Positive," Leilani said.

"We have a few open apartments at the compound. I'm sure Finn and Julianna would be cool with you guys staying there while you figure things out. I could ask Matt," Cody offered. "They left him in charge while they're on their honeymoon."

"Thanks, but I don't want to live there. Too many bad memories. I'd feel like I was in captivity all over again," Tristan explained. "Maybe Leilani and I will hang here in town while we figure things out."

"Cool. So, we're all staying?" Skylar asked.

Tristan looked to Leilani.

"I guess so," Leilani said. "But I do need to go home and take care of some things. It shouldn't take more than a day."

"I'll come with you," Tristan offered.

"No. It's safer if you stay here. I'll head out with Jake tonight and come back tomorrow. You won't even know I'm gone," Leilani said.

"Trust me. I'll know," Tristan said. "I just got you back. The last thing I want is to be apart from you, even if it's just for a day."

"Well then," she whispered in his ear, "what do you say we spend the rest of the day together, just the two of us?"

Tristan smiled. "You're on."

As they scuttled out the door, Leilani called over her shoulder, "Bye, guys. Jake, I'll see you at the ferry landing tonight."

# 137 – Varietals

Several hours later, Tristan took Leilani to the ferry and returned to his empty hotel room. He turned on the TV and channel surfed. Unable to find anything entertaining enough to take his mind off Leilani, he breathed a sigh of relief when he heard a knock at the door.

"I'm thinking about a midnight surf session. You in?" Skylar asked.

"I don't know," Tristan said.

"Ocean. Waves. Fun. What don't you know?" she asked.

"I don't know what I feel like doing," he said. "Nothing feels right."

"You're moping because Leilani's gone."

"I'm not moping," he said.

"Liar," she teased. "Let's hit the water. C'mon, you'll feel better. I promise."

After catching a few small waves and enjoying a vigorous swim under the silver glow of the crescent moon, they returned to the hotel.

Skylar searched for her room key in the bottom of her bag. "That was fun. Thanks for coming with me."

"I should be the one thanking you," Tristan said.

"Yeah, I know," she giggled. "Let's have a drink. When I was in Monterey County, I picked up some amazing wines."

Tristan hesitated, thinking of Leilani.

"C'mon, dude, it's just one glass of wine," Skylar said. "That sounds a lot more appealing than sitting alone in your room, feeling sorry for yourself. You're not going to question me again, are you?"

"No, I guess not."

Skylar opened the door to her room and rummaged through

her luggage. She retrieved a bottle of Pinot Noir and held it out to Tristan. "This is from the Santa Lucia Highlands," she said. "The vineyards get fog and breezes off the Monterey Bay. That's what makes this area so spectacular for these grapes."

Tristan smiled. "I forgot how into wine you are. So, it's really good?"

"See for yourself." She poured two large glasses and handed one to Tristan. She swirled the wine in her glass and inhaled. She took a sip and sighed with satisfaction. "Now that is a fine Pinot. You like?"

Tristan took a large gulp and smiled. "I like."

"You know, I've discovered I have a lot in common with Pinot Noir grapes," she said.

"You mean like the guy in that movie, Sideways?"

"No, I'm like Pinot Noir in a different way. Pinot Noir grapes can be risky and temperamental, but they can also be soft and romantic. The main thing is, when treated with care, they create a lasting impression—one that's well worth all the care and attention." Skylar took a sip of her wine and grinned. "They're quite tantalizing, actually."

"Interesting," Tristan said. "But I disagree. I think you're more like a Syrah."

"Really? How so?"

"A Syrah is spicy and intense. It's a wine that packs a punch."

"Is that a bad thing?" she asked.

"Not at all. It's got backbone. It cuts through the sweetness of other wines, but it also has a lot of heart," Tristan said. "So, what varietal am I?"

"Hmmm, a lot of people would say you're a Cabernet Sauvignon—strong, regal, full of depth and character, and you age very, very well." Skylar let her gaze wander from Tristan's head to his feet and back. "But I think you're a Zinfandel—big, strong, and full-bodied."

"Full-bodied, huh?" he smirked.

"Definitely, and I mean that in the best possible way," she said, flashing a flirtatious smile. "And like an old vine California Zin, you've got some years on you but that just makes you better—darker, more exciting, and oh-so-sinfully sweet."

Tristan smiled uneasily. He couldn't tell if Skylar was coming on to him or simply having fun with him.

"What's that look?" she asked.

"Nothing. I'm just glad we're friends. I was worried after we had that fight—the night you and Jake broke up—that you might be done with me for good."

"I will never be done with you," Skylar assured him.

"Even when I marry Leilani?" Tristan asked. He hated to bring up a subject he knew might upset Skylar, but he wanted to be clear that their friends-with-benefits days were over.

"Yes. You're my best friend! I hope you're always in my life," she said. "Don't you want me in your life?"

"Of course! I just want to make sure ..."

"We're good, Tristan. And I want to thank you and Leilani for listening to me about not going back to San Diego. I couldn't stand the thought of you getting locked up again," she said. "And I've really missed hanging out with you."

"So have I," he said.

"Now that we're here for a while—or at least until the next attack—I have to ask you something. Do you trust the finners?"

"Most of them," Tristan said. "It might take me a while to warm up to Finn since he's the one who kept me locked up. But if they can trust us, I think we can trust them."

"Okay. If you trust them, that's good enough for me." Skylar swirled the wine in her glass and watched the crimson liquid swish up against the sides like a wave of blood. "So ... can I ask you something else?"

"What?" Tristan asked.

"I'm worried about the promise you made to Leilani to not kill any humans, and the promise you made to Julianna to stop creating graysuits. I don't think you should limit yourself like that. We don't know what's going to happen in the future. You might need to do those things," Skylar said.

"I think Julianna's going to let me off the hook," he said.

"How do you know?"

"She's a graysuit now. She'll see things our way. We just need to give her a little time," he said.

"What about Leilani?" Skylar asked.

"She's tougher. I think half of the reason she's so freaked out about killing is because of her job. It goes against everything she's believed in and worked for her entire life. Even if a human is rotten to the core, she thinks there's still some hope for redemption or something. She's too wrapped up in the human idea of law and order. We know their system doesn't work. She thinks it does. But I'm pretty sure she'll come around after she's been with us awhile. If she decides to quit her job, that might happen even sooner."

"But what if we want to take out some humans? By the Rules, of course," she added. "They're still part of the food chain, right?"

"Right," Tristan smiled. "The thing to remember, Skylar, is that *I* made that promise to Leilani about not killing people. *You* didn't."

Skylar smiled to herself. *Good. So, he's not totally under her spell. He's still got some of the old Tristan in him.* "That's a relief. Can I ask you another question?"

Tristan nodded and refilled their glasses, emptying the bottle. "You're right. This is a tantalizing Pinot."

"Sometimes tantalizing isn't all it's cracked up to be." Skylar studied the wine in her glass to avoid gazing into Tristan's dark, alluring eyes. "It's hard to admit this, but as you know,

I haven't had the best track record with men lately. So, what I want to ask is, how did you know Leilani was different? That she was the one you wanted to commit to? And how did you know with Julianna?"

Tristan took a big gulp of wine. He remembered how hurt Skylar was when he had to tell her that he never loved her—and never would love her.

"Don't worry. I know I was upset the last time we talked about this, but I'm over it," she assured him. "And I really want to know. I'd like to find someone someday, but I'm obviously doing something wrong. With Torrey and Cruz gone, you're the only one I can ask about this stuff."

"Well, um, it's not any one thing. It's a feeling more than anything," he explained. "I met Julianna right after I became a vampire shark, so I was already feeling pretty incredible. But that first night I spent with her, I knew she was different from anyone I'd ever known. After that, I couldn't imagine being without her."

"What about Leilani?" Skylar asked.

"When I first looked into her eyes, before I even knew who she was, I felt something indescribable. It's like there was this magnetic connection—this soul connection—that made it impossible for me to turn away. Then when I saw her again, even though more than 10 years had passed, it was still there—just as strong. Once I got to know her, it deepened. She feels like home to me." He glanced at Skylar to gauge her mood but couldn't get a read on her. "I'm sorry. I'm probably not explaining this very well."

Skylar took a swig of Pinot Noir to wash down the bile rising in her throat at the thought of Leilani having a connection with Tristan that was stronger than hers. "No, you are. I get that you're attracted to Leilani. But I don't understand how you can feel so confident about spending a lifetime with her when a long-term relationship has never really been your thing—at least since I've known you."

"I know. That's what I can't explain," Tristan said. "I love the way I feel when I'm with her. When I picture my life, I can't picture it without her. She has to be in it or …"

"Or what?" Skylar asked.

"I don't know. Without her, all I see is darkness. Like there's no road ahead for me if she's not there. She's my present. She's my future. She's … it."

Skylar nodded. She understood perfectly—because ever since she met Tristan, that's exactly how she felt about him.

"Have you ever felt that way about anyone, Sky?" As soon as the words escaped Tristan's lips, he wished he could take them back.

Skylar opened a second bottle of wine from the Santa Lucia Highlands—a Lucienne Pinot Noir from Hahn Family Wines—and filled their glasses. "The better question is, has anyone ever felt that way about me? Sadly, the answer is no. But that's okay. I might not have it today, but I will eventually. Life is long and especially long for us. I just need to be patient."

Tristan chuckled. "Patience isn't exactly one of your virtues."

"Screw you, dude," Skylar laughed.

"Hey, I'm just keepin' it real," he grinned.

"Well, in this matter, I guess I have no choice. I'd like to make a toast." She raised her glass. "To love and patience."

Tristan clinked his glass to hers. "To love and patience."

# 138 – The Hangover

After consuming a Pierce Ranch Vineyards Tempranillo from the San Antonio Valley, a De Tierra Vineyards Syrah from Arroyo Seco, and an Odonata Petite Sirah from the Santa Clara Valley, Skylar and Tristan passed out in her bed.

When Tristan awoke a few hours later, he turned to caress Leilani and was startled to find a brunette next to him. *Skylar?! No! What happened last night?* He peeked under the sheets. Seeing they were both fully clothed, he sighed with relief. Next to the bed, he spied five empty wine bottles and two half-full glasses on the bedside table.

Skylar rustled next to him. "What time is it?"

"I dunno. Do you have any aspirin?" he asked.

"In my purse," she answered, half-awake.

Tristan climbed from bed and reached for her purse on the armchair across the room.

As soon as Skylar heard Tristan unzip her purse, she remembered she had Leilani's engagement ring buried at the bottom. "Wait!"

"What?"

"Give it to me," she said hurriedly. "I've got a ton of stuff in there. I'll be able to find it quicker."

He handed the purse to her. "You seem grumpy."

"I'm just hungover like you." She removed two aspirin from a small pillbox and handed them to Tristan. She took two, even though her head didn't hurt.

# 139 — Career Counseling

On the ferry from Avalon, Leilani remained quiet for most of the ride. As they climbed into their rental car in Dana Point, Jake broke the silence. "Is something wrong? You haven't said much since we left."

"I'm just trying to figure out my life. I've got a little over two weeks left on my leave, and I've never been more confused. Since I was a teenager, I knew I wanted to go into law enforcement. But is that still what I want? I keep asking myself that question, and I don't know," she said.

"Well, what do you like about your work?" Jake asked.

"Catching bad guys. Getting them off the streets so they can't hurt people," Leilani said.

"Okay. What else?"

"The order. The structure. People take things seriously. It's the complete opposite of what I had growing up," she said.

"Is that why you gravitated toward law enforcement? It was the ultimate fuck-you to your parents?" he asked.

Leilani sat motionless, taken aback by Jake's question.

"Having met them, I'd totally understand if it was," he added.

"You know, if you'd asked me that six weeks ago, I would've said, 'No. I love what I do. It has nothing to do with my parents.' But now? I don't know. Maybe it does. It's like when Tristan and I went on our first date. I was telling him about my parents and how terrible they were—and I realized that I gave up surfing to spite them but, really, I only ended up hurting myself. I wonder if it's the same with my job. Maybe I went into law enforcement to spite them. I like my career, but maybe it's served its purpose. Maybe it's not who I am anymore," Leilani said.

"Maybe not."

"Now I understand something Torrey told me once," Leilani

said. "It was before I knew about the whole graysuit thing. She said that after she completed med school, when she was thinking about going into private practice, she realized she didn't have the same passion for medicine she once did, so she quit. At the time, I didn't understand how after all that time and money and hard work she could leave it behind. But now I get what she was saying. People change. I've changed, and the path I took 10 years ago might not be the right path for me anymore."

"If you're not in the FBI, what would you want to do?"

"I don't know. I really like investigating—questioning, digging, putting pieces together. I've always had this, like, intense curiosity about things. It used to drive my parents crazy," she said.

"Then find something else where you can put those skills to use. How about the work Finn and Julianna do? Maybe oceanography or marine biology or some kind of research? Cody said Finn is some kind of hotshot marine biologist or something," Jake said.

"Maybe. Ugh! I thought I was past all this. What about you? What are you going to do?" she asked.

"Me? I still like designing and programming websites. But it's a little hard imagining myself dealing with clients and then taking off in the middle of a job to go hunt a rogue vampire shark. I mean, what do I tell my client? 'Sorry, Mr. So-and-So. I can't get to your site for a couple of days. I've gotta go kill this supernatural creature you're not even aware exists so I can save some innocent beachgoers. You understand, right?'"

Leilani laughed. "I can see how that might be difficult."

"But to live on Tristan's money? I'd feel like a total leech," Jake said.

"Exactly! I need to do something—not just lounge at the beach, drink mojitos, and spend my fiancé's money. That's so not me," Leilani said.

Jake grinned. "I've got it! We could go into business together. Ryder & Waters Investigations. I can see the commercial now. 'Hi. I'm Jake Ryder. Think that pale, creepy neighbor who never goes out in sunlight is a vampire? Call 1-800-bloodsukr. We'll let you know if he's just weird or if he actually wants to drain you of your blood.'"

Leilani giggled. "Ooh, how about this? 'Hi. I'm Leilani Waters, former pro surfer and co-owner of Waters & Ryder Investigations. Is your beach infested with vampire sharks? Call 1-800-graysuit. Whether we stake 'em or bake 'em, you'll get your beach back. Guaranteed! Want 10% off your first service appointment? Call within the next hour, and tell 'em Heavenly Flower sent you.'"

Jake laughed. "Stake 'em or bake 'em? That's good. Maybe you should go into advertising."

Leilani sighed loudly. "I guess I'll figure it out sooner or later."

As they approached Leilani's freeway exit off Interstate 5, Jake asked, "Is it okay if I drop you off and take the car to my place? I gave away my truck to a friend right before we left for Oahu. In hindsight, that might've been a mistake because now I've got no wheels," he chuckled.

"That's fine," she said. "You can pick me up tomorrow night on our way back to the ferry."

"Okay. Call if you need me."

# 140 – Presence

At home, Leilani emptied her luggage. While her clothes churned in the washer, she watered her plants and cleared the rotting food from her refrigerator. After she caught up on several days of emails and tossed her clothes into the dryer, she settled into bed around 1 a.m.

Two hours later, she bolted upright. She felt like someone was in the bedroom with her. She sat motionless in the darkness. After a few seconds of listening to her heart pound in her ears, she mustered the courage to get out of bed and look around. She quietly reached for the flashlight next to her bed and removed the gun from the lockbox in her nightstand.

She crept from room to room in her bare feet. She checked the doors and windows. Everything was locked and secure, so she returned to bed. She tucked the flashlight and gun beneath the pillow next to her. She drifted into a restless sleep.

Leilani awoke with a start. She felt something on her leg, like a mouth pressing against her skin. Sharp fangs pierced her flesh. She cried out. She grabbed the flashlight and turned it on her legs. She saw nothing but the marks from Dean and Logan. She noticed one of the wounds on her right leg had opened up and was bleeding again. She got a bandage from the bathroom and placed it on her leg.

She sat down on her bed. She tried to slow her breathing, but the more she tried to calm herself, the more anxious she became. Tears streamed down her face. She couldn't stop them. She began crying. Again, she tried to calm herself, but she couldn't stop sobbing.

As the minutes passed, Leilani became more and more alarmed that she couldn't stop crying no matter how hard she tried. She reached for her phone. She heard a groggy voice say, "Yeah?"

"Can you ... come over? Something's ... wrong," she sputtered, unable to catch her breath.

"I'm on my way. Are you safe? Is someone there?"

"No. No one's ... here. But ... it feels like ... someone is. And ... I can't stop ... crying," she said.

"It'll be okay. I'll be right there. Just stay on the phone with me till I get there."

A few minutes later, Leilani heard a banging at her door.

"It's me! Let me in."

Leilani flung open the door and rushed into Jake's arms.

# 141 – Carson

Carson Lo watched Jake enter Leilani's house. He pulled his cell phone from his pocket. "Mara, it's Carson. Leilani's here at her house tonight."

"Is Tristan with her?" Mara asked.

"No. And I didn't see any of his things inside except an old photo album," Carson said.

"How'd you get in? I'm guessing she didn't invite you into her house," Mara said.

"Earlier I dressed up like a gas & electric guy and got the landlord to invite me in. Now I can enter whenever I want," Carson said.

"Where are you now?" she asked.

"In my car, across the street. Have you seen her, by the way? She's cute—and she tastes good too." Carson ran his tongue over his fangs, savoring the flavor of Leilani's blood. "Tristan's got great taste in women. I'll give him that."

Mara sighed. "Don't get distracted. You're there to do a job, not feed."

"I know," Carson said. "I was just curious."

"Did you find anything to give us any clue as to where Tristan is?" Mara asked.

"No. Leilani woke up, so I had to hightail it out of there. I slipped out through a sliding glass door and re-engaged the lock from the outside. She'll never know I was there."

"You're sure?" Mara asked.

"Yep," Carson said. "When I left, she called over some guy—early 20s, brown hair, medium height and build. I only caught a quick whiff, but I'm pretty sure he's a graysuit."

"One of Tristan's?"

"Probably," Carson guessed. "He doesn't look familiar

though. Maybe Tristan's creating again?"

"I doubt it. He might be the graysuit who was with Skylar in the Monterey Bay when our friends got killed."

"What happened?" Carson asked. "I thought Dean and his buddies were finally going to kill Leilani."

"That was the plan, but only Spencer survived. He got shot in the head with some kind of tranquilizer just as things were getting started. When he woke up, everyone was dead," Mara explained.

"I'm sorry about Dean," Carson said. "I know you guys were really close."

"Yeah. We were friends for 30 years," she sighed. "Now he's just another casualty of the war Tristan chooses to wage against his own kind."

"What now?" Carson asked. "If we kidnap Leilani, that'll definitely draw Tristan out."

"No. I have other plans for Tristan. Don't touch Leilani, and don't let her see you. Stay with her and the graysuit. If they split up, stick with Leilani. Keep me posted."

Mara Sombra leaned back in her office chair and smiled. *Your days are numbered, Tristan. Leilani's too.*

# 142 – Coping

Jake wrapped his arms around Leilani. "It's okay. I'm here. C'mon, let's sit down." He led her to the couch and sat beside her. "What's wrong? Did something happen?"

"No," she said. "But I can't calm down. I can't stop crying."

"C'mere." He enveloped Leilani in his arms again. He didn't know how long he held her until her sobs began to subside.

"Can you tell me what's wrong?" he asked gently.

Leilani reached for the box of tissue on the coffee table and wiped her eyes and nose. "I don't know. I was in bed, and all of a sudden, it felt like someone was in the room with me. I looked around the house, but no one was here. I went back to bed, and then it felt like it did with Dean and Logan. I could feel a mouth on my leg, the fangs … and then my leg started bleeding."

Jake wrapped his arm around Leilani and stroked her hair. "Do you want me to look around the house?"

"No. I already did," she said.

"Do you want to go back to bed?" he asked.

"No! Every time I close my eyes, I feel them on my arms and legs, biting me …"

"Shh, it's okay. You're safe. I'm here," Jake soothed.

"No. I can't shake this feeling—this anxiety. I can't calm myself down. Something's wrong with me," she said.

"Nothing's wrong with you. My god, Leilani, you were just attacked 10 days ago. What happened to you would mess anyone up. I'm still messed up, and what I went through was nothing like what you or Cody did," Jake said. "Before Cody came back, I kept seeing his body when it washed up. And then when I saw you tied to that chair, drenched in your own blood—it's seared into my brain. Every time I remember it and see you there like that, I want to kill Logan and Dean. Even though they're dead, I can't shake that feeling. That rage, that revulsion is still there. I don't know how to get rid of it. And that's just from seeing that stuff. I'm not the one who had to experience it."

"I keep thinking about Torrey and Cruz. They came to Tristan's house because they heard me scream. Now I'm alive, and they're not. I feel guilty. They tried to help me, and now they're dead. I just … I feel so weak. I should be stronger than this," Leilani said.

"Bullshit. You are strong. You're probably the strongest person I know. But you're still human, Leilani. You feel things, and that's good. If this didn't mess you up, then I'd be worried. What happened to you was horrible. With all the running around we've been doing, you haven't had time to deal with it. Your brain and body are just telling you it's time to deal with it— because if you don't, you're gonna make yourself sick. So, let it out. Let go."

She looked into Jake's caring eyes and began sobbing again. He pulled her close. He could feel each sob violently rack her body.

After a while, Jake felt her loosen her grip on him. "Are you feeling better?"

"I think so. I'll be right back," she said.

As Leilani splashed cold water over her face at the bathroom sink, she could remember only one other time when she'd completely lost control of her emotions. It was the night she confessed to Tristan that she was an FBI agent and that it was no accident they met. But she knew that this was much worse. She'd never felt so helpless in her life.

She dried her face and walked back to the couch but didn't see Jake. Panic set in. "Jake?"

"In the kitchen. I'll be right there." He returned to the couch with two steaming mugs of tea. "Drink this. The label says it's 'calming and soothing,' so it must be, right?"

They drank their tea in silence and set their empty mugs on the coffee table.

"I'm sorry for that earlier—all the crying," she said. "I don't know what came over me."

"Don't do that, Leilani," he said softly. "You never have to apologize for being you."

Leilani gazed appreciatively at Jake and lifted her head to kiss his cheek. At the same moment, he turned his head to kiss her forehead. Their lips connected.

All the electroreceptors in Jake's head lit up. He felt a rush of warmth travel across his forehead, over the top of his head, and down his spine.

Leilani, too, felt a surprising rush when their lips touched. Before she knew what was happening, she felt Jake's lips moving against hers. She felt his tongue enter her mouth and touch hers. She pulled away. "I'm sorry. I shouldn't have …"

"No, it's my fault," Jake said. "I was going to kiss your forehead and …"

"No, it's me. I was going to kiss your cheek, and I guess I missed. I'm sorry. Can you forgive me?"

"If you can forgive me." Jake lay back against the couch and groaned.

"What?" she asked.

"Oh, nothing. It's just that Tristan's going to want to kick my ass when he hears about this, and I don't blame him. I would too."

"Tristan's not going to hear about this," she assured him. "It was an accident, right?"

"Well, yeah. I mean, it's not like we planned for this to happen," Jake said, "but I still feel kind of guilty."

"I know. But like you said, we didn't mean for this to

happen. And it won't happen again, so I say we let sleeping graysuits lie. Telling Tristan about this wouldn't accomplish anything," Leilani said. "It would only hurt him. And it didn't mean anything."

Jake winced.

"I didn't mean it like that. I just meant …"

"I know what you meant. Don't worry about it. I'm cool with not telling Tristan if you are. Plus, I think kissing the creator's fiancée is probably a stake-able offense in the vampire shark community," he said. "So, why don't we call it a night? I'll stay here on the couch. We can pack your stuff tomorrow and then go to my apartment and get my things."

"You don't have to stay. I think I'll be okay now."

"Dude, I'm staying," Jake said firmly. "Now get some sleep."

# 143 – Other Sharks

The next night, Leilani and Jake drove back to Dana Point. They didn't mention the kiss again.

When they boarded the ferry, they didn't notice Carson Lo following several feet behind them. With his wispy black hair buried beneath a black skull cap, bronze skin, friendly eyes, and hey-dude-let's-party smile, he looked like just another surfer—which made it easy to stalk his prey.

When the ferry arrived in Avalon, Carson spotted Tristan waiting on the pier. He sent a text to Mara: "tristan in avalon. will tail & report back 2 u."

While Carson watched from the shadows, Tristan wrapped his arms around Leilani and gave her a kiss. "I missed you!"

"Me too," she said.

Tristan released her and patted Jake's shoulder. "Good to see you, man."

"Yeah," Jake muttered.

"Everything go okay?" Tristan asked.

"Mmhmmm," Leilani said.

Tristan eyed them suspiciously. "Doesn't seem like it. What happened?"

Leilani quickly glanced at Jake. "I had a rough time last night. Jake helped me, but I was pretty much a mess."

"Are you all right?" Tristan asked.

"I'm fine. I'll tell you about it later." She reached for Tristan's hand and entwined her fingers with his.

"I have something that'll cheer you up." Tristan's eyes danced as he reached into his pocket.

"What?" she asked.

"This!" He opened a small box to reveal Leilani's new engagement ring. "It arrived today."

"It's beautiful! It looks just like the one you gave me before," Leilani said.

"Let's get this back where it belongs." Tristan slipped the ring on her finger.

Jake turned away, feeling like a third wheel—and feeling guilty about his kiss with Leilani, how much he enjoyed it, and how much he wished it hadn't stopped. Seeing the ring back on Leilani's finger made his heart ache, even though he knew it was what she wanted.

"This'll keep the other sharks away," Tristan joked.

"Yeah," Leilani laughed nervously. "It really is beautiful, Tristan. Thank you."

"You're welcome." Tristan wondered why Leilani didn't seem like herself and why Jake seemed so distant. "Jake, can we drop you off at the compound?"

"Yeah, thanks."

Both Jake and Leilani remained silent during the ride, which made Tristan worry.

# 144 – Dealing

As soon as Tristan closed the door to their hotel room, he wrapped his arms around Leilani and gave her a deep, soulful kiss. "Welcome home."

She glanced around. "Home, huh?"

"Anyplace you are is home." Tristan peered into her eyes. "Now tell me what's wrong. What happened last night?"

She told him about everything except the kiss with Jake.

"Why didn't you call? I would've come for you," he said.

"You were here, and it was too far. I thought I was losing my mind. I needed someone right there, right then, so I called Jake," she explained.

"I'm glad he was there, but I wish I could've been there for you. I'm so sorry you had to go through that." Tristan's eyes darkened. "You know, I almost wish Skylar hadn't killed Dean so I could do it myself. I'd like to tear him limb from limb and then have Finn stitch him up so that I can tear him apart all over again. Fuck! I should've never trusted him, let him into my house, let him be anywhere near you ..."

"Tristan, calm down. I'm okay. I'd been carrying all that around since that night, and I just needed to get it out of my system—or at least start to deal with it. I feel better. Really. And now that I'm better, I don't want you getting all worked up. The best thing we can do is forget about Dean and Logan. They already took so much from us. I don't want them to take any more," she said.

"You're right." He rubbed his thumb over her engagement ring. "This is all that matters—that I have you here with me. I meant what I said when I slipped this ring on your finger the first time. I will love you forever, Leilani."

She wrapped her arms around him. "Forever."

# 145 – Sandwiches

The next day, Tristan and Leilani decided to head to the compound to see if the finners had spotted any nefarious graysuit activity in the last 24 hours. They ran into Skylar in the hotel lobby on their way out.

"Leilani! It's good to have you back here," Skylar said. "Tristan was so moody without you."

"Really?" Leilani asked.

"I wasn't moody, Skylar. I just missed her," Tristan said.

"No, dude. You were moody." Skylar turned to Leilani. "I had to take him out surfing to cheer him up. Then we ended up drinking way too much wine and falling asleep in my bed."

Leilani narrowed her eyes at Tristan.

"We passed out," he clarified.

"Nothing happened, of course," Skylar said. "Just too much good wine in one sitting."

"Right. Anyway, we're on our way out. See you later, Skylar." Tristan reached for Leilani's hand, and they walked out the front door. When they were a few steps down the sidewalk, he turned to her. "I'm so sorry about that. Nothing happened with Skylar. I swear. I was going to tell you about it, but then you started telling me about what happened with Jake—when you were upset and couldn't stop crying. Then I got upset thinking about Dean, and I totally forgot. Are you mad?"

Leilani thought back to her accidental kiss with Jake. "No. I'm not mad. I just wish you would've told me so I wouldn't have had to hear about it from Skylar first."

"I know, and I'm sorry," Tristan said.

"Okay. Just don't let it happen again," Leilani said.

They arrived at the compound and greeted Jake and Cody in the mess hall.

"Hey guys, what's up? You feeling better, Leilani?" Jake asked.

"I'm okay," she replied.

Cody smiled at her. "Just okay? Nah. You look beautiful today."

Leilani blushed.

"She looks beautiful every day," Tristan said. "So, is everything still quiet on the graysuit front?"

"Seems to be," Cody answered. "Matt's monitoring things in Finn's office if you want to go ask him."

"I will. Leilani, why don't you make us some sandwiches while I take care of business?" Tristan asked.

"I'll come with you," she said.

"No need. I won't be long," Tristan replied.

"But I can help," Leilani said. "I can …"

"I've got this," he said. "I'll be back soon."

"But Tristan, I really want to …"

"Don't worry about it. Relax here with Jake and Cody." Tristan kissed her forehead. "Oh, if they have any salmon, I'll take that." He left the mess hall and set out to find Matt.

Leilani sat, speechless. *What just happened? Does he actually think I came here to make sandwiches? And after that whole thing with Skylar, he thinks he can just boss me around? Seriously?! I'm an FBI agent. Not his personal chef. Is this how he thinks it's going to be from now on? Because I'm not giving up my career for this.* She marched to the refrigerator. She slapped a piece of salmon between two dry pieces of sourdough bread and made a raw veggie sandwich for herself. She slid Tristan's plate in front of his empty seat. The top piece of bread fell off the salmon. She didn't bother to fix it. Instead, she tore into her sandwich.

"I have an idea," Jake said excitedly, oblivious to Leilani's dark mood.

"*We* have an idea," Cody corrected. "Give credit where credit is due, man."

"Whatever, dude. Anyway, *we* have an idea. I know what I can do so I feel like I'm doing something useful and not leeching off of Tristan," Jake said.

"That makes one of us," Leilani mumbled to herself.

"What? Is something wrong?" Jake asked.

"No. Sorry. Go ahead," she said.

"I want to create a website where surfers can report shark sightings and attacks. I figure that surfers know the ocean better than anyone. They're in the water all the time, so they'll be the first to see anything suspicious. And they can be pretty specific about the sightings because they know every beach, every break …"

"That sounds cool," Leilani interrupted, "but don't websites like that already exist?"

"Yeah, there are other sites that do stuff like this. But they don't know what we do, so we can create the best site," Jake said.

"The thing about Jake is he's super-modest about his work," Cody interjected with a grin.

"Shut up, dude. I said 'we.' Anyway, I think *we* can create the best site for this, and if it works, maybe we can prevent some killings," Jake said. "What d'ya think?"

"It sounds like a great idea," she replied.

"Do you think Tristan will like it?" Jake asked.

"I think he'll love it. I'm sure he really values your professional skills and experience," Leilani said. "Unlike mine," she muttered under her breath.

# 146 — Crush

Tristan wandered down the hall. He spotted a door with Finn's name on it. He knocked and pressed the buzzer outside the door. "Hello? Matt?"

Hearing no response, Tristan punched Julianna's code into the keypad. He stepped inside and closed the door. He saw a wall of monitors with video and audio from each lab. He wondered if Julianna had a similar office. *Though if she did*, he thought, *she probably would've discovered I was here earlier than she did.*

Tristan's gaze moved from monitor to monitor, lab to lab. Labs 1 through 3 were empty. He paused when he got to the monitor for lab #4. He spotted something gray on the hospital bed. *Ash. I wonder who they had in there. Maybe that woman Finn mentioned? What was her name? Lily?*

On the monitor, Tristan saw the door open to lab #4. Matt and Lucia entered.

"I guess Finn forgot to take out the trash before he left." Matt scooped the remains of the vampire shark into a dustpan and dumped it in the trashcan. He stripped the bed and tossed the soiled sheets by the door so he could take them to the laundry room on his way out.

"You better not let Tristan hear you call one of his friends 'trash,'" Lucia said.

"How do you know it was one of his friends?" he asked.

"Because they were all his friends at one time, weren't they? He created them all," she said.

"Yeah, but he might have created this one 40 years ago and then never saw her again," Matt said.

"Seriously? It's nice to know he set the bar so high for those he gifted with near-immortality. Smart guy, that Tristan," Lucia mocked. "A real visionary."

Matt shook his head. "Well, we're working with him now, and Julianna and Finn trust him so …"

"Yeah, yeah, so we do too," she said.

When Tristan saw them head for the lab door, he hurried into the hall. He walked toward the door that connected the ground floor to the subterranean level so he'd run into them.

"Hi, Matt, Lucia," he said warmly as they entered the hallway.

"Hi, Tristan." Matt dumped the dirty sheets in the laundry room and shut the door. "Lucia, you remember Tristan from the wedding?"

Tristan smiled and extended his hand. As soon as Lucia grasped his hand and peered into his espresso-brown eyes, she lost track of space and time. It was just her, Tristan, his hand on hers, and the infinite depth of his mesmerizing eyes.

Noticing that Lucia refused to release Tristan's hand, Matt turned to her. "Lucia?"

No response.

"Lucia?" he asked again.

Still no response.

Tristan couldn't suppress his grin. He knew the effect he often had on women and found it amusing that Lucia was so taken with him after dissing him only a minute before.

"Lucia!" Matt grasped her hand and pried it from Tristan's.

"What?" Lucia asked, her voice far away. Slowly, she realized where she was. She saw Matt staring at her. "What?!"

"I dunno. You tell me," Matt said.

"Tell you what?" she asked.

"Nothing," Matt sighed. "Tristan, what can we do for you?"

"I wanted to ask if there's any graysuit activity to see if we can help," Tristan replied.

"Not since the last time I checked. Why don't I finish up here with Lucia and meet you outside Finn's office in a minute?" Matt suggested.

"Sure." Tristan turned and walked back toward Finn's office.

Lucia watched him go, admiring the view of his rear-end.

"You're unbelievable," Matt muttered.

"What?" Lucia asked.

"You're totally crushing on him. Lucia—crushing on a graysuit! That's something I never thought I'd see," Matt said. "Plus, I thought you were only into women."

"No, I like men too—just not the men around here," Lucia said. "But him? He's gorgeous!"

"You are so shallow," Matt teased.

"What about you?" Lucia retorted. "You're the one crushing on a graysuit."

"What are you talking about? I'm not the one who was just checking out Tristan's ass."

"You like Julianna. You *looove* her. You pretend you're best friends, but I know it's more than that for you," she taunted.

"You don't know anything," Matt insisted.

"You can say it all you want, but I don't believe you. You get all gooey-eyed every time you're around her," Lucia said.

"You're so wrong. I can't even believe we're having this conversation," Matt said. "I've gotta go meet Tristan."

# 147 — Red Devil

Matt unlocked Finn's office and opened the door.

Tristan glanced around the room and pretended to be surprised. "Are all these labs monitored?"

"Yep," Matt replied.

"Are they all for vampire sharks? Or do you study other things here?" Tristan asked.

"Labs 1, 4, and 6 are for vampire sharks. Labs 2, 3, and 5 are for finners who get hurt capturing vampire sharks," Matt said.

"Does that happen a lot?" Tristan asked.

"More often than we'd like. I recently spent time in lab #2," Matt said.

"I heard. Are you okay now?" Tristan asked.

"Yeah, except for the post-traumatic stress disorder," Matt said. "But who doesn't have a touch of PTSD from vampire sharks, right?"

Tristan couldn't tell if Matt was joking. "Right," he said as he scanned the monitors. "Is there a reason certain labs are designated for vampire sharks and others are for finners?"

"Yeah. It was kind of an inside joke of Terrell's. He used to go off on these rants about scientists trying to communicate with whoever might be listening in outer space. A lot of them thought they'd be able to communicate with an alien species using math—prime numbers and stuff. But Terrell thought it was stupid to reach all the way out into space to find intelligent species when we have them right here on earth—dolphins, whales, elephants ... Of course, dolphins were Terrell's favorite, even before he became the first finner. When he was still human, he used to try to convince these other scientists to use their math-based communication—if, in fact, it was such a great communication tool—with dolphins, but they weren't interested. So, Terrell bought this compound and embarked on his own research."

"And he assigned the labs with prime numbers—2, 3, and 5—to finners?" Tristan smiled at Matt. "That's funny."

"Yeah, he was a pretty cool dude. He's Finn and Julianna's hero. I guess he's mine too," Matt said. "He's the reason finners exist. Without him, I'd be dead."

"How did you end up a finner? Were you killed by a vampire shark when you were human?" Tristan asked, dreading the answer.

"No. I was scuba diving," Matt said. "I got separated from my friends. I was down pretty deep, shooting video, and I got attacked by a Humboldt squid. He was, like, 7 feet long—about a foot longer than me anyway. I guess he didn't like me recording him because he tore off my face mask, pulled my breathing apparatus from my mouth, and ripped off my scuba tank and fins. Then he wrapped himself around my head and yanked on my left arm, which dislocated my shoulder. I ended up drowning—but not before I saw him swim off with my video camera."

"I've heard of them attacking divers before, but that's pretty crazy," Tristan said. "I guess that's why they're called 'red devils,' right?"

"Totally. You see my hair? It used to be black. But that incident scared me so bad that when I became a finner and morphed for the first time, my hair was gray," Matt said. "Anyway, Julianna is the one who saved me and brought me here. So, it all worked out okay. Finn arrived shortly after that, and we've all been working together ever since."

Tristan decided to indirectly ask Matt about the pile of ash in lab #4—a test to see if he'd be open and honest with him. Tristan pointed to the monitor. "This lab here. There's no bedding. Did you have a vampire shark in there?"

"Her name was Lily. Julianna and I caught her right around the time you arrived," Matt replied. "Julianna removed her fangs and sacs so we could analyze her venom. She didn't last very long after that."

The hairs on the back of Tristan's neck stood up. *If Cody hadn't been here, that easily could've happened to me.*

"What did Lily do?" Tristan asked casually.

"We're not killing vampire sharks for no reason if that's what you're wondering," Matt said. "I'm part dolphin, remember? Smarter than a human. If you want to know something, just ask."

"Right. Sorry. Yes, that's what I was wondering," Tristan admitted.

"Okay, let me show you what Lily did so you'll see why we couldn't let her go." Matt scrolled through a few folders on Finn's computer until he located the right one. He opened it and clicked on the video file.

Tristan watched the screen and heard Julianna narrating, "We're searching for a vampire shark named Lily ..." As soon as he saw the shark snatch the stranded kayaker and crush him between her jaws, he stopped the video. "I've seen enough." Tristan rubbed his eyes. "So much senseless killing. Where did it all go so wrong?"

Matt stared blankly at Tristan. He didn't expect this reaction from the creator of all graysuits. He didn't expect to see regret.

Tristan pointed to another monitor. "What about lab #6? It looks like the bedding in there is stripped."

"Yeah," Matt said quietly. "That was the one who attacked me. He died too. I'm not sure how. It happened when I was recovering."

"I'm really sorry you got hurt," Tristan said.

Matt shrugged. "It wasn't you that attacked me."

"No, but I still feel responsible, and I'm deeply sorry." Tristan gripped Matt's shoulder. "Thank you for what you're doing to save people. You guys are all incredibly brave, and I'm sure you've saved a great many lives."

"We try."

"We do too. Maybe now that we're working together we can finally get this thing under control," Tristan said.

"You really think so?" Matt asked.

Tristan smiled ruefully. "A graysuit can dream, can't he?"

# 148 — Just Tired

Tristan arrived back in the mess hall long after Leilani had finished her lunch. "Sorry. I got caught up with Matt. We were talking business. He told me what happened to the last two graysuits who were brought in. It was pretty ugly."

"Here's your sandwich." Leilani pointed to the plate in front of him but snatched her hand back before he could touch her.

Tristan looked at her, but she wouldn't make eye contact. "What's up?"

"Nothing. Jake has an idea he wants to share with you. I'm going back to the hotel," she said flatly.

"Wait, I'll go with you," he offered.

"No. You stay and 'talk business' with Jake," Leilani said.

"Is something wrong?" Tristan asked. "Is it that thing with Skylar?"

"No, it's not that at all. I'm just tired. Stay. Talk. I'll see you later." Leilani stepped away from the table. "Bye, guys."

"Bye," Jake and Cody said.

When Leilani exited the room, Tristan turned to Jake. "Is she mad about something?"

"I don't know," Jake said.

"Maybe …" Cody stopped, wondering if he should continue.

"Maybe what?" Tristan asked.

"Maybe she's pissed because you went to go 'take care of business,' and you left her here to 'make sandwiches,'" Cody said.

"She's mad because I was gone too long?" Tristan asked.

"No, dude. She's mad because … Listen, I haven't known Leilani very long, but she doesn't seem like the kind of woman who's content to make sandwiches while her partner goes off to do his important business—especially now when she's feeling really unsure about her career," Cody said.

Tristan sighed. "But I just asked her to make us lunch. We were hungry. I thought it would save time if she did that while I did what I needed to do. I didn't mean it like she's subservient to me or something."

"Maybe not. But I think that's how it made her feel," Cody said.

"Huh." Tristan leaned back in his chair, dazed. "And all this time I thought I knew a lot about women."

"Yeah, Cody has a way with women," Jake chuckled. "A bunch of the younger guys at the beach used to call him the 'wahine whisperer.'"

Cody shook his head. "I always hated that. It sounds so condescending to women—like they have no choice in the matter."

"Oh, they have a choice," Jake laughed, "and they always choose you."

"I just understand women is all," Cody said. "Everyone says women want to be loved and cherished, and that's true. But they also want to be heard and respected."

"How do you know so much about women?" Tristan asked.

"My dad split before I was born, so my mom raised me all by herself," Cody said. "She worked hard every day of her life to provide for me. I'd see the way guys treated her. Some were cool. Some weren't. My mom was a tough lady though. She had a lot of self-respect. She was really nice, but she didn't put up with crap. If a guy disrespected her, he was gone. She wanted to set an example for me of how I should treat women by showing me what was okay and what wasn't with her own relationships.

"The thing with Leilani is, right now, she probably doesn't feel like she's being respected," Cody continued. "When a woman is pissed and you ask her what's wrong and she tells you she's 'just tired,' you're probably in serious trouble, dude. I know because my mom used to say the same thing to guys right before she'd dump them. She'd be tired because she was working too much and they weren't working enough. Or she'd be tired because they weren't doing their fair share of work around the house or in the relationship. You need to ask Leilani what she needs that she's not getting. Then step up and do it, or step aside."

"You got all that from her saying she's 'just tired'?" Tristan asked.

"That look on her face when she said it? I've seen it before—lots of times—on my mom's face and other women, and it never ends well," Cody said.

"So, I should go after her and apologize? And ask her what she needs?" Tristan asked.

Cody nodded and smiled. "Now you're getting it."

"You know, Cody, Skylar's single," Tristan said. "She could use a good man who knows how to treat women."

"No way, dude," Jake said. "Don't even think it!"

"Sorry, Jake," Tristan chuckled. "I'm out. Thanks, guys."

# 149 – Purpose

Tristan entered the hotel room. "Leilani?"

"In here," she called from the bathroom.

He walked in and found her soaking in a bubble bath. He couldn't tell if she was angry. He sat on the edge of the tub. "I'm sorry about before. I didn't mean to leave you behind to fix us food while I went off to talk business with Matt. That was stupid of me. I didn't mean it like that."

"I know you didn't mean anything by it. It's just that I've been thinking about my career. A lot. And I've come to the conclusion that I might not want to continue with it—in its current form anyway. I don't see how our relationship can work with me holding down a job like that. We'd never see each other," Leilani said.

"But if it's what you want to do, we can make it work."

"No, we can't. That's reality, Tristan. I've been doing this job awhile now. It's demanding. With all the traveling you do, we'd never see each other. That's not the kind of marriage I want."

Tristan's jaw dropped. "You don't want to marry me?!"

"That's not what I'm saying. Of course, I want to marry you," she said.

Tristan exhaled a huge sigh of relief.

"How could you even ask that? I love you," she said.

"But something's not working for you. You said you were tired. What are you tired of?" he asked.

"I'm tired of trying to figure out what I'm going to do with my life. I know you said I don't have to work anymore, but that's not me. I like working. I like having a purpose every day. I need that. It fills me up. I can't be happy without that," she explained.

"That's fine. But if you don't want to continue as an FBI

agent, then what do you want to do?"

"I want to find a way to use my interests and talents in a way that's useful and fulfilling—like Jake has."

"Jake?" Tristan asked.

"Didn't he tell you his idea?"

"No."

"Then what did you guys talk about after I left?" she asked.

"I dunno. Guy stuff." Tristan hoped Leilani wouldn't press him since they spent the entire time talking about her. "What's Jake's idea?"

Leilani told him about the website.

"That sounds awesome! How soon can he start?" Tristan asked.

"Probably as soon as you want him to," Leilani replied.

"Okay, but what about you? How do you want to use your interests and talents to make the world a better place?" he asked.

"I'm not sure yet," she said. "What's so frustrating is that I feel lost. If I'm not an FBI agent, then who am I?"

"You know, I went through something similar to this when I was still human," Tristan recalled. "I was 29. I was staring 30 in the face, and I felt like the world wanted me to find my life's purpose and become my own man. It was kind of intimidating. I felt like I was being pushed to do something, but I didn't know what."

"That's how I feel," Leilani said.

"And you're 29 now?" he asked.

"Yep, 30 is just around the corner," she said.

"Yeah, you're probably feeling like it's time for you to step up and find your destiny or at least get on the path to your destiny, right?" he asked.

"Exactly. So, what did you do?" she asked.

Tristan flashed an embarrassed smile. "I wish I could say I did something. I woke up the morning of my birthday and felt really melancholy. It felt like the whole universe was disappointed I hadn't found my way yet. I continued to wander kind of aimlessly through my life until I turned 31. That's when I got turned into a vampire. I guess if you don't find your way, something else finds you. It might not be the path you'd choose for yourself, but it is what it is."

"Ugh, this is depressing me even more," Leilani said.

"Sorry. But if you think about it, there's a happy ending. I found my path the night I became a vampire because it eventually led me to you—and here we are," he said.

"Here we are."

"Hey, maybe you and I are together for a reason that's bigger than the two of us," Tristan said. "Maybe we're meant to work together to save people—like I'm now working with Finn and Julianna, and maybe Jake and Cody too."

"So, I'd continue to do what I'm doing but just not as an employee of the FBI?" Leilani asked.

"Yeah. If you love what you do, why not do it for us, the Nomads?"

"Because I'd have no resources. When I flash my badge, doors open, people talk to me. I have access to all these different databases and files and stuff. I'd lose all that if I resign. It'd be like trying to work with one hand tied behind my back," she said.

"No, it wouldn't," Tristan smiled. "I can hook you up with the access you need."

"What? How?" she asked.

"The thing about vampires and vampire sharks is we live under the radar. We have to because humans wouldn't be able to deal with knowing they're not at the top of the food chain anymore. And most vampires and graysuits need to work, just like everyone else, to have things like shelter and clothing. So, we have people all over the place—mostly vampires because there are a lot more of them, but some graysuits too. Some are with the FBI, CIA, police, government, hospitals, banks, schools, corporations. Basically, almost anyplace you have humans, you have at least one vampire on the payroll. And we help each other. The vampire at the DMV will adjust birthdates on IDs. The vampire at the police station will let his friends know if another officer is getting too close to a vampire nest."

"So, you'd hook me up with your moles?" Leilani teased.

"They're not moles," Tristan said. "They take pride in their work, just like humans do. And, like us, many of them work to protect humans."

"I have to say, I'm intrigued. Do you really think it could work?" she asked.

"I know it could. We'd set you up with the right credentials and passwords, or get you into the databases you need through back doors in the code. I've been alive a long time. I have friends in a lot of different places. I can get you whatever you need. The question is, what do you want?"

Leilani pondered the question. "I don't know exactly. But this could be a good place to start. It could be a test—to figure out if this is still what I want and if it actually works."

"So, is that a yes?" he asked.

"Yes!" Leilani sank down in the tub. The fragrant bubbles tickled her chin as they popped. "I feel so relieved! It's like a huge weight just lifted off my shoulders."

"When do you want to start? I can make a few calls now," Tristan offered.

"How about tomorrow? For now, why don't you climb in here with me and celebrate?"

In a flash, Tristan's clothes fell into a pile on the bathroom floor. "You don't have to ask me twice." He splashed into the tub. "Let's get this party started."

# 150 — Mara

Carson stood beneath the green awning covering the entrance of the hotel where Tristan and Leilani were staying. He dialed Mara, admiring the view of the boats docked in Avalon Bay. "Hey, Mara. I've got an update for you. Tristan and Leilani are staying at a hotel on Crescent Avenue. Earlier today, they visited a building on the outskirts of Avalon—past Descanso Bay and White Rock but not as far as Frog Rock."

"What building?" Mara asked.

"I don't know," Carson replied.

"How can you not know?"

"Well, it looks pretty normal, kind of like an office building with residences above it. It's totally secure though. There's only one entrance off the street, and it's locked. You can't see inside the windows at all. I tried to find a way in. But it looks like they have cameras everywhere, so I didn't want to spend too much time poking around. You think the building could be Tristan's?" Carson asked.

"He's never spent much time in Catalina, and I've never heard anything about him having a building there," she said.

"Here's the thing, Mara … I get a really skeevy feeling around that place, like some bad shit has gone down there. I've asked around, but no one's sure who owns it or what goes on inside. Most people think it's some kind of research facility, like maybe the R&D arm of some secret technology company or something. What's even weirder is that there's no address on the building, and it doesn't show up on Google or any other search engine. Anywhere. When you search for the location, nothing shows up on the street map or the satellite images. It's like the building doesn't exist."

"Okay. I'll see what I can find out about it," Mara said.

"Do you want me to keep tailing Tristan and Leilani?" he asked.

"For now. Thanks, Carson. You're doing a great job."

Carson grinned into the phone. "Thanks, Mara. Talk to you later."

Mara leaned back in her black leather chair in her elegantly appointed office. Her thick, blunt-cut, raven-colored hair shone beneath the recessed lighting, contrasting beautifully with her flawless pale skin and soft red lips. She gazed at a picture of Dean and herself, positioned next to her computer on her desk. It was taken when they met at an Oingo Boingo concert in early 1986 at the Del Mar Fairgrounds during the Dead Man's Party tour.

She traced the edge of the pewter picture frame with her fingertip. *Dean, baby, I don't know why you thought you could convince Tristan to see things our way. You and Lance should've just killed him and Leilani when you first arrived on his doorstep two-and-a-half weeks ago. Your affection for Tristan and the memory of the friendship you had 40 years ago was your fatal flaw. And Tristan's self-righteousness—that's his.*

# 151 — Perks

The next morning, Leilani called the special agent in charge of the FBI's San Diego Division and resigned. She completed all the paperwork, transferred her open case files to her boss, and closed her laptop with a flourish. "I guess I'm an independent contractor now. I have to say, it feels good to be my own boss."

"And what a beautiful boss you are." Tristan leaned over and kissed her. "I'm happy you're so happy about this."

"I am. Even better, my old boss said since I still had another couple of weeks on my leave of absence, he'd consider that my two weeks notice. He also said I should give him a call if I ever need anything, so maybe that little favor will come in handy someday," she said.

"Do you have anything you need to get from work, like personal belongings?" he asked.

"No. I'm not the type to decorate my office. You should know that. I believe on our first date you made a pretty rude comment about my home decorating," she teased. "I may have left a mug on my desk, but the FBI can keep it as my parting gift."

"I'll get you a new mug," Tristan said magnanimously. "It's the least I can do for the newest member of the Nomads."

"A new mug? Wow! I didn't know being a Nomad had so many perks," Leilani grinned. "Did Jake and Cody get mugs, or are you playing favorites with me?"

Tristan kissed her. "Oh, I'm definitely playing favorites."

"Good. I like being your favorite." She smiled and kissed him back. "Speaking of Jake and Cody, we should go tell them you like their idea for the website."

"Now?" he asked.

"No time like the present," she said.

"All right," he agreed, "but it would be much more fun to

stay here with you."

When they arrived at Cody's apartment, Leilani revealed that she'd be working with the Nomads as their very own special agent. Then Tristan told them he loved the idea for the website for surfers to report shark sightings and attacks.

"That's great! When do you want us to start?" Jake asked.

"Whenever you want," Tristan replied. "Hey, Leilani, Jake, do you mind if I step outside and talk with Cody? He helped me out with something yesterday, and I haven't had a chance to thank him."

Leilani and Jake shook their heads. Once Cody and Tristan stepped into the hallway and closed the door, Jake turned to Leilani. "So, I guess we're both Nomads now."

"I guess so," she said.

"And you and Tristan are good?" he asked.

"We're great. We talked yesterday, and he helped me come up with this idea. He said he can get me the access I need to continue my work, even if I'm no longer in the FBI."

"Good. We're still agreed we're not telling Tristan about what happened with the, uh, accidental kiss?" Jake asked.

"Yeah. It's better that way. And we're good? You're not upset about what happened?" Leilani asked.

"No. I'm fine," he assured her. "It was an accident, and it will never happen again. You're with Tristan, and I'm happy for you guys. We're cool."

# 152 – Getting Away

In the hallway, Tristan and Cody talked quietly.

"Thanks again for yesterday," Tristan said.

"I'm glad it all worked out," Cody replied.

"It's funny. All this time I thought I understood women. But yesterday with Leilani … Then right before I met you, some stuff went down with Skylar … And before that, other women and, of course, Julianna … Anyway, I've come to realize I don't have a clue. Were you this smart when you were human, or does being part dolphin help?" Tristan asked.

"I dunno. I like women. Women like me." Cody frowned. "Or at least they used to. There aren't many single women around here. I think I need to get out more. I know Jake definitely does."

"Oh yeah?" Tristan asked.

Cody stopped. *Yeah, he's in love with your fiancée, dude. He needs a woman to take his mind off her so he doesn't drive himself crazy,* he thought.

"Yeah," Cody said. "Seeing as how he was last involved with Skylar and that didn't turn out so well, it might be good if he meets some new women."

"You're right," Tristan said. "Things seem pretty quiet now. There haven't been any attacks. Maybe we can all get some R&R. You and Jake can take off. And Leilani and I can take some time for ourselves and get away from all this for a while."

# 153 – Paradise

Across the Pacific Ocean, Finn and Julianna sat in bed, eating tropical fruit from an ornately carved wooden platter. They listened to the soothing sounds of the ocean through the open windows of their rented condo in Poipu Beach.

Julianna took a bite of pineapple. "I'm famished!"

"Me too. But I guess four days of nonstop honeymoon sex will do that to you whether you're a human, a finner, or a graysuit," Finn chuckled.

"I thought sex as a human was fantastic. But as a vampire with heightened senses? There are no words," she said. "You're incredible, Finn. I love you so much."

"I love you, and I love being married to you. It's even better than I thought it would be. Even though we've been together a long time, it feels different—like our relationship is deeper somehow. Is it like that for you?" he asked.

"Being married to you is awesome, Finn. Really. I don't know why I waited so long. But I wouldn't say it feels different—and that's a good thing. I didn't want it to feel different. I wanted it to feel exactly the same and it does, and that makes me so happy."

"Should we go for a moonlight swim?" he asked. "It's a beautiful night."

She grinned playfully. "That depends on what you mean by 'swim.'"

"What would you like it to mean?"

"How about if we finish this platter and then go work up an appetite again?" she suggested.

Finn and Julianna strolled down the path to Brennecke's Beach. Seeing the beach deserted, they removed their swimsuits, set them on their towels in the sand, and splashed into the water. They made love in the ocean. Afterward they floated, feeling the earth lazily spin around them as the stars carved glittery arcs into the sky.

"This is perfect. Maybe we should close the compound and move to Kauai," Finn joked.

Julianna smiled. "You might be onto something, Dr. Finnegan. This is paradise."

"You are paradise."

After they floated a few minutes more, Finn announced he was ready to return to the condo. "I'm beat. I may power down both brain hemispheres tonight. I need a deep, deep sleep."

"I'd like to stay out here a little longer. I'm hungry again. I'll morph and find something to eat—a fresh Hawaiian seafood dinner," Julianna said.

"Okay. Just make sure you come back before sunrise. I'll leave your bikini and towel where they are in the sand." Finn kissed her and returned to shore.

Julianna turned into a great white shark and headed deeper into the sea.

# 154 – Prey

Julianna started with small prey. She moved from bright yellow triggerfish to iridescent silver bonefish to brilliant green and yellow mahi mahi to dark blue and silver ono. As the size of each kill increased, so did her excitement. Adrenaline surged through her body. She felt elated, intoxicated. After killing the ono, conscious thought stopped and instinct took over. Julianna felt … free.

By the time she returned to shore, she couldn't remember the last kills. It was all so exhilarating that everything faded together into a frenzy of splashing and gnashing. Still dazed from her underwater adventures, Julianna forgot about her bathing suit and towel on the beach. Naked, she ambled through the sand, across the street, and back up the path to the condo. She collapsed on the bed. "The thrill of the kill," she mumbled to herself as she slipped into a deep sleep.

Finn awoke first. He gazed at Julianna and saw her eyes darting beneath her eyelids. He quietly climbed from bed and pulled on his trunks for a quick bodysurfing session. He knew that early morning was a prime feeding time for sharks, but it was also one of his favorite times in the ocean. He set out on the short walk to the beach, feeling grateful to be alive, here on this beautiful island with the love of his life.

As he padded toward the ocean, he felt something other than grains of sand beneath his feet. He looked down and saw he'd stepped on Julianna's towel. Her bikini lay on top of it, exactly where he'd left it. *Did she forget to put this on before she came home?*

At that moment, a wave of noxious air struck Finn's nostrils. It smelled like death. He crept closer to the ocean, his senses alert, his heart thumping like a taiko drum in his chest. He waded into the water up to his knees, scanning the surface for the carnage he knew he'd find. He cast his eyes down. The ocean looked like tarnished copper—swashes of turquoise blue mixed with a rusty reddish-brown color. *Blood.* He could smell it around him.

Finn scoured the ocean again and spotted something in the waves. He watched it tumble and churn as the surf pushed it closer and closer to shore. He waded deeper to get a closer look as the object drifted toward him. He reached down to examine it and instantly recoiled his hand. *An arm. Oh my god! It's an arm.* He saw a larger object hurtling toward him. He jumped out of the way. Not wanting to look but knowing he had to, he steeled himself against what he might see. He edged toward the object. It was long. He stood over it. *A leg.* Finn felt his stomach sink, inducing a wave of nausea. He forced himself to take deep breaths despite the smell of death around him. Even though he'd seen dead bodies and body parts many times before, it never got any easier for him. Each time felt like the first.

He looked up and saw more things being pushed toward the shore by the breaking waves. He waded from object to object, horrified. Half of a torso. A foot and ankle. A head. Part of a hand. A few whole bodies riddled with shark bites. More body parts. He estimated there were parts from at least 10 different bodies strewn in the shallow water across the beach. He'd never seen anything like it—so many dead bodies at once.

Another wave of nausea surged inside his stomach and pressed up against his throat. He couldn't fight it any longer. He vomited. When the contents of his stomach had been emptied into the Pacific Ocean, he dry heaved. He had to leave. He knew there were no survivors. There was no one to save. There was only death.

Finn picked up Julianna's bikini and towel, and he ran back to their condo. He didn't want to have to tell Julianna about this. Not on their honeymoon. Not on the only real vacation they'd ever taken together. But he knew he had to. It was only a matter of time before other people would arrive at the beach and discover the gruesome truth. Then the police would arrive and the TV cameras. Soon it would be splashed across the news around the world: Shark Attack!!!

*If they only knew,* Finn thought. *Then again, it's probably better they don't.*

He crept to the bedroom. He bent down and woke Julianna with a whisper-soft kiss on her cheek. "Hey, J."

"Shh, I'm still sleeping," she mumbled. "We can do that later."

"No, sweetie. I need you to get up."

"I don't want breakfast," she grumbled. "You go ahead. I'm so full I'm not going to eat for days."

"No, it's not about breakfast." Finn stopped abruptly. He looked at the bikini and towel in his hand. *No,* he told himself. *Julianna couldn't do this. She was tired from swimming. That's why she forgot her stuff in the sand. She fed on fish. That's why she's full. She would never ...*

Feeling Finn's gaze bore into her, Julianna's eyes fluttered open. One look at Finn's face told her something was wrong. Really wrong. "Finn? What is it?"

"What happened last night after I went home?" he asked quietly.

She sat up in bed. "I went for a swim. I ate some fish."

"What kind of fish?" he asked.

"Triggerfish. Bonefish. Mahi mahi. Ono. Why?"

"Is that all you ate?" he asked.

Julianna tried to remember the evening. She recalled eating all the fish she mentioned and how each catch felt more exciting than the one before it. She remembered the rush of hunting and killing larger and larger prey. It was intoxicating. Her face flushed with the memory.

"Is. That. All. You. Ate?" Finn repeated.

Julianna struggled to recall what happened after she ate the ono, but she couldn't. The next thing she remembered was Finn kissing her cheek. "Yes, that's all I ate. Why?"

"You need to see something." Finn clutched Julianna's arm and led her toward the door.

"Wait! I'm not even dressed." She reached for her nightgown and pulled it over her naked body.

Finn opened the front door and pulled her toward it.

Julianna jerked away. "What are you doing?! I can't go out in sunlight!"

Finn's blue eyes darkened. Julianna had never seen him look so disturbed. "Finn, what is it? You're scaring me."

He pointed toward the ocean. "You see that? Strewn across the beach?"

Julianna squinted. "What is it?"

"It's bodies and parts of bodies. They're all dead."

"Who's dead?" she asked.

"Ten people!" Finn shouted. "They're torn apart. I've never seen anything like it—so much death in one place."

"We have to call Matt and Tristan!" She ran to retrieve her cell phone from her purse.

"Are you sure you want to do that?" Finn asked.

"Yes. Why are you acting so weird? I know what you saw was terrible, but we need to get on this." She picked up her phone and glanced at Finn again. "Why are you looking at me like that? Wait. You don't think that … that I could do something like this?"

"No, I don't want to think that, but I have to ask the obvious question. I know there's a graysuit here because she's my wife. I also know she has a strong prey drive and an intense craving for blood because she told me. I don't want to believe she'd kill a human—or many humans—but I have to ask because I haven't seen any other graysuits around. Are you telling me everything about last night? Are you absolutely certain you did not kill those people?"

Julianna shot a withering glare at Finn, marched to the bathroom, and slammed the door. *How can he ask me that? I'm his wife!* She gazed in the mirror. *But what happened? After the ono, I must've blacked out or something. I don't even remember how I got back here. But there's no way I could kill someone and not remember it, let alone 10 people!*

She flung open the bathroom door. "No, I did not kill those people. How could you even ask me that?"

Finn rushed to Julianna and threw his arms around her. "I'm sorry, baby. I'm so sorry. No, of course, I don't think you killed those people. But I had to ask. I had to be sure. You understand that, right?"

Julianna sighed loudly. "No. Not really."

"J, it's bad. It's so bad. You're right. We need to get everyone here. Now."

Julianna grasped Finn tightly. She knew she didn't kill those people, but with a significant portion of the night missing from her memory, a tiny part of her wondered, *What if I did?*

# 155 — Alert

Matt activated the yellow siren at the compound. Cody notified Tristan and Leilani, while Jake called Skylar. Ten minutes later, everyone assembled in the compound's conference room.

"We're going to Kauai. Finn said he found a massacre at the beach this morning. It's like nothing he's ever seen or even heard of before," Matt explained. "He and Julianna want four of us finners to join them—me, Lucia, Jamal, and Cody. The others will stay here and monitor things to see if any other unusual sightings or attacks occur. Tristan, they want your entire team."

"How many are dead?" Tristan asked.

"At least 10," Matt reported.

"Ten!" Skylar said. "All in one place?!"

"Yeah. Finn says it's mostly body parts—limbs, torsos, heads. Only a couple of bodies are intact, and they're covered with shark bites. Tristan, have you ever seen that many bodies and parts in one place?" Matt asked.

"No," Tristan said. "Never."

"Let's get the first flight to Lihue out of LAX," Matt said.

"No. I'll charter us a jet from there. It'll be faster," Tristan said. "You all get whatever you need, and let's meet back here. Jake, Sky, you guys too. Bring stuff for at least a week or two, maybe longer. It's hard to say how long we'll be gone until we get there and check things out."

Everyone raced from the room to gather their things.

"Leilani, what about you?" Tristan asked.

"I'm coming with you," she said.

Tristan enveloped her in his arms. "I was hoping you'd say that. But at the same time, I was hoping you wouldn't. If what Finn and Julianna say is true and graysuits did this, it's like nothing I've ever seen. This level of recklessness isn't typical graysuit behavior. I don't want to put you in harm's way, especially if we don't know what we're dealing with."

"Tristan, this is my job now. It's no different than when I worked for the FBI. If this is going to work, I need to be able to do my job without you interfering," Leilani said. "I understand you have to go because it's what you do. I have to go because this is what I do."

Tristan knew she was right, but that didn't mean he liked it. "Let's go pack."

# 156 – Stay

Carson followed Tristan and Leilani to their hotel. Five minutes later, he saw them leave with their bags. He followed them back to the mystery building.

Shortly after that, he saw the two of them, their graysuit friend, and five other people rush out of the building. Everyone carried luggage and moved quickly—like lives depended on it. He dialed Mara.

"Tristan and his crew are on the move. I heard them say something about the Airport in the Sky—that's the Catalina airport. Want me to tail them?" Carson asked.

"Don't bother," Mara said. "I know where they're headed."

"So, am I done?" Carson asked. "It's pretty boring here. Not a lot of night life, if you know what I mean."

"I know," Mara said. "But I'd like you to do some more digging into that building you told me about. I haven't been able to find anything on it. What bothers me even more is that Tristan knows what that place is, and I don't. I don't want to be caught by surprise if he's up to something."

"I'm on it."

# 157 – Sail to the Sun

The finners and Nomads climbed the steps to a private jet waiting for them on the tarmac at LAX. Tristan closed all the window shades as the jet sailed toward the sun.

An hour into the five-and-a-half-hour flight, Leilani noticed Tristan hadn't said much. She nudged him and saw that his eyes looked cold and distant. "What's wrong?"

"I've got a bad feeling about this," Tristan whispered. "I've been thinking about what Finn saw. When Rogues kill, they might take out a group of people, like Andi and Andy did with that family in Santa Cruz. They might even leave a body behind. But 10 kills in one place at one time? That's insane. First, because it's so conspicuous. It'll draw a ton of attention, which no vampire wants. Second, because it's a level of brutality I've never seen. I've only been able to come up with two possible explanations, and I don't know which is worse."

"What?" Leilani asked.

"One, we're dealing with one or more vampire sharks with no regard for the Rules or for keeping a low profile, which is dangerous for all of us. Or, two, we're being set up. The massacre is intended to draw attention. With such a conspicuous killing, they know I'll have to come deal with it," Tristan said. "I never thought I had enemies. But after what happened with Dean and his friends in San Diego and the Monterey Bay, it looks like there's a faction of graysuits who are done with the Rules and with me. Either way, this is incredibly dangerous. I need to warn everybody so they know what they're getting into."

Tristan stood and called for everyone's attention. "There's no easy way to say this. I think we're walking into a trap—a trap that's being set for me. I can't ask any of you to risk your lives. And, honestly, I hope you won't. If you don't want to do this, as soon as we land, I'll have the jet refuel and take you home." Tristan made eye contact with everyone on the plane, silently imploring them to return home.

"I'm going," Skylar said. "It might be the worst killing we've ever seen, but it's no different than any other time. I have your back. If they mess with you, they mess with me—and if they know what's good for them, they really don't want to do that."

Jake and Cody turned to each other and nodded.

"We're in this too," Jake said. "This is what we signed up for. We're not going to leave just because it looks bad. That's all the more reason to go. The more of us there are, the better our chances to take them out."

"That's right," Matt said. "We're not going to turn and run. Plus, since no one else knows we're working together, maybe that'll give us the advantage we need to stop them."

"You already know I'm going, Tristan," Leilani said. "Nothing you say will change that."

Tristan sighed heavily. "Okay, but the offer stands if anyone changes their mind. Once we get there, it's important that we stick together. No one goes off on their own. We don't know what we're dealing with, and until we do, we take the highest level of precaution. Agreed?"

Everyone nodded.

Tristan settled into his seat and grasped Leilani's hand in his. "Then let's go kill some Rogues."

# THE END

# Thank You

Thank you for reading RISING,
the second book in the DARK SURF series.

If you enjoyed it, would you please take a moment to leave
a review at your favorite online retailer? Mahalo!

# For More Info

For information about T.C. Zmak
and the DARK SURF series, visit:
**TCZmak.com**
**DarkSurf.com**

Follow T.C. Zmak:
**Facebook.com/TCZmak**
**@TCZmak**

# Acknowledgments

Thank you to:

My family and friends for their love, encouragement,
and unwavering support.

My generous test readers: Robert Alexander, Christine
Arenson, Susan Boettner, Paula Criswell, Christina Grant,
Jeanette Nicely, Claire Zmak, and Steve Zmak.

You for continuing this journey with me!

# Also by T.C. Zmak

**DARK SURF**
(The first book in the DARK SURF series)

"This debut novel is so good—so insanely audacious—I
actually stood up and applauded when I finished reading it!"
— *Paul Goat Allen for BlueInk Review*

"Dark Surf by TC Zmak was an amazing story! I was
hooked right from page one and could not put it down
until the very end."
— *Anne-Marie Reynolds for Readers' Favorite*

# About the Author

T.C. ZMAK was born and raised in San Diego, and graduated
from the University of California, San Diego (UCSD) with a
bachelor of arts degree in communication. T.C. now lives in
Marina, California on the picturesque Monterey Bay. Read
more about T.C. Zmak at TCZmak.com.